# The Dragon Ring

Guinevere
Book One

## Fil Reid

## ARE YOU SIGNED UP FOR DRAGONBLADE'S BLOG?

You'll get the latest news and information on exclusive giveaways, exclusive excerpts, coming releases, sales, free books, cover reveals and more.

Check out our complete list of authors, too!

No spam, no junk. That's a promise!

### Sign Up Here

www.dragonbladepublishing.com

*Dearest Reader;*

*Thank you for your support of a small press. At Dragonblade Publishing, we strive to bring you the highest quality Historical Romance from some of the best authors in the business. Without your support, there is no 'us', so we sincerely hope you adore these stories and find some new favorite authors along the way.*

*Happy Reading!*

*CEO, Dragonblade Publishing*

# Dedication

*For Patrick, my ever-supportive husband and the love of my life.*

## The Legend of King Arthur

L ong ago, after the Roman legions abandoned Britain to defend their city of Rome, a time of turbulence came upon the land, and many men fought for the right to rule. A proud tyrant named Vortigern seized power, making himself High King above all other kings. At first, he ruled well, but when he was old and beleaguered on all sides by his enemies, he retreated into the mountains of Wales. Here he planned to build a great fortress and lock himself safely inside, leaving his people to their fate at the hands of the invading Saxons.

Each morning, the workers found the walls they'd built the day before had fallen down, and they had to start again. After many days, despairing, Vortigern called his wise men to him and sought their counsel. They told him to find a boy born with no mortal father and sacrifice him, and only then would the walls of his fortress stay standing.

Vortigern sent his knights out to search the length and breadth of Britain for a boy who fitted this description. At last, they brought such a boy to him, who, when questioned, answered that he had no mortal father, being supposedly the son of a demon. His name was Merlin Emrys. The wise men were about to sacrifice this boy when he asked why they had need of him. On being told that the walls would not stay standing, he informed Vortigern and his wise men that if they dug down into the hill, they would find a lake. Vortigern ordered this done, and the wise men found a lake beneath the hill.

Merlin then asked the wise men what was in the lake, but they knew not. So he told them that if they had the lake drained, they would find two dragons fighting – one white and one red. The wise men did so, and sure enough, there were the two dragons, fighting. Some of the time the white one gained the upper hand, and some of the time the red one appeared to be winning.

Merlin asked the wise men if they knew what the two fighting dragons meant, but they knew not. So he told the High King that the white dragon represented the Saxons, and the red the British who would eventually, under a great leader, defeat the Saxons.

Vortigern was able to build his fortress and, needless to say, he didn't have the boy sacrificed. Instead, he named the fortress Dinas Emrys after the boy. And thanks to the High King's patronage, young Merlin Emrys became the king's chief advisor and enchanter.

When Vortigern died, a new High King came to power – Uther Pendragon, who was a brave and successful warrior, and was also, in his turn, advised by Merlin. He ruled for many years from his capital in London, with much strife against the enemies of the British: the Saxons from the eastern seas, the Irish from the western seas and the Picts from beyond the wall.

At Pentecost one year, Uther called together his knights for a tournament in London. Gorlois, Duke of Cornwall, left his home of Tintagel Castle in Cornwall and journeyed to London to take part, bringing his young wife, Ygraine. At the tournament, King Uther fell deeply in love with Ygraine, and seeing this, Gorlois fled with her back to Tintagel.

Uther was angry, and ordered Gorlois to return, but the duke did not. So, taking his army, Uther marched into Cornwall and fought against Gorlois at his castle of Dimilioc. Desperate to have Ygraine for himself, Uther persuaded Merlin, his enchanter, to help him. Merlin said that he would as long as Uther gave him the child who would result from this union to bring up himself. Consumed with lust, Uther readily agreed, and one night, while Gorlois was engaged in battle at Dimilioc, he came to Tintagel disguised as Ygraine's husband. Allowed inside by the unsuspecting guards, he spent the night with Ygraine and his son, Arthur, was conceived.

The following morning news came to the castle that Gorlois had been killed, and Ygraine realized she had been fooled by Uther. As the victor, he now took her as his wife, but when her child, Arthur, was born, Uther had to fulfill his promise to give the child up to Merlin as the price he paid for the enchanter's help.

Merlin took the baby far away to the home of the knight Sir Ector for the boy to be brought up as his own son, stepbrother to Kay. And there Arthur grew to be a young man of sixteen. Sir Ector was ignorant of who his young ward was.

King Uther, meanwhile, took a wound in battle that was incurable, and eventually he sickened and died without ever seeing his heir. On his death there was dispute as to who should reign after him, and to settle this, Merlin set up a sword embedded in a stone, with the instruction that whosoever could draw the sword from the stone was the true-born king of Britain. Many came and tried their hands, but none could draw the sword.

A tournament was held, to which all the knights in the land were invited. Sir Ector came with his son, Sir Kay, and young Arthur accompanied them as Kay's squire. On the morning of the tournament Sir Kay realised he'd left his sword in their lodgings and sent his squire to fetch it. On the way, Arthur spied the sword in the stone, and thinking to be quicker, drew the sword and brought it back to Sir Kay. The young knight recognised the sword and asked his father if this meant that he was king, but wise Sir Ector realised his stepson was the one who should be king. The boy was taken back to the stone, and the sword returned to it. Before all the knights in the realm, Arthur drew the sword a second time and Merlin proclaimed him king.

Arthur became a great king, ruling wisely for a long time from his capital of Camelot. Many great knights came to his castle – Bedivere, Gawaine, Agrivaine, Tristan and Percival, to name but a few. At length the sword from the stone broke in battle, and riding past a lake Arthur saw a hand rise from the water holding a new sword – Excalibur. Taking a small boat he rowed toward the hand, and took the sword for himself. The hand retreated into the water.

For a wife, Arthur took the beautiful Guinevere, daughter of King Leodegrance, and for a long time they were both very happy. He fought many battles against the Saxons, culminating in his famous Battle of Mount Badon, where he bore the image of the Virgin Mary upon his shield and drove the Saxons back once and for all.

But he had two sisters, born of his father's marriage with Ygraine: Morgana and Morgawse. And unwittingly, before he knew Morgawse was his sister, he lay with her and the boy Mordred was born. Morgawse married King Lot of Lothian and bore other sons, and eventually these sons all came to Camelot to become knights of the Round Table which Merlin had provided for Arthur.

When Arthur took his army to fight in Gaul, he left Mordred as his regent, and Mordred, knowing his parentage and thinking that the kingdom could be his, seduced Guinevere and took her for his own. When Arthur returned, he and Mordred came to the final battle of Camlann, where Mordred was eventually slain, and where Arthur was sorely wounded.

Dying, Arthur called his faithful knight Bedivere to his side and, giving him the sword Excalibur, asked him to take it to the nearby lake and throw it in. Bedivere went to the lake, but he could not bring himself to throw away so beautiful a sword. He returned to Arthur and told him he'd done as he'd asked. Arthur asked him what had happened, and Bedivere could not say, so Arthur knew he had lied. A second time he sent Bedivere to the lake, and a second time that knight could not throw the sword away, and Arthur knew he lied. Finally, on the third time of asking, Bedivere threw the sword as far as he could into the water and a hand emerged to grasp it by the hilt. As he watched, hand and sword disappeared beneath the surface of the lake. When Bedivere told him what had happened, Arthur knew Bedivere had at last done as he was asked.

The dying Arthur was then carried to the edge of the lakes around the Island of Avalon. Here, a boat bearing three queens came to carry him away from the land of the living to be cured of his wounds and put into a deep sleep from which he would only waken when the island of Britain was in dire need of his help. To this day, he sleeps there still, waiting for the moment when he is needed again.

# Place Names

**Din Cadan:** South Cadbury Castle in Somerset, refortified Iron Age Hill Fort

**Ynys Witrin:** Glastonbury, which once was an island surrounded by marshes

**Viroconium:** Wroxeter Roman Town (near Shrewsbury)

**Caer Baddan:** Bath (Roman Aquae Sulis)

**Caer Ceri:** Cirencester (Roman Corinium)

**Caer Gloui:** Gloucester (Roman Glevum)

**Caer Luit Coyt:** Wall (Roman Letocetum)

**Caer Legeion guar Uisc:** Caerleon (Roman Isca Silurem) South Wales

**Caerwysg:** Exeter (Roman Isca Dumnoniorum)

**Castle Dore:** Stronghold of King Mark of Cornubia (Cornwall) near Fowey

**Tintagel:** North coast of Cornwall

**Caer Pensa:** Ilchester (Roman Lindinis)

**Caer Gwinntguic:** Winchester (Roman Venta Belgarum) Hampshire

**Caer Lundein:** London

**Caer Ebrauc:** York

**Caer Ligualid:** Carlisle (on Hadrian's Wall)

**Caer Lind Colun:** Lincoln

**Linnuis:** kingdom centred on Lincoln

**Sabrina Sea:** Estuary of the River Severn (Sabrina)

**Metaris Estuary:** The Wash

# Chapter One

W HEN I WENT to scatter my father's ashes, I didn't expect to get kidnapped.

On that chilly Sunday morning in November, I wanted to be alone for the last words I'd ever say to him. With Dad in my backpack, and leaving my boyfriend, Nathan, asleep in bed in our Glastonbury hotel, I climbed the steep path to the Tor.

In the half-light of early morning, thick mist lay over the town, and no one else was about. For miles around only the odd dark treetop and the tip of a church spire emerged from the sea of white.

Easy to see why some people believed this hill could have been part of Avalon, that mystical land King Arthur had vanished to after being mortally wounded in his last battle. My father had been one of those people.

Shouldering off my backpack, I pulled out Dad's urn. It weighed surprisingly heavily in my hands for someone who'd only been skin and bones when he'd died. I stood him on the grass beside the roofless church tower.

"I wish Artie could be here, Dad."

No answer, of course. My twin brother was on the far side of the world on a prolonged trip with his mates, and I'd have to imagine him here with me, spiritually, despite the fact he hadn't made the effort to get back. Typical.

A bitter frost sparkled on the short grass. For a minute or two, I stood looking at the bleak hilltop, remembering the last time I'd been up here seventeen years ago. Artie and I were seven, our mother was already dying. Although being so young we weren't aware of the limitation on our time with her. I remember it so well because it was the first time I saw the Fancy-Dress-Man.

THE TREES' NAKED branches rattle in the wind beneath a dull grey sky. Damp cold penetrates to my very bones. My mother's skin is parchment pale, her once glorious auburn hair wispy and colorless beneath her hand-knitted hat.

My father, over-enthusiastic as usual, expounds on the history of the Tor. He looks old, with his bush of grey hair, jutting eyebrows and thick-lensed spectacles. He's a university professor and obsessive Arthurian scholar, which is how my brother and I have come to be called Arthur and Guinevere. Although my mother shortens those to Artie and Gwennie.

The hump of Glastonbury Tor rises out of the surrounding flat farmland, long since reclaimed from ancient marshes. Dad parks our Land Rover on a rutted grass verge, and we take the shortest route to the summit.

Artie and I run on ahead, our boots splashing through the puddles. We're oblivious to the quiet suffering of our mother as she and our father slog along behind us. It's a pilgrimage for them, as it will be the last time she sees the Tor. But to exuberant seven-year-olds, she just seems annoyingly slow.

We reach the summit together, well ahead of our parents. For a moment the gaunt outline of the tower holds me mesmerized, even though I've seen it countless times before. Artie and I have been visiting Glastonbury since just after we were born.

"Race you to the tower." Artie gives me a backward push and sets off at a run. I sprint after him, but he's long-legged and athletic and taller than I am, and besides, he's given himself a cheating head start. He wins, of course. I pretend I haven't been trying. We walk round to the far side of the tower and look out at the view over the Somerset Levels.

Voices carry on the wind. I peer through the arches of the tower. Our parents appear at the far end of the hilltop.

"Race you back." Artie's off again, legs hammering down the slight slope. This time I ignore him.

I'm alone. The wind blows through the empty shell of the tower. Below me, the town lies quiet. I turn on the spot, my short arms outstretched, my face uplifted to the slate grey sky overhead, eyes stretched wide to take it all in. Strands of my long chestnut hair whip across my cheeks.

Above the whistling of the wind, a faint musical note sounds. I close my eyes and open my ears. Such a sweet sound. To a seven-year-old brought up on bedtime tales of Celtic heroes it carries all the allure of fairyland. My lips curl in a smile. My small feet take tentative steps toward the sound.

I open my eyes. I'm standing inside the tower. The wicked wind has died to nothing. All I can hear is that single faint musical note. Beyond the stone arches the world has blurred out of focus, yet within, every stone is crystal clear. I turn around, pushing loose strands of my hair out of my eyes.

He's standing watching me. A man in strange old-fashioned clothing. Immediately, in my head, I dub him the *Fancy-Dress-Man*. He's tall and slim and as out of place as a hawk on a garden bird table. His clothes remind me of a picture of the Pied Piper of Hamelin in one of my books. A long russet cloak hangs below his knees. I'm not afraid.

He smiles at me, dark eyes crinkling in a thin, tanned face. His shoulder-length hair's a darker shade of brown, his clothes like autumn leaves. I smile back, just a little shyly.

He extends a hand. Something sparkles in it. Without thinking, I reach for what he offers. My fingers close over warm metal. It shimmers like solid gold. He releases his hold, and I look down in curiosity.

Heavy in my hand lies an open-ended gold bracelet, at each end an intricately worked dragon's head. It takes my breath away. I've never seen anything so beautiful.

I lift my eyes, words of surprise and, I like to think, of thanks on my lips. But he's gone. The wind whistles through the tower again and my parents approach up the grassy slope, Artie between them. I've never felt more alone.

What a fuss this causes.

There's nothing secretive about me at seven, and the first thing I do is show my parents, proudly, what I've been given.

"The Fancy-Dress-Man gave it to me," sounds feeble, even though it's true.

Artie goes green with envy and runs off round the tower looking for the Fancy-Dress-Man until our father brings him back and anchors him down with a firm grip on his hand.

"A stranger?" my mother asks, rising panic in her voice, her sunken eyes darting over the empty hilltop but finding nothing.

"Haven't we always told you never to talk to strangers?" Every father would say the same.

My mother goes to the brow of the hill and looks down the path to the town. She shakes her head. Artie tries to free himself from our father's iron grasp and can't. He whines his hand is hurting.

My mother comes back, and my father holds out his hand for the bracelet.

I hesitate. I don't want to let it go. It's mine. The Fancy-Dress-Man gave it to me. I've seen the kindness in his dark eyes, telling me the gift is meant for me alone. My jaw juts in rebellion. I'm angry that my parents think differently.

"Let me see it," my father says.

With great reluctance I hand it over. Immediately, I feel naked without it, my hand where it nestled warm against my palm, cold and lost. A tear sneaks its way out of the corner of my eye and runs down my cheek.

"Look at the work on the dragon head terminals. This is exquisite craftsmanship. It's old, very old."

"It's mine," I say tearfully. "The Fancy-Dress-Man gave it me."

My mother's gloved hand, tight around mine, reassures rather than admonishes. "Of course it's yours." There's strain in her voice and an unhealthy flush to her thin cheeks. "You shall have it as soon as Daddy has taken a good look at it."

And so I do eventually, after my father has completed his research and shown it to his fellow Dark Age scholars. He never tells me what he's concluded, and I never ask. It's enough that it's mine again, my present from the Fancy-Dress-Man.

Too big for my wrist for years, I keep it in the little wooden jewelry chest my mother gives me before she dies. I have her to thank for it. She insists my father let me keep it, so it's a present from her as well as the Fancy-Dress-Man.

That isn't to be the only time I see him, though.

ROUSED FROM MY reverie, I stroked the warm gold of the bracelet and it chased away the cold.

"Well, I can't stand here all day reminiscing," I said to Dad's urn, "or someone's likely to come up the hill, and then I won't be able to scatter you."

I bent and picked him up, the feeling strong that he was here, in this urn, still with me.

I unscrewed the top. This was something I'd vowed to do – something I'd promised Artie. I swallowed the lump that threatened to rise in my throat and walked the few steps to the brow of the hill.

I cleared my throat. "Dad." My voice cracked with emotion, "I've brought you here, like you wanted. You'll always be a part of Glastonbury now. You'll be here for all eternity…" My voice trailed off. Shimmering through the cold air came a musical note, high and pure and lovely. It felt like a salutation to my father. More tears trickled down my cheeks.

No way would I let it interrupt me. "I'll never forget you. You were the best dad ever. I know you're with Mum now, and one day Artie and I will see you again. I love you, Dad." I upended the urn. A sudden breeze took the ashes, spreading them across the hillside like fine snow.

The musical note swelled. Was I just overcome with the emotion of the moment and imagining it? Or was the Fancy-Dress-Man up here too, stalking me when I most wanted to be alone? Indignation welled up in me at the thought.

Because that's what I half-believed he was. A stalker.

⋙⋘

THE SUMMER AFTER our thirteenth birthday, Artie and I miss the last two weeks of school to go on a dig with Dad at Glastonbury Abbey. Piled into our Land Rover amidst all the paraphernalia of archaeology, we travel from our Berkshire home and set up camp in a couple of ridge pole tents on site.

Like dutiful little budding archaeologists, Artie and I set to with the mix of students and volunteers to scrape away, millimeter by millimeter, the layers of soil in the trenches that have been opened.

The end of the summer holidays arrives, and we only have a few days left on the dig. It's evening. Everyone else has gone home or to the pub. I sit outside my tent twirling my gold bracelet in my fingers.

Under my touch, the warm metal throbs with heat and for the first time in years I think about the Fancy-Dress-Man.

From where I'm sitting, the taped off area of the dig lies between me and the deserted abbey ruins. A slight movement, glimpsed from the corner of my eye, draws my gaze, and I turn my head. A faint ringing starts. Just beyond the far tape barrier stands a lone figure. A man, in tunic, trousers and a long cloak – fancy dress.

It's him.

Memories come flooding back to me as clear as though they happened yesterday, memories I didn't know I still had.

The bracelet burns hot against my skin as though it, too, recognizes him. I remember the earthy shades of his clothing, the russet cloak, the soft brown boots splattered with dried mud. For a long minute his dark eyes hold mine across an acre of open ground, and then he turns toward the path up to the Tor.

Without thinking, I follow him.

On a warm summer's evening, to encounter not a single other person on the Tor path is strange. Ahead of me the Fancy-Dress-Man, his russet cloak swishing, strides always out of reach, no matter how I hurry.

It's quiet, too. No noise penetrates from the town. I'm inside a bubble of silence broken only by the lonely cries of a colony of rooks in the treetops.

Emerging from the trees, I spot him above me on the summit, silhouetted against the evening sky. I hurry. He turns away, vanishing from sight over the brow. I want to shout "wait for me" but can't find my voice.

Out of breath, I reach the top of the hill. And there he is, leaning against the wall of the tower.

I approach in curiosity. In the background the thrumming musical note I remember from our first encounter swells to fill the air.

"Who *are* you?" I ask, my hand automatically going to the hot bracelet on my wrist.

I'm up close now. He smiles, and his eyes crinkle just as I remember, and I can't be afraid of him. But now I look at him with more interest than I did as a seven-year-old. Brown wavy hair reaches his shoulders and a shadow of stubble covers his chin.

"A friend." There's a lilt to his voice that's pleasant and reassuring. Like no voice I've heard before. A voice for reciting poetry.

"Why are you watching me?" I'm still unafraid, despite the fact that I'm alone with a strange man.

He tilts his head to one side. His face is unlined yet full of wisdom.

"To make sure you're safe."

"That's a funny answer. Why wouldn't I be safe? I'm with my dad."

"Not now you're not."

I frown. "That's because I followed you."

He grins. "How do you know you're safe then?"

Of course, I don't. Any amount of danger might be lurking. He can't be the source of it though, because for some reason I know he means me no harm.

A different tack is needed. "What d'you want? Why me? Why do I need a guardian angel?"

This makes him laugh out loud. "No one's ever called me that before."

I scowl. I don't like being laughed at. "Why me?"

He doesn't answer but indicates the bracelet on my wrist with a nod of his head. "I'm glad to see your mother let you wear it. Keep it on. Never take it off. It's your protection when I'm not here."

With all the wisdom of my thirteen years it begins to dawn on me that he might just be a teeny bit nutty. After all, this *is* Glastonbury, and he's wearing fancy-dress as though he's off to a party or is maybe an actor playing a part. But there's also something deep within my mind that urges me to believe him.

"My mother's dead." It's a ploy I've used a number of times to put people on the back foot. It usually works a treat.

It doesn't with him. He just nods. "I know."

"How do you know? How do you know me? Are you a stalker?"

He holds his hand up to silence me. "Your name is Guinevere. You're thirteen years old. Your father is Professor Andrew Fry. Your twin brother is Arthur Fry. Your mother Alison died when you were eight."

"You *are* a stalker." I'm still not afraid, even though he knows so much about me, but I take a wary step back, just the same.

"I'm here to keep you safe. You're not ready yet. Go back now to your father and brother. Never take your bracelet off. Others seek you. One day we'll meet again."

He straightens up from where he's been leaning against the wall and steps inside the ruined tower. I follow him, to have it out. He hasn't answered my questions properly at all. He's only left me with more, and I'm angry.

The tower is empty.

>>><<<

THE MEMORY BLEW away.

My father's ashes settled, leaving the air empty once again, but the musical note continued. I put the open urn beside my backpack and walked around the tower, half expecting to find the Fancy-Dress-Man lurking there, intruding on my grief.

Not a soul. I surveyed the frosty hillside in every direction. Still no one. Yet that musical note swelled until it filled the crisp, early morning air.

"I know you're here." My voice sounded small and lost in the stillness of the morning. Anger made me bold. "Come out right now."

Nothing. I walked around the tower again, then paused and looked inside. Low sunlight slanted across the uneven paving slabs, but it seemed as empty as everywhere else. Or was it?

Something shone on the ground in one corner.

I stepped inside. The note, loud in my ears, rose to a crescendo. A ring. Lying on the flagstones.

I took another step. The morning sun filled the ancient building, bouncing off the uneven walls, magnified so much I had to screw up my eyes against the glare. On the floor at my feet, the ring shone as though a star had fallen from the sky. The musical note rose. I bent, reaching for the ring. It looked like solid gold, with a dragon, like the ones on my bracelet, carved on its face. My outstretched fingers touched it.

A powerful force yanked me forwards and I fell, arms outstretched, fingers clenched tight around the ring. The sunlight vanished, and the stone walls of the tower melted away as bright lights exploded in my head. Air rushed past my ears, and a high-pitched wailing joined the musical note. It might have been me making it.

# Chapter Two

T HE GROUND CAME up to meet me, bumpy and cold and wet. I rolled, mud and grass finding their way into my mouth, hands scrabbling to stop my fall. Finally, I slithered to a halt, facedown, eyes shut, head spinning.

My fingers clutched soft wet grass. Bile rose in my throat. The musical note had died to nothing.

After some steadying breaths, the feeling of imminent sickness passed. I raised my head a little and took a peep. I'd finished my downhill roll lying face down in the mud, my hat lost and my hair a tangled mess. Grass, and treetops shrouded in mist, sloped steeply away below. And now I was definitely going to puke.

Retching only brought bile up as I'd not eaten breakfast. What was happening? Had there been an earthquake? Ridiculous as that sounded, what other explanation was there?

I sat up and surveyed my filthy clothes. No doubt my face matched them. Opening my hand, I studied the golden dragon ring. At a loss what to do with it, I slipped it onto my forefinger where it fit perfectly, then rubbed my hands together to get rid of the worst of the dirt.

The mist had crept up the hill and thickened. I needed to get my backpack and Dad's empty urn and return to Nathan. The thought of snuggling up with him in our nice warm hotel bed was a great incentive.

The climb back up the hill took a lot longer than my roll down it.

The frost had vanished, leaving the ground damp and slippery. Sheep droppings peppered the grass, which I'd probably rolled in as much as the mud. The effort made me pant.

Reaching the brow, I gazed across the hilltop. Instead of the tower, a circle of uneven standing stones now stood gauntly outlined against the grey sky. And with the tower had disappeared both my backpack and Dad's urn.

More ridiculous thoughts popped in and out of my aching head. Was I dreaming? Hallucinating after a bump on the head? A church tower couldn't just vanish into thin air.

I approached the stones. They looked real enough. With a tentative hand I touched the nearest one. Cold, damp and hard. I walked around the others touching them all in turn. Every one of them felt real, the grass growing rank and tall around their bases, as though they'd been planted there a long time. Weird.

I pinched the back of my hand hard, but nothing changed except the back of my hand hurt. Could you have dreams as real as this one? Could you get stuck in them? The idea that I might be hallucinating resurfaced. The only thing to do now was to go back down the hill into the town, to the staid normality that was Nathan, who'd probably think I'd gone mad. Perhaps I had. Perhaps I was imagining all of this. Perhaps the shaking I'd given my brain as I rolled down the hill was playing tricks on me? That was an awful lot of *perhapses*.

Then I remembered my phone. In a hurry, I pulled it out of my coat pocket. Ninety-five percent battery but zero signal. An annoyed shake made no difference. Still only zero bars showing. Typical. You have a mobile phone just in case of an emergency and the moment you need it, it decides not to work.

I put the phone back in my pocket. Thinking about Nathan and a shower, I set off toward town, plunging downhill into a sea of mist so thick it was hard to find the path. Well, impossible. I ended up sliding on my bottom part of the way, bumping into trees I wasn't expecting to find and making a bit of a hash of the descent. I felt both grumpy and hungry, even a little tearful – not at all like me. I put it down to the shock of my fall.

The land at the foot of the hill leveled out. I should have been approaching the A361 road and houses on the edge of town by now, but no sign of civilization appeared. Just more grass, more trees and even more mist. An eerie silence, too. A glance at my phone told me it was now nearly a quarter to nine. Surely I should have seen cars and heard the town waking up even though it was a Sunday? Maybe even a church bell or two. My stomach twisted with anxiety.

Just as that thought crossed my mind, the faint sound of a single bell tolled through the mist. Relief washed over me, quickening my steps almost to a run. I'd been thinking I'd come down on the wrong side of the hill in the confusion after my fall, but the sound of the bell reassured me I must be nearly back. It rang out again and again, but the mist stole the sound, playing with it and making it impossible to tell where it was coming from. I broke into a run. Any minute now I'd see the buildings of the town and be safe.

*From what?*

More trees loomed out of the mist like ghostly specters. I tripped over a root and went sprawling face down in the dirt. For a moment I lay there, hands and face pressed to the ground. The bell sounded no closer. Where had the town gone? And where was the sound of that bell coming from? I struggled to my feet and ran a few more paces. This time I fell into a swampy pool.

Luckily for me it wasn't deep. I struggled out, wet now as well as muddy and sheep-shitty, and very annoyed. What was Nathan, who was fastidiously clean, going to say when he saw me? Thoughts of Nathan and a hot shower, and things he might do to comfort me after my adventure, spurred me on.

Watching out for more swampy pools, I jogged toward the bell for a few more minutes. But I was too late. The ringing ceased, and silence enveloped me. I stood still, ears straining, hoping it would start up again.

"This is ridiculous," I said out loud, then wished I hadn't. The mist swirling between the forlorn trees deadened my voice to nothing. The silence had been making me feel very alone, but breaking it was worse. I took my phone out of my pocket again. Thank goodness it hadn't got wet in the swampy pool, but it still said zero bars. I must be in the back end of beyond for phone service. I shoved it back into my pocket.

All around me the mist swirled and eddied.

Twigs crackled.

Footsteps on dead leaves.

Coming toward me through the mist.

I swung round, heart pounding. Who was it? *What* was it?

A sheep emerged from the gloom and bleated at me. A small, brown sheep, nothing like the round, white woolly creatures most farmers keep. In fact, it looked more like a goat than a sheep. A second, similar sheep materialized out of the mist, then a third. They stood in a row looking at me out of their narrow-pupiled eyes. Nothing to be afraid of in sheep. My heart steadied.

Then I saw the boy. The mist thinned to reveal his small, sturdy figure standing behind the sheep. He couldn't have been more than eight. Thick, dark hair hung in a tangle to his shoulders and his urchin face was as grubby as mine must have been. But the strangest thing about him was his clothing. A dirty, checked tunic hung to his bare, muddy knees, and a sheepskin, slung over his shoulders like a cloak, fastened on his chest with a bronze clasp. On his feet were boots of a sort, but more like bits of animal skin tied on with strips of leather. A wooden shepherd's crook hung over his right arm, and in the other hand he held a slingshot. A loaded slingshot. Aimed at me. We stared at one another.

"Who're ye?" His voice was wary and strongly accented, but I couldn't place its origin. With large, dark eyes he surveyed me from head to toe and obviously found what he was looking at to be wanting.

I smiled as I might smile at any child to put them at their ease with an adult stranger. He needed humoring. In all my time coming to Glastonbury with my father, I'd come to understand that nothing here could ever surprise me. This child's eccentric appearance must have been something to do with the many hippies who congregated here.

"My name's Gwen," I said. "I'm lost, and I'm trying to get back to the town. I think I've come down the wrong side of the hill in the mist. Can you show me the way back, please?"

"Don't ye come any closerer t'me." He held the slingshot out in front of him as though he thought I might hurt him, his lips curling back in a snarl. "How'd ye get 'ere?"

That slingshot looked dangerous. "I walked, of course. And now I want to get back to my hotel and get a nice hot shower and some clean clothes. I've got no phone signal so I can't ring anyone for help. Can you show me the way, please?"

From the blank look on his face he didn't seem to have understood what I'd said. I'd have to spell it out. I held out one of my wet, jeans-clad legs. "Look. I'm all muddy and wet. I need to get home. Which way is the town?"

He stared back at me as though I were an idiot, and for a moment we stood at an impasse. Then he gave a jerk of his shaggy head and turned away. I took that as an indication to follow. The sheep did too, and all four of us trailed behind him through the thinning mist, me hurrying to make sure he didn't get out of sight.

Scrubby trees and bushes opened out in front of me, more sheep droppings, a muddy track and even more sheep. Not a very promising aspect. The three who were accompanying us broke away and went off to graze with their fellows. Ignoring them, the boy kept on walking, glancing back from time to time as if to make sure I was following him. Or maybe to make sure I didn't get too close.

I didn't recognize any of this. I should have crossed the main road and been almost at the hotel in the middle of the town by now, but instead, all I saw was soggy grassland and stunted trees. Until the first hut loomed up out of the mist.

It was rectangular with a low, thatched roof sloping steeply up to where smoke was escaping through the apex to mingle with the mist. The wall beneath the thatch's overhang appeared to be made of wattle and daub.

Aha. A historical re-enactment site. Of course. Hence the hut and the oddly dressed boy. Surely someone here would be able to tell me how to get back to the town. Maybe even give me a lift in their car. Especially if I told them who my father was. He'd been well known in re-enactment circles.

It wasn't the only hut. A dozen similar buildings made a rough circle, the smoke from their fires hanging over them in a pall. Between lay wooden pens where pigs rooted in the mud, their stench mingling with the acrid wood-smoke. Bedraggled chickens scratched in the dirt, stacks of firewood stood near each house, and several heaped middens steamed in the cold air. A very authentic re-enactment both to look at and to smell.

This piqued my scholarly instinct. My father would have liked this place.

A woman emerged from the low door of the first hut. She straightened and stared at the boy and me, and I gazed back at her hopefully. She was about my age with greasy dark hair tied back in a thick, waist-length plait and a rather plain face that creased into a frown as soon as she saw me.

"Hello," I said in my best librarian friendly-to-the-public voice. "Your little boy found me on the side of the hill, and I asked him to show me the way back to town. But he brought me here instead." Maybe the little boy was backward. "I'm sorry to bother you, but is there someone here who could tell me how to get back? Or even better, give me a lift back themselves? Has anyone here got a car?"

The woman's hand rose to her chest and her fingers sketched a shape in the air, fear etched onto her face. I realized with a start that she was warding off evil. In fact, she thought I *was* evil.

The boy went to her side, the slingshot aimed at me afresh. "She do talk funny," he said in a low voice. "I thought I'd best bring 'er 'ere. I think she be fairy folk."

*Fairy folk?*

The woman's frown deepened, making her look older than I'd thought at first. "Or a Yeller 'air spy. You done right." She looked me up and down with open suspicion. "She's not from round 'ere, thass for sure. Look at 'er clothes. 'Ow'd she get through the marshes by 'erself? Someone must've showed 'er." Her voice grated with the same fear I'd felt in the boy. Why would she be frightened of me, and what was she talking about? Was this some sort of secret project I'd stumbled on?

"I'm not a fairy," I said, grasping onto the boy's words. This conversation was taking a very strange direction. "And I'm not a spy. I don't know what marshes you're talking about unless you count the stinking pond I just fell into, which is why I'm so dirty." I encompassed my muddy apparel with a gesture of my hands that made both of them take a step back as though they thought I might be about to attack them. "I was up on the Tor scattering my father's ashes. I just need to get back to my hotel so I can get a hot shower and some clean clothes. If you can't help me, can you get someone who can?"

"See?" said the boy, "I don't unnerstand most of what she sez."

The woman nodded. "Got that last bit though, din't we? Go fetch Geraint. 'E'll know what to do with 'er. And gimme your crook. If she do anything odd, I'll fetch 'er one wi'it." She glared at me. "Ye stand there and don't budge. Ye're our prisoner now." The boy thrust the crook into her waiting hands and ran off toward the biggest of the huts shouting Geraint's name.

*Her prisoner?* This felt surreal. I decided to wait and see what this Geraint might say. Hopefully, his would be the voice of reason. I didn't want to risk her giving me a whack with that crook. Beneath her rough tunic she looked tough and strong and well capable of dealing me a heavy blow.

A huge bear of a man emerged from the biggest hut, and roused no doubt by the boy's shouts, a fair number more men and women came out of the lesser huts, followed by a cluster of tatty children. Their costumes were much the same as the woman's – tunics and trousers for the men, ankle length homespun gowns for the women. None of them clean.

Geraint strode toward me as the boy ran at his side, gabbling his story. I noticed with a pang of unease that he and all the men had come out carrying spears, and most of the women had wooden clubs in their hands. Even the children had weapons.

The woman guarding me stepped back, a look of relief on her face. Geraint stopped in front of me, heavy brows knitted in aggression, bearded square jaw jutting. Bushy grey hair reached his shoulders, and an ugly, thickened white scar ran from above his left eye down to his chin. Where his eye should have been was a puckered reddish hollow. I swallowed. Surely this was taking realism a bit too far?

He didn't need to wave his spear to frighten me. One look from that grim face had already done that. The rest of the men and women gathered round in a threatening circle, the children peering between the bodies of their elders. If anything, the women looked fiercer than their menfolk. No use appealing to them for help.

"Who're ye?" Geraint demanded.

"Gwen," I said. "My name's Gwen. I'm here by mistake. I –"

Geraint gave a growl of annoyance. "Jus' answer my questions, woman." His eye ran over my clothing, which was so unlike theirs. "Where did ye come from?"

That was a question I wanted an answer to myself. I pointed toward the Tor. "Up there. I went to scatter my father's ashes, but when I came down, I got lost and ended up here. I don't know where I am. I'm lost."

"No one ends up 'ere unless it's by intention," Geraint spat at me. All around, the others muttered their agreement in a hissing chorus. "There's no way in 'less ye know the way. And I'll be bound ye don't. Who was it brought ye in and why?"

I was drowning in a sea of mud, bogged down and being sucked under. "I came here to Glastonbury in my boyfriend's car," I said, guessing this answer wouldn't do. "I walked up to the Tor, and then I walked back down, and fell in a bog. Look at me. I'm wet and filthy, and all I want to do is get back home for a shower and clean clothes." My voice rose in desperation.

"She 'as the clothes of an 'eathen," came a rough voice from behind me, followed by grunts of assent.

"She's not one of we," said another. A rumble of approval ran through them all.

"String 'er up right now." That came from a woman. No sisterhood here, then. Did she mean it?

Real fear gripped me. "I haven't done anything. I just need to see someone who can help me. Please, I need your help. I'm not a spy or a fairy or anything else you don't like." A sea of blank faces greeted my outburst. "I'm just an ordinary person who got here by mistake. Please help me." My voice rose an octave higher.

One of the women, a wrinkled, toothless crone, held a coil of rope in her hands. She edged closer, running it through her fingers.

Geraint pushed her away. "We don't know what she be or what she be about, but the abbot will. 'E'll know for sure what to do with 'er. We'll take 'er there. If 'e thinks she needs 'anging then 'e'll do it. It's not for us to deal out justice – much as you'd like to, Old Mother Nia." The crone licked her thin lips, but let the rope drop to her side.

*Yes.* An abbot was a person in authority. He sounded like he'd be helpful. "Please," I said. "Take me to the abbot."

One of the men snatched the rope from the crone. "We don't know what she might do. Better bind 'er 'ands, Geraint." He thrust the rope at Geraint, who took it and turned back to me. As well as aggression, his eyes held fear, superstitious, unreasoning fear. That was it. They were all afraid of me.

"Stick out yer 'ands, woman, and don't do nothin' unexpected, for if ye do I'll not be able to stop these good people meting out their own justice on ye. Strangers aren't welcome 'ere."

I believed him. Terrified of what they might do if I made a wrong move, I held out my dirty hands to him, palms together. He seized them and the sleeve of my coat slipped backwards. The bracelet on my wrist caught the dim light. Every eye in the crowd fixed on it.

Geraint froze.

"Where'd ye get that?" he asked, at length. As one, the eyes of the crowd moved to my face.

I trembled. "It was given to me when I was a child."

Was that the right answer? What would I do if they tried to steal it? My bracelet had been part of my life so long, and was so inextricably tied up with my mother's death, I knew if they tried to take it I would fight them for it, despite the threat of being beaten.

"She've stole it." A man spoke out.

"'Tis the royal dragon on it," the old woman who'd had the rope said.

"Stolen or not, the abbot'll know what to do with 'er." Geraint wrapped the rope round my wrists, binding them together. "We'll take 'er there and 'e can deal with 'er."

Wherever I was, they were so enmeshed in the authenticity of their lives they feared me and meant me harm. I glanced around at them. Ordinarily, I might have admired their commitment to realism. Their costumes had the appearance of having been lived in for a long time, and their weapons could well be the real things. Every one of them looked and smelled in need of a good bath, as you'd expect people in an ancient village would. The fact that I'd rolled in sheep droppings and was smelly seemed as though it wouldn't matter to them at all. A shiver of fear ran down my spine.

Holding the end of the rope that bound me, Geraint nodded to a few of the younger men. "I'll need ye to come along o'me and take 'er to the abbot. We don't know she's by 'erself, do we? Rest of ye, stay 'ere and guard the village. Ye women get knives 'stead o' those clubs. Give the young'uns the clubs. We'll be quick as we can. We'll leave 'er with the abbot and get back straightaway."

He pointed the tip of his spear at me threateningly. "Ye keep yer 'ands right where I can see 'em and none o' yer strange talk."

They were taking their remit for authenticity a bit far, but it was probably best to go along with them, just in case they were mad. Well, it looked more and more likely that either that was true, or they were so absorbed in their reenactment they'd shut themselves off from reality.

"Thank you very much," I said.

"You mind she don't disappear on you, Geraint," the first woman said. "Con's right. There's no way she could've got 'ere by chance. She's not one of us. I never seen clothes like that afore. She might've come out o' the 'ill itself."

Geraint nodded. "I can see that for meself, woman. I'll 'ave Meb, Rab 'n' Rath wi' me. And I 'ave 'er tied. She'll not get away. And if she do, she'll drown in the marshes. Abbot'll know what to do with 'er."

That didn't sound very reassuring, but I had no choice. They were all armed, and I could do nothing other than go along with their plan. At least they weren't hanging me as the old woman had wanted. Seeing the abbot sounded much the safest bet. Surely he'd be an educated authority figure.

Three unsavory men joined the escort. Geraint, holding the rope, led the way. The other three encircled me as I followed him but kept their distance as though they thought I might bite, each of them with a deadly looking spear pointed in my direction. Behind them, the small boy, Con, his sheep forgotten, brought up the rear, as though the fact that he was the one who'd found me gave him proprietorial rights.

The villagers watched me go with the same look of fearfulness I'd surprised in Geraint's eyes. There must have been close to a hundred people ranging in age from babes in arms, to the old, would-be hangwoman with no teeth. A lot for a re-enactment. If I hadn't known better, I'd have thought they'd never seen anyone like me before. There's such a thing as over-the-top on recreating the past.

I was glad of my walking boots in the mud, but wished they hadn't tied my hands. If I slowed at all due to the slippery footing Geraint gave the rope a vicious tug, which sent me staggering forward in danger of falling flat on my face again. And I was frightened. Frightened of the nagging doubt that this wasn't a reenactment at all, but something much more real.

The clearing mist revealed trees clustering close by the village, the path we took snaking between them. Beyond, small brown sheep dotted the steep rise of the hillside.

I had a rather nasty feeling about this. The hill emerging from the mist was definitely the Tor. I knew its shape well and couldn't have been mistaken. Judging from the view, I should be walking right through the town of Glastonbury at this very moment. Which I wasn't.

What I was doing was emerging from a scrubby wood into a wide clearing with the Tor outlined to our right and a group of low, thatched buildings in front of us. Small fields surrounded the buildings, fallow and muddy now in early winter, bristly coated pigs rooting about amongst the stubble. A cobbled path wound between the fields, leading us up to an open gateway and into the courtyard beyond.

The cobbles here had been swept clean. Opposite the gateway

stood a wattle and daub church, a small tower squatting on its thatched roof. A single small bell hung in the tower, silent now, but surely the bell I'd heard tolling earlier. Down the other three sides lay a range of low buildings. This must be the Abbey, but an abbey unlike any I'd ever seen before.

I hesitated, and one of the men extended the blunt end of his spear and gave me a prod with it as though afraid I might explode if prodded too hard. I stumbled forward, staring around myself in amazement. If this was a historical recreation I'd been plunged into, it was frighteningly well done, and I didn't like it. If indeed it was just a recreation. Part of me, a part I was trying to ignore, was suggesting that maybe this wasn't fake, that maybe it was real. Maybe this *was* Glastonbury, and that *was* the Tor and this *was* the Abbey, not as it was now but as it used to be. Maybe when I touched that ring it had transported me back in time. It was the only explanation that made sense.

Ridiculous.

The rest of me, the sensible part, was adamant that wasn't possible. It was silly even to contemplate. There had to be a logical explanation. Time travel was impossible. I knew it because, as a teenager, Artie had gone through a physics phase when he'd told me a lot about time travel and why it was impossible, in between other boring stuff. So I knew I couldn't be in an ancient version of Glastonbury Abbey and these people, smelly and dirty as they were, couldn't be people from the past.

Could they?

The door of the church swung open. A string of monks filed out, dull brown robes skimming their ankles. The man at their head strode up to us, coming to a halt in front of Geraint, who stepped to one side so I was visible. He was a tall, thin man with a long ascetic face and eyes so heavy-lidded eyes they made him look sleepy, although the bright intelligence in them gave the lie to that. Thick dark hair peppered with grey grew in a bush around his tonsure, matched by heavy eyebrows.

"Geraint," he barked. "What do we have here?" His gimlet gaze ran from my head to my feet, and then returned to my face.

"Father Abbot." Geraint genuflected. "The boy 'ere found this woman on the Tor." He gestured at Con, who stepped forward with a look of pride on his face. "Don't know how she could've found 'er way through the marshes without a guide, though she's well covered in mud and must've fallen in a good once or twice. Talks all weird too. Asked to see someone who could 'elp her – dunno what with. We all thought as 'ow she might be a Yeller 'air spy. Old Mother Nia wanted to 'ang 'er there and then, but I thought ye'd want to see 'er first. Question 'er, like."

The Abbot, who had been looking at me the whole time Geraint spoke, raised his bushy eyebrows in curiosity. "What is your name, child?" he asked in a gentle voice.

"Gwen." I wanted to say a lot more, but common sense stopped me. I wanted to find out what was going on here before I said too much and made him, too, think I might be a fairy. A case of once bitten, twice shy.

"Hmmm." He gestured to my surrounding guards. "I think you may lower your weapons now. She is but a woman, and unarmed and bound at that. Here, within the confines of the abbey, we frown upon weapons. If she were indeed a Yellow Hair spy, do you think she would waste her time here, with our poor community? What do we have that is worth spying upon? Ask yourselves that."

Begrudgingly, Geraint jerked his head, and his men lowered their spears and stood leaning on them, their suspicious eyes still fixed on me.

"She've got a royal bracelet on 'er wrist," Geraint said, jerking the rope and pulling me forwards. "Roll back yer sleeve and show Father Abbot what ye've stole."

"I can't," I retorted. "You've got my hands tied."

Geraint gave a sigh and jerked back the sleeve on my right arm, displaying the gold bracelet. "Sez she's 'ad it from a child."

"Well, thass a lie," one of Geraint's men said. "Tis plain. So everything else she've said be a lie, too. Can't trust 'er further than she can be thrown. And that wouldn't be far, from the size of 'er."

Ignoring the insult about my size, which, although taller than the women I'd met so far, wasn't out of the ordinary, I took a deep breath. "Could I ask your name, Father Abbot?" My voice quavered.

A faint smile touched his thin lips. "You may," he said. "My name is Jerome, and I am head of the abbey here at Ynys Witrin and master of these people." His gesture encompassed both the gaggle of monks, who had approached more closely, and Geraint and his comrades.

Jerome. An old-fashioned name. "Abbot Jerome. And you're abbot of...Ynys Witrin?"

I'd heard that name before. I hadn't grown up with an Arthurian-obsessed father without knowing that in the past Glastonbury was known as Ynys Witrin – the Isle of Glass.

He smiled at me, and for the first time I felt a little reassured. "You seem surprised. Do you not know where you are?"

I stammered. "I thought I was at Glastonbury," was all I could manage, which didn't quite do justice to how I was feeling.

"'Tis an 'eathen name she speaks," Geraint said. "She be a barbarian spy, sent by the Yeller 'airs. Thinkin' that a woman might go unremarked."

Abbot Jerome shook his head with a frown. "I know not the name Glastonbury. Have you journeyed far?"

I shook my head, too. Whether I was intending to answer *no*, or just to clear my brain, I had no idea.

"Perhaps you can tell me why you are here and where you have come from?" His eyes narrowed. "You seem to have aroused the suspicions of these good people."

"An' well she might," said Geraint, "appearin' on the Tor with no reason for 'ow she did get there. You know well that the ways into this island be a close guarded secret. None save those initiated do know the pathways through the marshes. Only the boats from the Lake Village come to our wharf. How'd she get 'ere's what I want to know. And who was it what showed 'er the way?"

"I'm lost," I said, feeling as though my answer was on the inadequate side. "I went up the Tor on one day and came down it on quite another." I didn't think it would be a good idea to tell any of them I suspected I'd parachuted in from the future. If this really was the past, then it was hundreds of years before I was born, and if we didn't think time travel possible in the twenty-first century, then who knew what they'd think of it in what appeared to be the Dark Ages. Witchcraft, probably – since it couldn't be science.

Abbot Jerome bowed his head. "Geraint, you have good reason to think this woman, Gwen, should not be here. She bears a bracelet clearly marked with the sign of the kings of Dumnonia, and offers no reasonable explanation as to how she has come by it."

Dumnonia? I knew that name. I opened my mouth to speak.

Jerome went on. "You did well to bring her to me. It may be it was thought the bracelet would vouchsafe her passage and ease her spying. But I fear we must turn to a greater authority. If she is indeed a spy, then we must deliver her to the Prince. And to do that we must first take her to Din Cadan. They will know what to do with her there. Your name will be mentioned when the story is told. The Prince himself will know you as a faithful subject."

Geraint looked pleased. "D'ye want us to 'elp escort 'er to Din Cadan, Father Abbot?"

Abbot Jerome shook his head. "I have laymen here for that. You may return to your village and reassure them we have the matter in hand. Pass the rope to Brother Caius."

One of the monks held out a pudgy hand. He was a small, rotund man of middle-age with several wobbling chins. Unwillingly, Geraint handed him the rope, and Brother Caius wound it in until we were standing only a few feet apart. He didn't seem as scared of me as

Geraint had been.

Abbot Jerome nodded. "She is safe in our custody. You may take your men back to your village." His eyes rested on me. "There's no way off the island for her unless one of us shows her the way."

With marked reluctance and discontented mutterings, Geraint and his men took their leave. Only the little boy who'd first found me remained. I was glad to see them go. Surely I'd be safer with a bunch of monks than a quartet of ignorant villagers?

Abbot Jerome fixed the boy with a firm gaze. "And you, Con, must return to your sheep. I can see from here that they're scattered all over the Tor. Off with you." With a rueful backward glance, the little boy scuttled off through the gates.

Jerome raised his right hand, and another monk stepped forward. He was small and wiry with a ring of red hair above a thin ratty face.

"Brother Mark," Jerome said, "we must escort our prisoner to Din Cadan. Promptly, for the day wears on. Find four of our laymen and tell them to fetch horses. One for the prisoner as well."

This was all very well, but I wanted to get home. I didn't want to go to Din Cadan, wherever that was, under armed escort. "I need to go back," I said, without much hope. "I need to go back where I came from. I'm not from here."

Jerome turned back to me. "I can tell from your speech that you are nobly born, and yet you present a puzzle. This is a small island. All those who live here are known to me. There is just Geraint's village and our abbey. The ways in are hidden and secret. We have no need of fortifications because the marshes are our walls. Yet you are here. And you offer us no explanation as to how this has come to pass. And your clothes," he gestured at my jeans and muddy jacket, "are not like ours. There is some mystery to you which is not for me to judge. Hence, I must send you to one who can. You will go to Din Cadan with my laymen. And there you will be judged." He turned away.

I was dismissed.

# Chapter Three

THE OTHER MONKS dispersed, and Brother Caius kept a beady eye on me until Brother Mark returned with four burly young men. They brought five sturdy ponies, which they tethered in front of one of the thatched buildings and began brushing.

I didn't much like the look of the men. Feeling desperate, I scanned the dark thatch of the roofs that overhung the cobbles, the silent church, and the gates standing open onto the outside world.

Could I really be in the Dark Ages? The shape of the hill that loomed over the landscape, the thatched, wattle and daub abbey crouching in its shadow and the extreme authenticity of the village all indicated that possibility. But common sense told me I had to be wrong. For one thing, I realized for the first time, if I really was fifteen hundred years back in time, I wouldn't be able to understand what anyone said to me. They'd all have been speaking some kind of archaic Welsh or maybe even Latin. So no, I couldn't be in the Dark Ages, whatever the evidence I'd seen. The only possible conclusion was that there was some kind of trickery at work.

But why? What reason could anyone have for wanting me to think I'd travelled back in time?

I pounded my forehead with my bound fists as though I could beat an answer out of my brain. It didn't work. I just came up with another ridiculous scenario born of watching too many sci-fi programs. Perhaps I'd somehow found myself in an alternate reality, where nothing had progressed since the Dark Ages, but where everyone spoke English. Desperation at my situation was making me silly.

Beside me, Abbot Jerome gazed up at the sky as though for inspiration, his ascetic face composed and peaceful. He possessed an air of spiritual serenity that encompassed everyone about him. My thumping heart calmed, and the nervous tremble in my hands diminished as I studied his face. Abbot Jerome didn't look like someone who would allow me to get hurt.

I hoped.

The four laymen led the ponies across the cobbles toward us.

Abbot Jerome descended from wherever it was his thoughts had been, and turned to face me. He had the hands of a workman – rough and calloused, nails ingrained with dirt. I raised my head and his eyes held mine.

"Now, I realize you are a stranger, as did my villagers. And you yourself say you shouldn't be here, which is true. In these times the presence of a stranger, even a woman of high birth, such as yourself, rouses suspicion. And getting you back to where you come from depends greatly on where that is."

"It's rather hard to explain…" I began, shoulders sagging.

"Yet," Jerome continued, "I can see you could be one of us because you speak our tongue like a native. Although that, perhaps, is why you were chosen to spy here, if indeed you are a spy. I find it hard to believe that the heathens would want to spy on us in Ynys Witrin. We have no armies, no warriors, no gold to speak of. But the mystery of how you come to be here still remains. You must go now with my men and plead your cause in Din Cadan and be judged."

*Speak his tongue like a native?*

"But you're speaking English," I protested, ignoring the rest of his speech. "Just like me."

His dark brows furrowed. "I do not know this word, 'English'. You are speaking my tongue, which is Celtic, but I remarked that you also understood when I addressed you in Latin, so I can see you are a lady of education."

I'd never learned a word of Latin in my life. Not to mention Celtic. I probably knew what "Welcome to Wales" was in Welsh because it was written on the western side of the Severn Bridge, but that was all I knew of anything that might be thought of as Celtic. What was he talking about? How could I be speaking and understanding two languages I had no knowledge of? Impossible.

I rubbed my forehead with the back of my hand, and as I did so, the rather muddy ring on my finger must have caught the feeble sunlight. The abbot gave a gasp of surprise, and lifted his hand, long fingers extended. Taken aback, I stepped away from him, but Brother Caius jerked on the rope to stop me.

"Give me your hands." The abbot's command sliced through the damp air.

I had no option but to do as I was told.

As he bent his head over my hand, the golden ring glowed as though a flame burnt within it. He raised curious eyes to gaze into mine, this time clearly searching for something. After a moment a look of satisfaction came over him.

"This is a very old ring. Like the bracelet, it is marked as the property of the kings of Dumnonia. Where did you get it?"

Now I was really confused. Of course I'd heard of Dumnonia. Glastonbury was in it. At least, it had been in the Dark Ages. The ancient Dark Age kingdom of Dumnonia had once encompassed the modern counties of Devon and Somerset. I looked down at the ring again, but it was still just a ring. Nothing special other than its beauty, and, of course, the fact that I'd found it inside the tower on the Tor, and as soon as I'd touched it all these strange things had started happening.

But the abbot didn't know that, so there was nothing to make him think it was special. Yet from his expression I could see he was thinking just that. He let go of my hand, and I drew it close to my chest, fist clenched.

I kept my face blank, but my mind was whirring again. Could the ring be keeping me here? What if I took it off? I moistened my dry lips. What wouldn't I give for a nice cup of tea?

"I found it on the ground up on the Tor. And when I picked it up, I found myself here. And I want to go back, not stay." If I could have done so I would have pulled the ring off my finger and given it to the abbot, but my bonds prevented me. "You can have it. I don't want it." I offered him my bound hands.

After a moment's hesitation, the abbot slid the ring off my finger and turned it over in his hands.

Nothing happened. I was still standing in the cold on the cobbles in what seemed more and more likely to be a genuine Dark Age abbey with a man who belonged in a history book.

He twirled the ring, examining it closely. After a moment, he pushed it back onto my finger.

"The ring is yours by the ancient law of finders. It was made for your finger and now it has found its place. Keep it."

Well, wasn't that an odd thing to say to someone he suspected of ill-doing? I'd expected him to hang onto it. Why did he think I had a right to it?

I could think of no reason to refuse, so I gave it a surreptitious little polish against my coat, thinking of Aladdin and his lamp, and whispering under my breath, "There's no place like home." But it didn't work like the lamp or the ruby slippers, and nothing changed. I was still looking at Abbot Jerome in the middle of the cobbled yard on a cold misty day in early winter.

The four lay brothers vaulted into their saddles, leaving the fifth pony's reins held by Brother Mark, waiting for me to mount.

I finally ruled out the possibility that this was a re-enactment. I was being sent to Din Cadan, which surely had to be the iron age hill fort of South Cadbury Castle, the only fortified stronghold in riding distance. Were things going to look up, or was I just getting deeper and deeper into danger? Part of me wanted to throw myself on the mercy of Abbot Jerome, whose whole being made me feel the safest I'd felt since I'd picked up the ring.

However, I couldn't, and riding a horse sounded as good a proposition as any. I'd spent my teenage years, when I wasn't on digs with my father, down at the local riding school working in return for rides and was proud of my riding skills.

I quailed at the thought of having to put myself at the mercy of the four rough and ready lay brothers. Their persons bristled fearsomely with knives and swords at their belts, and spears slung from their saddles. Their shaggy ponies, about the size and build of Welsh cobs, stood maybe fourteen hands high. However, the saddles looked unlike anything I'd seen before. Four solid horns jutted up, one at each corner, a little like the one on the front of a Western saddle. They would wedge a rider into position on the horse's back far more securely than a modern saddle – a useful feature, as there were no stirrups.

Luckily for me, there was, at least, a mounting block.

I climbed onto the block and took hold of the front far-side horn, then swung my right leg over the pony's back and settled into the surprisingly comfortable saddle. Brother Mark passed my pony's reins to one of the lay brothers, and Brother Caius handed over the coiled rope that was attached to my wrists.

Abbot Jerome stepped up to my pony's shoulder. "My people will escort you to Din Cadan and deliver you safely. Speak the truth, and if you are not guilty, then you will not be punished. Hide nothing from our prince." He nodded to the man holding my pony's reins. "Watch her well, Corwyn, and take care on your passage through the marshes. She must arrive safely at Din Cadan."

I had no time to wonder about who I was being sent to because the lay brothers were in a hurry. Corwyn kicked his pony into a trot and behind him my pony and his three fellows followed.

We rode under the wooden archway and out of the courtyard. While we'd been waiting, the morning mist had vanished. Swiveling in my saddle, I saw the Tor high above the squat abbey buildings, still bare of the tower I was so used to. Turning my back on it, I looked instead at the track ahead, winding southwards between the earthen banks and scrubby hawthorn hedges that divided the land into the patchwork of fields I'd seen earlier.

I soon discovered that Dark Age Glastonbury was indeed the island modern day scholars thought it had been – an island in a sea of marshland and open waterways. The path branched, and Corwyn led us off to the left where the ground fell away, and dark water glimmered through gaps in the grim undergrowth. The narrow pathway snaked between stunted willows and stagnant pools, skirting dark reaches of water and thick reedbeds. Corwyn followed the path as though it was as familiar as the route a child takes took every day to school. The cold air was redolent with the smell of the damp land and still water. I was soon chilled to the bone despite my thick jacket.

Corwyn spoke only once. "Stay on the path. Don't think o' throwin' yerself off and runnin', because if ye stray even a step off the path ye'll be swallowed up and never seen again." He leered at me. "And these marshes be 'aunted. The Old Ones used to sacrifice men 'ere and throw their bodies into the water. On a full moon it's said ye can see their ghostly faces looking back up at ye outta the pools."

I shivered at the thought. I wasn't a believer in ghosts, but then, I hadn't been a believer in time travel either.

After that, we rode in silence, which gave me time to think. Jerome had claimed I was speaking his own language. On the whole, it might be best to assume he was telling the truth, which would mean this really *was* the Dark Ages and he *was* a real Abbot called Jerome.

But how I could have both travelled back in time, unlikely as that sounded, and on top of that acquired the power to speak their languages, even more unlikely, I had no clue.

But if it was true, and I was fifteen hundred years back in the past, I had no idea how to get back to my own time, to Nathan and my comfortable modern life. I would just have to make the best of it and see if I could find out how I'd got here, as that might help me to get back. That it had something to do with the ring on my right hand seemed a real possibility. However, as it didn't seem to function like either Aladdin's lamp or Dorothy's shoes, I had no idea how to make it work to take me home.

Yet.

My brain followed as convoluted a path as the one we were taking through the marshes. I would never have been able to find the way again, as even though we left deep muddy hoofprints behind us, the marsh swallowed these up nearly as quickly as we made them. My body rocking gently with the pace of my pony, inside my head I followed dead end path after dead end path, turning over what I knew so many times my brain felt as though it was spinning.

Overhead, the clouds thickened again and a thin drizzle fell. With difficulty, thanks to my bonds, I managed to pull my hood up then hunched my shoulders against the cold. My hands were frozen, and my feet like blocks of ice despite my fur-lined walking boots. Exhaustion crept over me. I didn't like the Dark Ages one bit.

At last, the land began to rise, and the marshes fell behind us. Forest closed in about our path on both sides, thick and dark and uninviting. Corwyn didn't need to warn me again – there was no way I would have run away into that. Who knew what sorts of wild animals prowled its inner recesses.

After what felt like hours, the forest thinned. In rain that was now heavy, we emerged onto a track that led between small fields. Shaggy cattle and tatty sheep grazed there, and pigs ploughed the ground with their snouts, all of them oblivious to the weather. Houses crouched inside defensive banks and ditches, many with wooden palisade walls on top of the banks. Smoke drifted up from the darkly thatched rooftops, but no one was about.

Then I saw it. Ahead of us, rising out of the plain, steep sided and shorn of the trees that covered its slopes in my time, South Cadbury Castle. Great earthen banks rose one after another to a flat-topped summit where a huge wooden wall topped its inner ring of defenses. I would have recognized it anywhere.

The thought that this was truly Dark Age Britain filled my head. A time when a local king had refortified this ancient Iron Age fortress. A king who was probably the basis for the legends of King Arthur. Was this his Camelot I was heading toward? Was the man I was about to be brought before the original King Arthur himself?

# Chapter Four

THE MUDDY PATH we followed around the hill foot became a
cobbled road, wide enough for a horse drawn cart, leading
between clustered farms. But the structure looming above us drew all
my attention. The steep hill rose far more spectacular and impressive
than in my time. The fortress looked impregnable, with its massive
earthen banks topped by high defensive walls. Once I went in there, I
wouldn't be coming out again unless whoever held it wanted me to. A
sobering thought. I shivered, acutely aware that just because our
modern stories of King Arthur cast him as a chivalrous hero, it didn't
mean he was one.

The road snaked up the steep hillside, through the concentric
earthen banks, toward a towering wooden gateway. Timber walls to
either side stood on a sturdy stonework base, and a lookout platform
that spanned their full width topped the gates. Above the wooden
battlements, warriors in chainmail shirts and rounded helmets peered
over as our little column made its way up the road. As we drew
nearer, the gates swung open, and we rode beneath the gatehouse and
into the fortress.

My head whirled at what lay within the walls. I couldn't get over
the idea that this was some surreal dream or that I was part of some
realistic reenactment, even though I'd pretty much decided to go with
the flow and believe I was in the past. Easier said than done, even in
the face of all this evidence. I kept hoping I'd wake up soon in bed with

Nathan.

I was treading land I'd walked across many times as a child. Only now, instead of long grass blowing in the wind, before me I saw scores of huts and pens, muddy pathways, cattle, stacks of firewood, store houses, steaming middens, and bedraggled chickens scratching in the dirt. Armored sentries manned the walkway that ran along the inside of the wall, and smoke curled from a hundred roof tops. The damp air hung heavy with the smell of woodsmoke and the middens' stench. In the center, on the highest ground, the great whale-like hump of the Great Hall dwarfed all the other buildings.

I didn't have long to digest the sight. Evening was drawing in, and the rain still sleeted down. Icy water dripped off the front of my hood and ran down my cheeks as my pony followed Corwyn's toward the Great Hall. Despite my trepidation, by now I was feeling pleased to see it. I wanted nothing more than to get off this pony and inside some-where warm.

In the courtyard in front of the Great Hall, Corwyn and his men dismounted, and I slithered down in an awkward frozen heap onto the cobbles. Not that anyone was looking. They were probably all as cold as I was.

Corwyn yanked me to my feet with the rope and handed our po-nies' reins to one of his men. He jerked the rope again as though I might run away if he didn't hang onto me. Hadn't he noticed the awful weather and all the armed men?

"This way." He pushed me toward the Hall doors, where two disgruntled looking guards stood beneath the shelter of the overhang-ing thatch. They'd been leaning against their spears, but as we approached, they straightened and banged their spear butts on the ground in acknowledgement.

"I've a present from the Abbot of Ynys Witrin." Corwyn indicated me with a nod. "So ye'd best let us inside."

I didn't much fancy the idea of being described as a present but was too cold and fed up to argue. As the guards stood aside, I let myself be pushed through the doors and into the Great Hall.

I'd seen drawings of great halls showing how historians imagined them. On paper, they didn't look or sound that big when compared to modern buildings, but in reality, this one felt huge. It must have been at least twenty-five yards long and half as wide. Although from the outside, the walls had looked low because the thatch came down so far, inside, the roof arched out of sight into a smoke-filled raftered gloom above my head.

Stout posts down each side supported the roof, each with an iron bracket bearing a burning torch that lit up the gloomy hall with a flickering glow. A layer of rushes covered the paved floor, and shields adorned the walls, empty trestle tables and benches standing to one side.

In the center, a huge fire burned in a rectangular pit where a single, scrawny, red-faced boy, dressed only in a thin tunic, tended a spit bearing the carcass of a deer. I broke away from Corwyn's grip and hurried to the fire, holding out my frozen hands to the flames.

The boy, a sandy-haired lad of about twelve, eyed me like a frightened puppy, but didn't stop basting the meat.

Corwyn approached the fire, but not to warm himself. Instead he caught hold of the boy by one ear and yanked him away from his task. The boy gave a cry of pain.

Gut reaction made me angry. "Hey, leave him alone," I said, my bravery returning with the warmth of the fire. "You've no need to do that to him."

Corwyn ignored me. "Where's yer lord, Yeller 'air?" he barked at the boy, giving him a shake but not letting go of his ear, which had gone as red as his cheeks.

"N-not 'ere," the boy stuttered and Corwyn released him. He fell to the ground clutching his ear with both hands. Tears pooled in his blue eyes, and I bent to comfort him, but he shied away from my hand

and scuttled backwards as though I was some kind of monster.

I straightened up.

"Wait 'ere." Corwyn dropped his end of the soggy rope to the ground. I'd have tried to get free, but my hands were still too cold, although the heat of the fire was beginning to warm them. He strode across the Hall toward a door in the back wall and knocked hard. It opened, and after a hushed conversation I couldn't catch, he disappeared inside.

Left alone, I stood over the fire, warming myself. If only I could get out of my coat, which was steaming in the heat. On the far side of the fire, the boy got to his feet. Keeping a wary eye on me, he returned to basting the meat, which was spitting into the fire and smelled heavenly. My stomach gave a plaintive rumble. I hadn't eaten anything in nearly twenty-four hours, and I was starving – hungry enough to hack off a great chunk of that roast and eat it bloody. Trying not to think about food, I held out my hands to the flames again and bathed in the warmth. I felt my cheeks begin to glow with heat like the boy's.

Why had Corwyn called him Yellow Hair? It sounded like an insult.

Just as I was thinking I'd try speaking to the boy again, the door in the back wall opened, and Corwyn strode out with three other men. They walked down the Hall toward me, their booted feet swishing in the rushes.

Looking at the newcomers, I forgot the boy. Two were bearded and grizzled with age, but the one who walked between them was younger and clean-shaven. His shoulder length hair was russet brown, and he was a few inches taller than his companions. I would have known him anywhere.

My Fancy-Dress-Man.

I could only stare at him in shock. I blinked a few times, thinking my eyes were deceiving me, but each time I looked at him again, he was still my Fancy-Dress-Man. And he was smiling. Did this mean I was safe now?

He came and took my cold hands in his. "Gwen," he said, as though I'd just dropped in for tea. "I knew you'd come. How lovely to see you."

"You know her?" Corwyn asked, nonplussed.

Why wouldn't he be? He thought he'd caught a spy.

The Fancy-Dress-Man nodded. Now, in the Great Hall of Cadbury Castle, he no longer looked out of place.

I was the one in Fancy Dress.

"I invited her," my Fancy-Dress-Man said. "Give me your knife, Corwyn, and I'll cut these ropes. Her hands are frozen."

Corwyn found his knife, a long-bladed, vicious looking thing, in double-quick time. He passed it to my Fancy-Dress-Man, who slid it in amongst my bindings and cut me loose. Handing back the knife, he took my hands in his again, the warmth of his touch reassuring. My fears that I might be meeting with someone else who would think me a spy began to dissipate. I felt as though I was with an old friend, even though I'd seen him so infrequently in my world. He was a link back to my own time, and I was prepared to hang on tight to him.

"You're wet," he said, his eyes travelling over my soaked attire. "Clothes must be found for you. More suitable ones. Stand closer to the fire."

I found my voice at last. "How is it you're here? And who are you, really?"

"I live here. And I'm your friend. I told you that when last we met."

I bristled. "If you invited me, do you know how I got here? You were in my world, and now you're in this one. And so am I. Do you know the way back?"

His hands tightened around mine. "You're here because I called you. You came up the Tor and answered my call. You came to Ynys Witrin as I knew you would, and now you're in Din Cadan, where you're meant to be."

I was *not* meant to be here, but perhaps it wasn't the right time to tell him that.

I knitted my brows. "And you – who *are* you?"

His fingers found the ring on my finger and rubbed it clean of mud. It shone in the firelight. "Can you not guess?"

I looked down at it, then back up at him. "Abbot Jerome said it was a royal ring of the Kings of Dumnonia. Is it yours? Are you – are you a *king?*"

He shook his head. "Not I. But the man I serve is of the royal line and with your help may yet be king. His bracelet has protected you all these years, and his ring brought you here."

Where I had no intention of staying. Bloody cheek, really. Taking it upon himself to bring me here. To kidnap me. That was what it was. I'd been kidnapped in time.

"Well, who is he, then? And you – what's your name? You have to tell me. I've got a right to know who's abducted me."

His lips curled in a smile. "Me? I'm unimportant, other than for the fact that it's through me you're here. I'm no one, but I've watched and waited for you to grow into the woman I knew you'd become. Waited until this very day. I am Merlin, advisor to Prince Arthur Pendragon, son of the High King. And this is his fortress."

My mouth fell open in shock.

"Your name is *Merlin?*" I repeated, sounding as incredulous as I felt.

He nodded. The two grizzled men beside him must have taken my words as disbelief. "Aye," one of them growled. "He's Merlin all right." The second one nodded his head and so did Corwyn.

"*The* Merlin?" I couldn't think of anything else to say. It was such a surprise, I forgot to be afraid.

"You've heard of me?"

I nodded.

He looked even more puzzled. "How? Did Abbot Jerome mention

me?"

"Everyone's heard of Merlin," I said, without thinking, and then wished I hadn't.

He seized upon my words. "Everyone? What do you mean?"

I shook my head. In for a penny. It couldn't do any harm telling him. "Back where I've come from everyone knows who Merlin was...*is*. And King Arthur."

Corwyn and the two grizzled men looked puzzled now. Was Merlin the only person who knew the truth of where I'd come from? He must have noticed their expressions.

"Bors," he said, addressing the man on his right. "Take Corwyn and his men to stable their ponies, then bring them back to the Hall to eat. They'll have to ride back tomorrow. It's late now and too far for them to return safely by nightfall." He turned to the other man. "Garth, can you fetch Cottia, and tell her that the lady has arrived, and the warm clothing I asked her to have ready is required."

The two men departed, taking Corwyn with them. Only the boy remained, still basting the spitted deer.

A silence settled on the hall. It stretched into minutes. The boy kept his eyes fixed on his task, but I could guess his ears were flapping.

"Your hands feel warmer," Merlin said at last.

I snatched them from his grasp. I was feeling warmer all over, standing this close to the fire. "I've got a lot of questions I need answers to," I said.

"I'm sure you have. I'll try to answer them as best I can. But first you must have dry clothes and food."

"Are you telling me this place is Camelot?" I asked, not wanting him to dodge the questions welling up in my head.

"Where?"

"Camelot. King Arthur's castle."

"His what?"

"His castle." I searched for another word. "His fortress."

He shook his head. "This is Din Cadan. The High King, Prince Arthur's father, named it for his older son, Prince Cadwy. And Prince Arthur is not in line to be king. Yet. He is the younger son. When Uthyr Pendragon dies, Cadwy should follow him."

Uthyr Pendragon, legendary father of King Arthur. Wouldn't my own father be crowing with delight.

"Well, in my time everyone knows about *King* Arthur," I said. "And no one's ever heard of King Cadwy."

One of the double doors at the end of the hall opened, and a woman came staggering in, hastened on her way by a gust of rain that rattled against the wood of the doors. She was short and stout with wispy grey hair for the most part hidden beneath a voluminous hooded cloak. From beneath it, she drew out a bundle and came hurrying up the hall.

"Milord Merlin," she puffed. From the mud on her cloak and the hem of her too-tight green gown, I guessed she'd run through the rain from somewhere, clutching her precious bundle to her ample chest. "I 'ave the clothing ye asked for."

Her eyes fell on me, travelling from my lank wet hair to my skinny jeans and walking boots. They went wide with surprise.

Merlin nodded. "Cottia, welcome. You see why we need the clothes, I take it." Then by way of explanation. "The Lady Guinevere is from Gaul."

*The Lady Guinevere? Me?*

Cottia nodded, and, tutting her tongue against her teeth, approached me. "Ye were right about 'er size, it seems. These should fit 'er fine enough."

Merlin nodded toward the door he'd appeared from. "You may take her into the solar. She's to have Arthur's chamber, as it's the best. Fetch me when she's ready."

The chamber beyond the door was not as wide as the great hall. In place of rushes, furs covered the flagstones, and woven rugs hung on the walls. A brazier burned on a bare patch of floor, the smoke rising slowly upward to mingle with that from a couple of wall torches and filter its way through the blackened thatch out into the wet air. The room was warm, but I was still in wet clothes, so I went and stood by the brazier to toast myself a little bit more.

Cottia followed me. "You're soaking wet, Milady," she tutted. "Let's get ye outta these clothes, shall we?"

Exhaustion was creeping over me. I stifled a yawn.

Cottia looked at my jacket in perplexity. I unzipped it and her eyes widened with surprise once again.

I was too tired to cope with explanations. "It's a zip," I said. "Get over it."

I shrugged my jacket off and let it drop to the furs on the ground. My hoody, emblazoned with the name of my old university, followed suit, eliciting an indrawn breath of shock. I tugged off my long-sleeved t-shirt, my boots and my jeans, which peeled wetly off my cold legs, and stood before Cottia in the red lacy knickers and matching underwire bra I'd bought for my weekend away with Nathan.

Her eyes widened with amazement as she took in my underwear. It was easy to tell no one had ever had anything like that on under their Dark Age clothing.

She pointed at my bra as the most outlandish of the garments. "What is *that*?" Her accusatory finger wavered.

"It's from Gaul," I improvised. "A very new idea. Look, it supports your breasts. Stops them from hanging down to your navel when you get old." I could see that was where hers were, like a pair of deflated balloons resting on her rounded stomach.

She frowned. "I don't think ye should be wearing it 'ere," she said. "Ye're not in Gaul now."

Let her disapprove. I wasn't taking it off. I did wish I had clean knickers to wear, though. The ones I was wearing brought another heavy frown. She was going to love my Brazilian.

Her eyes went to the bracelet on my left wrist, sharpening. I covered it with my hand. It was mine and I wasn't taking it off. The action made the ring shimmer in the torchlight. She gave it a hard look but didn't pass comment.

Tutting to herself, she produced a bowl of warm water from beside the brazier and a clean cloth for me to wash myself, which I did with some relief. It felt wonderful to use warm water even if there was no proper soap or moisturizer.

While I was performing my ablutions, she set her bundle down on the bed and spread out what she'd brought. A strong smell of lavender permeated the smoky atmosphere of the bedchamber. I dried myself with a large piece of rough cloth and turned to see what she had to offer by way of clothing.

First, she slipped a cream linen hip-length undershirt on over my head. Then I pulled on soft woolen stockings, gartered above my knees. Finally, she helped me into a long-sleeved, pale-blue gown which hung in soft folds almost to the ground, the linen of my shirt showing at the neck and wrists and open underarms. The lavender scented clothes were warm and comfortable, and I liked them. I slid my feet back into my walking boots, though, before she could find me something different to wear.

"That's better," she said. "Now ye look as though ye're fit to be a bride."

*What? A bride?*

My brain did a few somersaults. She was dressing me up to be a bride. Whose, I'd like to know? I was getting in deeper and deeper when all I wanted was to escape back to my own world, and the man I loved, out of this ever-worsening nightmare. One thing I did not want to do was to become anyone's bride. Not even Nathan's.

She touched my tangled hair that was drying in the heat from the brazier. "Let me brush yer 'air. 'Tis a lovely color, but my, so full o' knots. How did ye let it get like this?" She ushered me over to the bed, pushed me down onto it, and started to tease through my hair with a bone comb. It wasn't an easy job after the day I'd had.

After a while, I took a deep breath. "Cottia? Why is it you think I should look like a bride?"

She paused in her combing. She was being very gentle and managing not to pull my hair too much despite the mess it was in. "The prophecy," she said. "Ye being 'ere fulfills the prophecy made years ago. Afore Uthyr were 'igh King. Even afore 'is brother were 'igh King."

I was sidetracked. "His brother? Who was that?"

She teased out a particularly difficult bit, breathing heavily through her mouth. "Ambrosius, last o' the Romans."

Ambrosius. A name from my father's textbooks, a name whose authenticity was historically more verifiable than Arthur's. And it seemed as though he must have been Arthur's uncle.

"What was the prophecy, then? And who made it?"

She ran her hands through my hair with a sigh of satisfaction. "That's gettin' better now." She patted my head. "I'll braid it for ye to keep it neat."

"The prophecy?" I prompted.

She started to plait my hair. "Well, this story goes back ter the last days o' the legions, when there were king after king declared, emperors they called theirselves back then. My old mother told me all about it. She were but a girl 'erself back then. There were fighting 'mongst the men what wanted to be kings, there were fightin' 'gainst the painted people from beyond the wall, and along the western coast 'gainst the Irish raiders. As well as that, the man what would be king, 'e'd invited in them Yeller 'aired warriors to 'elp 'im fight 'is enemies."

Yellow Hairs. Of course. Saxons with their traditional blond hair and beards. The boy working the spit must be a Saxon prisoner. That would account for his sandy hair and startling blue eyes.

"D'you know what his name was? This man who wanted to be king and use the Yellow Haired warriors to fight his enemies?" I thought I knew it already, but I wanted her to verify it for me.

She shook her head. "I misremember 'is proper name, but 'e were called the Guorthegirn. The Tyrant. It was 'is own wise men what made the prophecy."

Guorthegirn. Vortigern. It had to be. The man who traditionally gave the Saxons their foothold in Britain, the man who gave them an inch and found they took a mile.

She reached the end of the plait and started binding it with something I couldn't see, that might well have been string for all I knew. Oh, for elastic bands and scrunchies. I waited for her to go on.

"It was when them Yeller 'airs turned against 'im that the Guorthegirn called 'is wise men to 'im, and asked 'em to tell 'im what 'e needed to do to defeat 'em, and free 'is land." She was into her stride now, a natural storyteller, despite the difficult accent.

"They put their 'eads together and cast their stones to see what they could foretell. And they come up with nothin' that would 'elp 'im. 'Cept a boy what told 'im about a red dragon and a white one. My mother told me – she 'ad it from one o' the Guorthegirn's own servants at the Council o' Kings – that 'is wise men told 'im 'e'd die alone and forgot. 'E'd lose all 'is sons, and there were nothin' anyone could do to prevent it. That bit were certainly true." She finished fastening my plait. "But what they also said were another'd come, unborn then, who'd be the red dragon that'd defeat the Yeller 'airs, them that were the white dragon."

"But how does that affect me? I don't understand."

She wagged a finger at me. "Let me finish, then. What were said were that a woman'd come, a woman with no past. She'd 'ave the golden dragon ring of Dumnonia, and she'd 'erald the rise o' the red dragon. This ring 'ere." She jabbed her finger at my right hand. "This dragon warrior'd finish off them Yeller 'airs and free us from 'em, an' there'd be a new golden age. My old mother knew – no, we all knew, that the red dragon they'd seen were the dragon o' the royal 'ouse o' Dumnonia." She paused. "And now you're 'ere. With yer ring."

I turned the ring on my finger. "And I'm supposed to be the woman who precedes the rise of this red dragon?"

Cottia finished fastening my plait and nodded. "Aye, that ye are."

I turned my head to look at her. "And who is the man whose rise my arrival heralds? And what makes you think I need to marry him, for him to fulfill his role?"

She smoothed the sleeve of my gown with her gnarled brown fingers. "Merlin told the 'igh King it were one of 'is sons who'd fulfill the prophecy. That one of 'em would marry the ring bearer when she came. Prince Cadwy's already wed. Only Arthur's still free. When Merlin told me ye were coming 'e told me you was to be Arthur's bride."

Oh, did he? I was amazed at his effrontery. It seemed he'd been coming to my world for years, waiting for the right time to snatch me and marry me to his protégé. I'd only seen him twice, but who was to say how many times he'd watched me in secret? I'd accused him of being a stalker, and it turned out I'd been right. Who did he think he was?

Quite frankly, I considered myself to have been kidnapped. He couldn't just decide my future because it suited him, and he needed to be told. Besides which, Cottia was talking hokum about prophecies, and although she sounded as though she believed it, I, with my twenty-first-century common sense, knew it was a load of bollocks. Just like I knew time travel was...

A knock on the door that led into the great hall disturbed us. Cottia opened it, and Merlin stepped inside. He'd changed his clothes and now wore a dark green tunic edged with elaborate embroidery, brown trousers and soft tan boots that came halfway up his calves. Like me, he had the cream of an undershirt showing at his throat and cuffs. The smartest person I'd seen so far, he stood out as an island of normality in a sea of strangeness. I scolded myself for thinking anything nice about him. I had to remember he was one of them – my enemy, not my friend.

He looked me up and down in satisfaction, with a smile on his lips. It softened his thin face, making him look friendly and approachable. If I hadn't been so cross with his colossal cheek, I might have liked what I saw. Instead, I scowled at him.

"I've just found out what you want me for," I said, cutting to the chase. "Cottia told me about your so-called 'prophecy', which I have to say is just nonsense, and I don't believe it at all."

He opened his mouth to speak, but I held up my hand, on which that bloody dragon ring shone in the torchlight. "If you think you're going to marry me off to your Arthur, you've got another thing coming. I don't believe in prophecies. I don't belong here. And I certainly don't intend to hang about while a husband of mine conquers the Saxons."

He closed his mouth, a frown replacing the smile.

I surged on. "That's who the Yellow Hairs are, isn't it? That boy in the Great Hall's a Saxon captive, isn't he? Is that why Corwyn shouted at him? And while we're at it, I don't like people who get hold of children by their ears. It's probably against the Geneva Convention."

Of course, he would never have heard of that, but I just felt like saying it.

I ground to a halt.

A picture of Nathan popped into my head – of him waiting for me in the hotel, wondering where I'd got to, maybe taking a walk up the Tor himself. He'd find my backpack and my father's urn abandoned by the tower, and maybe my lost hat lying on the hillside, and all the while I was here, out of the reach of anyone in my world, facing the prospect of imminent marriage to someone I hadn't even met.

Merlin looked aggrieved. He shot a cross look at Cottia, who was

49

gathering up her things and ignoring my outraged outburst and her own part in triggering it.

"I've left ye a choice o' gowns, spare stockings, clean undershirts and a cloak," she said, not even looking at Merlin. "An' I'll be back later and 'elp ye get ready for yer bed." She bustled past Merlin and the door banged shut behind her.

"When were you going to tell me?" I asked, as soon as she'd gone, "Or were you just going to spring it on me when you were walking me up the aisle?"

To do him credit he looked uneasy. "Of course I was going to tell you. But I was going to explain it better than that old bat probably did. What did she say? No, let me guess, she told you what Guorthegirn's wise men, if you could call them that, said. That was all very vague. It could have been interpreted in lots of different ways. You need to know why I chose you."

I opened my mouth to speak but it was his turn to hold a hand up.

"Any woman could have been given a dragon ring to present to the High King and he'd have believed it was the fulfillment of the prophecy. But I chose you for a reason. It had to be you. Why else d'you think I came and found you when you were just a child? Because I'd seen you. Right across the great void of time that separated us, I'd seen you climbing the hill to the top of the Tor, a little girl in a red coat with ribbons in your hair. You were shown to me. I saw you there, so I came to find you. I knew you were the one."

"Wait a moment. You saw me? How did you see me?" I had a big pile of questions, but this one would do to start with.

I narrowed my eyes at him. The torch nearest to us crackled with flames, and our shadows danced on the walls.

"I was on the Tor myself. In the center of the stone circle. There's a spot where I stand where sometimes I'm given visions."

*Was there?*

I mentally catalogued that fact for future reference. Perhaps if I went and stood on that same spot, I might find my way back home. It was a straw to be clutched at.

I put it to the back of my mind. "And? What? You saw me, in my time, when I was a child?" How ridiculous that sounded when I said it.

He nodded. "I saw your parents coming up the hill with you and your brother running on ahead, racing you to the summit. Toward me. Where the tower stands in your time is where the stone circle stands in mine."

Of course, I'd been dragged back into his time when I was standing inside the tower, the moment I'd touched the ring. If so, surely this could be reversed?

"You were laughing. You were happy, even though your mother was dying. You were shown to me for a reason. I stepped forward out of my world into yours and gave you your bracelet, a bracelet I'd been keeping safely for just that moment. I knew you were the one that had been foretold. I knew that only you would do. But you were not ready. I would have to wait."

Well, that was a blessing, at least.

"So, you didn't snatch me when I was a child because I 'wasn't ready'?"

He nodded. From beyond the door to my left came raised voices. Something was going on out there in the great hall.

Merlin had heard them too. He stepped closer. "The evening meal is about to begin. They'll be waiting for us. With Arthur absent, the High Table is mine and so yours, also." He held out his hand.

I hesitated. I had so many more questions I wanted to ask him, but my stomach was growling with hunger and the thought of that roasting venison was more than tempting. I put my hand in his.

"Do you promise to answer all my questions later?"

His fingers, long and lean and brown, closed over mine. "I promise I will do my best to answer them."

Deciding that I would have to accept his promise for the sake of my stomach, I let him lead me through the door and out into the great hall.

# Chapter Five

T HE HALL BLAZED with light. Torches burned in iron brackets on every pillar, and in the center, where the deer had been roasting, the fire now blazed afresh. Some of the tables had been pulled out from the sides, and a crowd of outlandish looking people were seated at them on long benches. At this end of the Hall the high table stood on a raised dais, two ornately carved, high-backed chairs set behind it.

The noise of the people died down as Merlin led me onto the dais. Every eye fixed on us. A sweating, ruddy-faced man, who was cutting great wedges of the venison, stopped what he was doing and wiped his glistening forehead on his sleeve. I hesitated, blinking in the smoky atmosphere, as Merlin's hand at the small of my back urged me forward.

He pulled back one of the chairs, and I sank onto the cushioned seat as graciously as I could, conscious of how every person present was scrutinizing me. Cheeks flaming with embarrassment, I arranged my skirts.

Merlin didn't take the other seat straight away. Instead, he set his feet wide apart, chin up, and addressed the listening assembly. "The Lady Guinevere is here at last." He possessed all the flair of a ringmaster introducing the lions in a circus. "She is the Lady of the Ring. The prophecy you all know has been fulfilled. Today is the first day of a new era."

A roar of approval went around the Hall as people thumped the tables with fists and goblets and shouted their delight. The story of my arrival must have spread around the fort like wildfire.

Someone to the right shouted, "The ring, show us the ring!" Others echoed the call.

Merlin seized my hand and held it up, the torchlight catching the gold and making it shine like a star.

An awed gasp sibilated around the Hall. Merlin returned my hand, and I folded it in my lap, overcome by how easily the crowd had accepted his words.

I gazed at the faces of the people to whom my arrival meant so much. They were a mixed bag of grey headed older men, women of all ages, and spotty youths boasting sparsely whiskered chins, but few men of fighting age. Perhaps they were away somewhere with Arthur.

But the women were more of a cross-section, from fresh faced young girls through women in their twenties and thirties to the older, wrinkled and gap-toothed ones of Cottia's generation. She was there herself, wedged between two young women who looked enough like her to be her daughters, their round rosy cheeked faces full of excitement as the sound of voices rose to the rafters.

Merlin sat down beside me at the High Table, sweat beading on his forehead as though he'd just done something strenuous. Had he been nervous? Had he doubted they would accept what he told them? Whatever he'd been feeling before, he now looked relieved.

A servant brought us a platter of the sliced venison, and another laid bowls of stew on the table in front of us. A dish of beets in a heavy sauce, a plate of charred leeks and some thick pottage joined them. A third servant filled my pewter goblet with rich red wine.

I took a thirsty gulp, which I really needed, then helped myself to the meat, some stew and the vegetables. A boy brought dark bread cut into hunks, so I took some of that, too, and for the next ten minutes or so concentrated on ridding myself of the aching hole in my belly.

The food was good, but with some strange flavors I didn't recognize. Better not to know the ingredients. The last thing I wanted was to ruin my appetite. Eating was not so easy, though. All I had beside my plate was a knife, which was only useful for cutting and stabbing things. I watched Merlin to see how he coped, which involved a mixture of fingers and using the bread as a scoop for the stew and runnier purees.

We didn't talk. Perhaps he was afraid I'd bombard him with questions again, and as for me, I was too busy taking in my surroundings for conversation. The people, the smoky interior of the Hall, the hounds beneath the tables squabbling over discarded bones, the servants, and the different foods held my attention. A living history lesson. No one else from my time had ever done what I was doing. No one else had ever seen what I was seeing.

The smoke from the fire and the torches curled upwards, disappearing into blackened rafters, leaving its eye-watering pungency in the air. Voices rose in argument and conversation. People shouted for servants to bring more food. One of the hounds bit a man's ankle and there was a momentary disturbance as a servant evicted the offending dog. The rich aroma of roasted meat mingled with the smell of sweating humans, damp dogs and smoke.

"Do you eat like this every night?" I asked Merlin as we were served more venison slices, dripping fat across the wooden table.

He nodded. "Most nights. It's easier to cook once for many than it is for each household to cook for themselves. There's nothing wasted because what's not eaten goes tomorrow to the small children who don't eat in the hall, or to break our fast. This way every family gets to eat meat most days." He gestured round at the menfolk. "And that's important for warriors. You can't fight on a diet of bread and cabbages."

After the venison came sausages, but not like any sausage I'd ever eaten before. I was having a lot of experiences I'd never had before. Some were made of fish and some a bit like black pudding. I tasted them all, getting into the swing of things, and liking most of what I tried. I washed them down with more of the strong red wine.

Then came a thick meaty soup served in wooden bowls and mopped up with more bread, but by then I was getting full and could only manage a small helping. Quickly following on from the sensation of satiety came the renewed sensation of exhaustion. The noise in the Hall of people eating and shouting to one another washed over me, and my eyelids began to droop.

Merlin's hand touched my arm. I blinked myself back to wakefulness, jerking upright and hoping he was the only one who'd seen.

"You're tired." He sounded solicitous. "I think you need your bed."

I managed a sleepy nod. "It's been a long day." A vague feeling of disappointment that I hadn't managed to ask him any more questions nagged at me. Now I was too tired to try.

He lifted a hand toward Cottia, and she managed to extricate herself from between two stout younger women who might have been her daughters. They immediately slid over to take up the space she'd vacated. Heads turned as Cottia helped me to my feet and escorted me back through the door into the chamber of the absent Arthur.

Glancing back over my shoulder, I saw Merlin lean back in his master's chair, his eyes still brightly alert.

The door closed behind us, and the hubbub of noise fell to more acceptable proportions.

Cottia turned back the plaid blankets on the bed. It looked inviting. "Don't ee worry 'bout the noise, it'll be finished soon. In winter we're all to bed early. They'll not be stopping ye from sleeping."

I walked over to the bed. All I wanted was to collapse onto it and go straight to sleep. But she had other ideas.

"Let me 'elp you get out o' them clothes."

I realized with a jolt that these were indeed the sort of clothes you couldn't get out of by yourself. My gown fastened down the back with laces that only another person could undo. It took what felt like ages, but eventually I stood in just the long undershirt and my bra and panties, which luckily the undershirt hid, so Cottia couldn't see them and tut again. I spotted the dirty clothes I'd arrived in, folded up and set in a pile on the top of a big ironbound trunk. A thought struck me.

"Cottia, can you wash clothes for me?"

She looked pleased. "I'm 'ere to do as Milady wishes, and to keep yer clothes clean is one o' them things." I'd never had a servant before, someone at my beck and call. The sensation felt odd, to say the least, but more pleasing than I'd like to have admitted.

I nodded to my old clothes. "Can you wash those for me – and bring them back?" I didn't want to lose them. They were a lifeline connecting me with the reality of where I'd come from. "And if I take these off, can you get them washed and dried for tomorrow morning, d'you think?" Under my shirt, I wriggled out of my panties, and my bra followed. I passed them over to her. "They're important, and I want them back quickly. Can you do that?"

Cottia turned over the flimsy-looking lace in her hands. "Well, they looks as though they'll take no time to dry if I puts 'em by the fire in my 'ouse. But the rest..." She looked at my jeans and sweatshirt with a frown. "Them'll take longer."

I picked up my muddy coat. "You'll only need to sponge this off, not soak it. It's waterproof, you see."

She looked blankly at me. I fell back on my previous excuse. "A new process from Gaul. If you treat the material properly, it keeps the water off."

She felt the cloth between her fingers. "Like lanolin from sheep's wool, ye mean? Only this don't 'ave the feel o' that about it. Somethin' similar?"

I nodded. Then I thought of something else. All that wine had filled my bladder, and I had no idea what the toilet arrangements might be in the Dark Ages. Nothing my father had ever said had covered the possibility that I might require the Dark Age loo. I looked about uncertainly.

Cottia must have read my mind, because she trotted off into a corner and returned with a leather bucket. It smelled a bit, but was empty, thank goodness. I took it with a sigh and waited for her to go out. She didn't.

I could see I'd have to lay down the law, which would be a step in the right direction, even if it was only about the toilet.

"I'm the Lady Guinevere," I said, thinking how odd that sounded. "I don't use this bucket with anyone watching me. Good night."

It worked. She departed, taking my clothes with her. Left alone at last, I managed a much needed wee. That was so good. I hadn't had one since the morning. I returned the bucket to its shadowy corner and put one of the rugs off the floor over the top of it, to stop its smell permeating the chamber.

The torches guttered, and their light began to fade. I crossed to the bed and climbed onto it. I would have liked another wash and my electric toothbrush and dental floss and moisturizer, but I felt too tired to search for anything that might suffice to take their place. Snuggling down, I pulled the thick blankets and furs up to my chin. Someone had taken the trouble to put a wrapped hot stone in the bed. I put my cold feet on it and lay back, looking up at the smoke-blackened thatch where the torchlight danced across the rafters.

The sounds from the Great Hall diminished as everyone departed for their own beds. The clatter of dishes, the growl of a dog, and the muffled sounds of conversation came to me through the wall. Rolling onto my side, I closed my eyes.

Something rustled in the far corner of the room. For a fleeting moment I thought of mice, or, even worse, rats. Then came a familiar sound. A cat meowed in the dark shadows and running footsteps sounded, followed by a soft thump as the cat jumped onto the end of the bed. Confident of its reception, the cat walked up the covers to settle itself down next to me. It began to purr.

I stroked its sleek fur, and the purring went up a gear. A lump rose into my throat, my thoughts going to my own cat, Socks. I swallowed the lump, and the leaden weight transferred itself to my chest. I had to think about something else or I was going to break down and cry. How odd that thoughts of my cat had made me feel like that, and not thoughts of Nathan. Was I missing Socks more than him? Was I, perish the thought, actually half enjoying the adventure of all this?

Nathan's face rose before me in the darkness, the floppy fringe that overhung his sea grey eyes, and the infectious grin that had been the first thing to attract me to him at university. He'd have missed me for sure by now and would have called the police. They'd look at my abandoned backpack and the empty urn and think I'd been abducted. And they'd be right, because I certainly had, but nothing they could possibly do was ever going to find me. I was lost, unreachable in a time long forgotten, with people who'd been dry bones for hundreds of years.

A terrifying thought occurred to me. What if I never did get back and had to live out my life here in the past? In Nathan's time, I would still be here, somewhere. But I'd just be bones, as dry as everyone else's from the Dark Ages. I would be as long dead as Arthur and Merlin.

The lead weight in my stomach became a gaping hollow, and a tear oozed out of the corner of my eye and made its way down my cheek. I wouldn't think about that. It would do me no good to dwell on it. I needed to concentrate on how to get back to Nathan, but that was easier said than done.

I had to face the fact that he was fifteen hundred years away, quite unaware of my whereabouts. If I never got back, my disappearance would be one of those unsolved mysteries sometimes shown on documentary channels. *The woman who disappeared on Glastonbury Tor, leaving no trace but her abandoned hat and backpack.*

Nathan would mourn me for a while, maybe for a long time, but he'd get over it eventually, and he'd go on with his life and forget about me. People did get over loss, even the inexplicable loss of a missing person. In time, he'd meet someone else, marry, have the children I should have had with him, grow old with her.

But what would happen to me? Stuck here in the Dark Ages, I probably wouldn't make old bones, that's what. Merlin wanted me to marry his Arthur, and unless I could find out how I'd got here, and with it how to get back, I couldn't see an easy way out of that.

I was as vulnerable as if I'd been dumped on Mars. I had nobody to help me and no knowledge of the land I found myself lost in. If I did have to marry Arthur, there was no contraception, and no health care. If I got pregnant, which would probably be inevitable, then I'd be taking potluck as to whether I'd survive a delivery. I might be safe for a while, thanks to my contraceptive injection which I'd only had a booster for a few weeks ago, but at some point the effects would wear off and I'd be at risk. Not to mention the horrible thought of sex with a man I didn't know.

But I was getting a long way ahead of myself. Arthur wasn't even here. I had time before he returned to persuade Merlin to take me back to the Tor and up to the stones. Once there, I could use the ring to take me home. If only I could convince him.

I wouldn't think about that now. I rolled onto my side, cuddling the cat, who seemed more than satisfied by the arrangement. I needed sleep. I'd feel better in the morning, and I could get to work on Merlin straight away. I might be back at the Tor by tomorrow lunchtime if I played my cards right.

# Chapter Six

I WOKE UP with a hangover. For a moment, before opening my eyes, I forgot what had happened and reached out for Nathan. Then a cockerel crowed, and realization swept over me.

A waft of air blew chill on my face, and morning light filtered in where the thatch met the top of the wall. The torches had died and the cat had gone. Off hunting probably. There was bound to be a lot for a cat to catch in a place like this.

I rolled onto my back and stared up at the rafters disappearing into the gloom above my head. Would my body clock that awoke me at half-past six every morning have functioned now I'd slid backwards in time?

I felt warm and comfortable in the big bed, but now I was properly awake and fully rested, curiosity, which hadn't hit me yesterday, consumed me. The inquisitive scholarly part of me I'd inherited from my father took over from the awestruck girl of last night. I pushed back the covers and got out of bed, my bare feet sinking into a thick fur rug. My mouth felt gummy and sour. I badly needed to brush my teeth.

Cottia had put my dress from the previous evening on one of the chests, but I couldn't put it on by myself because of the lacing up the back.

I dumped it on the floor and opened the chest to find it satisfyingly full of clothes, all neatly folded and interspersed with the dried herbs

I'd smelled on my dress. They were men's clothes, as you'd expect in a man's bedroom. Much more useful than a dress and probably a lot easier to get into without help.

I found myself a pair of trousers and a tunic and put them on. The trousers were much too long. I pulled them up as far as they'd go and did up the drawstring waist to keep them up, but was still left with a concertina effect around my ankles. Further investigation produced some long leather thongs and, after pulling on my boot socks and boots, I proceeded to cross garter my lower legs with them in a satisfactory way that kept the spare trouser legs under control. The owner of these clothes must be a fair bit taller than I was. Arthur, of course. I put him out of my mind. His tunic went on over my undershirt and I cinched it round my waist with a thick leather belt. That was better.

Now I had clothes on it dawned on me that I was starving, as well as a little hungover. That wine had been very strong. Coffee was what I needed, and failing that, as it undoubtedly would, water, lots of it.

I was just heading to the door into the Great Hall when one of the doors I'd not yet explored opened, and Cottia came in. She came to a halt, her mouth a round O of astonishment as she took in my clothes. But it wasn't her face that interested me, it was the steaming bowl in her hands.

She put it down on the table and stepped back, arms folded in a look of belligerence. "I brought ye some breakfast," she said. "And came to get ye dressed." Between the lines it was easy to read her true meaning – dressed like a prospective princess.

I ignored the second part of her sentence. "What is it?"

Some very stodgy porridge with melting honey dribbled over its contours had been dolloped into the bowl. I picked the bowl and the proffered wooden spoon up and prised some off.

The honey was runny and sweet, and the porridge tasted of nutty grains with more flavor than any modern instant porridge could ever have had. I sat down on the bench by the table in my undershirt and ate it, scraping the bowl to get all the bits. Cottia beamed.

"That was delicious," I said, standing up again. "The best porridge I ever tasted. Thanks. But I'm also really thirsty, and I've a terrible headache. D'you have any water?"

Cottia, who, hands on hips, had been watching me eat in a proprietorial fashion, had a second reason to look shocked.

"Water?" she exclaimed, "Be ye a horse? D'ye want to get sick? We've small ale. I'll fetch ye some from the Hall." She paused, "But ye wait 'ere. Ye'll not be wanting to be seen dressed like ye are now. D'ye understand me?"

I nodded. The need for something to drink conquered my determination not to be dressed up like a prospective princess once again. While Cottia went out into the Hall, I took another look round at the bedchamber.

Last night I'd been too shocked and tired to take everything in. But now the historian lurking within my soul took over. The room was roughly square with three heavy wooden doors, all with ornately worked metal hinges and simple latches. On two sides of the room, pairs of wooden window shutters were set into the walls, closed now against the cold, although draughts of air seeped in to stir the cobwebs in the rafters above my head.

The meagre light illuminated the interior only gloomily. It allowed me to see there was a second, smaller chest, and a rack where several spears, along with a bow and arrows, were stored. On the wall between the window shutters a round shield hung, white with the image of a black bear rearing up on its hind legs painted across it. When I took a closer look at the flaking paintwork, I found the surface was chipped and pockmarked from what must have been many blows. The shield of a warrior.

Before I had chance to open the shutters and see the view, Cottia returned. She had a big jug in one hand and in the other, a goblet. She set these on the table. The weak ale tasted good as I gulped it down, but I doubted it would do much for my headache, and no one here would have any headache pills.

"D'you know what time it is?" I asked, before realizing that where I was now, numerical time as I knew it most likely didn't count.

"Morning," said Cottia, not very informatively. "Time to be up and about. But not dressed like that. Ye're to wed my Arthur, so ye need to look yer best."

Her Arthur. Hers as well as Merlin's. It seemed like several people felt proprietorial toward his person.

I wanted to question several things in that pronouncement. I went for the most obvious first, dodging the subject of my clothing as she helped me out of it.

"Where exactly is Arthur? If this is his fortress, why isn't he here?"

Cottia picked up a russet colored woolen tunic from the pile she'd brought the night before. "This be a military fortress. Six days ago 'e 'ad word there were unrest to the south, along the coast. 'E took 'is warband to sort it. They should be back soon." There was an unmistakable edge of anxiety in her voice. More than the worry of a serving woman for her lord. I seized upon it.

"You're worried about him. And you called him 'my Arthur'. What's he to you? Are you his mother?" It was the only thing I could think she might be, although why she should be serving me if she was, I had no idea.

She put the tunic on over my head, tutting loudly, but I couldn't see her face to read her expression. "Lordy, no. Eigr the Cornish woman be 'is mother. I were there when 'e were born, and then became 'is wetnurse after me own boy up an' died, and after that 'is nursemaid when 'e were a littlun." She straightened out the folds of my new tunic, which reached mid-calf.

"My 'usband died in battle the year afore, and my girls was growed and I 'ad no more babbies of me own. I might not 'ave birthed 'im, but 'e felt like 'e were mine, all right. Then when little Arthur were no more'n three-year-old, I met my second 'usband at the Council o' Kings and 'e brought me down 'ere, bein' 'e were Dumnonian born an' bred. 'Twas when Prince Geraint ruled 'ere." She smiled at a memory.

"I were right pleased when my boy turned up 'ere a good few years after that, almost a man grown. Geraint'd bin killed at Llongborth, and Arthur were sent to rule in 'is stead. 'E's like my own. I worry for 'im as a mother does 'er son." She tutted again. "Which is more than 'is own mother do."

My ears pricked. Was that just jealousy speaking, or was it the truth? "Where is his mother?"

She tutted again as she handed me my clean panties.

"I couldn't put that dress on again," I explained. "I wanted to take a look around the fortress. Can I do that?"

"Not dressed like a lad." She was kneeling down now, rolling the same stockings as last night onto my feet. I bent down and pulled them up over my knees.

A darker over tunic a bit like a tabard went on next, then my walking boots, which Cottia eyed with open admiration.

"They're fine workmanship," she said. "Where'd ye get 'em?"

I couldn't tell her from the giant Sports Direct store not far from where I lived. I thought for a moment, and then resorted to my earlier answer.

"Gaul."

That was going to have to be my default retort to a lot of things. I was banking on none of them ever having been there. Maybe if they had, I'd have to go further afield, and say Rome. Surely none of them would have travelled that far.

"Yer other clothes 're still dryin' by my fire," she said, standing back to admire the effect. "And now yer 'air."

Ten minutes later, having had the decidedly odd experience of cleaning my teeth with a frayed twig and a paste made of powdered charcoal and mint leaves, and with my face and hands washed and my hair brushed and plaited afresh, I emerged into the Great Hall once again, a thick fur-lined cloak around my shoulders.

Winter sunlight streamed into the empty Hall through the open double doors at the far end, and in the hearth, the remains of the fire from the night before smoldered and glowed. The tables had been pushed back to the sides again, and the Hall felt bigger than when it had been thronged with people. I walked down the wide aisle and out of the doors.

The rain of the day before had vanished, leaving the fortress sparkling, but wet. There were people everywhere.

I stood on the threshold, trying to take in a prospect that assaulted every sense. The steady rhythm of a hammer striking metal in a blacksmith's forge pierced the morning. A cockerel, probably the one I'd heard when I'd woken, crowed proudly on top of a steaming midden. A group of children played a noisy game of chase between a row of granaries, and busy men and women bustled everywhere, through the mud and along the paved roadways. As they saw me, their faces creased in wide smiles and their heads bobbed in little bows.

To my left lay a long, low, open-fronted building, smelling strongly of horses. Beyond it, the glow of a forge told me that was the source of the sounds of the blacksmith working. On my right, thatched buildings clustered round a small courtyard, where a stout woman I recognized as one of Cottia's daughters was sweeping out her front door. Inside another door I caught sight of a woman at a loom, her hands darting swiftly back and forth. A tabby cat, perhaps the one that had spent the night with me, sinuously curled itself about the loom's feet.

Looking down the slope toward the main gateway, I saw its massive gates standing closed once again. To each side, a thick stone-revetted platform ran around the walls beneath the wooden crenellations, providing a wide and solid walkway for the guards. The watery morning sunlight glinted on their chainmail shirts. South Cadbury Castle was certainly well fortified, just as my father had surmised it would be. A flush of satisfaction for him swept over me.

Turning my back on the main gates, I set off northwards over the brow of the plateau, the possibility of scouting out a means of escape foremost in my mind. The cobbled road led diagonally in the direction of where I knew the lesser, north-eastern entrance should lie, the entrance people used in my time.

I passed houses, barns, stables and workshops clustered about the roadside, small fields and animal pens jumbled behind them in no apparent order. Stacks of hay and straw and piles of firewood stood up against open fronted barns, and storehouses sat safe from rats on mushroom-shaped staddle stones.

An empty wagon leaned drunkenly outside a wide-open building, its shafts resting in the mud, one wheel off and propped up against the wall. A thickset, red-maned man was working at a primitive lathe, fashioning on a new spoke for it. Peering in as I passed, I saw that two men sat waiting for him inside, taking their ease on a couple of large log seats. They glanced up, and recognizing me, tugged their shaggy forelocks in deference. Flustered, I hurried on down the slope.

Wherever I went, people's heads turned to watch me. I braced my back and held my head up high, striding out as though I owned the place, advice my father had once given me when I was nervous. The long tunic, and the cloak Cottia had finished my ensemble with, swished as I walked.

It was a pity I didn't have a camera. Wait a minute – I did. My phone. It was still with my coat, though, drying in front of Cottia's fire. I might not be able to phone Nathan, but at least I could take pictures. However, the longer it was out of my possession, the more the battery would be running flat, and once dead I had no way to charge it.

A large part of me still believed this was going to come to an end, and that at some point I'd be going home. Photos would come in very useful when I had to explain where I'd been. Which was Cottia's house? Probably close to the Great Hall as she'd got to it so quickly last night. Maybe in the courtyard where I'd seen her daughter. Close to *her* Arthur.

I reached the north-eastern entrance to find it as impressive, though on a smaller scale, as the main gatehouse. Here, one of the robust double wooden gates stood open, allowing the passage of people in and out. Armed guards stood to either side of it and above it on the wall-walk.

I approached the ones on the ground. A man, roughly but warmly dressed, had just gone out through the gates carrying a hoe, its metal blade gleaming with newness. Maybe he'd been to the smith to get it mended. I decided to follow him. The guard, who'd allowed the man to pass unhindered, stepped into my path.

"Sorry, Milady, it's not safe to wander out the gates. Merlin's orders." He was gruff voiced and rough looking, but the kindness in his dark eyes gave the lie to his demeanor. I stopped. I could hardly walk through him, and a struggle to get out would be one I'd lose and would be embarrassing.

"I only wanted to see what's outside," I said, aware that I sounded petulant.

There was relief in his eyes. Had Merlin warned him I might try to make a run for it?

"Sorry, Milady, but orders is orders."

But what was outside that was so dangerous? Considering how insecure I felt inside the walls of the fortress, I was inclined to think that outside couldn't be much worse. But I could see it would be no use arguing. His face was set with an immovable determination. I turned away from the gate. Maybe it would be easier to sneak out at night under cover of darkness? What I would do if I did get out I had no idea, as it was a good ten miles through unknown wintry country-side to Glastonbury. It was rather a silly plan, really, as I couldn't get back by myself through those endless marshes into Ynys Witrin. But it was the only plan I had so far if I wanted to avoid ending up as Arthur's wife.

I climbed the wooden steps to the wall-walk and stood looking out across the plain. As the cold wind snatched at my cloak, I drew it closer about myself. Below, the plain lay scattered with farms, and in the far distance, beyond the darkness of winter forest that began where the farmsteads finished, the little hump of Glastonbury Tor rose out of a sea of mist.

I didn't know how long I'd been standing there, staring out at the familiar, yet unfamiliar landscape, when my reverie was interrupted.

"Gwen?"

I turned my head. Merlin stood on the wall-walk a few feet away.

Looking him up and down with as much scorn as I could muster, I asked, "Come to gloat?"

He shook his head. This morning he was smartly dressed in a deep red tunic over dark trousers and a fur lined cloak fastened with a heavy golden brooch of a bird in flight. A merlin falcon.

"I think you've got a lot of explaining to do." I fixed him with my hardest stare. He deserved it. He'd ducked out of it the night before, but I'd had a whole extra half-a-day to think about my situation, and I was full of questions.

"What is it you want to know? I'll answer your questions if I can." He moved closer and leaned on the parapet beside me, staring out toward the Tor. His eyes narrowed in the feeble sunshine. The smell of lavender on his clothing was strong. I'd read once somewhere that it repelled lice and fleas.

"What am I doing here?" I asked. "What are you really playing at?"

He smiled. "Fulfilling your destiny."

I bristled. "Talking about destiny is a load of bollocks. I'm not meant to be here, and I know it's got something to do with you that I am. You need to take me back home right now, before things get any more complicated. I have a boyfriend in my world who loves me. He'll be looking for me."

He turned his head. I tried to read his expression but couldn't. Was he on my side? Was he working against me? Common sense inclined me to think the latter.

"The man you were with, in your world, isn't important. Here, you're destined to be a queen."

If I could have bristled any more, I'd have looked like a hedgehog. "Where I come from, women get a choice in whom they marry, thank you very much. I've no intention of marrying anyone. And my boyfriend, who has a name – Nathan – is very important to me, even if he isn't to you." I paused. "And he'll be looking for me by now, and he'll probably have called the police. I want to go home to him. Right now."

"That's impossible."

Frustration coursed through me. He had to be lying. "It better hadn't be," I snapped. "For a start, then, you can tell me exactly how it was you got me here. Because if I came one way, surely I can get back using the same method?"

He shook his head. "I don't think you can. There was but one moment when you could pass through the tear in time. Yesterday morning. Now the tear is healed. It no longer exists. Your passing plugged the hole."

A tear in time. A tear that had linked the twenty-first century with the fifth, just when I'd come too close to it. A tear that somehow had mended when I passed through it. A bit of a coincidence. Did I believe him? If he thought there might be a way back, would he even tell me?

"How did the tear come to be made? I saw you at least twice in my world, so either the tear lasted for ages or there was more than one."

"Time is ragged." He had the air of someone choosing his words carefully. "But it's tied to lives. Seventeen years ago, when I served Arthur's father, the High King, and Arthur was just a boy, I found the ragged edges of time in Ynys Witrin's stone circle and knew that you would come. The tear was tied to you. It opened when you were in Ynys Witrin in your world, and allowed me through so I could find you when you were a child."

I seized upon his words. "Then if I go back to the circle it might open again. If I stand in the middle of it."

He shook his head. The wind caught his long brown hair and whipped it across his face so he had to put up a hand and push it back, a gesture that reminded me of Nathan.

"No. That's not how it works. In fact, even I don't know exactly how it does. But I do know you're now where you're meant to be, so there's no need for a tear to exist."

"But you don't know it won't. Take me back to Glastonbury and let me try to get back to my world."

He shook his head again. "I can't. I brought you here for a purpose. To fulfill a prophecy. Because whenever I use my magic to see what lies ahead for Arthur, I see it lies with you, his future intertwined with yours."

I frowned in frustration. "*Magic*? Is that what all this is? Are you trying to tell me you got me here by *magic*? That doesn't even exist."

Merlin gave a shrug. "Call it what you will. I was born with power. But I don't fully control it. It comes and goes when it's needed. It's hard to explain."

"You mean you have real magic?"

He smiled, almost apologetically.

I paused, thinking about what he'd just said, but it proved very hard to get my head around.

"Wait a minute. You said you were serving Arthur's father seventeen years ago. So, how old are you?" He looked young. Well, older than me, but still young. Definitely not old. Surely seventeen years ago he couldn't have been much more than a boy himself. There were lines about his eyes from squinting against the sun, but not a gray hair on his head, and he moved with all the suppleness of youth. It was hard to believe he was a day over thirty.

His smile became a wicked grin. "Old. I served the High King's brother, Ambrosius, before him, and before that I was with the wise men of Guorthegirn. I'm older than you think."

I had no idea of the time spans he was talking about. But I could see he looked too young to have done all that. Yet something in me accepted what he'd just said as truth. If he'd used magic to bring me here, then why not to keep himself young? None of the laws of physics seemed to apply to the situation I found myself in.

The feeling of being trapped was overwhelming. "You're not going to let me go back, are you?"

After an awkward moment he made a sweeping gesture with his arm across the plain toward distant Glastonbury Tor.

"If you escape and go to Ynys Witrin to try to find a way back, we will come after you. We can't let you perish in the marshes, which you most certainly would. And even if by some lucky chance you could find your way through the marshes, you wouldn't be safe. The Abbot controls the island, but his people are superstitious and already think you either a spy or a bog spirit."

I preferred fairy to bog spirit. "Then help me."

He turned around and leaned on the palisade wall, his back to the Tor. Four grey-haired horsemen clattered down the cobbled road toward the gates. He raised a hand in salute, and they all shook their spears back at him and shouted friendly greetings. Then they were through and riding down the steep path away from the gates toward the plain below.

He looked back at me. "I'll help you as much as I can, but not back to your world. There's very little possibility what you want to do would work, anyway. I'll help you settle in, adjust to the changes you'll meet. And one day soon, you'll be a queen to Arthur's king."

At this rate I couldn't see how I could avoid it. I had one thing that Merlin didn't have though, visions of the future or not. I had all the knowledge of the twenty-first century. I knew Arthur was remembered as a great king, I knew the list of his supposed twelve battles, and I knew what would happen to him at Camlann, his last battle, when his nephew Mordred would betray him, leading to both their deaths. But I also knew that by Arthur's side all that time was his wife, Queen Guinevere. A woman who, according to legend, was destined not to help him, but to betray him with one of his closest friends. A woman I'd been named after.

I changed tack. "If you want me to marry Arthur, I think you'd better tell me all about him."

Merlin's face changed. Was that relief I saw flash in his eyes? Did he think I was about to capitulate? He didn't understand independent twenty-first-century women if he did.

"What do you want to know?" he asked.

I looked back up the slope at the dark hump of the Great Hall's roof while I searched for what I wanted. "Everything. Where he was born, where he grew up, what he's like now. You're planning I should marry him, it's the least you can do."

Who would swerve the opportunity to find out more about the real King Arthur? What wouldn't my father have given for such a chance. I might as well seize it with both hands. The knowledge would be useful if I met Arthur, if – perish the thought – I had to marry him, but also if I made it back to my world.

A buzzard mewed in the sky overhead, soaring on the wind against the tattered clouds. I pulled my cloak more closely about myself and reflected that coats with sleeves and zipped or buttoned fronts were a useful invention.

"His father is King Uthyr Pendragon, High King of all Britain. Arthur's family have worn the purple, but he boasts British blood as well as Roman. Through his father's mother, he can trace his line back to Cunedda of the Votadini, who once ruled north of the Wall, but whose descendants now hold power in Gwynnedd and Ceredigion in the far west, keeping the Irish at bay. Through them he has blood ties with most of Britain's ruling families."

Interesting as that all was, it didn't tell me much about Arthur himself.

"Who was his mother? This Cornish woman?"

"Eigr." Merlin smiled as though a memory stirred him. "She was wife to Gorlois of Tintagel, with a small son, Cei. Gorlois unwisely brought her to the Council of the Kings of Britain."

"Uthyr fell in love with her," I said, filling in the story I knew, and hoping I was getting it right. "And when Gorlois went back to Cornwall, Uthyr followed."

Merlin looked surprised. "You know already?"

I shrugged. "Probably. I've no idea how much is true, though. Gorlois was killed and Uthyr took Eigr as his wife, and Arthur was born."

Merlin nodded. "Uthyr had put aside his first wife, a Saxon princess named Aelfled, so nothing prevented him taking Eigr to wife but Gorlois. It was well her husband died in battle, but some still whisper that in taking another man's wife, Uthyr did wrong and that's why he's afflicted now."

"Afflicted? What's wrong with him?"

Merlin frowned. "The High King took a wound in battle some years ago. At first it seemed to heal, but then it broke open anew, and now nothing will heal it. His whole leg is ulcerated, and he has to ride in a litter. Some say he shouldn't still be High King if he can't straddle a horse and lead his warriors into battle."

"Who leads his army, then?"

"Prince Cadwy, his son by Aelfled. Cadwy is King of Powys and Dumnonia in all but name."

"And Arthur?" We were back to him again. "Is he a good man?" Might a Dark Age warrior be judged on a different scale to a man from the twenty-first century?

Merlin smiled. "Arthur is a good man. He's a strong and brave warrior, who's killed many a foe in battle. He's a fair judge of men, he's kind to his women and his horses, and has learned wisdom in all his dealings."

I guessed that was a fair summing up, but then, Merlin was biased. I had an urge to ask what Arthur looked like, but I refrained. Instead, I turned back to gaze out again over the wooded plain. Rain clouds were scudding in from the west, dark and threatening. The day was not going to stay dry for long.

Merlin pushed himself off the wooden wall. "Walk with me," he said, taking my arm and guiding me along the walkway. I went with him, the sharp wind whipping loose tendrils of my hair across my face.

To our right, the little fields of the fortress reached almost as far as the wall, fenced with woven hurdles around vegetable patches, or banks and thorny hedges and rough-hewn posts and rails to keep livestock in. Between where we were walking and the small fields ran a narrow strip of land pockmarked with hoof prints. A place to exercise horses, perhaps.

Beneath a darkening sky we reached another small gateway facing due east. A cobbled road led up from it toward the Great Hall, flanked on both sides by more houses and workshops. I was surprised by how much was crammed into the eighteen acres lying inside the walls.

My footsteps slowed and I came to a halt, surveying the hive of industry spread out before me. Hard to imagine the deserted green farmland of my time with only a few cows to be seen between the still high grassy banks, where once these soldiers had stood. Were standing right now.

Every time I thought about what had happened to me, I felt confused and flustered. Best not to think of it too much.

"Who refortified this place?" I asked, to take my mind off my thoughts.

Merlin's grip tightened on my arm, encouraging me forward. "Uthyr, initially." He quickened his pace as a few drops of rain spattered around us. "Then it fell to Arthur to finish the work he'd started. Before Uthyr's brother, Ambrosius, became High King, under Guorthegirn the Usurper, we still had the old Roman towns, just as they'd been for centuries. But the rot was already there, like a canker waiting to find the weakest spot." He hurried me on.

"When Uthyr took over from his brother twenty years ago, everything had changed from when their father ruled before Guorthegirn. A lot can happen in fifty years. A lot. The people in the East had fled from the Saxon threat. They'd abandoned their towns. Now there's nothing left there but haunted ruins and heathen villages, and we in the West live in the old hillforts just as our ancestors did."

"Iron Age hillforts," I put in.

He raised a puzzled eyebrow. Too late, I realized the Iron Age was a name coined by historians long after his time. Choosing not to comment, he went on. "These forts were built by our ancestors long before the legions came. Even though none of us can claim to possess blood untainted by the Empire, they're still our ancestral homes." He gestured to the sizeable wall. "And as they're smaller and usually on high ground, they can be defended far more easily than a sprawling town."

I was fascinated, despite myself. He was a walking history lesson, and I wanted to learn. There was a lot of my father in me.

More raindrops fell now, splatting onto the walkway. I pulled the hood of my cloak up over my head. "How far have the Saxons progressed? How much of Britain have they taken?"

We descended some wooden steps and took the cobbled roadway back toward the Great Hall before he answered.

"They've made inroads in the east. Guorthegirn the Usurper invited them in when he was Imperator, as foederati – mercenaries – because he couldn't raise a big enough army himself to defend our shores. His problem was that in the East, or the far west, where the dangers lay, and still do lie, the people there had little money to pay in taxes to support the army, whereas in the fat south and center the people felt insulated and safe. Since Guorthegirn had reduced all the taxes when he came to power to make himself popular, it was very hard for him to raise them again unopposed."

"Taxation is always unpopular." I stepped over a pile of horse droppings. "Even in my world it's a problem."

He nodded. Raindrops sparkled like jewels in his brown hair. "No one wants to pay for someone else's defense, do they? Not when they feel they themselves are safe. So Guorthegirn called in the Saxons, Hengest, and his brother, Horsa, with their Yellow Haired warriors. I was there when they came to meet Guorthegirn, young and brave and boastful. I heard their empty promises to help him in return for land to settle."

His brows came together in a heavy frown.

"They said one thing to his face, but they meant another. From two hundred, they've grown to many thousands today. Ambrosius inherited Guorthegirn's problem and now those problems are Uthyr's. The High King isn't strong enough to drive them out, and because they know he's maimed, they press us hard. All Uthyr can do is hope to curb their spread. And that's nigh impossible."

"Which parts of the East do they have?" We were nearly at the Great Hall, whose doors stood open. With the rain had come low cloud, making it impossible to see the wooded plain that lay between us and the Tor.

"Ceint, southeast of Caer Lundein, where Guorthegirn originally granted Hengest and his men lands," Merlin said, guiding me toward the doors.

Kent – I knew that was the first Saxon territory gained in Britain.

He went on. "And sixty miles north of Caer Lundein, toward the coast. They've good natural defenses there – the marshes and the forests protect them from us, but they also put a barrier on their expansion. We've not much to worry about from them. But there's another settlement up toward the Wall, under Hengest's son, Octha, and they're growing in strength. Guorthegirn sent them up there to protect us from the Picts, but now they're more of a danger than the Picts themselves, and Guorthegirn's been in his grave these thirty years."

I stopped under the overhanging thatch in front of the Hall doors. Two guards were there as usual, the butts of their long spears resting on the ground. They looked at me with interest.

"Where are you getting the most trouble from?" I asked.

Merlin shrugged. "As easy to ask which ant in an anthill bites the worst. It varies. Now they've established permanent settlements in Britain, they're free to bring over more keels of raiders, to sail along our coastline and attack where they will. The fact that it's nearly winter doesn't seem to put them off over much. News of a couple of keels of Saxons raiding near Caer Durnac took Arthur off about a week ago."

I had no idea where that was.

"The weather's been wet, but there's been wind for sailing, and even when there's no wind, they've oars to their boats that're faster than sails. They're shallow bottomed and easy to pull up on a beach so their warriors can leap ashore and be inland before warning is raised. They pillage – taking food and weapons and gold if they can find it. And women, too. There's a ready market for slaves across the sea in Gaul and further on into the Mediterranean."

It was weird hearing him talk about geography. I'd expected him to have little knowledge of the world outside Britain, perhaps to only have known his own small part of it. But until not so long ago Britain had been part of the Roman Empire. There might even be maps he could have seen.

From where we were standing we could see the main gates, and now something seemed to be going on down there. Guards ran along the wall-walk and down the steps to fling the gates open. A trumpet blew, its voice strident in the wet air. People's heads turned toward the sound. A rider came through the gates, then another and another. I couldn't see them clearly, but I could see they were carrying shields. And on the white shield of the foremost rider a black bear reared up on its back legs aggressively. I didn't need telling.

Arthur was back.

# Chapter Seven

THE RAIN DRIPPED from the thatch and splashed into puddles on the cobbled roadway that led up from the gatehouse. Standing in the shadows, I watched as the riders made their way toward the Great Hall. The man with the big black bear on his shield was joined by another, whose shield bore a leaping silver fish on a black background.

I watched their approach in a curiously detached way, as though at home in my sitting room, and this the opening scene of a film unfolding before me, none of which could touch me.

But of course, it could.

I didn't need Merlin to tell me who the warrior with the bear emblem was. I knew without a doubt that the man riding up the slope toward us was Arthur. I think I would have known even if I hadn't recognized his shield from the duplicate hanging in his bedchamber. Forty yards away, boys came running out of the stables to take their horses. It seemed that when you were a prince you didn't need to look after your own animal.

Arthur dismounted.

He was tall, his long dark hair plastered to his head by the rain. A voluminous cloak draped around his shoulders partly obscured the glitter of a ring mail shirt. Beside him, the red-headed fish warrior said something that made him laugh, and he punched the other man playfully in the shoulder. Laughter rippled through the rest of the warriors, as they too swung down from their horses with the exhausted air of men who'd ridden all night.

"Wait here. Don't move." Merlin strode down the slope, leaving me with only the two guards for company.

He reached Arthur and his red-headed companion. I watched him speak to them, saw their heads turn and look up the slope toward the Hall and me, saw Merlin put his hand on Arthur's arm, and the red-headed warrior return Arthur's playful punch. The three of them began to walk up the slope toward me.

I put a hand on one of the door posts to steady myself. The roughness under my fingers grounded me in reality. Here, walking up the rise through the rain, was living, breathing proof that everything my father had believed was true. I took a deep breath and raised my chin.

They stopped in front of me. The fish warrior stood the tallest, solidly built and wide shouldered. Arthur, in the center, was an altogether leaner specimen than the fish warrior. I stared at him: heavy, black brows above eyes so dark they could have been black, too, a long aquiline nose, and a week's growth of dark beard. A white scar puckered his left cheek from just below the eye, and a blood-stained bandage covered his left hand.

"Welcome to Din Cadan, Lady Guinevere," he said. His voice was deeper than Merlin's, a voice for issuing orders, not reading poetry.

Should I curtsey? Bow? What?

"May I present my brother, Cei of Tintagel."

The red-haired fish warrior bowed, and when he straightened, I saw he was finding something about this funny. Blue eyes sparkled with mirth. I couldn't for the life of me see what it might be.

"Shall we go inside out of this rain?" Merlin said, nodding to the two guards, and they stepped aside.

The hearth fire now blazed, and torches flamed brightly on several pillars in the Hall. After the grey rain outside, the interior glowed with warm light. Arthur thumped his shield down on the nearest table, and having undone the clasp on his wet cloak, threw that down on top of it, revealing his heavy, ring mail shirt.

"We well and truly walloped them," he said, unbuckling his sword belt.

Merlin took the sword and laid it on the table. "How many were there?"

"Two keels of raiders. They'd burnt a fishing village to the ground and loaded the young women into their boats when we came on them."

Cei helped him pull the mail shirt over his head, leaving him standing in a sandy-brown quilted tunic and close-fitting leather braccae.

Arthur gave Merlin a grin. "Their ships were still drawn up on the sands. We attacked as they tried to launch them."

He began to help his brother out of his armor.

"And the women? Did you manage to save them?" Merlin's eyes were on the bandaged hand. There was dried blood encrusted on it.

Cei nodded. He was a big man even without his armor, raw boned with a square-jawed face and high cheek bones. Beside him, both Arthur and Merlin looked slight, which they weren't. "We got 'em all. And a fair number of the raiders – but we took no prisoners. Not worth it. We put 'em all to the sword as they'd done to the men of the fishing village."

They were casually talking about killing people, and it meant nothing because it wasn't real. I should be feeling something. Men had died. Probably women and children, too, at least on the British side. Yet I felt nothing.

Merlin's brow furrowed. "And the ships?"

Arthur answered this time. "They managed to get one of them into the surf, so we sent fire arrows after it. Their sails burnt, but they put the fires out and rowed away with what men they had left. The other one we burnt on the beach."

"Any casualties?"

Arthur's face clouded. "Many, amongst the villagers, and a couple of our men wounded. None dead."

"Your hand?"

Arthur glanced down at it as though seeing it for the first time. "Oh that. It's nothing. I'll get Tinwaun to take a look at it later."

Merlin frowned. "What did you put on it?"

"A poultice of sage leaves Bedwyr had in his pouch."

That didn't sound ideal. The bandage looked anything but clean, the outer part grey and wet, the edges crusted with dried blood. It needed to be taken off as soon as possible and the wound dressed properly. But dare I say so? Neither Arthur nor Cei had so much as glanced at me once we'd entered the Hall and they'd started telling Merlin how their expedition had gone. It was as though I didn't exist, which was ironic, as most of my father's academic friends had been convinced it was they who had never existed.

I took a deep breath. "That bandage is dirty. Infection can get in even the smallest of cuts if they're not kept clean. You need to change it and wash out the wound with something antiseptic."

The three men stared at me as though at a dog that had suddenly gained the power of speech.

"Bedwyr saw to it," Arthur said, "it should be fine." There was a glint of amusement in his solemn dark eyes, as though surprised I had a voice. They were going to have to learn I wasn't like the women they knew.

"Well, I don't think it will be," I said, feeling as though I was getting onto home ground because the library where I worked had recently sent me on a fairly extensive first aid course. "Let me take a look at it."

Our eyes met, and I held his gaze. His weren't actually black but a dark brown, flecked with gold. Silence stretched between us before he sat down on the bench and held out the offending hand. Ignoring Cei and Merlin, I settled beside him and took a sniff at the bandage. It wasn't a pleasant sight but at least it didn't smell infected.

"I need hot water and clean cloths and spirits – something stronger than wine if you have it." I paused. "And honey." My parents had been very keen on alternative medicines, and I'd grown up being doctored with natural everything. Honey would be a good antibiotic substitute.

At a nod from Arthur, Merlin departed through the open double doors.

I looked back down at the blood encrusted bandage, racking my brains as to what I should do.

On the far side of the table, Cei sat down with a thud. A big hand went up to push his mane of thick red hair out of his eyes, and he fixed me with a hard stare. Unnerved, I turned my attention back to Arthur.

"How did you get this wound?" I asked, to fill the silence that had fallen in the Hall.

Arthur pulled a face, and for a moment I had a glimpse of the boy he might have been not so long ago. "Fighting, of course. It's a knife cut, that's all. It's nothing."

"We'll see about that." I began to work at the tight knot Bedwyr had made of the ends of the bandage. It was matted with dried blood and determined not to be undone.

Silently, Cei drew out a long, sharp knife and laid it on the table. The blade glimmered in the torchlight as he shunted it across the table toward me. I picked it up and slipped it under the knot. It sliced through the rough material like a Samurai sword through silk. Hurriedly, I laid it down again.

"So, you're the woman with the dragon ring," Arthur said. "The woman Merlin wants me to marry."

I stopped picking at the bandage and looked up at him. "I suppose so." How to tell him without offense that I had no intention of becoming anyone's wife?

"To fulfill some old prophecy." His tone was sardonic.

He didn't sound like he believed in prophecies any more than I did. My hopes, which had hit rock bottom as soon as I'd seen him and his men ride through the fortress gates, began to rise at last. "That's what he told me."

He looked troubled, as though wrestling with some inner torment. However, I didn't get to find out what, because just then Merlin came back in with a bowl of hot water and the clean cloths I'd asked for. He was closely followed by Cottia carrying an earthenware bottle and a jar.

Arthur stiffened, and a frown of annoyance furrowed his brow.

Cottia, bustling like a mother hen, set the bottle down on the table and approached Arthur as though ready to clutch him to her ample bosom. He held up his good hand to stop her.

"Ye're hurt." Her voice was accusing, as though he'd injured himself on purpose.

He shook his head. I could feel his annoyance. "It's nothing."

Her face contorted as though she wanted to say more but didn't dare.

Instead, she turned on me. "What're ye doing? D'ye have the skills of an 'ealer?" She looked at Merlin for support. "Send for Tinwaun. Don't let 'er touch 'im. Tis best to use our own 'ealer. None of us know what she might do. None of us do know 'er." She was into her stride. "Corwyn from Ynys Witrin thought she were a Yellow 'air spy and what'd be better for 'em than if she were to poison our Prince? Or she may 'ave been sent by Prince Cadwy. That's more like to be the truth of it."

So much for her wanting me to be "her Arthur's" bride.

The last bit was addressed to Arthur, who gave an impatient sigh and pointed an angry finger at her. "Be quiet, woman. Why will no one listen to me? It's just a scratch, that's all. Bedwyr already treated it."

Cottia looked very much as though the last thing she wanted to be was quiet. She set her hands on her wide hips and glared at Arthur and Merlin. They both ignored her.

Cei, also ignoring her, had uncorked the bottle, so I picked it up and took a sniff. It smelled like whisky, which I didn't like, but I needed Dutch courage, so I took a swig of it to make sure it was strong enough. I swilled it round my teeth and swallowed. A fiery path burnt its way down to my stomach. It was definitely strong enough, plus it calmed my nerves. After all, it wasn't as if I dealt with battle wounds on a regular basis in the library.

Taking Arthur's hand, I put it into the bowl of warm water to soak.

"Tell me if it hurts." I worked at the softening bandages, peeling them off as gently as possible. The water darkened with blood. "What happened?"

"A Saxon warrior. He came off worse than I did, though." He reached for where his sword belt lay and drew a vicious looking short-bladed knife from a tooled leather scabbard. "I have his knife here. He has no more use for it."

A dead man's knife. Could that make this any more real? No, it was still like a bad dream.

The softened bandages came away in the water with a mess of bloody sage leaves, revealing a nasty gash across the back of his hand. With a fresh cloth, I dabbed away the congealed blood until I could see the wound properly. The edges looked clean and infection-free, but it was gaping and needed stitching.

"When did you get this?"

"Yesterday. We followed sightings of Saxon raiders along the coast from Caer Durnac. They didn't attack the town because they only had the two keels. Eighty men at most. Less than half that now."

"Forty less south coast raiders is forty less to fight against in the East," Merlin said.

I lifted Arthur's hand out of the water and laid it on a clean cloth to dry, gently dabbing at it with a corner. "You see how wide this cut is. It needs stitching to hold it together or it'll never heal properly. We'll need another bowl and a needle and strong thread." And scissors. Would they have scissors, or even know what they were? I had no idea. I'd have to use Cei's knife, still lying on the table beside me.

Merlin departed with Cottia in search of what I'd asked for. They weren't gone long. Cottia had the sewing equipment. Rather unwillingly, she handed it over, then sat down next to Cei, where she could best keep her eye on me and make sure I didn't hurt her precious Arthur.

I poured some of the spirit into the emptied bowl and then soaked the threaded needle, hoping it would be enough to sterilize them both, and that twenty-four hours wasn't too long after the wound had been made for stitching. Then I poured a liberal dose of the spirits over the open wound, drawing a short gasp and wince of pain from Arthur. I finally dowsed my own hands in spirit as an afterthought, mentally crossing my fingers. I wasn't working in what I'd have called clinical conditions.

"This is going to hurt," I warned him, taking his hand again.

Cottia's knuckles whitened on the edge of the table. If looks could have killed...

"Go on," he said, "it's no matter. I'll have had worse."

The needle was sharp, thank goodness, but even so I had difficulty getting it through the tough skin on the back of his hand. However, all I heard was a sharp intake of breath from him, and his hand never moved. Carefully, I made a stitch holding the wound together and tied it off. Merlin cut the thread for me, and I moved on to a second stitch. Beads of sweat formed on Arthur's forehead, but as they were on mine too, I ignored them. The mouth of the wound began to come together, until at last, after six more stitches, I had it closed entirely from end to end. Merlin cut the last thread, and I set down the needle with a sigh I couldn't hide.

Arthur looked up. "I don't know who was more worried about that, you or me. You keep a steady hand for one so nervous."

A laugh of relief escaped me. "It's not as easy as it looks."

Cei picked up the now half-empty bottle of spirits and took a long swig from it, then passed it to Arthur. He did the same, and putting it down, wiped the sweat from his forehead with the back of his sleeve. "A bit more of that and I won't feel a thing."

"I'll have a bit more." I picked up the bottle with a slightly shaking hand and took a mouthful. It ran fiery hot down my throat again. "And now a fresh bandage – which must stay clean and dry. You mustn't use this hand for anything that might make the stitches come apart, or make it dirty. That's very important." He really needed a course of antibiotics, but that was impossible. He'd have to take his chances. Having applied honey to the wound, I carefully bound the hand with a clean linen pad and fresh bandages.

Arthur looked up at me. His solemn face softened into a smile. He gave a little bow of his head. "Thank you, Lady Guinevere." His dark eyes twinkled. "I think you've come to us at an opportune moment, and already proved your worth. Will you tend to my other warriors who also have been wounded?"

Others? Of course, there'd be others after a battle. For the first time I felt there was a real reason for my being there. I couldn't say no. I nodded.

"Bring them here and I'll look at them, but I'll need a lot more hot water and cloths and spirit. It's the spirit that cleanses the wound. If dirt's in a wound, even dirt you can't see, it can fester. And if the invisible dirt gets into the blood, then sickness follows, and soon after that, death." It was the best explanation I could think of, especially as I was only a first aider and was just going on information I'd read in the papers about sepsis. I was glad I'd watched so many hospital soap operas. You can learn a lot from television.

Arthur nodded to his brother, who, like Cottia, was still glaring at me. "You'd better fetch Bran and Tegid."

Cei got to his feet, pushing back the solid wooden bench he was sitting on as though it weighed nothing, and disappeared out of the Hall to fulfill his mission. Merlin went in search of more spirits, and Cottia, muttering under her breath, left to get more hot water and clean cloths. Arthur and I were alone.

It was quiet in the Great Hall. The flames in the hearth fire crackled loudly in the silence, and from outside came the sound of voices calling and a dog barking. I was much too close to Arthur and his raw masculinity for my own liking.

He looked me up and down in a speculative fashion.

"Do you like what you see?" I asked him in annoyance. Was I a horse to be judged by my appearance?

The corners of his eyes crinkled in a smile. One thing I'd never have expected the real Arthur to be was so full of good humor. "What's not to like?" he retorted. "You're beautiful, you fill your gown well, you look strong and have good child-bearing hips. What more could a man want?"

*A lot,* I thought crossly, but what I said was, "That's a bit shallow."

He frowned. "I don't understand. What d'you mean, shallow?"

"Judging someone by their appearance only, not by personality."

"Well, so far your personality seems pleasing, too." He paused. "And you have some very useful skills." He held up his bandaged hand. "I can almost bring myself to agree with Merlin that it would be a good idea to marry you."

"Almost?"

Why did I feel offended? After all, I didn't want to marry him myself.

He shrugged. "I'm not looking for a wife. Merlin is. Well, he's looking for one for me. I don't need a wife. Not yet. Now's not the time."

"What about the prophecy?"

"Huh." He got to his feet. "You believe that story?"

I shook my head. "Why would I? How could anyone predict the

future?"

As I said the words it occurred to me that he was, in fact, talking to the one person on earth who could do just that. If he only knew. However, everything known about Arthur in my time could be written on the back of a penny piece, and all the rest dismissed as speculation. So I could only begin to guess at his future. I had no idea what bits of the hundreds of legends about him were true and which were made up.

"Merlin thinks he can," he said. He'd picked up his sword belt and was examining the ornate hilt of the sword as though he'd never seen it before.

"Yes, well, Merlin's wrong."

He was very good-looking in a dark, earthy fashion, his looks only enhanced by the presence of the scar on his face. It gave him a piratical air. I thought of Nathan with his floppy, sandy brown hair and his kind, intelligent face. There was nothing about Arthur that was remotely like Nathan – and yet his amused smile, long, dark hair and almost black eyes were undeniably attractive.

He pushed his damp hair back from his face. "He says you're vital to my future. That you're the key." He looked into my eyes, puzzled. "Yet you're just a woman. A stranger. Not some highborn princess whose father I want to make an alliance with. Not someone who brings an enormous dowry or even a kingdom. You're the girl with no past. The one that bloody prophecy says I have to marry." He shook his head in frustration. "And yet I can't see how any woman could be the key to anything."

Well, there was one thing you could definitely say about Arthur: he wasn't into girl-power. I didn't know whether to laugh or get angry. I was saved from either by Merlin coming back.

He was closely followed by Cottia and her two daughters, carrying bowls of hot water. They set everything down on the table, while Arthur moved closer to the fire, his left hand cradled to his chest. It was probably throbbing painfully. I hoped he was going to heed my warnings about keeping it clean.

Luckily, neither Bran nor Tegid proved to be too seriously wounded. They came nervously into the Hall with a crowd of onlookers, all damp with the rain, and directed by Merlin, sat down at the table so I could treat them.

Bran was a young man with mousy hair and a wispy beard. Someone had given him a slice to his upper arm. Having soaked his bandages off, I stitched his wound, rebandaged him, and told him not to use his arm until I said he could. He sat silent throughout, gazing at me out of wide blue eyes like a wounded puppy. I rewarded his stoic attitude to the stitching of his wound with a generous swig of spirits.

Tegid was an older man with a head wound. On removing his horrible dressing, I found a long graze running from up in his hairline right down the side of his face. This wasn't gaping open, so I doused it with spirits, which made him shout, and then bandaged it up again. He took a much longer swig at the bottle afterwards than young Bran had. Cei had to wrest it from his hands with a word of rebuke. The watching crowd laughed. Tegid seemed to be well known for his predilection for strong alcohol.

I was nervous about doing all this. After all, if they should sicken and die from their wounds, which they well might, I was setting myself up to take the blame. But as someone with the knowledge, scanty as it was, of germs and infections, I owed it to them to at least try to improve their chances. Merlin might fight my corner if things didn't go as planned – I hoped.

"What're you all staring at?" Cei asked my audience genially. "Never seen a healer work?"

"Probably not," Arthur said, as the crowd dispersed with Tegid and Bran, the show over. "How often do we see a real healer here in Din Cadan? How often did we see one in Viroconium, even? My father could do with someone like this." He looked at Merlin. "You didn't tell us she was a healer."

"I'm not a healer," I said, "I just happen to know a bit about first aid. Only as much as the next person, though."

They all gave me disbelieving looks. Well, maybe not Cottia, who looked as though she might like it if I turned out not to be as capable as the others thought. I hoped my ministrations were going to work because they were showing a touching faith in me. Still, small as my knowledge was, it was probably a great deal better than theirs. That, at least, gave me comfort.

Arthur stretched. "My hand feels almost better. If you're not a healer, then you're the next best thing." He looked at Cei. "I don't know about you, but I need a bath. Six days in the saddle in the middle of winter's left me feeling sore to my very bones. Cottia, can you organize that?"

My mouth fell open. "You've got somewhere you can have a bath?"

Why hadn't they told me? It was two days since I'd had a shower and I felt the dirtiest I'd ever been.

Arthur nodded. "We have a bath house. It's not like the one in my father's palace. Not like the old Roman ones, but it's nearly as good. Would you like a bath too?"

Would I? Was water wet?

I nodded. My hair hadn't quite reached the stage where it hurt with being dirty, but I thought it soon would.

Cei slapped Arthur on the back. "Me too. Let's get out of these clothes and into some hot water."

The very thought was delirious.

The bath house was an oblong thatched building in the courtyard where I'd seen Cottia's daughter working that morning, divided into one half for men and one for women. Armed with my returned clean underwear and a big rough cloth to serve as a towel, I entered the women's half in trepidation. I needn't have worried. Inside, a young girl helped me out of my clothes and took me through a door into a room with a big wooden tub in it, steam rising off its contents in a promising manner.

The only drawback was I couldn't have my bath by myself. The girl, Maia, insisted on helping me with every step of my ablutions. I hadn't had my hair washed by anyone else apart from the hairdresser since I was a child, so it was strange to sink back into the tub and let her rub a treatment into it. It didn't lather like modern shampoo and smelled quite strongly of vinegar, but when she rinsed it off, it left my hair feeling super clean. It was quite a while before I emerged, my skin glowing pink, in my clean underwear and russet gown.

The rain had cleared a bit, but the cloud still hung low as I walked back to the Great Hall. Inside, I found Merlin sitting on a stool by the fire, plucking the strings of a musical instrument a little like a small guitar. It reminded me of the note I'd heard up on the Tor, pure and sweet and high. He stopped when he saw me and set the instrument down.

I came and sat beside him, feeling much better now I was clean. My bath had made me feel more up to coping with the situation, more in control. Maia had even provided me with a twig and some powdered charcoal paste for cleaning my teeth again. This had entailed much rinsing to get rid of the bits of charcoal, which Maia had insisted I did with a cup of beer.

"What's that?" I asked, pointing at his instrument.

He plucked a string. "My lyre."

"I think I heard it when I saw you, back in my world. At least, something that sounded very like it."

He nodded. "You may well have. I take it everywhere with me."

We sat in silence for a few minutes, me playing with the braided cord Maia had knotted round my waist, him sitting quietly.

Eventually, he broke the silence. I'd been waiting for him to do that. "He's not so bad, is he?"

I shrugged. "He seems to be –" I nearly said *nice*, but that wasn't the right word for him, nor for anyone in the Dark Ages. None of them were nice. "He seems to be a good man." Such as I could judge after a brief hour's acquaintance.

"He'll make a good High King one day."

"Will he?" I had no idea about the qualities required to become a leader in the Dark Ages, so I couldn't pass an opinion. "What about his brother? I thought you said he had an older brother?"

"He does. But it's not Cadwy's destiny to be High King. It's Arthur's."

I thought about that for a moment. "So you say. I guess this Cadwy might have a different opinion of that himself. Although it might explain why in my time I've never heard anything about him."

"But you know of Arthur?"

I nodded. "Everyone does. But hardly anyone believes he really existed. There's nothing written down, no records of his reign, just legends. My father was an Arthurian scholar. He knew everything there was to know about the Dark Ages. Despite his colleagues insisting it was unlikely there'd ever really been a King Arthur, he stuck to his belief that there had been. He believed there'd been a real man all the stories were based on. And believe me, there are plenty of stories."

"And his wife? What was her name in your stories?"

He had me there. Why had my parents named me after her? What had possessed them? "Guinevere."

He smiled with just a hint of triumph, of having talked me into a corner I couldn't get out of. "See. You are indeed the one. It was foretold by others, not just by me, that you would come."

I gritted my teeth that I'd fallen into his trap and that he was so difficult to deflect from what he wanted. I was angry with myself because against my better judgement I liked him.

"Yes, but me having the right name doesn't mean I'm the one

you're searching for." I felt as though I was banging my head against a brick wall. "The only reason I'm called Guinevere is because I was named after the real one. Named after the woman you should be looking for. She must be out there somewhere in this world, but I'm not her."

He shook his head. "You're the one. I've looked into the future, and I've seen you, solid and real, a point about which the future pivots. An immovable point. You are the one."

A thought crossed my mind. "Maybe you're right." I put my hand on his sleeve. "Maybe you're right, but you've not interpreted it correctly. Maybe what I was meant to do, I've already done. Maybe I stopped Arthur from getting an infection through his wound. Maybe that's why he can go on and become High King. Maybe without me he would have died."

Merlin shook his head. "If that were true, it would have been clear to me. No, you have much more significance than that. Without you, he will be nothing. With you, he will be great."

Why couldn't I make him listen? "But I'm not from your world," I protested. "You've left a gap in my world that I should be occupying. I belong there, not here. I have to get back."

He frowned. "Even if a way back existed, I wouldn't show it to you. But it doesn't. You're here, and here is where you have to remain. Arthur is your destiny, and you are his. Nothing you can do will change that. It was written before either of you were born. He is the one who will defeat the Saxons, and you are the queen who will be by his side."

I shook my head again, feeling frustrated. "Arthur becoming king has nothing to do with me." I knew this story. Could I make him believe it? "It's you that makes him king, not me."

I had his attention.

"When his father dies, you take a sword and you stick it in a stone, and you say that whoever can draw the sword out of the stone will be the true born King of Britain. Everyone tries, but no one can draw out the sword. And then Arthur does. That's what happens. That's how he becomes king."

Merlin's eyes narrowed thoughtfully. I could almost hear the cogs turning.

# Chapter Eight

I N THE HALL that night I sat beside Arthur at the High Table, wearing the beautiful russet gown, my hair plaited, with bad grace and golden thread, by Cottia. It appeared that almost everyone who lived in the fortress had come to celebrate the safe return of their prince. Warriors and their womenfolk crammed every bench, cheek by jowl with the older men and youths who'd been left behind to guard the fortress while he'd been away, and noise rose to the smoky rafters.

This time, not so dazed with shock as before, I had more opportunity to observe the revelers and the goings on around me. The food was better than the night before. As well as venison dripping with juices, we ate hare and pheasant and partridge, with dishes of cooked vegetables like beets and parsnips and leeks, all served with savory sauces. I restricted myself to small amounts, drinking sparingly of the red wine that was topped up every time I set my goblet down on the table. I didn't want another hangover.

Arthur went out of his way to be pleasant, making every effort to talk as we ate. He wore the plain dark tunic and braccae he'd appeared in after what must have been a very long soak in his bath, his bandage still remarkably clean and dry. Round his neck a golden torc shone warm against his skin, its dragon-headed finials grinning at each other, reminding me of my bracelet and ring. He caught me looking at it.

"May I see your ring?"

I offered him my hand, which he took in his, the better to see.

"So, this is Merlin's dragon ring?" His warm touch was curiously disturbing. He turned my hand this way and that, my cheeks flushing in betrayal of my confusion. He seemed oblivious. "It's not a ring I've ever seen before. Not part of the royal jewelry collection or I'd know it. I'd have seen my mother wear it."

He glanced down the Hall to where Merlin sat with Cei and a gaggle of other warriors in their evening finery, their heads turned away.

"Where is your mother?" I asked, to cover up my discomfiture. "Is she still living?" If she were here in Din Cadan, surely I'd have met her.

His face hardened and he released my hand. "She's in Tintagel. Cei's fortress."

I put my hand in my lap, out of his reach. "Why isn't she with your father?"

He frowned into his wine, and I looked away, down into the body of the Hall at the boisterous crowd, feeling as though I'd said the wrong thing.

Arthur set his goblet down. "I don't speak of my mother. You weren't to know."

"My mother died when I was eight," I said, to break the ice that had somehow formed between us.

He nodded. "Merlin told me. And your father is also dead."

The flames in the hearth leapt toward the rafters, and sweat ran down the faces of the revelers nearest to it. The fug of hot humanity hung heavy in the smoky air.

My turn to nod. How my father would have loved this, though. Could he see me from wherever he was? Did he know I was living his dream? Even though it was hardly mine.

"And your father?" I asked, feeling more at ease now he was no longer touching me.

He gave a shrug. "He's the High King. What more is there to say than that?"

Lots. I was going to have to draw this out of him. "Where's his court?"

"Viroconium." Wroxeter, near Shrewsbury, whose impressive bath house ruins I'd once visited with my father.

He pushed the food on his plate about absent-mindedly with his knife, those dark eyes veiled by enviably long lashes. "Capital of Powys. It's been the seat of the Imperators and then the High Kings since the Romans left."

I was instantly interested, and distracted from his physical presence. This might allow me to orient myself in time. I knew the Romans had withdrawn from Britain in AD 410.

"How long ago was that?"

His brow furrowed. "My grandfather was just a young man. And he died forty years ago, long before I was born. Poisoned, my grandmother swore. He was overthrown and exiled by the usurper Guorthegirn before my uncle and father were even born."

I raised my hand. "Wait a moment. Poisoned? By whom? And where was your grandfather exiled to?"

He gave me a wry smile. "To Gaul. My great grandfather, his father, was the Imperator Constantine the third, killed there fighting to defend the Western Roman empire."

"He was a Roman?"

He nodded. "His family – *my* family wore the purple. His son, my grandfather, Ambrosius the Elder, was named Imperator, *last* Imperator, when his father was killed. He was just a young man. Constantine had left him to rule Britain while he fought in Gaul for his empire."

He picked up his wine goblet again but didn't drink from it, swirling the contents about ruminatively instead. "Guorthegirn, the Usurper, served as my grandfather Ambrosius' Magister Militum – and his friend. So my grandfather thought. But it was he who overthrew my grandfather and drove him across the southern sea to Gaul. He who abolished the title of Imperator and declared himself High King. My father and his brother were born in exile."

Guorthegirn the Usurper, whose wise men had prophesied my arrival and my destiny.

"And the poisoning? What happened?"

"My grandfather was a determined man. He made every effort to seize back what was his by right, but Guorthegirn had bought himself a Saxon army, and my grandfather was defeated at the battle of Guoloppum, many miles to the east of here. He retreated to Armorica, in Gaul, a beaten man."

Guoloppum? Nowhere I'd ever heard of. Somewhere to the east could be as far as Kent.

"He died in his bed, of a sickness no one could cure. My grand-mother swore Guorthegirn had sent someone to poison him. She refused to eat anything not tasted by a slave beforehand, and made my father and uncle do the same."

"So, what did your father and uncle do?"

He gave a shake of his head. "Do? Nothing. When they were grown they went to Guorthegirn and offered him their services."

"Didn't they want revenge?"

He nodded. "Of course. But they were young men with few fol-lowers. The king of Armorica, their mother's kin, couldn't offer them support. His men had been decimated following my grandfather back to Britain. They no longer had the strength of arms to overcome Guorthegirn, who was still in his prime. And don't forget, he had the Saxons at his beck and call."

"What happened to Guorthegirn? Merlin told me your uncle be-came High King, and then your father. How did that come about?"

The noise in the hall was deafening. No one could have overheard our conversation. I felt at liberty to ask him what I liked. And besides which, I was enjoying talking to him because there was something very attractive about his frankness.

"The Saxons were not reliable allies. They wanted more and more – they still do – and Guorthegirn couldn't pay what they demanded, so they rose up to take it for themselves. As is their habit." He waved away the slave offering the flagon of wine. "My uncle Ambrosius, and Guorthegirn's oldest son Vortimer, drove them back toward the sea in Ceint, forcing them to their ships. Many Saxons drowned. My uncle lost many British warriors. Even so, it was a great victory. After that, the fighting went back and forth, and eventually the Saxons sued for peace."

I wanted to ask the sort of probing questions my father would have posed, but for the moment I stayed silent, listening. This wasn't the time for them. I just wanted him to talk.

"Guorthegirn trusted them. My father and uncle did not. If they had, then I wouldn't be here now."

He was such a vital life force I found myself wondering how he could have been snuffed out before he was born – how the whole canon of myth about him might so easily never have happened, how the legends of King Arthur might never have been.

He went on. "Three hundred men, British kings and princes with their followers, went to meet the Saxons. Guorthegirn amongst them. Ceint was allotted to the Saxons for settling. They all sat down to feast, Britons alongside their Saxon hosts." His brows knitted in a scowl. "As High King, Guorthegirn had agreed that none should come bearing weapons as a sign of peace. They left these outside and went to eat undefended. And when much wine and mead had been drunk, the Saxons rose up and each slew the Briton by his side. It was called the Night of the Long Knives. All died except for Guorthegirn."

If Ambrosius and Uthyr had joined their king, Arthur would never have been born. His whole being had hinged on their distrust for the Saxons. I didn't know what to say. I didn't need to, though, because he went on.

"Guorthegirn was married to a Saxon princess, Ronweinna, daughter of Hengest. Some said he was spared by her pleadings. Whatever the reason, after that, Guorthegirn was a broken man, a puppet in the hands of Hengest. That was when my uncle began his campaign to snatch back what had been stolen from his father by the Usurper."

He took a long draught of the wine, then wiped his mouth with the back of his hand. "All this was long before I was born."

I met his eyes; they were like dark peaty pools. Flustered, I asked, "When was that?" The date of birth of King Arthur would be a choice piece of knowledge.

He hesitated before answering, staring so hard into my eyes I had to drag my gaze away. "Seven years into the reign of my uncle." He flushed and looked away. "My mother was not my father's first wife. First, he took a Saxon bride, Aelfled. A match organized by my uncle to broker a cease in hostilities. She was the granddaughter of Hengest and an important pawn in the game of kings. With Hengest dead, my father put her aside so that he might take my mother to wife. I was born ten years after my brother Cadwy, three years before my father became High King."

His lips came together in a firm line. Was he as discomfited and awkward as I was? Had he felt the electricity that I'd sensed flickering between us?

A fat little man in a costume made of many different colored patches came cartwheeling down the central aisle of the hall to land on his feet in front of us. He swept off his tasseled hat and made a deep bow. He had a large, red, bulbous nose, and one side of his face was much larger than the other, giving him an odd, lopsided appearance. He came up grinning and Arthur threw him a lump of venison from his plate. Catching it deftly between his teeth as a dog would, he flipped over backwards onto his hands, then set off down the hall on them, his legs waving in the air. Shouts of encouragement rang from the benches.

Arthur gave a shout of laughter as the little man fell over a couple of quarrelling hounds.

Despite myself, I liked him. He was intelligent with a quick wit, and even with the quantity of wine being served, he drank as sparingly as I did. He talked about his people, pointing them out in the noisy throng of the Great Hall, catching their eyes, raising his goblet to them in salute. Their faces revealed how much this meant to them. He seemed a much-loved leader. And there was something about him that I found undeniably attractive.

I WOKE LATE the next morning, curled amongst the furs and rather scratchy plaid blankets of the bed that should by rights have been Arthur's. I had no idea where he, having given up his chamber, had been forced to sleep, and I didn't care. If I were going to suffer the downside of being trapped in the Dark Ages, there was no way I was going to give up the perks.

I lay there for a few minutes, in that sleepy half-awake morning state, not wanting to open my eyes. After a bit, the sound of voices drifted in from the Hall on the far side of the dividing wall. I rolled over to face the door. Women's voices. One of them was singing, but I couldn't catch the words. Servants, probably. I was already thinking like a potential princess and taking it for granted that someone else would do the clearing up.

My thoughts drifted to Arthur, which made me think about Nathan as well. Two very different men. Today was the beginning of the third day of my disappearance, and surely Nathan would be panic-stricken by now, and the police would be searching for me. Maybe they'd have dogs out. What would they find, though? Nothing. My scent would have disappeared as though by magic. Definitely by magic if Merlin was right. Something no one's believed in for centuries. And yet what else could it have been?

I blinked away tears as I thought about Nathan. You can't just forget someone if you think you're never going to see them again. I felt like he'd died and I'd been left behind, although in truth it was the other way around. If I was stuck here, then I really was dead –dead and buried in Nathan's time, just an archaeological find waiting to be discovered, pored over and labelled. Put in a museum, maybe. Horrible thought. A lump rose in my throat.

The opening of the Hall door disturbed my wallowing in self-pity. Maia, the girl from the bath house, came in carrying a steaming bowl of hot water. Just as I'd asked her at the baths. The lump in my throat subsided, and I pushed the covers back off the bed, feeling a little better.

Washed and dressed, my hair in one thick plait down my back, I took breakfast at the table in my chamber, this time of thick slices of hot bacon and scrambled eggs lightly flecked with soot. Who'd have thought the traditional full English was actually Celtic?

The meal over, I ventured through the Hall, empty now of the women who'd been clearing up and tending the fire. By its glowing embers, a pile of hounds twitched and snored, long tails stirring the reeds. They ignored me as I passed them. Some guard dogs they were.

Outside, the day matched my rising mood. It was one of those rare, cold winter days when the sky is an almost cloudless blue and everything beneath it sparkles afresh. The fortress buzzed with activity. A man nearby was sharpening his sword on a whetstone. In the stables, men tended their horses, and cheerful singing came from one of the barns.

Investigation proved the singers to be a group of young women rhythmically beating wheat to loosen the grain from the husks. Winnowing. A cloud of dust rose around them in a haze, but they didn't seem to mind. I stood and watched for a minute or so, until they, aware of my scrutiny, became self-conscious and their singing died away.

Embarrassed they should feel they needed to be silent because of me, I turned away from the barn door and took a narrow alleyway between the barn and the house next door. Mud squelched under my boots, and drips from the dark thatch spattered my head. I emerged between an earthen bank enclosing the house's kitchen garden and a pen behind the barn, where pigs rooted in the mud. Beyond, a maze of railed paddocks checkered the hilltop. I'd found the horse pens, so I decided to take a look at the horses.

I threaded my way between the paddocks until I came to one where a group of sturdy cobs grazed. Despite their dirty and shaggy appearance, they were good stock with strong legs and well filled-out bodies, better quality animals than the ones belonging to Abbot Jerome. I leaned on the fence and the horses raised their heads, ears pricked in curiosity, to stare at me. I clicked my tongue at them and a couple of them started to walk toward me.

"Hello."

I looked down at the sound of a voice.

I hadn't noticed the little boy who was standing watching them as well. He looked up at me out of large, dark eyes that peeped from under a mane of wild, curly hair.

"Are you the Lady of the Ring?"

I supposed I must be, so I nodded. "My name's Gwen, what's yours?"

"Llacheu."

He looked about six years old. His build was sturdy and strong, and he wore a fine dark blue tunic over matching braccae, and a short cloak. Not the child of one of the servants.

"That's a nice name."

His brow creased. "So's yours. It's Guinevere really, isn't it?"

I nodded. Did they all know about me? Down to the smallest child?

"Mine should be Llacheu Pendragon," the child said. "But it can't be, because my mother's not wed to my father. So I'm baseborn. But

I'm still from the dragon's line." He eyed me thoughtfully. "My mother says I would be a Pendragon if it weren't for you."

I blinked. Was this Arthur's child? I wasn't sure how to answer this pronouncement.

He kicked the toe of his ankle boot in the mud. "But I don't mind. If I were a Pendragon I'd be his heir, and if I were that, I'd have to be a king one day, because he's going to be a king. Now he's got you and the prophecy is coming true, he'll be the High King. And kings are never their own men. They can't do just what they like. They can't take off being a king at night like their cloaks. They have to be kings all the time. And I wouldn't like that."

"Who told you that?" It didn't sound like a conclusion a six-year-old would have reached all by himself.

"My friend Merlin."

Of course. The perpetrator of my problems. And this little boy's as well. If Merlin hadn't been promising the imminent arrival of the woman who would make him High King, Arthur might be married now to this child's mother.

"Lucky escape, then," I said, thinking I could do with a similar cop-out.

Llacheu grinned. "I want to be a warrior when I grow up and fight the Yellow Hairs and the Irish raiders and the Picts. Kings do get to do that. But I don't want to have to do court stuff. Merlin says they have to be wise and good and-and give out justice, and that sounds boring. It's hard being good all the time. I just want to do lots of fighting."

He pushed back his cloak and drew a short wooden sword from a scabbard on his belt. "See? My father gave me this. He says I'll be a great warrior, and they'll sing about me in kings' halls for years to come. I'd like that."

I smiled my admiration for his sword. The horses had their heads down grazing again.

"Want to see my pony?" Llacheu asked suddenly. "Want to see me ride it?"

Why not? I liked children, and it would be good to get to know this frank little boy better.

"All right. Lead the way."

He threaded his way through the network of pens to a small enclosure where a fat, grey pony was grazing by herself. He whistled, and she raised her head and started to walk toward us. She looked very much like the Welsh Mountain Pony I'd first learned to ride on when I, too, had been six. Llacheu unhooked a rope halter from one of the fence posts and slipping between the rails, stood on tiptoe to get the halter over his pony's small ears. The pony dropped her head, and Llacheu led her up to me.

"Her name's Seren," he said, one small grubby hand buried in her mane, "because she's so beautiful. Star. My father gave her to me on my last name day."

"Lucky you," I said, giving Seren's forehead a rub. She had a good growth of thick winter coat on her, covered in dried mud. "Have you got any brushes so we can groom her?"

Llacheu looped the halter rope over the fence. "I'll run and get them."

While he was gone, I had a bit of a conversation with Seren, who was convinced I might have something edible hidden about my person and kept nudging me with her soft, grey muzzle and nibbling at my sleeves. By the time Llacheu returned, she and I were good friends. He'd brought another older boy with him, and this boy carried a small saddle and a bridle, while Llacheu had a couple of bristly brushes and a toothed metal tool that reminded me of a modern currycomb.

"This is Tulac," Llacheu said, introducing the older boy. "Father gave him to me to be my body slave. He has to do what I say, but my mother keeps stealing him to do her chores. I had to go and get him back. I can't carry the saddle by myself. It's too heavy, and I trip over the girth." He stood on tiptoes to brush the mud off Seren's wide back.

"But I'm growing fast. I couldn't reach up here in the summer, and now I can."

I took a brush and started on the other side of Seren while Tulac watched, still holding the saddle. He was a lanky, sandy-haired boy of about twelve, with a wide mouth and thick smattering of freckles. When the pony was clean enough, Llacheu took the bridle and managed to get it onto her without too much difficulty. Tulac put a checked rug and then the saddle on her broad back, and Llacheu did up the girth. The pony puffed herself out as he tried to get it tight, so when he'd finished, I too gave it a tug and got it much more securely fastened. Tulac grinned at me out of wide-spaced tombstone teeth that looked too big for his bony head. Evidently puffing herself out was Seren's favorite trick.

"Where are you going to ride her so I can watch?" I asked.

Someone had put a wooden box outside the drop rails, and now Llacheu led her over to it, positioned her carefully, and used the box to leap up onto her saddle. The four horns gripped his thighs, making him look very secure despite the lack of stirrups.

"This way." He drummed Seren's fat sides with his heels and led the way, with Tulac and me following, through the pens toward the outer wall of the fortress. There, against the bank, lay the narrow strip of land I'd seen the day before from up on the wall-walk. Three other boys on ponies were already there, and someone had set up a round target for them. As we approached, one of the boys charged his pony at the target, short blunt spear in hand, and hit it hard in the center. It spun out of his way as he went galloping past.

They all looked older than Llacheu.

"Fetch me my spears, Tulac." He was very imperious. This was a child who knew his place, and it was high up. Maybe not as high up as it could have been, but it seemed that illegitimate or not, being Arthur's son had perks. Tulac loped off good-naturedly back the way we'd come.

The three boys rode over to greet Llacheu. They all rode small ponies like Seren. The boy who'd hit the target had long legs that hung down below his pony's belly. The sleeves of his tunic were well above his bony wrists, as though he'd recently undergone a growth spurt. Bright ginger hair peeked from under the leather helmet he wore. Might he be Cei's son?

"Hey, Llacheu, did you see me hit the target?" he cried excitedly. "I got it dead center."

"Who's she?" asked one of the other two, a rather chubby boy with a double chin, pointing a grubby finger at me.

Llacheu drew himself up. "She's the Lady of the Ring. The one foretold. She's come to watch me ride." Emphasis on the word *me*.

Chubby's mouth made a round O of astonishment, and his eyes went to my hand, where the dragon ring shone in the morning sunlight. But it was Long Legs who found his voice first. He did a little awkward bow to me from on top of his pony. "My Lady."

"She's going to marry my father," Llacheu went on. "And be queen when he's king."

Chubby did a little bow as well, his round face alight with interest. The third boy, nearly as dark as Llacheu, didn't look quite so impressed. "She's still just a girl. And girls can't fight so they're not important. It's a sword that makes a warrior, and it's warriors that make kings. Not girls."

I smiled. "I quite agree with you. It takes more than marrying someone to make a king."

Tulac came back lugging a couple of short spears, one of which he handed to Llacheu.

The little boy settled it in his right hand and, using his left on the reins, wheeled his pony toward the target. Seren was obviously used to this. She set off at a fast canter toward her target, hairy little legs pounding the muddy ground. The spear wavered a little, then hit the target, which spun round so fast it almost knocked Llacheu out of the saddle. He righted himself and managed to pull Seren up about a hundred yards away, looking very pleased.

"Let's fight next!" he shouted, kicking Seren into a trot toward us. "Take my spear, Tulac. Swords, Drem!" The dark boy, Drem, whipped out his own wooden sword and kicked his pony toward Seren. Llacheu drew his sword and waved it above his head.

"Wait a minute. Wait a minute."

I spun around at the sound of a deep, amused voice. Arthur was walking toward us across the trampled grass.

"No fighting without shields," he called. "Tulac, go and fetch them all some shields."

Tulac ran off once again.

"Father!" Llacheu shouted. "We don't need shields. We can fight like this. It's easy." But he and Drem had lowered their swords and brought their ponies to a halt.

"You know it's a rule," Arthur said, in a voice that brooked no argument. "You know you need to learn to use your shield as well as your sword. Once you've got your shield you can show me and the Lady Guinevere what you've been learning." He turned to me with a conspiratorial smile. "I take it that's why you've been invited down here?"

I returned his smile. It was infectious. Were his eyes twinkling at me? I was struck anew by how very attractive he was. It wasn't just his looks – something about him shone. What would it be like to have a man like him take me in his arms and kiss me? My cheeks grew warm at the disturbing thought.

"Yes, sir." Clearly disappointed, Llacheu shoved his sword back into its scabbard and trotted over to us. "Did you see me hit the target? It nearly swung round and got me, but I didn't fall off. I'm getting better at that, aren't I?"

Seeing them side by side, I was struck by how very much alike they were. Arthur himself must have been like this child when he was young.

Arthur nodded. "You're certainly improving. As you should be. Here comes Tulac. Put on your shield. Here, take yours, Drem." The two boys donned their small round shields, both white painted and devoid of any emblem.

"We'll do the Battle of Llongborth. You be the Saxon Cerdic, and I'll be Prince Geraint." Llacheu drew his sword again and waved it in the air, pulling his pony round to meet Drem's. The wooden swords clashed as they rode knee to knee, and Llacheu managed to get in a sound blow to Drem's shield. "Got you!" he shouted.

"Geraint dies," remarked Chubby, who had brought his pony over to stand next to Arthur and me. "Cerdic kills him."

FOR A MOMENT something akin to anger flitted across Arthur's face, then he laughed. "I think my son is keen to rewrite history."

I studied his face, sure there was something here I'd missed. But no, he was watching the two boys begin their fight with only the love of a proud father in his eyes.

For such a young boy, Llacheu was a ferocious warrior. He rained blows down on Drem, who must have been a year or two older than him, and took those Drem inflicted on him as though he hardly noticed them. After a few minutes, he got in a blow to the stomach while Drem had his shield arm back, pulling his pony to the left. With a gasp of pain Drem toppled sideways and landed with a thud on the ground.

I clapped my hands as the victorious Prince Geraint trotted over to us, his face pink with exertion. Drem picked himself up and went to catch his pony.

"D'you think I'm going to be a great warrior?" Llacheu asked boldly.

I laughed.

"A great warrior should never openly seek praise," his father scolded and turned to me. "Don't answer him. He's getting too big-headed as it is."

I laughed again. If I imagined we were standing on the lines of a football match the boys had been playing, we could have been in my world. That we had just watched a rehearsal for the deadly reality of adulthood that awaited these small boys sent a cold trickle of appre-hension running down my spine. My laugh died away as I had a momentary mental image of them fighting with real swords, and how that blow to the stomach would have run Drem through if it had been real, and his entrails would have come spilling out onto the muddy turf. Envisioning the violence of this way of life sobered me.

Arthur took my arm. "She's mine now," he said to his son. "Be-have yourselves and don't fight without your shields. Remember."

He steered me across the muddy riding track toward the wall, and we climbed up the steps that led to the walkway where I'd stood the day before with Merlin. Behind us, the four boys kicked their ponies into a race, small hooves thundering across the turf, howls of encour-agement to their mounts rending the air.

To my right and left, guards stood along the wall at intervals, gaz-ing out across the surrounding farmlands. I turned away from Arthur to look down the steep slope of the hill. Was that the wooden spire of a church nestled amongst a small thicket of trees at the hill's foot? Arthur came and stood next to me.

"Your son's very charming," I said.

He smiled. "And very cheeky. I can see he's taken to you."

"He's very much like you."

"So I'm told." His dark eyes regarded me. "Does that mean you think I, too, am charming?" He was teasing me. Wasn't he?

I'd fallen into that one. "I mean, he looks like you. Who's his mother? Have I seen her?" I could feel my cheeks reddening.

"Tangwyn." He leaned against the crenelated parapet, the wind ruffling his hair. "She was in the Hall last night. A red-haired woman with eyes like a cat."

I couldn't remember anyone like that.

"Are there more children? Yours, I mean?"

He shook his head. "No. Tangwyn had two others but neither lived." His face was suddenly serious. Was he thinking of his dead children? The death of babies was pretty much to be expected, I supposed. Infant mortality would be high in the Dark Ages. I didn't press him.

"Nothing since the last one," he said, "I've been away a lot. She'd like another, I know, but these things don't always happen. She knows it. She has Llacheu. He's strong and brave and past the age when he might be carried off by illness."

"He's a son to be proud of."

The smile came back, lighting up his face. "I know."

He turned his head and looked northwards. On the horizon clouds were gathering in grey tatters. Was more rain coming? I hoped not. Din Cadan was almost pleasant in the winter sunshine.

He lifted a hand and pointed. "Riders from the North."

I looked. At first, I couldn't see them, and he had to lean nearer to me so that I could look down his pointing arm. His breath was warm on my cheek. I felt myself flush, which was silly. And then I saw them, tiny specks emerging from the forest on the rough road. Riders. I counted ten.

"Who are they?"

He shrugged. "No idea. But whatever they're about, it must be important for them to be abroad in winter when the roads are this bad. They'll be headed here. There's nowhere else they could be going."

"How d'you know they're not your enemies?"

He gave a short laugh. "They're on horseback. The Saxons are foot soldiers. Plus, there are only ten of them. The Saxons would never send out so small a war party, and they would never attack us here in Din Cadan. We're too well defended for that." He took my arm again and started around the wall-walk. "Come, we'll go to the gates and see what it is they want."

At the gates we climbed the ladder to the top viewing platform and watched the progress of the riders along the road and around the base of the hill between the farmsteads. As they began the climb toward the gates, they dipped out of sight until they emerged onto the plateau and wove their way between the offset entrance banks, their horses' hooves clattering on the cobbles. Every one of them was an armed warrior.

"Theodoric!" Arthur called out as the lead rider came into view. The rider, a big man on a solid black cob, raised his hand and took off his round helmet, letting a mane of dark blond hair blow out in the wind. He was mustached, but not bearded, and nearly as big a man as Cei, long legs dangling below his sweaty horse's girth.

"Arthur!' he shouted back.

Arthur was at the ladder sliding down it to the floor below, as Theodoric and the other nine riders passed beneath us through the gateway. I followed him more sedately, thanks to my long gown. By the time I'd reached the roadway, Theodoric had dismounted, and he and Arthur were embracing one another like old friends.

As they parted, I saw the look on the newcomer's face. Whatever he was here for, it wasn't something good.

Arthur had seen it as well. "What is it?" he asked, "What's wrong?"

Theodoric pulled the long ends of his sandy moustache. "I'm sorry," he said. "It's your father. He's dying."

# Chapter Nine

T HE GREAT HALL thronged with men. I sat completely forgotten
on one of the benches, watching and listening.

Arthur and Theodoric, followed by his nine men, had walked up
the cobbled road to the Hall, where Arthur called for servants to lead
their horses away. More instructions produced food and drink for the
warriors. They'd ridden flat out from Viroconium and were travel-
stained and exhausted. Now most of them sat at the trestle tables in
the Hall, eating last night's leftovers hungrily, while around them
Arthur's men donned their armor and readied to leave.

Theodoric downed a brimming goblet of wine in one long
draught, then held it out for a refill. Dark circles shadowed his startling
blue eyes. With his blond hair, he looked different from the rest of the
men in the Hall. Could he be a Saxon mercenary himself? His blond
moustache glistened red as he wiped his mouth on his sleeve. Fortified
by the wine, he seized a cold haunch of venison and bit into it with
strong teeth.

Arthur paced back and forth, his feet scuffing up the dusty reeds.
Merlin, coming into the Hall hot on the heels of the party from
Viroconium, urged him to caution. "An escort can be ready within the
hour. Rushing won't make it happen quicker." His gaze slid past his
master to rest on me. "And you should take her with you."

Was that to make sure I didn't try to sneak back to Glastonbury
while they were away? Did Merlin want to keep me where he could

see me?

Theodoric's blond eyebrows rose over the haunch of venison. He looked from Merlin to me, then back again.

"She's the Lady of the Ring," Merlin said quickly. Theodoric's eyebrows went up even further and he stared in open curiosity.

Arthur barely seemed to register Merlin's words. He didn't even glance at me. I was no longer important.

"Cei," he called out to his brother as Cei came striding into the Hall, fully armored, cloak flapping out behind him. "How soon can the men be ready?"

"Quickly. I'm having our horses prepared as we speak." Cei turned to Theodoric, who was standing beside the smoldering fire, still looking at me. "Well met." He slapped him on the back. "But I hear you're the bearer of this bad news."

Theodoric, eye to eye with him, two big men together, clasped Cei's forearm with his free hand. "I rode as fast as I could. When it was obvious the king wouldn't rally, I knew the time had come to fetch Arthur. Cadwy's already there, of course. Because of that, we had to sneak out like thieves in the night."

My ears pricked. Why had he been forced to sneak out of Viroconium? Who would have wanted to prevent him coming to Arthur with this news? Cadwy? Arthur's own brother?

A servant arrived with Arthur's armor and put it on the table in front of me with a loud clatter. Arthur picked up the heavy quilted tunic lying on top of the pile and pulled it over his head. Stepping up, Cei helped him into the awkward ring mail shirt. His sword lay on the table. Could it be Excalibur? Its hilt lay close to my hand. I could stretch out and touch it if I tried. What would my father have had to say about that?

I didn't, though, because just then Arthur looked at me, his dark eyes narrowed. I was back in his thoughts.

"Yes, you're right," he said to Merlin. "We should take her with us.

Can she ride?" He didn't ask me, and he didn't wait for an answer. "She's your responsibility." He looked back at Cei. "Can you go and hurry things along?" He buckled his sword belt.

"I'm going. The horses were nearly ready as I left them."

"I'm coming as well," Theodoric said. "If you've fresh horses for my men, we'll all ride with you. You need to be at full strength." Looking at him, it was impossible to tell he'd already ridden so far. Only the dark shadows under his blue eyes gave that away. "Do you think you can furnish me with a fresh horse? Mine is spent."

Arthur gave him a tight-lipped nod. "Take your pick of the horse pens. There should be one there up to your weight. We manage to horse Cei well enough." And picking up his shield, he swept out of the Hall. Cei and Theodoric followed in his wake, the latter still carrying the now half-eaten haunch of venison.

Merlin turned to me. "There'll be a horse prepared for you. Can you ride alone? Or do you need to be led?"

He'd only seen me arriving from Ynys Witrin led like a rank novice. I tried not to be insulted. "I've ridden for years."

My mind was churning over plans. Would we be going via Glastonbury? Or near enough for me to persuade someone in the party to take me there? Maybe I'd be able to sneak away unnoticed. It was a pretty feeble idea, but it was the only one I had.

I looked down at my long skirts. "I can't ride dressed like this, though."

I expected him to tell me I'd have to, but he nodded distractedly. "Of course. You'll need braccae if we're to make good time. It'll be a hard ride."

He was right. South Cadbury to Wroxeter is far enough as the crow flies and would be even farther along the roads of Dark Age Britain. I might have ridden a lot in my teens, but I'd barely ridden in the last few years since meeting Nathan and starting work in the library. And it would be on a saddle without stirrups.

Cottia rose to the occasion and managed to produce braccae that fitted me well enough. Tutting over the outlandishness of me dressing like a boy, she packed my dresses into saddle bags.

"Be sure and put a dress on afore ye meet the High King," she advised.

Supposing he was still alive. It must have taken days for Theodoric and his men to reach us, and it would take just as long to get back. The dying king might well be a dead and buried king before we got there.

Something puzzled me though – Arthur's reaction to the news of his father's imminent death. He'd given the impression he didn't get on with him. Yet now he was desperate to rush to his bedside. Perhaps the indifference had been all show. I'd find out soon enough. Whatever the reason, it seemed vitally important to him to get there in as short a time as possible.

I changed out of my dress with relief. I was a jeans and T-shirt girl, really. The braccae had been made for a youth and fitted me snugly, and the tunic, embroidered around the neckline and hems, only came to mid-thigh. A woven belt gathered it round my waist, and I finished by lacing up my walking boots.

I was so absorbed in thinking how I could turn these events to my favor that I didn't speak to Cottia as she worked. Instead, I planned how to get away from the Viroconium-bound party without them noticing. I would have to take the first chance that offered itself.

After about ten minutes, Merlin came in to find me fastening a thick fur-lined riding cloak about my shoulders with a fibula brooch in the shape of a dragon.

He paused on the threshold, then nodded his approval. "Safer to travel as a boy. You're to stick with me, and I'll keep you safe. If anything should happen, we're to get away as fast as we can. D'you understand?"

That sounded ominous. "Why? What d'you think might happen?" I asked. "Are you telling me we might meet Saxon raiding parties between here and Viroconium?"

He gave a shrug. "Not just Saxons. We have to pass through neighboring kingdoms and subkingdoms. In name they're united beneath the High King and come together for the Council of Kings every year, but in practice they're rarely on good terms – still less now the High King lies dying."

Not a comforting thought.

"So you stick with me," he repeated.

I nodded.

It seemed I was important again though. I was the bearer of the dragon ring, after all. If we were attacked, I certainly wouldn't want to stay around, and I'd be no good in a fight. It might even be my opportunity to get away from them. "Do I get a weapon?" I asked. "Just in case I need to defend myself?" Better to be safe than sorry.

Merlin nodded. "Good idea. Cottia, the small dagger in the weapons chest. The one with the serpent's head."

She brought it, and he drew it from its tooled leather scabbard to show me a slim, lethal-looking blade that glowed with life in the torch-lit chamber. The hilt was formed in the shape of a sinuous snake, its blunt head wicked and dangerous. A belt that came with it fastened round my waist, the knife sitting on my left hip. It felt as though it belonged there, and I had a sudden unnerving vision of me whipping it out and holding it between myself and threatened but unspecified dangers.

I faltered. What was I doing? I now had a knife of my own, and I was even considering using it. What was to stop me? Only my twenty-first-century sensibilities, and how long would they withstand the temptations of the fifth? They already felt as though they were crumbling. How swiftly one's morals could change.

Cei's bulky and helmeted self appeared in the doorway. "Time to leave." Then he was gone.

I followed Merlin out into the now empty Hall. The rushes rustled softly underfoot as we passed, embers glowed in the hearth, and smoke curled around the rafters. Suddenly, it felt like a safe haven, the only one I knew, and that I was heading into the terrifying unknown. I wanted to stay here with Cottia, despite her huffy attitude. My stomach churned, but I stayed silent. We stepped out into the raw daylight.

Riders and people milled everywhere. Tulac was holding the reins of a sturdy bay cob, already strapped with my saddle bags. Merlin gave me a powerful leg up into the saddle, and I gathered my reins as I settled myself. Tulac released his hold and stepped out of the way. This horse felt very different from Corwyn's half broken-down old nag. He fidgeted beneath me, and I tightened the reins one-handed, running my other hand down his neck under the thick mane, whispering to quieten him. His ears flickered back toward me as he listened.

"Gwen!"

Startled, I looked up.

Near the doors to the Great Hall, Llacheu stood with a tall, slender young woman, her long auburn hair in two thick braids that reached her waist. Her pretty face had a pointed chin and catlike eyes. His mother, Tangwyn. There was very little of her in Llacheu; he was all Arthur's.

Instinctively, I didn't like her. I didn't know why. She'd done nothing to me, and I'd not met her yet. I liked her son, probably because he was so like his father, but for her, all I could feel was a sense of foreboding and distrust. I raised my hand and smiled at the little boy, and he waved back. His grandfather's imminent demise didn't seem to have bothered him at all. He'd probably never met him. His mother watched me out of her sleepy cat's eyes, her face expressionless. I couldn't tell what she was thinking. For that I liked her even less.

Arthur emerged from the press of men mounting their horses and milling about in front of the Hall. He had his round leather helmet, studded with metal plates, tucked under his arm. A lanky boy led forward a big, dapple-grey cob, and I saw why Llacheu had a grey pony himself. It was to be like his father. The child was jumping up and down on the steps of the Hall, every inch of him aching to be noticed.

Leaving his helmet hooked onto his saddle, Arthur came striding over, bulky and solid in his padded armor, and swept the little boy up into the air. Llacheu let out a shriek of delighted excitement. Beside him, Tangwyn gazed up at the two of them together, a smile curving her pretty mouth, and Arthur passed the boy into her arms. She laughed, setting him down on the ground again. It was a carefree laugh, but as her eyes flicked toward me, I knew it was done for a purpose. She held out her arms to Arthur and he folded her to him. As she lifted her face to his, he gave her a long kiss on the lips.

I was annoyed. And then I was annoyed with myself for being annoyed. What on earth was I feeling like that for? He wasn't mine. In fact, I didn't even want him, did I? But she must have thought I wanted him, and that was why she'd done it. The equivalent of a dog pissing up against a tree to mark its territory. So why did I feel so annoyed that he'd kissed the mother of his child? I had to ask myself; was I actually jealous? It was a sobering thought. I pushed it out of my head and turned my horse downhill so I didn't have to look at them and see him kiss her again, see his hands on her hips holding her body to his. I had to get a hold of myself. This was utterly ridiculous.

It wouldn't go out of my head, though. I'd thought he liked me. In fact, when he'd smiled down into my eyes last night in the Great Hall I'd thought he wanted me. Me, that was, not just the possibility of the power his marriage to me might bring. I didn't want him though, did I? Reluctantly, I acknowledged that I wanted him to want me. I'd thought he did, and now I wasn't so sure. Maybe he'd just been being polite. Maybe I'd mistaken friendliness and warmth for flirting. Maybe he flirted with every woman he met.

Merlin brought his horse up beside me, his knee pressing hard against mine. He too wore a mail shirt and helmet, his sword thrust into a scabbard carried on his back, his shield hanging from one of the horns on his saddle. His emblem was a swooping bird, blue on a yellow background – a merlin falcon. "Everything all right with you?" he asked, a single eyebrow raised.

I was annoyed with him this time. Had he seen me watching Arthur and Tangwyn and guessed why I'd turned my horse away? Did he have any inkling as to how I felt? I had a horrible feeling he did. I felt myself coloring.

"Fine, thank you." I paused. "How many of us are going?" Anything to change the subject.

"Fifty, and you. All warriors. Theodoric and his men, and forty of ours. Enough to make any raiders we might come across think twice before attacking us. Few enough to be able to move swiftly. Viroconium is at least four days ride from here, and our journey is of the most urgent kind."

I wanted to know more. I had questions, but there wasn't time.

His horse spun away from mine, and I was alone amongst a throng of riders I didn't know. Searching for Bran or Tegid, I found nothing but grim faces I couldn't remember having seen before beneath heavy helms. Faces that would have been out of place in my twenty-first-century world, even amongst the armed forces. They looked what they were – tough, hardened killing machines, men for whom warfare was the most important thing in their lives. If the good guys looked like this, what might the bad guys, the Saxons, look like?

Arthur rode through the milling riders, his shield with its rampant black bear hanging from his saddle. Theodoric, slightly underhorsed on a heavily built brown cob, pressed up close on one side of him, Cei on the other. Arthur raised his gloved fist above his head. "To Viroconium," he shouted above the hubbub, and started down the cobbled road toward the main gateway. Behind him, the rest of the riders fell in, me included, Merlin by my side like the guard dog I suspected he was. Shaking him off would not be easy. If I went missing he was going to notice.

We passed beneath the guard tower and emerged through the gates onto the steeply sloping hillside. Before us, the road snaked down through the encircling ring ditches and banks, toward the farmland. The sun was already beyond its zenith, and we had a long ride ahead of us.

I was disappointed in my plan of escape.

We didn't take the road I'd hoped for, through the forest toward Ynys Witrin. Instead, we followed a track that branched northwards, across open grassland where sheep grazed in little groups, and smoke rose from village rooftops.

Once on the flat land, the horses quickened their pace and broke into a canter, clods of mud flying. I'd ridden without stirrups before, and even bareback, so this wasn't too difficult, but the muddy ground underfoot made me nervous my horse would slip and fall, and I was unused to being part of such a large group. After about a mile, we slowed the horses and let them walk on a long rein until their breathing returned to normal. Then everyone slid down out of their saddles to walk beside the horses for another mile.

I was at the very back of the column with Merlin. Without his company it might have been easy to gradually fall behind and then slip away, but he dogged my footsteps.

"We march like the Romans did," he explained, walking beside me in the mud. "Gallop a mile, walk a mile, get off for a mile. It saves the horses, and it stops us getting too stiff in the saddle. We don't trot. Too uncomfortable."

"In my time we still ride but only for pleasure," I said, rubbing my horse's sweaty ears. "And we have something that makes riding a lot easier. We have stirrups."

He raised his eyebrows. "What's a stirrup?"

"It's an iron loop on the end of a leather strap that a rider's foot goes in. There's one on each side of the saddle for getting on, like a step, and when a rider's mounted, he can rest his feet in them. It stops the rider's legs aching so much and it makes trotting much more comfortable. I can draw a picture of one. If I'm going to do much more riding, I want someone to make stirrups for my saddle."

Was that me acknowledging I was stuck here?

"Sounds interesting," he said. "I'd like to see your picture."

My picture. If I was at home, I'd just have done a quick internet search on my phone and shown him a photo of a stirrup. Job done. If I'd had my phone. I'd quite forgotten about it. Cottia still had it. My coat and jeans and hoody as well. Had she hung onto them because she thought them so strange, or in case I wanted to put them back on again? She'd given me back my underwear, but that was badly in need of another wash. What did Dark Age women wear as undergarments? I could see I was going to have to find out some time soon. There was only so much wear lacy knickers could take.

Thinking about my phone, left behind in Din Cadan, made me angry with myself. Too much was going on. I couldn't keep track of every thread and it was making me careless. Now I was stuck without it, whatever actual good it would have done me. I was beginning to doubt I would ever get back to my world. That thought, which I'd been shoving to one side and ignoring, swept back over me in a wave, leaving my stomach with a hollow ache and tears springing in the corners of my eyes. I looked away from Merlin and gave them a surreptitious wipe with my sleeve.

"Mount up," came a shout from the front of the column. I had no more time to dwell on my predicament. Merlin gave me a leg up into the saddle, then leapt onto his own horse. We cantered again, the wind whipping my plait and cloak out behind me. It was exhilarating, and despite the way I felt, I couldn't help but enjoy it, even though I also couldn't help but think a hard hat would have been a good idea. It had been drummed into me in the riding school as the most important part of my riding gear.

My horse's hooves thundered, and ahead of me the other riders urged their mounts on with whoops of encouragement, as full of enjoyment as I was, despite their gloomy mission. When we finally pulled up at the edge of a forest, the horses were sweating and snorting, clouds of steam rising from their slick coats, and I was well splattered with mud.

"Now we walk." Merlin brought his horse next to mine. The constant guard dog.

I looked over my shoulder. Din Cadan was just a distant hill, hazy in the autumnal damp, hidden now as the forest closed over us, and the path wound beneath bare, wintry branches. Our horses' hooves swished in the dead leaves underfoot and I pushed thoughts of home out of my head.

In this way, a good three hours passed before we came to something I would call a proper road. In front of us, the road ran away straight and paved to left and right, its surface gently curving to a deep ditch on either side, wheel ruts graven in the gravelly surface. A proper Roman road. I racked my brains for which it might be, trying to recall the map of Roman Britain my father used to have on the wall in his study. Maybe the Fosse Way, which led all the way from Exeter in the south-west to Lincoln in the north-east.

"This'll be better," Merlin said. "We stay on the Roman roads all the way to Viroconium. The Romans knew how to build a road to last. We'll make faster time now."

He was right. We did make better time on the Roman road. It led straight as an arrow across farmland, through forest, up and down hills, across fords and over slabbed stone bridges. In the distance, farms and villages and small fields checkered the landscape, smoke rising from every hearth fire. But we didn't meet anyone. It was winter; sensible people were not about. Britain had ground to a halt with the advent of the cold wet weather.

Before long, we came upon the tumbled ruins of a Roman way station that must once have boasted an inn and changes of horses for passing travelers. Rank grass grew between the fallen stones. Buildings where men once sat down to eat and drink now stood open to the sky.

I was struck by how alien the landscape seemed. And how empty. It felt as though I were exploring somewhere far distant from the Britain I knew, with its endless tarmac, its road signs, cars, houses, ugly pylons marching across the countryside and countless people. I was a stranger in a strange land, and nothing I saw could quiet my uneasy mind.

# Chapter Ten

W E ARRIVED AT Caer Baddan, modern day Bath, just as the sun set. The good weather had lasted all day, and only now were clouds mustering on the pink horizon. I'm not sure what I'd been expecting when Merlin told me where we were heading that first day, but it wasn't what we found. I suppose I'd assumed there'd be a sort of mildly decayed Roman township, its people still clinging doggedly to the ways of their ancestors. I never for a moment imagined the level of destruction I was to find.

Hovels, their walls leaning drunkenly and roofs covered in ancient, blackened thatch, were sparsely scattered in a shantytown along both sides of the road that led to the tumble-down city gates. Hearing the clatter of our hooves, the inhabitants emerged to stand and stare. Their clothes were little better than rags, and their filthy feet were bare. The sullen looks on their faces, giving no hint of animation or intelligence, shocked me. I was familiar with the word "peasant", but I'd never expected to see the embodiment of that word. Was that what they were? I glanced across at Merlin, but he was talking to Bedwyr, the young warrior in charge of treating battle wounds.

The once towering walls of what must have been an impressive city had been looted for stone down to ground level in places. Timber and rocks lay haphazardly in the gaps as though there'd been the necessity for speedy reconstruction. The gates, which should have been a key point in the defenses of the city, hung crookedly, half broken and patched, only one of them standing open to let us pass inside.

Despite my exhaustion and abominably aching legs, I gazed about myself with avid curiosity. The town's narrow cobbled street stank of shit and rotting vegetation. The roofs of half the houses had fallen in, and pigeons roosted on their exposed and rotting rafters. Under our horses' hooves, the cobbles were thick with dirt, and pigs snuffled in the rubbish-filled gutter, searching for tasty morsels.

A movement in a dark alleyway caught my eye; children, their scrawny bodies barely covered with filthy rags, scavenged in the muck that covered the street and alley.

I couldn't suppress a gasp of horror. Merlin was so close he must have heard me, but he didn't spare the children a glance. Ahead, the column of well-fed, well-clothed warriors rode on past all the poverty, their horses' hooves clattering on the cobbles.

I reached over and put my hand on Merlin's arm. "The children. Look at them. They're starving. We have to stop and do something."

He turned uncomprehending eyes to me. "What?" Looking where I was pointing, he frowned, but at me, not them. "What d'you expect me to do? This isn't our city. They're not our responsibility." He could have been talking about some distant report on "News at Ten", not these children, whose hollow eyes were devoid of hope, standing in the road, staring after us, barefoot and frozen.

For a moment, I was furious. "How can you just ride past them? None of you even looked at them. They need help." My voice rose several notes.

He gave a dismissive shrug. "What do you expect me to do? There are people like this all over Britain – in every kingdom. I may not like what I see, but there's nothing I can do to change it. And nor can you."

Realization dawned. He was used to sights like this. They all were. I was just a visitor to his world, an observer of the poverty to which they were all inured. He was right; there was nothing I could do to change anything. No welfare state in the Dark Ages. No benefits if you were poor or unable to work. No help if your father or mother died. No handouts. No hospitals. No social workers if you were ill-treated. Nothing. Just poverty. And death.

A resolve seized me. If I was going to have to stay here and marry Arthur and become his queen, then I would make it my mission to help children like these. I twisted in my saddle to look back at them. They hadn't moved. Their gaunt faces imprinted themselves on my retinas. *This* was what a town in fifth-century Britain looked like. My father would have been shocked.

Further along, women leaned on a balcony overlooking the street. Not quite as dirty as the children, they were unlike any women I'd seen before. Greasy hair sat piled on top of their heads in sloppy curls above painted faces – lips bright red, cheeks rouged, black eye liner giving them a hint of the Egyptian. Grubby gowns slipped from pale shoulders to reveal pendulous breasts, the nipples artificially reddened like their cheeks.

One of them tossed her head carelessly at Theodoric as he rode beneath the balcony. "Hey, goldilocks, come up 'ere and tickle me with that moustache o' yours!"

Theodoric, who must have been more tired than any of us, threw back his head and guffawed with laughter. "You wouldn't be the first in this place to get a tickle out of me. I think I had your sisters last night." He tossed her a coin, which she caught deftly in her hand and tucked into her cleavage. "Come to the Imperial Palace tonight and bring a friend, and there'll be more of that."

Another woman leaned forward over the balcony, bare breasts dangling. "Take a look at these bubbies, then. Ain't they enough to get yer cock 'ard?" She put her hands underneath them and waved them at the passing riders.

Arthur turned in his saddle, a frown on his face, and said something in an undertone to Cei. Did he disapprove? The coarse cries of the women were left behind as we rode deeper into the decrepit center of the city.

I turned to Merlin. "What's happened here? I thought this was a Roman city?"

Merlin grimaced. "It was. But things have changed since the legions left. We had plague in Britain forty years ago. It spreads like wildfire in crowded cities. The people died, and there were none to replace them. Empty houses quickly fall into disrepair." He gestured at the tumbledown buildings we were passing. "Feeling against the Romans has been hostile since they left, because they wouldn't come to help us when we begged them. The people decided they didn't want Roman laws any longer, or reminding of the Empire. They pulled down the forums and basilicas to replace them with buildings of their own. Caer Baddan isn't the only place this has happened."

"I've been here in my time. I've seen the baths. They're famous. Can you still use them?"

He gave a shrug. "After a fashion. I wouldn't go there, though. You saw those women?" He didn't wait for me to answer. "Well, the baths are full of others like them, and boys too. They cater for all tastes. And cut-purses. You go there, you take your life in your hands."

"What happened to the people who survived the plague?"

"They left. Cities are hard to defend. The length of the walls is huge – if they're still standing. It takes too many men to garrison a city against the Saxons or against the Irish."

"You get raids by the Irish here?"

"From time to time they sail their ships up the Sabrina Sea."

The estuary of the river I knew as the Severn. "But where are all the people?"

He gave a shrug. "Most of the people of Caer Baddan left forty years ago after the plague, when the Saxon raids were at their worst. They did the same thing as we've done at Din Cadan. They refortified the old hill forts, took to their farms if they had them, became tenant farmers if they didn't. They went where they could defend themselves and where they could scratch a living. There's only the dregs left in the city now."

The road began to widen and the houses to look less seedy and dilapidated. In places they'd been cleared away, and barns had been built in their footprints, with livestock pens filled with scrawny cattle and pigs and small brown sheep. The farmyard stench was overwhelming.

"They bring the livestock in at nights for safety," Merlin said, seeing the look on my face. "And all the grain stores are within the walls. Ramshackle as the defenses look, they're enough to keep out the small raiding parties that might venture this far west. For the time being."

The light was failing fast as we emerged into what must once have been the forum, the center of the Roman city. The stone remains of Roman splendor, pillars, and porticos with their brickwork showing through the cracked marble, stood forlornly cheek by jowl amongst the thatched buildings and animal pens. Here, in the gathering darkness, men were watering and feeding their livestock, pushing handcarts of hay across the uneven paving stones of the forum from the stacks of fodder beside the barns. Our horses' hooves clattered, and heads turned to look at us in weary indifference.

Arthur threaded his way between the jumble of barns and pens toward a long, low building not unlike the hall at Din Cadan. The blackened thatch needed repair, and the whole place had an air of genteel dilapidation about it. Halfway along the side, double gates barred an archway.

Cei swung down from his saddle in front of the gates. He gave the heavy iron knocker on the right-hand gate a resounding thump, and then stepped back, hands on hips, waiting.

After a minute or two, the gate swung open, and a short, bandy-legged old man hobbled out.

"Oo's that?" he grumbled, squinting at Cei in the evening gloom.

"Wotcher want?"

Theodoric kicked his horse forwards. "It's me, you lazy old bastard. Back again. And this time I've brought Prince Arthur with me. Get those gates open and let us in."

The old man's gaze slid to Arthur, recognition dawning in his rheumy eyes. Hastily, he tugged his scanty forelock. "Milord."

He swung the gates open, then stood back out of the way while we rode through. The archway was so high we didn't need to duck our heads as we passed through a huge storage barn filled with bulging sacks.

Beyond the thatched building lay a cobbled courtyard, and to its left, a stable block with stacks of hay and straw beside it. Opposite the gates, a high wall loomed, white paint flaking from its crevassed surface, the long, withered arms of a grapevine crawling over it on a trellis. To the right, facing the stables, rose the most Roman building I'd seen so far. Terracotta tiles covered the roof, and wide steps led up to a veranda, but it was now too dark for me to make anything else out.

Behind us, the old man closed the gates and slipped home a heavy wooden beam with a thud. Was it to keep us in, or those desperate looking peasants out? Everyone slid down from their saddles, so I followed suit. It was a great relief to have my feet on the ground again. At this rate I'd be bow-legged by the time we got to Viroconium.

As the old man pushed his way between the damp flanks of our horses, Theodoric caught his bony wrist. "Go tell your master Prince Arthur has arrived. We need food and wine, and beds for fifty. And some whores will be coming knocking – see they come to my quarters. No pretending to be asleep, or I'll be after you." He released the wrist, and the old chap went hurrying off up the steps toward the house.

I followed the men into the gloomy stables where I could just make out a row of stalls. Someone lit a torch in a wall bracket, and warm light and black shadows flooded the interior. My horse shoved his nose hopefully into the manger in his stall but came out aggrieved and snorting, with nothing more than dust. I undid his girth and lifted off the saddle and under blanket.

As everyone else was rubbing their horses down with twists of straw, I did the same. A horse with a heavy winter coat that's been ridden for over thirty miles, ten of them at a canter, gets hot and sweaty but he doesn't dry; his sweat just gets cold and then he risks a chill. Oh, for a set of horse clippers. Wouldn't that make life easier. Copying Merlin, who was dealing with his own horse next to mine, I took the saddle blanket, unfolded it, and slung it over my horse's back, fastening it in place with a long strap round his girth.

Farther up the line of horses, Arthur did the same for his grey, his face a picture of concentration. He seemed to have no airs at all, although perhaps caring for his horse took his mind off the purpose of our journey.

When the horses had been settled, it was time to tend to their tack. Merlin gave me a rag and shared his pot of grease with me as we gave saddles and bridles a good clean. It was clear that for these men their horses were their top priority. Probably higher than their women.

When we'd finished, Merlin picked up my saddle bags and, shouldering them as well as his own, led me out of the stables and across the courtyard to the steps up to the house, where we joined Arthur, Theodoric and Cei.

Arthur seemed to have come out of his reflective mood. "This is the Imperial Palace," he said, as Merlin and I reached the top of the steps. "It was built by my great-grandfather, Constantine, toward the end of his reign." He gestured back at the gateway in the long, thatched hall. "Not that bit. That was Claudius of Gloui. Before he was deposed and ran off to Armorica."

"Does the city have a king?" I asked, ignoring the tempting red herring of who Claudius of Gloui had been.

He shook his head. "There's a ruler, but he doesn't live here. This is my father's territory. Melwas holds it as a sub-kingdom, by the gift of my father. He's off at Dinas Brent to the west. The Isle of Frogs. He doesn't often come here."

I wasn't surprised.

Theodoric pushed open the door of the house, and we walked through into a shabby atrium where once a fountain must have played. Now the stone pool it had splashed into was broken and dry. Torches burned in iron brackets, leaving sooty patches on the faded wall paintings, and under our feet lay a black and white mosaic of stark geometric shapes.

Beside the broken fountain stood a stout, balding man in his late forties. His deep red toga half-covered his white tunic, and he wore sandals on his pudgy feet, which must have been cold. He clasped hands with Arthur, and then with Theodoric and Cei, then finally with Merlin.

"My Prince. Lord Cei. Lord Theodoric. Merlin." He rubbed his plump white hands together. "It is a regret to me that we should meet again under such difficult circumstances. The Imperial Palace is at the disposal of you and your men."

Something about this man seemed oily, with his wobbling double chins and his sunken piggy eyes. Something that set my skin crawling.

Leaning close, Merlin filled me in.

"Bassus, magistrate of Caer Baddan. Melwas's creature. Theodoric stayed here last night. I expect he's surprised to see him back so soon."

"Is he a Roman?"

Merlin shrugged. "Is anyone nowadays? He affects the gown, but he's no more a Roman than you or I."

Well, I wasn't a Roman at all, did he but know it. More likely an Anglo-Saxon than anything else. Did he imagine my world was a slightly updated version of his own? I doubted if he could have any conception of what my century was really like. Any more than we ourselves would have had any idea about fifteen hundred years in our own future.

Slaves came and showed us to our quarters. A girl in a long, cream-colored tunic led me through some doors and into a small garden courtyard. The fountain in its center was in no better condition than the one in the entrance hall, and the garden grew straggly and weed-filled, but the room wasn't as bad as I expected. A single bed stood close against one wall, an iron-bound chest beside it. Merlin unslung my saddle bags and bade me farewell, but he wasn't going far. He and Arthur, Theodoric and Cei all had rooms opening off this same courtyard.

I sat down on the bed. More tired than I'd ever been, I stretched my aching legs to ease the pain. My bottom and thighs were saddle-sore. Lying back with a little sigh of relief, I closed my eyes.

I must have fallen asleep instantaneously, something I'd never done before. A discreet cough woke me.

The girl stood at the foot of my bed holding a large bowl of steaming water.

"Milady," she mumbled, tongue-tied with embarrassment.

Reluctantly, I dragged myself away from sleep.

The water was pleasantly warm, and the soap almost usable. Knowing that animal fat was often used in ancient soap making, I tried not to think about its possible ingredients. What I longed for was a soak in a hot Radox bath, but a stand-up wash was all I got. And another strange look for my underwear, which she took from me as though I were handing her a hot coal.

Dressed in one of the gowns Cottia had packed, minus my underwear, which the girl was washing, I was finally escorted to a dining room with couches arranged around a central table. It appeared that not only did Bassus dress like a Roman, but he also ate like one. I'd always thought eating while lying down would be difficult, and I was about to discover I was right.

Arthur, Cei, Merlin, Theodoric and I ate with Bassus and his wife, Antonia, a small, thin, middle-aged woman with curled and hennaed hair and a slight moustache. I was given the couch between Arthur and Antonia, and had some difficulty settling comfortably due to my long gown. As I propped myself on my left elbow, I had a nasty feeling I was going to get indigestion.

The food was excellent and far more elaborate than anything laid on at Din Cadan. There were little parcels of spiced meat, rissoles made of crayfish caught in the River Avon, mussels cooked in a sauce of celery seed, rue, honey and pepper, stuffed marrows, leeks wrapped in cabbage leaves and cooked in coals, olives imported from the Mediterranean, beets dressed with mustard oil and vinegar, pigeon breasts sliced in a rich sauce, and a suckling pig cooked whole and served on a decorated platter. The splendor of their table was in sharp contrast with the poverty I'd seen on the streets, but I'm ashamed to say that not even thoughts of those poor children diminished the appetite I'd worked up that day.

The wine was good, too.

"We have it brought in by ship from the Mediterranean," Antonia told me with more than a hint of pride. "Our river here flows into the Sabrina Sea. Our wharves are quite cosmopolitan, you know."

She followed this up with a whole host of other remarks that went right over my head. She talked non-stop about everything – about her children, who were angels, and her slaves, who were not, and her clothes, which she bemoaned were not the height of Roman fashion, and her food, which was not up to the standard she was used to, and her ailments, which were many.

I was so tired I had to limit myself to smiling and nodding when required. The small amount of wine I drank went straight to my head, and my eyelids soon grew heavy.

Beside me, Arthur ate little and drank even less, listening while Bassus waxed as loquaciously as his wife, although his diatribe was one long complaint about his posting here at Caer Baddan, and a request for Arthur to have him moved elsewhere. I stifled a yawn and fidgeted my aching legs. I would be glad to get to my bed that night.

At last, the interminable meal was finished. I made my polite goodnights to Antonia and Bassus, and Merlin led me back to my bedroom, while Arthur remained to talk to Bassus in his study. Cei and Theodoric went off jovially, arm in arm, presumably in search of the women Theodoric had paid a deposit for.

At my door, Merlin and I halted. Torches burned in brackets on the pillars of the porticoed veranda, smoke rising to the starry sky. Somewhere outside the walls a dog barked. The cold night air had given me a second wind, and now I was wide awake.

Merlin pushed open my door for me. "Sleep well. I'll have you called at first light. We need to be off early. Today was an easy stage. We've a lot more ground to cover tomorrow."

I had questions on the tip of my tongue. Questions I felt I couldn't ask Arthur, but that I wanted answers to. I put my hand on his arm as he turned away. "Wait a minute."

He turned to face me, his back to the torchlight, his face thrown into dark shadow.

"I want to know why Arthur and his father don't get on. I want to know the reason why Theodoric had to sneak out of Viroconium to bring his news to Arthur. If I'm really who you think I am, then I deserve to be told. Tell me about Uthyr Pendragon."

A dog, the same dog perhaps, howled out in the desolate city, and another dog joined in, their voices rising heavenwards.

Merlin tilted his head to one side. "What do you want to know?"

I hesitated. What to ask first? Verify the legends maybe?

"Did he – was Arthur brought up by his father? How is Cei his brother?" I was thinking of the legend that Arthur had been taken by Merlin as a baby to be brought up by Sir Ector with his son Sir Kay, away from his father and the court. I'd already met Cei, so had there been an Ector as well? Because if it was true, and Arthur had been brought up away from his parents, that might explain his indifference to them. Or was I just projecting twenty-first-century social mores onto Dark Age reality?

Merlin nodded. "Why would he not have been brought up by his parents? And as for Cei, Arthur's mother is Queen Eigr. Her first husband was Gorlois of Tintagel. Cei is Gorlois' son and Arthur's milk brother. Gorlois being dead, both boys grew up in Viroconium at the court of Arthur's father. Cadwy is Uthyr's son by his first wife, so also Arthur's brother."

I drew my cloak more closely about me against the cold. It sounded like Arthur's family was a bit of a soap opera.

"What sort of a relationship did he have with his father? I mean, does he have?" It was hard to think of the man we were headed to see as being in the present. In fact, it was hard to think of him as being real. To me, he was still a legend who'd lived and died hundreds of years ago.

He paused, and I could sense him mulling over what to tell me. "I taught all three of them as boys. Arthur was an apt pupil. The youngest, but the best of the three. Good at everything I taught him, and good at his battle training as well. As keen with a book in his hands as with a sword. His father was well pleased with him, as you would expect. And now he is a man..." He hesitated. "Arthur is a strong and brave warrior, a son to be proud of. But...there has always been dissent between father and son. Arthur and Cadwy do not get along, and Cadwy played his younger brother and their father against one another. He drove a wedge between them, as he'd always wanted. It's long since we've been to Viroconium."

"So, he fell out with his father?"

"Not quite. His father is very...autocratic. He's the High King. Uthyr waited a long time in the shadow of his brother to gain that position. He's held onto it now for more than twenty years. He tolerates no argument. Cadwy does as his father orders him. Or he appears to. Arthur never has."

I wasn't surprised. Arthur had the look of a rebel.

"That doesn't explain why he seems not to like his father."

Merlin shifted slightly. "That goes back to when he was a boy. The Queen, his mother, took it into her head that she wanted Arthur to enter the church. Second sons do that quite frequently. She wanted him to become a bishop."

"Why would she have wanted that for him?"

Merlin bridled. "She has the second sight. Some say she looked into his future and was afraid."

I felt sympathy for her. If she'd seen anything approaching what I knew of the legends of King Arthur, I didn't blame her for having wanted to save her son from the fate that might be lying in wait for him.

Merlin shrugged. "The King refused her. He had other plans for Arthur. They fought. She refused him her bed. He took another woman to his. Things escalated. The King banished her to Tintagel, her first husband's stronghold. She took her younger daughter with her, but Uthyr wouldn't let her take her son. She's been there ever since. Arthur blamed his father for everything."

"How old was he when this happened?"

"A child only. Seven, maybe eight years old."

The same age I'd been when I'd lost my mother. I felt a rush of sympathy for him.

Merlin continued. "The rift with his father never healed. All to Cadwy's advantage. Arthur was a rival not just for their father's affections but also for his inheritance. There's no love lost between Arthur and Cadwy."

"So, Arthur is at Din Cadan because he doesn't get on with his father?"

Merlin nodded. "Their relationship is...strained. Uthyr sees in him the makings of a great leader. No great leader is ever a great follower. The King's not stupid. He saw how the land lay between his sons. He gave Arthur Dumnonia and the West to rule, sending him far from court. Cadwy saw it as banishment and was pleased. Arthur too, until he'd been there a while and began to realize his father had given him a little kingdom of his own to rule."

"And now his father is dying."

He nodded. "Just so. And a dutiful son returns to the deathbed of his father."

I began to think I could see what lay behind this headlong ride.

"If his father is High King, and Cadwy is the oldest son, will Cadwy succeed his father? When Uthyr dies, will Cadwy become High King?"

Merlin gave a half shrug. "The role of High King isn't hereditary. He's elected by the Council of Kings. Uthyr took the title after his brother Ambrosius died, not by right of birth but by election. It's doubtful the kings will elect Cadwy in his stead, even if he asks it of them. He's not popular."

"But they may elect Arthur?"

"He is not a king."

I was silent for a few moments. The cold night air pressed in around us, making me shiver.

"Does he need to be?"

Merlin shrugged his shoulders again. "Yes. But there are ways and means for that to be achieved."

I pulled my cloak tighter about me as a chill breeze tugged at it. Merlin stepped away from me.

"Now, you must sleep. Tomorrow we rise early and must make fifty miles or more before darkness falls."

He left me standing on the threshold of my room, with more questions than I'd started with, farther from home than I'd ever been.

# Chapter Eleven

W E ROSE EARLY, as Merlin had planned. The same timid girl brought bread and olives and a flagon of mead to my bedroom. Then Merlin knocked on my door to escort me down to the stables where one of the men had prepared my horse. Someone, Merlin I suspected, had found a sheepskin and fixed it to my saddle, so I was more comfortable than I'd expected to be.

It was barely light when we clattered out of the courtyard and into the dirty old forum of Caer Baddan, leaving behind Bassus and his wife. I was glad to see the back of the place. The bed had been surprisingly comfortable, and I'd slept well, but there'd been something scurrying about on the floor of my bedroom on tiny feet. A mouse, I hoped, but it could just as well have been a rat. I was glad to be on my horse again, especially with the luxury of the sheepskin.

The eastern horizon began to redden as we rode out through another dilapidated gate onto the northbound Fosse Way. Mist lay pale over the trees and fields in shrouds of silk. Water glimmered between a line of trees that marked the river Avon, and ducks rose to take flight in a shudder of wings. The morning was marred only by the thought that I was getting steadily farther from Glastonbury and whatever small chance I had of returning to my own time. The cold knot in my stomach was a constant reminder.

The land rose steeply as the road climbed into hills that would one day be called the Cotswolds. Small roads, scarcely more than muddy tracks, turned off to left and right, toward woodsmoke rising into the cold air from hidden dwellings. Herds of cattle and flocks of sheep grazed in the distance, and from time to time we saw shaggy horses. Again, we met no one on the road, as though Britain had closed down with the advent of winter. How busy the modern road that followed this route would be in my time, thick with noisy delivery lorries, cars, motorbikes and coaches.

I couldn't get used to the silence. No engine noise and fumes, no planes overhead leaving their vapor trails across the sky, no power lines buzzing, no crowded trains – nothing but the expanse of semi-wild countryside. Although, it wasn't as wild as I'd expected. Columns of smoke rose from isolated farmsteads, and clusters of smoke marked hidden villages like the one I'd seen at Glastonbury. I continued to be surprised by how populated Dark Age Britain was. I'd imagined it to consist of great tracts of uninhabited lands still covered in primordial forest.

The Roman road made quite a difference, and we made good time. At mid-morning we stopped to eat a meal of dark bread, cold meat and onions, washed down with cider, warm from having been carried against the hot sides of our horses. I was ravenous by then. The plain food tasted wonderful, and so did the cider, consumed standing up, while my horse grazed at the side of the road.

With the sun already descending toward the west, we passed the ruins of Caer Ceri, modern Cirencester. It was in an even worse state than Caer Baddan. Only the amphitheater outside the tumble-down walls seemed occupied, where crude huts clustered both inside and out. Armed men climbed up onto the walls to watch us ride by, in stony, brooding silence. I was glad we weren't stopping there for the night.

As the pale sun slid behind the high Welsh hills in the west, we came upon our second night's accommodation. It was a ruined way station, bigger than the one we'd passed the day before, but in just as bad a state.

We drew up in front of it, and everyone but me dismounted. My heart sank into my boots. There wasn't even a roof. Remaining on my horse, I looked toward where Arthur stood with Cei and Theodoric, surveying the jumble of stones and rank grass.

"This'll have to do," Arthur said. "We've had worse bivouacs. Needs must."

Theodoric led his horse through the entrance, which might have once been an archway, but now was nothing but fallen stones. Still mounted, I trailed in last, with Merlin walking by my side, leading his horse.

The roof of the old stables had fallen in, but with some work the beams were cleared, and we tethered our horses in the old stalls for the night. Leather nosebags came out, filled with grain, and soon they were hungrily eating their evening feed.

The men set up makeshift tents in no time and soon had a fire burning in what had once been the inn itself. The wood lying about from the roofs made a satisfying blaze. Cold meat and bread came out as we sat on our saddle bags around the fire, and the warriors passed a wineskin from man to man.

Thoughts of my brother sprang into my head, and how we used to camp out in our back garden when we were children. My father had let us do pretty much what we wanted, so we'd had fires and cooked baked beans and sausages and flour dampers. Where was he now? Would Nathan have contacted him when I didn't turn up? He'd be the only one of our family left. All alone.

"What're you thinking about?" Arthur had got up to throw another length of wood on the fire, and now he sat down beside me. "You look sad."

It was the first time he'd really acknowledged me since we'd left Din Cadan.

Taken aback, I told him the truth. "About my brother."

Across the fire, Merlin watched us.

"What's his name?" Arthur asked.

"Artie – Arthur, like you." I couldn't tell him Artie was named after him, could I?

"That's a coincidence. I've never met another Arthur."

That's because you're the first, I thought, but didn't say so.

"I've never met another Guinevere." Tit for tat. There certainly weren't many Guineveres about in twenty-first-century Britain, although there were a lot of Arthurs. Since my brother was born, it had become quite fashionable.

"Why're you sad, then? Where's your brother?"

"Far away." A lump rose in my throat. "I don't think I'll ever see him again."

The wineskin came around again and he took a long pull, then passed it on to me. I wiped its mouth and took a generous swig. It was strong red wine, so I took a second swallow then passed it to the man beside me.

Arthur shrugged. "You may see him one day. He may come to Din Cadan. Many men do."

I shook my head. "He's too far away. And I think I can never go back and see him."

"You care for your brother?"

I nodded. "My parents are dead. He's the only family I've got."

He smiled wryly. "I care for my brother Cei, but not my brother Cadwy. If I never saw him again, it would be too soon. But he's going to be at Viroconium when we get there."

"Will that be so bad?"

"Probably. He hates me. He won't be pleased Theodoric's fetched me. He'll have wanted to keep my father's imminent death to himself. The better to ensure his inheritance."

"And what do you want?"

He shifted a little. The flames of the fire leapt up toward the inky sky. On the far side, one of the men, a wiry little fellow with spiky short brown hair and brown skin, fetched a flute out of his saddle bags and began to play. The haunting music filled the quiet of the night with plaintive notes. The fire crackled and a log hissed. I could have been in our old back garden with Artie, only the music then would have been his guitar.

"What do I want?" he repeated. "I'm not sure. I know what I don't want, though. I don't want Cadwy to be voted the next High King. That would be a huge mistake."

"Have you thought about being High King yourself?"

There was a silence. Even the flute player had stopped. Everyone was listening.

Arthur laughed. "I'm not a king." He sounded bitter. "The Council of Kings elects someone from amongst their ranks. I'd prefer to be Dux Britanniarum. The old Roman office. No one's held that position in years. Not since the time of the Usurper Guorthegirn. But I'd like that. Better than being High King."

Theodoric, who was holding the wineskin, spoke up. "Things change. If…when your father dies, the Council of Kings will be called. A High King will have to be elected. Or a Dux. Better a good Dux than a bad High King."

Cei took the wineskin out of his hands. "And we have the Lady of the Ring. Look at her. The prophecy's coming true. We can show her to the Council. With her by your side, you'll be the greatest warrior the kingdoms of Britain have ever seen." He took a gulp of wine.

*Don't ask the Lady of the Ring herself what she wants to do.*

"We need to take this one step at a time." Merlin's voice rose over the buzz of agreement from the men. "First, we must get to Viroconium and see for ourselves how near to death King Uthyr is. And when we're there, we must assess what Cadwy intends."

Theodoric kicked some dirt into the fire. "He intends no good at all."

The fire died down and we turned in for the night. The man on first watch climbed to the highest point of the ruined way station and wrapped himself against the cold in his cloak. Merlin had made me a tent out of a woolen blanket and spread a bedroll beneath it. I couldn't fault him. He was living up to his assignment of looking after me. But the ground felt hard and cold, and I couldn't get comfortable. I tossed and turned on what felt like a bed of sharp stones for a long time. That everyone else seemed to have no trouble sleeping, if their snores were anything to go by, did nothing to improve my mood.

After what felt like hours, I got up and moved the bedroll and tried to find the lumpy things that had been sticking into me. It was pretty dark now because the fire had died down to just glowing embers, and I had to search by feel. Fed up, I rearranged the bedroll and was just about to lie down again when I heard a low whistle above the gentle snoring.

I sat bolt upright and cocked my head, every sense in my body on the alert. The sound came again, long and low, like a signal. Was it the lookout on top of the old inn's rickety wall? I couldn't make out his shape against the dark sky. Over in the tumble-down stables the horses moved restlessly.

I could have just ignored it and lain down and tried to get back to sleep. But I didn't. I crawled the couple of feet to where Merlin had erected his own shelter, and reached out for him in the darkness. My hand touched his back and he moved. I gave him a poke. He came wide awake in an instant. By the dim glow of the fire I saw his eyes.

"It's me, Gwen," I whispered. "I just heard a funny noise."

He pushed himself up on his elbows. "What did you hear?"

"A whistle."

"Stay right here." And he was gone. I sat on his bed. Did it feel less lumpy than mine?

He moved almost silently. Then I heard more whispers. The snoring stopped. He was waking the others. I leaned back against the crumbling wall of the inn and pulled Merlin's blanket round myself. The faint swish of swords being drawn came to me. I made myself as small as I could, feeling very vulnerable indeed. Then I remembered the dagger Merlin had given me. But it was in my saddlebag, which I'd been using as a pillow. I didn't dare go and get it.

Silence fell. My heart, which had been beating fast and hard, began to steady. Perhaps it had been my imagination, after all. I thought again about going back to my own bed.

Then the world exploded around me. Dark shapes came pouring over the low walls of the way station, and the space that had been so empty and silent was filled with the sounds of fighting, and men silhouetted against the night sky. Swords clashed, men shouted, shields thudded with muffled blows, and feet scuffled in the dirt. The horses squealed and whinnied in alarm.

From my position on the ground up against one of the walls I couldn't see much. Booted feet scuffed past me, grunts filled the air, swearing, cries of pain. More metal on metal. Someone fell like a tree, and by the dim glow of the fire I saw his face dark with blood, spread blond hair and wide-open eyes staring sightlessly at the night sky. Then the melee of fighters was between me and the fire again, and in it, kicking up glowing embers.

I shrank back against the wall, remembering that Merlin had told me to run away if we were attacked, but too frightened to move. At least down here, crouched almost out of sight, I might go unnoticed, but if I got up to run away someone would see me for sure.

My heart pounded. Who were these men? Saxons? The yellow hair of the dead warrior still lying only a foot away from me suggested that. What if they killed all of Arthur's warriors? What would they do to me? Kill me if they thought I was a boy, but if they discovered I was a woman I dreaded to think what would happen.

I thought of the dagger again. I needed it. My bed was close by. I got up onto my hands and knees and began to crawl toward it.

Someone grabbed me by the back of my tunic. My fingers scrabbled in the dirt, shoulder blades shrinking from the touch of cold steel I thought was only milliseconds away. I screamed. My stretching fingers found the saddle bags I'd been using as a pillow and pulled them toward me. The dagger was tucked inside one of them. My feet kicked wildly and connected with something. I heard a grunt of pain. The grip on my tunic shifted. Someone had hold of my long plait, wrenching my head backwards.

My fingers found the hilt of the dagger. I couldn't breathe. My head was going to be pulled off backwards. My assailant dragged me to my feet as I choked for breath. I dropped the saddlebags, my fingers tight around the dagger's hilt. He had me now, my back pressed hard against his body, the side of my face up against his, but I could breathe again at last. He was wearing chain mail. The smell of his rank sweat and oniony breath was strong. His stubble rasped against my skin. One vicelike arm snaked around my waist, holding me firm, pinning my left arm to my side. But my right hand, the one holding the dagger, was free.

Instinct kicked in. I sagged against my captor, letting all my weight fall on him, and stepped back hard onto his instep. At the same time, I drove the dagger into his thigh. I couldn't see what I was doing, but my aim was good. The dagger sank in up to the hilt, grating as it struck bone. It was surprisingly easy. The blade was sharp, and I was desperate.

He gave a roar of pain. I had a moment when my hand felt hot and wet as the blood poured out over it. Then my captor released me, and the knife slipped out of my fingers. I fell to the ground in a heap, my head banging hard against the inn wall.

A dark shape loomed over me, and instinctively I screwed myself up into a fetal ball and closed my eyes tight. He was going to cut off my head, run me through, kill me.

Thud. Something hit the ground beside me and lay still. I didn't open my eyes. Anything might happen. I didn't want to see it. I didn't want to see anything at all.

I don't know how long I lay like that. It could have been hours, or it could have been seconds.

Someone grabbed my shoulder and pulled me upright. Hands forced my arms apart from where I'd been holding them in front of my face.

"Open your eyes. Are you hurt?" Arthur's voice was rough and urgent.

I blinked open my eyes. I could see barely see him in only the dim light of the fire's embers. Someone was kicking them back together from where they'd been scattered during the fight.

"Are you hurt?" he repeated, more gently.

I shook my head. Words wouldn't come.

Merlin stepped up. There was a graze on his forehead and blood had run down the side of his face.

"Is she all right?"

Arthur nodded. "Shaken."

That was an understatement. I'd just stabbed a man. I'd plunged a knife into living flesh, and I could feel the blade grating on the bone again and again in my head. Yes, I'd done it to save myself. Yes, he'd been an enemy. But he'd still been a living breathing human being. I couldn't get the feel of it out of my head. What was I turning into?

Merlin picked up my blanket from my overturned bed and put it round my shoulders. "Come and have some wine. It'll make you feel better."

I looked down. The man who'd attacked me lay face down by my feet. My dagger still stuck out of his right thigh. Someone had sliced halfway through his neck, and the ground was slick with his blood. I could smell the iron in it. Someone had killed him – for me. But in the heat of the moment I would have done the same. It had been him or me.

Arthur put a booted foot on the dead man and turned him over. His helmet rolled off his head revealing long golden hair stained black by the congealing blood. He had a long moustache much like Theodoric's.

"Saxons."

Merlin nodded, his arms still round me, holding the blanket in place.

Arthur bent down and pulled my dagger out. Before straightening up, he wiped it clean on the Saxon's clothing. Then he handed it to me.

I couldn't touch it. Even if I'd wanted to, my hands were shaking too much. There was still blood on it. I looked down at my right hand. The man's blood was all over me too, drying on my skin and dark on the sleeve of my tunic. The bile rose in my throat, and I bent forward and vomited on the ground.

Merlin took the dagger and tossed it onto my bed. Then he ushered me toward the fire and found me the wineskin. There was some left in it, and he made me drink it. When I lifted it to my mouth I smelled the blood on my sleeve again and vomited a second time.

Tears of delayed shock streamed down my cheeks. "I'm sorry," I mumbled. "I've never seen a dead man before. At least, not a man who's died like that." I'd seen my father, but that had been different. No one had tried severing his head.

Merlin guided me to sit on a large cornerstone that lay close to the fire. "You'll feel better in a minute. Your first dead man's always a shock."

My sleeve was wet and cold. "I have to get out of these clothes. They're covered in his blood."

All around me Arthur's men were moving about. I didn't look at what they were doing, but from the sound of it they were stripping the bodies of armor. I didn't want to know how many bodies there were. I didn't want to see them.

Merlin fetched my saddle bags and rummaged through them until he found a clean undershirt and tunic. I didn't care that the men were still milling about in the dark. I wriggled out of my bloody clothes and into the clean ones as fast as my shaking hands would allow, and Merlin rinsed my hand in beer to get rid of the horrible iron smell. Then I had another swig of wine and managed to keep it down. Merlin put his arm around my shoulders again and I leaned against him. He had a slightly musky, masculine smell to him that was reassuring. As the shock began to wear off, exhaustion swept over me in a tidal wave.

After a while, Arthur and Theodoric returned to the fireside. Flames crackled now from the new wood piled onto it. The front of me glowed with warmth, but my back, away from the fire, felt chilled. It reminded me of Bonfire Night and fireworks. My eyelids began to droop, but I forced myself to stay awake and listen to what they had to say.

Arthur turned to Merlin. "This was meant to look like a Saxon raid. The ones we killed are all Saxons. To a man. But it wasn't. They were after one thing." He nodded at me. "They were after her."

I came properly awake.

"How do you know?" Merlin asked, his arm tightening around me protectively. He must surely have felt the responsibility of bringing me into this world. After all, I'd been here less than a week and he'd already nearly got me killed.

Arthur put his hand on his sword's hilt, caressing it almost loving-ly. "The one I killed wasn't trying to kill her. He was trying to snatch her. He knew she was a woman. He was looking for her. They all were."

"I don't understand how they could have known we'd have her with us," Theodoric said.

Merlin stiffened. "Morgana."

Arthur nodded. Blood spatters flecked his face, but they weren't his. "She used the Sight." He glanced beyond Theodoric, at where Cei was making his way toward us, sword still in hand, dark with blood. "If you knew Gwen was coming, Merlin, then she could have as well."

Merlin shifted uncomfortably. I racked my brains for what legends could tell me of Morgana. Was she Morgana le Fay? Didn't she learn magic from Merlin and then lock him up in a crystal cave for evermore? Or was that Nimuë? That could hardly be the Morgana they were talking about. Could it?

"We've got one that's still alive," Cei said, "What d'you want us to do with him?"

Arthur set his jaw. "We'll question him."

Bedwyr and another man dragged the Saxon into the firelight. He'd lost his helmet, one side of his head caked in blood, one of his trouser legs dark with it. Someone had almost cut off his left ear. It still hung by a piece of skin. They threw him down on the ground in front of Arthur, where he lay on his face, breathing heavily.

Theodoric kicked him. "Get on your knees, Saxon."

The Saxon turned his head and spat an oath at Theodoric in a language I couldn't understand. It sounded vituperative. Theodoric kicked him again and the man doubled up in pain. Already blood from his leg was pooling in a dark shadow on the ground. If no one did anything, he was going to die.

Theodoric and Bedwyr dragged him onto his knees. He knelt there, swaying slightly, blood running down his neck. It came as a shock to see that he was young. Scarcely more than a boy. No long moustache like Theodoric, just a blonde fuzz on upper lip and cheeks. He couldn't have been more than a teenager. I felt a pang of sorrow for him, until I saw his eyes.

From beneath a heavy brow they glared back at us in open defiance, full of hatred.

"Who sent you?" Arthur asked.

The young Saxon spat. A glob of bloody phlegm landed on Arthur's boots. Arthur stepped forwards and, seizing a large handful of that bloodstained blond hair, yanked the Saxon's head backwards. A dagger flashed in his hand and came to rest with the point just beneath the young man's right eye. "Who sent you? I won't ask again."

There was a pregnant silence. The tip of the dagger dug into the flesh of the Saxon's cheek, and fresh blood trickled down toward his chin. My heart was in my mouth. The boy was wavering. He was young, too young, and he was afraid of losing his eye.

"I not know." His thick, guttural accent was hard to understand. "Not tell me. Captain say take girl. That all I know."

"Where were you stationed?"

"City. Big city."

"What city?"

The boy's lower lip trembled. "Not know. British city."

The dagger didn't waver. Arthur looked back at Merlin. "Well? Is he telling the truth?"

Merlin was silent for a moment. I turned my head to look at him, but his face was veiled and I couldn't tell what he was thinking. Then he nodded.

Arthur let the dagger drop. The boy's body relaxed.

"Take him away and kill him." Arthur's voice cut through the silence.

Bedwyr and Theodoric started to drag the Saxon away. He began to scream. Had he thought that if he answered Arthur his life would be spared? The screaming was suddenly silenced. I was too shocked even to move.

"That's a pity," Arthur said, matter of factly. "I would have liked some evidence to prove my brother sent these men."

I found my voice at last. "You think these men were sent to kidnap me? By your brother?"

He nodded, sheathing his dagger. "My sister, Morgana, inherited the Sight from our mother. She learned her lessons alongside me, from Merlin, and then while Cei and I were at sword practice she learned his secrets – more than we ever could. She will have seen you coming."

The how was not important. If I decided to believe in magic, that was. The why was more intriguing.

So I asked him. "Why? Why would she send men after me?"

It was Merlin who answered. "She sides with Cadwy. She always has. It's my fault. She wanted to learn more from me and I refused to teach her. So she found her own way of learning, and Cadwy helped her. He's her brother as well as Arthur's. She won't have sent those men herself. She'll have warned Cadwy of our imminent arrival. It's he who's sent these Saxons against us. From amongst his Foederati."

"Foederati?"

"Saxon mercenaries. The usurper Guorthegirn hired them first more than sixty years ago. They came and settled, and now there are Saxons in every king's army. They're on our side. They have as little love for the new invaders as we have ourselves."

Theodoric came back. I looked up at him. Fresh blood speckled his hands and face. "Is *he* a Saxon Foederati?"

Merlin shook his head. "Theodoric is a Goth."

Overhearing my last remark, Theodoric burst out laughing. "I might look a bit like them, but my people are quite different. We are the civilized side of the Germanic tribes."

The blood on his hands gave the lie to that.

"So you claim!" Cei clapped him on the back, then turned to Arthur. "That's seventeen of them dead now, and the rest put to flight, with only Maccus of our men dead and no one else too badly hurt to ride. Shall we bury Maccus and leave the Saxons for the crows?"

Arthur nodded. I could see him better now as it was getting lighter. His once clean bandage was dirty, and his face bone weary. He nodded. "It's nearly dawn. We've a long way to go today. We'll eat, then saddle up. It's winter and the wolves will be hungry. Make sure we've got everything that's worth salvaging off the bodies."

*Wolves?* I was suddenly quite glad I hadn't been able to go off on my own, trying to get back to Glastonbury. It seemed there were more dangers than just the Saxons out there lying in wait.

# Chapter Twelve

O N THE THIRD day of our journey, we made it to a much more salubrious hostelry than the one we'd stayed at the night before. Although it would only have needed a roof and no raiding Saxons to have been a big improvement. Merlin told me its old Roman name was Letocetum, but the men called it Caer Luit Coyt.

A high and very thick wall, with a wide ditch on the outside, ran around an area of about five acres straddling the road. Within the wall lay quite a settlement: houses, shops, cultivation, and an inn. There was something altogether more vibrant and alive here than there had been in Caer Baddan. I felt as though we were at last entering a region where civilization existed.

People filled the streets – prosperous, cheerful-looking people in clean tunics and long cloaks, unlike the downtrodden peasants of Caer Baddan and Caer Ceri. Ox carts and horse-drawn wagons creaked past us, women carried shopping, children ran about underfoot, vendors packed market stalls away for the night, and dogs scavenged in the gutters. The smell of cooking food mingled with that of stale urine, wood smoke, and horses. Armed soldiers manned the walls, red dragon emblems stitched onto the fronts of their tunics. We were in Pendragon territory now.

"Only thirty miles to Viroconium," Merlin said. He looked as tired as I felt. "Less than a day's ride. Too close for Cadwy to stage another attack and pretend you've been taken by Saxon raiders. They don't come this close to Uthyr's capital. They daren't."

Our horses clattered down the main street between the close-packed houses – real houses with plastered walls, not huts or hovels. The cobbles underfoot had been swept clean of excrement, and running water in the roadside gutters took away household refuse. The whole place was cleaner than Caer Baddan and much more welcoming.

The inn itself proved a bit of a shambles, though. But at least it had a roof, so I was content. Dark thatch, much in need of renewing, overhung the walls. A heap of broken red roof tiles, overgrown with weeds, told me that once, probably a long time ago, the inn had been smarter and more Roman in appearance. But the bright spot in all this was a bath house, opposite the inn across a narrow, cobbled street. And from the smoke and steam issuing from its rooftop, I guessed it was in full working order.

On one side of the inn's courtyard stood stables, equipped with stacks of ample fodder. I piled my horse's manger with hay on top of a liberal ration of grain, and left him covered with his blanket, making the most of the comparative luxury. I was thinking about that bath house, and how good it would be to get clean again.

A big oak door in the porticoed front of the inn opened onto an inner atrium where a colonnade surrounded a tatty flower bed. The smell of herbs filled the air. Most of the bedraggled plants in the central bed must have been aromatics. Torches, already lit on the wooden pillars that held up the first-floor balcony, made the night rush headlong in on us.

A door opened, and the largest woman I'd ever seen came forward, looking not unlike one of those toys you push over that just bounces back again. A great iron ring, hung with large keys, was attached to her girdle.

"My Lord Theodoric," she said, "welcome to my humble hostelry. I'm honored to be able to offer you my hospitality once again." She made a little bow, her breath coming in wheezing puffs as though the short walk had been too much for her.

Theodoric made her a little bow back. "Madame Lucretia, may I introduce you to Prince Arthur Pendragon?"

A look of recognition slid over her face. Arthur took a step forward and she bowed as low as her bulk would allow. Taking his hand, she applied her lips to it enthusiastically with a loud smacking noise.

"My Prince." She straightened up. "You're most welcome to my humble abode. The best room will be yours. And the best food my servants can prepare."

Releasing Arthur, she clapped her plump hands together, and two young servant girls emerged from another door. When they saw the gaggle of men in the courtyard, they put their heads together and giggled. They were like less vivid echoes of the women I'd seen in Caer Baddan, but from the saucy looks they gave the warriors, I had the distinct impression they were probably just as free with their favors. I was really seeing the seedy side of Dark Age life.

Lucretia gave the nearest one a good-natured cuff round the ear. "Be quiet, you silly girls. Tegan, you can take these lords to our finest rooms and organize the communal hall for their men. And mind you see the Prince has the best you can offer." She accompanied this instruction with a meaningful leer. "Maeve, you get to the kitchens and help the cook. We've a pack of hungry men to feed tonight."

The two girls exchanged glances that told me exactly what the best they had to offer might be, and how they were thinking of presenting it. Maeve, whose ash blonde hair was piled up on top of her head in unruly curls, looked a little disappointed that she was assigned to the kitchens, but Tegan, the other girl, had the look of a cat that had got the cream.

I was surprised to find I was annoyed with them both. Just as annoyed as I'd been when Arthur had kissed Tangwyn farewell. If everything Merlin said was true, and I was still far from believing it myself, then he was mine. Not that I wanted him. I just didn't want anyone else to have him. I couldn't help but feel that he should be exclusively mine, and not the property of a mistress in Din Cadan, or a woman of loose morals met in a Roman way station.

Tegan, by far the prettier of the two with curly dark hair and dark skin, bobbed a little bow to Arthur, and came up smiling at him cheekily in a clear promise of things to come.

"Milord Prince." She licked her lips suggestively.

I bristled in silence.

Arthur laughed. I hadn't heard him laugh once since we'd left Din Cadan, so it was good to hear he could still do it. The girl laughed with him.

"Welcome as your offer of food is," he said, turning to Lucretia, "we need to use the bath house before we eat."

Lucretia was quick on the uptake. "Tegan can take you over there. She knows what to do."

Her intentions for Tegan were as plain as the nose on her round face. Could this be a brothel?

Tegan looked very pleased with herself. She shot a smug smile at poor Maeve, who was hovering nearby, probably in the hope that Lucretia would change her mind about sending her to the kitchens.

Taking Arthur by the arm in a proprietorial fashion, she beamed up at him. "This way, milord."

I wanted to slap her hand away from him, which shocked me. I should have felt sorry for her, plying the oldest trade in the world, but I didn't.

Still smiling, Arthur allowed himself to be led back toward the main doorway out into the courtyard, and his men fell in willingly behind him.

"Don't you worry," Lucretia said to them complacently. "There's plenty more girls working over in the bath house. Plenty to go around."

It was definitely a brothel. There was no other explanation. I hesitated, unsure what to do next. I'd certainly never been in one before, but I badly wanted a hot bath.

Merlin put a restraining hand on my arm. "Not you. It'll be no place for a woman. I'll have hot water brought to your room."

I bristled with indignation. "Typical! I've been looking forward to a hot bath since we got here. Why should only the men get one?" Not to mention whatever other services those girls had on offer.

Ignoring my annoyance, Merlin turned to Lucretia. "This is the Lady Guinevere. See her to your best room and provide her with the means to wash, and a maid to help her change into more becoming clothing for a lady. She's had a hard day, and she needs your best care." Lucretia's best care for a visiting lady wasn't up to much. I certainly didn't get a pretty, young maid. She must have been saving them up for the men. Instead, I got a scrawny old woman with no teeth and abnormally strong body odor. And the promised hot water turned out to be tepid. I had a very good wash all over and, even though I hadn't been able to soak my aching limbs, began to feel a bit more human.

I rinsed through my underwear myself, and the old woman, whose utterances were unintelligible but who seemed to have no problem understanding me, helped me into a terracotta-colored gown and laced it up the back.

The trouble was, unable to have a conversation with her, all I could do was think about that bath house and those girls and Tegan with her possessive hand on Arthur's arm and what might be going on over there. In my experience, men who are offered sex with no strings, take it. They'd have to be monks not to. And none of them were that. But you assign your own morals to other people, and I'd done that with Arthur and Merlin, and my morals were a bit prudish even for the twenty-first century.

Consequently, I was feeling disappointed they so obviously didn't have the moral fiber I'd invested them with. It was silly, really. They were free agents, both of them. They were living life very much from day to day, and barely twelve hours ago they'd been attacked by a band of ferocious Saxons. On top of that, Arthur was on his way to see his dying father. What better way to relieve stress than sex?

Okay, I'd forgive them. They were men and they couldn't help their urges. No, they were Dark Age warriors, whose urges might be more primitive than those of men like Nathan. That made me think of him. He and Arthur were so unlike each other. Nathan was well-educated, sensitive, caring, gentle, in touch with his feminine side and, above all, understanding. He'd always put me first at every turn. I didn't think any of the men I'd met here so far would do that for me or any woman. And they didn't appear to have a feminine side to get in touch with.

The old woman brushed out my hair for me, then picked up the ties and began to braid it with deft fingers.

When she'd finished, I stood up and looked myself up and down as best I could. The dress fitted my slim frame perfectly, sweeping down to just above ground level. Long enough to be elegant and yet short enough that I wouldn't get the hem all muddy or trip over it. On an impulse, I picked up my dagger and fastened the belt around my waist. Best to be on the safe side in a place I didn't know. Last night had made me wary.

The common room of the inn was full of mostly empty chairs and tables. A roaring fire blazed in a central hearth, and torches smoldered in iron brackets on the walls, their smoke rising into the rafters to filter through the thatch and out into the cold night air. In one corner of the room, planks had been set on barrels to form a makeshift bar and looking at them, I realized I must be inside a Dark Age pub. Was the fat man behind the bar some relation of Lucretia's? A son, maybe?

In one corner, two men playing dice glanced up at me in curiosity, and beside the fire an old man crouched on a stool, gumming a piece of bread to death with toothless jaws. Apart from them, the room was empty, and when I looked round I realized that my old maid had done a vanishing act as well.

But I was a twenty-first-century girl, and thirsty, and I wasn't about to let being the only woman in a pub put me off. I walked with dignity up to the bar and stood in front of it, waiting for the barman to notice me.

He was wiping out metal tankards with a grimy-looking cloth and standing them along the bar. They were a mixed bunch, size-wise. He wouldn't have got away with using such disparate vessels in my time, not with weights and measures inspectors on the prowl.

He went on polishing the tankards industriously.

I gave a polite little cough. Instead of looking at me, he spat enthusiastically into one of the tankards and proceeded to give it a vigorous polish, taking no notice. I made a mental note to avoid that particular vessel.

The two men who'd been dicing were staring at me. I began to feel a bit self-conscious, but I was determined not to be put off. I wanted a drink, and I was going to get one.

"Excuse me," I tried, and knocked my knuckles on the plank bar top.

Nothing. Was he deaf? He just took some more tankards out of a box behind the bar and started polishing them up, as well.

One of the dicing men got up and swaggered over to stand beside me. He was about my height but twice my width, with a disconcerting look of animal power about him.

"Morgan, gi' the lady a drink. She's standing 'ere dyin' o' thirst."

The barman looked up at me and gave an elaborate start, as though seeing me for the first time. His fat cheeks made his eyes into narrow slits, and his belly wobbled above a low-slung belt.

With a grunt, he picked up one of the tankards, not the one I knew he'd spat in, thank goodness, and turning to a row of barrels behind the counter, stuck it under the wooden tap. Golden liquid flowed, and when the tankard was brimming, he stood it on the counter in front of me.

"Thank you very much." Politeness cost nothing. I picked up the tankard and took a sip. Strong cider, sharp with the taste of apples. I took a thirsty gulp. It was very good indeed.

"An' I'll 'ave one, too," my rescuer said, plonking his own empty tankard down on the counter. While Morgan filled it, he turned back to me, and I caught his gaze sliding down to take in my figure-hugging gown.

I felt uncomfortable. Where were Merlin and Arthur and the rest of them? Carousing in that bloody bath house, of course. Men.

"Ye travelled far?" asked my rescuer conversationally.

I nodded. Even the attack of the night before hadn't quite taught me the caution I needed for Dark Age life yet.

He smiled at me. His teeth were yellow and crooked, and there were hairs poking out of his nostrils. Not a pretty picture. But he'd helped me get a drink, so I couldn't just ignore him.

I sought for polite small talk you could use on a Dark Age bar customer. "Do you live here?"

"Me? No. I'm a merchant. Came 'ere to meet up wi' someone. 'E's not turned up. Typical. Ye can't rely on no one nowadays."

The other man had been putting away his dice in a little leather pouch. Now he got to his feet and sauntered over to the bar, settling himself on the other side of me.

"What's a nice young lady like ye doin' in a place like this?" he asked. How corny could you get? Although, perhaps in the Dark Ages it was a novel approach to a woman.

He had a narrow, ratty face and sparse sandy hair. Both of his front teeth were conspicuous by their absence. In fact, neither man was an oil painting.

"I'm waiting for my friends," I said. "They should be along in a minute or two."

Now that I was virtually hemmed in from both sides, caution washed over me, and I felt more than a little uneasy.

"Drink up, girly," Hairy-Nose said, "and I'll make Morgan get ye another."

I didn't want to gulp down the cider. It was strong, and I had an empty stomach, and it would go to my head. I took another small sip.

Ratty leaned in toward me. His breath smelled of stale onions. The two of them were positioned in such a way that getting away from them would mean shouldering my way between them, and, as I didn't want to touch either of them, I recoiled from the idea. Surely Merlin at least, with his watching brief, would be along soon? What could be keeping them? Silly question. I knew very well what was keeping them, Merlin included. Hopefully they'd be quick about it.

"Ye got a man to take care o' ye?" asked Ratty, with a leer. Did he think I was one of the hostelry's employees? Horrible thought.

Fifty, but what use were they when they were all off getting their legs over in the bath house?

Hairy-Nose bristled with indignation at Ratty's muscling in. He laid his hand on my arm. The nails were broken and filthy. Were they the hands of a merchant? I doubted it very much. Was he bigging himself up to impress me? Well, it wasn't working.

He pulled me round to face him. "A nice lady like ye didn't ought to be alone in a bar."

I was just beginning to realize this fact. The strong implication was that I couldn't possibly be a nice lady. I really wished I'd been able to ask the old maid if it was the done thing to wait in the bar unattended. It looked very much like it wasn't.

Behind the counter, Morgan was busy sweeping the floor, his back to us. He wasn't going to be much help.

The old man by the fire made a horrible noise in his throat and then spat copiously into the flames. Yuck. No help from his direction, either. I put my right hand on the hilt of the dagger at my waist.

Ratty's hand came down on top of mine, vicelike, clamping my hand against the decorative hilt. His touch felt dirty and hot.

"Not so fast, girly, we ain't doing you no 'arm."

I stood very still. Neither of them was taller than me. I drew myself up, my free hand itching to slap him, my pinioned hand desperate to twitch away from his hot grasp.

"Let go of me," I said, as imperiously as I could. My heart was pounding so hard I was sure they'd both be able to hear it, and realize this was a last-ditch panicked attempt.

It must have worked, because Ratty's hand wavered on mine, and I snatched my hand away, but without the dagger. The action brought me up against Hairy-Nose by mistake, and his arm went around my waist from behind, his hand clamping down over my left breast. I was furious. But I'd done self-defense in university, and I knew what to do next. I stepped back hard onto the instep of his foot, grinding my booted heel down onto it. He let out a shout of pain and let go of me, and I pushed myself away from both of them.

I looked desperately round the room, but Morgan was no help at all, and the old man didn't even look at us. There was a flash of steel in the torchlight and a knife glittered in Ratty's hand.

"You want ter play the shy little virgin?" he sneered at me, holding out the knife and moving from one foot to the other like a boxer. "I likes a bit o' resistance in a whore."

He hadn't seen Merlin walk quietly into the room.

"No, she does not." Merlin's sword came down hard on the knife, knocking it from Ratty's hand. He let out a shout of rage and pain as blood spurted across the floor. Some small pink things lay in the straw underfoot. They were his fingers.

Hairy-Nose was not brave. He abandoned his friend and started to back away across the room. "We didn't mean no 'arm. Didn't know she were yours, milord. Gotta forgive a man for tryin'."

Ratty was crying, nursing his finger stumps to his chest.

I couldn't take my eyes off the fingers. They looked alien and horrible, as though they'd never been attached to a human body.

"Get out," Merlin snarled at the two men, the sword pointing directly at Hairy-Nose, who was pretty near crying himself. "And you, take your fingers with you."

A dog had crawled out from under one of the tables and already snatched up one of the fingers, but Ratty, sniveling terribly, went down on one knee, and while still trying to keep one eye on Merlin, gathered up the other three in his good hand.

Hairy-Nose didn't wait for him. The door slammed shut behind him. Ratty struggled back to his feet and followed his friend.

Merlin lowered his sword.

I raised my eyes from the pool of dark blood in the straw. "You cut his fingers off." I was so taken aback I couldn't think of anything else to say.

He nodded. "Would you have preferred it if I let him stick his knife in you? And then his cock?"

Of course not. But I didn't say so. I was outraged that he'd inflicted such an over-the-top punishment.

He picked up Morgan's discarded tankard cloth and, wiping the sword clean of blood, frowned at me. "What were you doing down here on your own anyway? I came to your room, but you weren't there. You're lucky I got here in time."

"Well, if you hadn't been so long in the baths this wouldn't have happened," I spat back, riled. "Have you brought me to a brothel?" My voice rose in indignation.

He sheathed his sword and gave a noncommittal shrug. "Sort of. As much as any inn is. They cater mostly to men, so of course they have a bit of extra comfort at their disposal."

I was furious. "But those awful men thought I was one of the women on offer!"

He was annoyed too, but with me. "Well, who could blame them when they found you in the taproom?"

"Oh, so there's a law stopping women getting drinks in taprooms, is there?"

He shook his head. "Of course not. It's just that well-born ladies don't do it. Only the sort that are free with their favors."

"Do I look like that?" I stormed indignantly.

I'd gone out of my way to look as different as possible to the blowsy Tegan and Maeve – particularly Tegan. I put my hands on my hips and glared at Merlin. "How was I supposed to know all this? In my time I can go in any pub – any inn I like and there's no problem. Women go out all the time by themselves. No one gives a damn what we do."

Actually, now I came to think about it, women in the twenty-first century weren't all that much safer than I was back in the fifth. There were rapes and attacks and dangers on as many sides as there were here, especially in cities. You only had to look at the papers to know that. Something Merlin would not have done on his brief excursions to my world, I was sure.

He pulled a face. "I'm sorry. I should have realized you don't know our ways yet. Next time you're somewhere new, ask me what you should be doing. That'll be best."

"Next time, don't go off with a whore, then," I snapped back.

His eyes widened. "I didn't. I went for a bath and a massage."

A euphemism, of course. A massage, my foot.

I glared hard at him. "Well, I didn't get a *massage* with my two buckets of tepid water."

A smile hovered on his lips. It was contagious. I found I was smiling back. He began to laugh, and I joined in.

"You got two buckets of tepid water?"

I was laughing so much now it was hard to answer. It was from delayed shock as well as mirth. All I could do for a moment was nod. Then I managed, "And a toothless old woman I couldn't understand. A smelly, toothless old woman." And that set me off again.

Which was how Arthur found us, leaning on a table, hysterically laughing together.

He came in with a bunch of his men, Theodoric conspicuous by his absence. Probably still enjoying his *massage*.

Merlin saw him and stopped laughing, straightening up and stepping away from me. Arthur's eyes slid from me to him, and then back to me. I composed myself and smoothed down my gown with slightly unsteady hands. It had done me good to laugh. God knows, I hadn't felt like doing so for what seemed a very long time. Nevertheless, this was an awkward moment.

Lucretia broke the silence as she came in, the sound of her wheezing arriving ahead of her. She'd put on a voluminous and not very clean apron, and was carrying a tray of steaming pies. "All worked up an appetite, have you?" she called as she set her tray down on the plank bar. "Get 'em all jugs of our finest cider, Morgan, you lazy good-for-nothing. Right now, not tomorrow. Chop-chop."

Morgan was galvanized into action, filling his supposedly clean tankards with cider and setting them on the bar. Arthur picked one up and took a long pull on it. I hoped it wasn't the one Morgan had spat in.

"What was so funny?" he asked Merlin.

Merlin gave a shrug. "Nothing. That's why we were laughing. Nothing was funny at all."

Arthur looked puzzled and slightly annoyed. Did he think we'd been laughing at him?

"The thing that wasn't funny," I explained, "was that while you lot were in the bath house getting *massages,* I was stuck with two buckets of tepid water and a stinky old hag."

Theodoric came breezing in. Catching the end of my words, he gave a great guffaw. "Best be careful what you say. That stinky old hag is Lucretia's mother. It's very much a family business here. Maeve and

Tegan are her daughters."

Were they? I was astonished. "They're not very alike."

He grinned, showing his large teeth, which gave him a distinctly wolfish air. "Different fathers, that's why. I don't believe Lucretia could tell you who their fathers were. There's never been a husband in her life, and she's free with her favors. She's over forty now, but she's still got her teeth and she's hotter in bed than any of her girls in the bath house. And I should know."

What? Too much information.

"Maeve looks like she could be yours," Bedwyr remarked. "She's got your yellow hair. Or I suppose she could be the get of a Saxon. Your doxy's not fussy who she opens her legs to."

Theodoric amiably shook his head. "Maeve's too old to be mine. I've only known Lucretia these last five years. But that blonde babe she was nursing last year, he could be mine. I'll not deny it."

Lucretia was organizing the tables. "Nonsense," she said briskly, overhearing Theodoric. "That babe could be anyone's. I'm not saying it's not yours, but you weren't even my only client that night."

"Has it got a moustache yet?" asked the wiry little flute player from the night before. "He marks his get with a big droopy one like his own."

That made everyone laugh.

Arthur took my arm. "Come and sit down."

Considering what he'd just been up to, this was a bit rich. I wrenched my arm free but went with him anyway.

The meal was served by Maeve and a boy with a harelip, whom I presumed must be another of Lucretia's relatives. The pies were crispy pastry filled with chunks of meat in a rich gravy. When the boy set a whole one in front of me, I was sure I couldn't eat all of it, but it was so good, and I was so hungry I managed the whole thing. We ate with our fingers, wiping the gravy off our mouths with our sleeves and washing the pies down with flagons of cider. It was one of the best meals I'd ever had.

When the food was finished, I thought we'd be going to bed, but several of the men started to call for music.

"Give us a song, Gwalchmei."

"Get your flute out."

"Play us a sad song."

Gwalchmei got up from his seat and went and stood in front of the fire.

His audience fell silent expectantly. He put his flute to his lips, and the smoky air filled with music. A mournful melody rose toward the rafters in coils of twisting sound. I sat back a little, letting the beautiful notes filter into my mind. It seemed appropriate not to play a happy tune when we were on such a sad journey. Nobody spoke. Even the old man stopped hawking and spitting into the fire and turned blind eyes toward Gwalchmei, a sad smile hovering on his thin lips.

It was magical. Inside my head the music conjured tall, snow-capped mountains and deep, dark lakes, thick forests beneath a night sky, and wolves howling on a ridge. A river ran through a rocky gorge, tumbling over piled rocks, the sound of its passing mingling with the music of the flute. I felt tears sting my eyes and a solid lump in my chest that wouldn't go away.

At last, the music ended, and Gwalchmei sat for a moment or two, the flute silent in his hands, head bowed. Nobody moved. Not even the dog that had eaten Ratty's finger stirred in the straw beneath his table.

# Chapter Thirteen

THE NEXT DAY we set off westwards along the graveled Roman road historians would come to know as Watling Street, but, to Arthur and his men, was simply the Viroconium Road. The weather held, with a sharp wind blowing from the north that bit through my cloak. I was glad of the sheepskin gloves I'd discovered in one of my saddle bags.

The horses were weary after three days of hard riding, and I felt as tired as they were. Arthur had said nothing to me as we'd readied our horses, but I noticed him and Merlin deep in conversation by the water trough in the middle of the inn courtyard. Were they arguing? There'd been too much noise in the stables to make out what they were saying, but Arthur had seemed agitated. Merlin had slipped into place by my side as we rode out of the inn gates, but there was no laughter about him this morning. In fact, the nearer we drew to Viroconium, the less anyone spoke. It was as if all the warriors were holding their breath and waiting for something to happen.

I'd been to Viroconium as a child. My father took me to visit the ruins of the gigantic bath house complex, which was all that could be seen above ground. In the twenty-first century, the majority of the city still lies buried under farmland, although archaeologists have a good idea of its size and layout. The part of me that was still a historian eagerly anticipated seeing something no modern scholar had ever seen, even though the rest of me viewed the approaching capital of post-Roman Britain with trepidation.

Long before we came in sight of the city, the land began to change. Left behind were the ridges of high ground with their wooded slopes and scattered sheep and cattle. Instead, we rode through rich agricultural lowland in the wide valley of the River Severn, a land of farms and prosperous, well-kept looking villages. It felt as though we'd reached the center of Dark Age Britain, heading to its beating heart with every step our horses took.

Nothing had prepared me for the city's size, though. It dwarfed tumble-down Caer Baddan and abandoned Caer Ceri. Its sturdy walls stood tall, showing no signs of having been pillaged for building stone. The gates, standing open in daylight hours, looked impregnable.

Our road ran straight as a die toward the huge north-eastern gates of the city, past stubble fields and grazing livestock. The late afternoon sun was already nearing the western horizon, where the hills of Wales stood shrouded in low, grey cloud. Between a scattering of trees, the River Severn glinted, and a flock of crows swept across the open sky to come to roost in a stand of naked willows where a row of masts marked the city's wharves.

We approached the gates, Arthur and Cei leading the column. Theodoric and Merlin rode behind them, while I had been promoted from my place toward the rear to ride behind Merlin, guarded by Bedwyr and Gwalchmei. As we were now so far from Din Cadan, and Merlin could no longer fear that I might run away, I reasoned it must be because he was anxious for my safety. Not a thought guaranteed to fill me with confidence.

The heavy gates banged shut behind us for the night. We were inside the capital of Dark Age Britain. An unwelcome shiver ran down my spine, and I wished, not for the first time, that we were still in Din Cadan. The farther we got from it, the more attractive it became.

Compared to Caer Baddan, Viroconium was a buzzing metropolis. The houses on both sides of the road had a well-to-do look about them. However, thatch had replaced the tiles on many of their roofs, and the plaster on their walls had flaked away in places to leave bare patches of brick and stone. Shops lined the road, and the smells of cooking mingled with the stench of unwashed humanity, of dogs and horses, of damp thatch and dirty gutters. This was like a much larger, more crowded version of Letocetum.

The streets thronged with people. Ox carts and horse-drawn wagons rumbled over the cobbles. A couple of boys drove a dozen reluctant sheep, and scruffy dogs ambled between the buildings, casually cocking their legs wherever they wanted. People ate in shop fronts, the men in tunics and braccae, or in flowing togas just as Bassus had worn, the women in an array of brightly colored gowns. Children ran about everywhere, getting in the way of our horses.

I stared about with interest, my anxieties pushed to the back of my mind as I took in the chaos that was the fifth-century capital of Britain. A different world to the earthily primitive Din Cadan, maybe an echo of what Imperial Rome's cities would once have looked like.

Passing a building with a wooden balcony on its upper floor, I looked up to see several heavily made-up young women leaning over it, and this time I had no doubts about their profession. Seeing the column of warriors, they slipped off their cloaks to reveal plump white shoulders and expanses of cleavage, licking their lips suggestively and calling out bawdy, and slightly ambitious, suggestions as to what they could do for a man.

But this time no one was being side-tracked, not even Theodoric. The warriors rode past them without a second glance, their horses' hooves loud on the cobbles. The disappointed calls of the women followed us down the road.

The Imperial Palace was the most Roman building I'd seen so far, dwarfing Bassus' house in Caer Baddan. In startlingly good repair compared with the majority of the city's buildings, it still boasted most of its red-tiled rooftops. Someone had even taken the trouble to patch up the flaking walls. The fresh patches stood out against the old plasterwork.

The stables stood outside the Palace in a low wattle-and-daub building of much more recent construction, surrounding a cobbled courtyard. We dismounted, and a servant came running to take Theodoric's horse. Two more took Arthur's and Cei's. Ignored by them all, I stood holding my reins, feeling lost and insignificant.

Merlin came to my rescue. He caught the arm of a passing stable boy. "Here, take the lady's horse. She's coming with us." He turned to Arthur. "We shouldn't leave her here unchaperoned."

Arthur nodded, but he was clearly distracted. Probably worrying about seeing his father for the first time in years. Or maybe worrying his father might already be dead. Or hoping he was.

"We'd better take our own guard with us, too," Theodoric put in, slinging his helmet on the horn of his saddle. "We shouldn't take any risks."

Cei commandeered a dozen of Arthur's warriors to accompany us.

I followed them out of the stables and across the narrow, cobbled road to the main entrance to the palace. Huge double doors studded with iron blocked our path. Two guards stood on either side, spears in hands, swords on hips. The plumed Roman helmets on their heads made them tower above even Cei and Theodoric.

"I don't like the look of this," Cei muttered to Arthur, loud enough for me, walking just behind them, to hear. "This place has taken on the look of somewhere you go into but never come out of."

*A bit like Din Cadan then.*

"Cadwy wouldn't dare." Arthur sounded confident of his welcome.

I wasn't.

"We won't be the only visitors here," Theodoric said, keeping his voice low. "The Seneschal sent messengers to all the members of the Council of Kings. Some will undoubtedly already be here."

"Cadwy's too clever to do anything in front of witnesses," Arthur said.

Merlin put his hand on the hilt of his sword, fingering the ornate carving, his face wary. The hairs on the back of my neck stood up, and my heart rate rocketed.

The guards stamped the butts of their spears hard on the cobbles and two of them threw open the doors for us. We walked inside.

"Too late to turn back now," Cei hissed to Arthur as the doors closed behind us with a resounding thud.

We were in the vestibulum of the palace, which opened into the atrium. So were a great many other people who all turned to stare at us. Some, mostly the younger men, were dressed in British braccae and tunics, while others, mostly the grey-haired, wore Roman togas. There were no women. I was glad I was disguised as a boy, although I had no confidence that close scrutiny wouldn't give me away.

There was a long silence.

"Prince Arthur." A man in a toga, with thinning grey hair cut very short, stepped forward, his arms held out, his bland pink face the picture of fawning welcome. He clasped hands with Arthur and then put his arms around him, holding him for a moment. Who was this? Not Arthur's father, surely, who was supposed to be on his deathbed? Whoever it was, I was deeply suspicious of him. Too oily by half.

As one, the rest of the assembled men bowed to Arthur.

The pink-faced man released Arthur and stood back, looking him up and down as though comparing the boy he used to know with the man before him.

"It's been too long since we saw you here in Viroconium. Although I hear you've been acquitting yourself well in the west. Where is it you're based? Din Cadan, isn't it? A primitive backwater, I've heard."

"Dubricius, it's good to see you, too." Arthur gave a quick, forced smile. But his attention wasn't on the older man, his eyes were sweeping the room, searching. For his father? Or his brother?

Merlin leaned toward me and whispered in my ear. "Dubricius, archbishop of Caer Legeion, to the south. He'll be here to give the King the last rites and officiate at the burial ceremony." He paused. "And crown the new High King."

Of course. They were all Christians. Yet there was nothing what-soever of holiness about this archbishop.

"My father? He still lives?" There was strain in Arthur's voice, and his dark brows were drawn together in a heavy frown.

Dubricius nodded. "He's weak. But he holds his own." He paused. "You and your men have come far. Allow me to provide you with food and drink. You will want to rest before you see your father."

Arthur frowned. "I'll see my father before I do anything else."

Dubricius' face changed as his pale grey eyes narrowed. "I believe your father to be sleeping now, and the doctor's instructions are that he is not to be disturbed." There was an edge to his voice, of impatience, of anger even.

Arthur must have known Dubricius of old. His lips came together in a hard line. His hand started to tap his leg.

"I have a healer with me," he said very clearly. "She needs to see him. Now."

*Did he mean me?*

Dubricius, who'd been standing resolutely in front of Arthur, took a step back.

"A healer? A woman? I did not know. But she will be no help, I fear. It's too late for healers."

The archbishop needed to make up his mind. Either there was no hurry for Arthur to see his father, who was holding his own, or he was so bad it was too late for the intervention of a healer. From my point of view, as the prospective healer, I would have preferred the latter option.

"Then don't stand here passing the time of day," Arthur said.

"Take me to him at once."

A second grey-haired man stepped out of the crowd and made a small bow. He was tall but still powerfully built, just a little pot belly that hung over the belt of his tunic betraying his age. "My Prince, you will not remember me. Euddolen of Rheged. I've been your father's Seneschal these last five years. Allow me to escort you to the royal bedchamber. Your father will want to see you straight away, I'm certain."

"Cadwy won't," muttered Cei, in an aside only I heard.

Arthur reached out a hand and took my wrist. "I'm taking her. She's the healer."

Did he think I was a miracle worker who could save a dying man? If he did, he was about to be sorely disappointed.

"And my men." He gestured at Merlin, Theodoric and Cei, and the warriors who'd come in with us. It wasn't a request. It was an order. Dubricius opened his mouth to object, but it was too late. Too late for him and too late for me.

Reluctantly, I allowed myself to be led away as we followed Euddolen across the atrium, which was crowded with important-looking men whose heads turned as we passed. A fountain played in the center under a square of open sky. Then we were out into a large courtyard filled with greenery and surrounded on all four sides by a colonnaded walkway. More guards, in fact, guards at every turn, and tiles underfoot and faded paintings on the plastered walls. I smelled rosemary and mint on the damp evening air and saw wood smoke curling up into the darkening sky. My heart filled with disquiet.

The royal bedchamber lay halfway down one side.

At the double oak doors, Euddolen and Arthur stopped. Arthur still had me by the wrist, but now he transferred his hold to my hand. His was hard and calloused, the grip firm. He wasn't about to let me go. I didn't find the contact in any way reassuring.

Euddolen knocked on the doors.

For a moment there was silence. Then one of the doors creaked open a crack and a wrinkled face peered out.

"Who is it?" asked the ancient owner of the face, squinting at us shortsightedly. It was impossible to say if it was male or female.

"Euddolen, Seneschal to the High King. I bring Prince Arthur to see his father."

The old face sucked its gums ruminatively.

"Best come inside then, the lot o' ye," it mumbled, spraying spit at us. Who'd have thought dentistry would be one of the things I'd miss most about the twenty-first century?

We found ourselves in a large antechamber illuminated by oil lamps set at intervals in niches on the walls. A powerful smell of decay struck me. It hung in the still air so thickly I could taste it. There being so many of us, we rather filled it up. On the far side of the room stood another set of double doors. Underfoot, furs partially covered an elaborate black and white mosaic, and a faded fresco of ancient Greek mythology decorated the walls. Two ornately carved wooden bench seats were piled with cushions, a long low table standing between them. A small man with a closely shaven head sprawled snoring on one of the seats. Could he be the doctor?

The little old person was a woman, to judge by her clothing. Her sparse white hair grew in a soft halo about her wrinkled face, and she had a stoop most likely caused by osteoporosis.

Arthur stared at her in the lamplight, a look of recognition dawning on his face. "Breanna?" He released my hand.

The old woman's withered apple face split into a smile, giving us a good view of her empty gums.

"Little Arthur," she spluttered. "I can't see so well now, and when the Seneschal said your name, I wasn't sure 'e 'ad it right. I 'adn't thought to see ye 'ere again afore I died."

Arthur dropped to his knees in front of her. She was so bent and withered that even then she was barely on eye level with him.

"Mother Breanna, I too never thought to see you again. I am indeed your Arthur, come back to you." He put his arms around her fragile, birdlike body and held her gently to his heart.

Who was she? And what was he to her? She'd clearly known him as a child and he'd called her Mother, but I knew his mother was Eigr, and that she was in Tintagel. A nurse perhaps? But hadn't Cottia been that?

Tears brimmed in her rheumy old eyes and ran down her corrugated cheeks. He held her as she cried, her face pressed to the rough links of his mail shirt, his unshaven cheek against her thin white hair.

She must have felt the chainmail on her skin. "But ye're dressed for war, not the sick room. Take time to get this off ye, and then I'll take ye in to see yer father. Cadwy sits with 'im now."

Arthur stiffened at the mention of his brother, his dark brows knitting in the familiar frown. Gently he put her to one side and got back to his feet. "No," he said firmly. "I'll see him now. He's a warrior king. He'll not find fault with me for coming in my armor. I've come to see him, and I'll not be delayed." He glanced at his men. "I'll go alone but for the Lady of the Ring."

She might not be able to see very well, but the trepidation in Breanna's face was clearly readable. She put out a skeletal bird's foot hand, but he was turning away from her already, heading toward the far doors. He caught me by the wrist again and pulled me with him, taking long strides across the mosaic floor. I was going to have bruises.

At the doors he gave a great shove to both of them, and they swung wide open. He strode into the room beyond, me in his wake like a piece of flotsam tossed in the waves.

The first thing I noticed was that the smell was much stronger here, catching me in the back of the throat and making me want to vomit. The stench brought Arthur to a halt, his face a mask of shock and thinly veiled disgust. No mistaking the smell of death hanging over the bed that stood in the center of the room. Even if you'd never smelled it before, like me, you'd have known there was nothing else that could smell like that. And it was hot, swelteringly hot, with a brazier burning near the bed and the window shutters firmly closed.

A slight hump beneath the piled bedclothes marked where the High King of Britain lay gasping out his final hours. In the shadows, a woman stood, her hands clasped in front of her, head bowed as if in prayer. Beside the bed, a figure lurched to its feet and turned toward us. For the first time, I saw Cadwy, Arthur's older brother.

# Chapter Fourteen

C ADWY WAS NOTHING like Arthur. Where Arthur was all whipcord strength, Cadwy was a bear. His wiry, dark hair, flecked with grey, grew in a bush about his head, merging into a thick black beard. This in turn merged into a mat of chest-hair trying to escape from the neck of his deep red tunic. His ears, his wrists and all his fingers were heavy with gold.

Having got to his feet, he didn't come any closer, but stood like a bull preparing to charge, glaring from under bushy, grizzled brows.

I didn't move. I was mostly obscured behind Arthur, and that was how I wanted to stay. I hadn't been keen to meet Cadwy in the first place, and now that I'd seen him, he looked as though he embodied every worry I'd been nurturing.

The woman in the shadows turned her head and looked at Arthur out of wide, dark eyes, which held no surprise. Dark hair hung loose in a cascade down her back.

"Brother," Cadwy growled. His voice matched his looks – deep and coarse and not at all friendly.

Arthur inclined his head infinitesimally. "Brother." His voice was ice and steel.

The mound in the bed stirred. Another wave of fetid odor assaulted my nostrils. Whatever was wrong with the High King, it must be bad for him to smell like this. The woman pressed pale hands together but made no other move.

Disregarding Cadwy's aggressive stance, Arthur took three steps closer to the bed to stand at its foot, looking down at the pathetically slight shape beneath the covers. I stayed as still as possible, dimly aware that the Seneschal and Breanna were in the open doorway behind me. Cadwy didn't seem to have noticed me or them, staring as he was with such malevolent intensity at Arthur.

In the shadows, the woman turned her head toward me, her gaze running from my untidy plaited hair, through my travel-stained masculine clothing, to my booted feet. I shifted uneasily. She knew I was a woman. She knew I was the Lady of the Ring. I don't know how I knew this; I just did.

The figure in the bed moved a hand as thin as Breanna's on the covers. Blue veins stood out like knotted cords. His shrunken face was paper pale upon the pillows, his features so sunken his head had the appearance of skin stretched tight over a bony skull. What little hair he had was wispy, and white as thistledown. This was all that remained of Uthyr Pendragon.

Arthur stepped around the bed to its head, opposite Cadwy and the woman. He stood for a moment looking down at his father, as though in two minds what to do, and then he went down on one knee. Reaching out, he took the thin hand in his own lean, brown grip.

Uthyr Pendragon turned his head and looked at his younger son out of bloodshot eyes. "Arthur." The word came out on a gasp, faint and barely audible. "You came."

Arthur bowed his head. "I came." He paused and swallowed. "Theodoric fetched me." His voice was thick with emotion.

There was a long silence before Uthyr spoke again. His breath came in wheezing puffs as though he smoked sixty a day. "Your brother said you would not come." The words were faint, but the silence in the room was total. The whispering voice of Uthyr Pendragon sibilated through the air.

Cadwy made a sharp movement. Anger emanated from him in

waves. Clearly he was furious Arthur was here, that Theodoric had fetched Arthur to his father's deathbed in defiance of his wishes.

Uthyr spoke again. "But I knew my boy would come." Was that a smile touching the cracked lips?

"Don't talk, Father," Arthur said gently. "Save your strength." He glanced in my direction. "I've brought a healer with me." He beckoned, and reluctantly I stepped away from the doors and up to the end of the bed. Euddolen's and Breanna's anxiety pressed in on me from behind.

Cadwy stared across the bed out of small dark eyes sunk in his overblown, ruddy cheeks. It was impossible to tell whether he took after his father or not – the High King's appearance was too far gone for that. Once, Cadwy might have been a handsome man, but now, consumed with scarcely concealed hatred for his younger brother, his face had contorted into lines of ugliness.

"What can this boy do that our father's own doctors could not?" he asked scornfully. He hadn't even noticed I was a woman.

Arthur released his father's hand and got to his feet. "Come here, Gwen."

I went on leaden feet. A first aid weekend was no preparation for this. The smell was appalling. I wanted desperately to be somewhere else, miles from this terrible death chamber.

I stood beside Arthur. As I looked down at Uthyr I drew a sharp intake of breath. Astute intelligence resided in his bright eyes, an intelligence that recognized this was his end already come upon him. He held up a shaking hand. "No."

Arthur took my hand in his firm grip. "Let her try, at least."

Uthyr waved his hand back and forth feebly. "No." It was a gasp. "You mean well, my son." He had to pause to regain his strength. "But nothing can be done. It's too late. My body already rots. Only my mind remains." The hand fell and his eyes closed. His breathing sounded loud in the silence, as though he were forcing the air in and out of his lungs in an active effort to stay alive. Above dry and fissured lips, his nose rose prominent as an eagle's beak from his ravaged face, his blue-veined eyelids thin as parchment.

"This is a girl?" Cadwy wasn't fast on the uptake, that was for sure. "Your healer is a *girl?*" His voice was heavy with scorn. Not very PC of him.

The woman from the shadows stepped forward. Her gown rustled slightly as she moved, and for a moment, a rich exotic scent overpowered the stench of decay. "This is the Lady of the Ring who was foretold." Her voice was deep and sweet, made for singing.

A leaf-green gown clung to her curves in all the right places, and for a woman she was tall. She had a pale, heart-shaped face with full lips, and a small dimple in her chin – a face that was not just beautiful, but absolutely stunning. I'd never seen anyone like her. I shifted uneasily in my dirty tunic and braccae and travel-stained cloak, feeling like a scullery maid brought before a duchess. A small smile curved her lips as she acknowledged the effect she'd had on me.

"The Lady of the Ring?" Cadwy echoed, staring from me to her and back again, and then at Arthur. "This is her?" He sounded disappointed. Should I feel insulted?

Arthur nodded. There was an air of triumph about him, as though he were playing cards and had just laid his winning hand on the table. "This is she." Words hung unsaid in the air between them. Perhaps Arthur was thinking of the supposed Saxon raid on our camp two days before. I certainly was. This was the man who'd sent them.

The woman's smile deepened. She looked as though she was enjoying Cadwy's surprise. "She has the ring, Brother. Look, and you will see."

Why did I have the feeling when she looked at me that she knew what I was thinking? Did she really have the "sight"?

Uthyr opened his eyes. They were fever bright. "You have the Lady of the Ring?" There was animation in his voice. He coughed, and the flecks of spit at the corner of his mouth were stained with blood. "Now? Here?"

Arthur dropped back down on one knee and took his father's hand in both of his. Bending his head, he touched his brow for a moment to the skeletal fingers. "Yes, Father, she is here." There was unmistakable exultation in his voice.

"Let me see her," the old man whispered. "I must see her before I die." His eyes closed again. The bed covers rose and fell as he struggled for breath.

A choked sob came from the door. Surely Breanna and not Euddolen.

Without being asked to do so, I knelt beside Arthur, our shoulders brushing. I stretched out my hand, the one with the dragon ring on it, and took Uthyr's hand from Arthur. There was nothing there but dry papery skin and fragile bones.

The old man's eyes opened again. He looked long and hard at the ring on my finger, then at my face. "I never thought I would see this day." His voice trailed off and for a moment his eyes wandered blankly from side to side, the bright intelligence lost.

The woman stepped closer. "Leave him." Her voice held command. She was used to being obeyed. "Let him rest. His time is fast approaching. By bothering him with this girl, you will only make it come all the faster."

Now that she was out of the shadows I could see she was young – younger than Arthur and younger than me. The fresh bloom of her cheeks gave that away.

Arthur turned angry eyes upon her. "He needs to see the Lady of the Ring. He's waited all his life for this."

The bony hand in mine twitched, and I squeezed it in instinctive reassurance. The skull-like head turned, and he looked up at me, the blank look replaced by that sharp intelligence once again. How old was he? Surely not as old as he appeared.

"You are the one foretold." Uthyr's whisper rasped in the silence. The stench was terrible.

His lips moved. "I'm glad I have lived long enough to look upon your face." He paused for breath. "And to see you married to my son."

"She's not married to him," Morgana interjected.

Arthur shifted beside me. Was it because he felt as unwilling as I did to be coerced into a marriage to fulfill a bloody prophecy?

The old man's eyes slid sideways to look at Cadwy, who was standing, hands on hips, an angry frown etched onto his face. Uthyr licked his dry lips. "Send for Dubricius."

There was a long moment when Uthyr held his elder son's rebellious gaze, and I thought Cadwy was considering whether to disobey his father. And then Cadwy caved in. He walked to the door, and I heard him tell Euddolen to send for the archbishop.

The dying king emitted a deep sigh and closed his eyes. For a long minute the bedclothes remained unmoving and then at last he took a rasping breath. He was asleep.

Arthur got to his feet, his jaw set. Breanna hobbled up to the bed and with a wary glance toward the brothers, drew up a low wooden stool and took Arthur's place beside me.

Arthur walked toward his brother.

I looked at Breanna. "What's wrong with the king? What's he dying of?" Memories of my own father's deathbed swarmed in on me.

Arthur stopped in front of Cadwy, feet squarely planted, as openly aggressive as his brother. There was no brotherly love between them at all, only simmering sibling rivalry and machismo. From her position on the far side of the bed, Morgana watched them, her tongue caught between her teeth in expectation, her thoughts written clearly on her face. She was excited. She wanted them to fight. She'd been waiting for this.

Breanna put out a frail hand and smoothed the High King's brow. "These ten year ago my sweet Lord took a wound from a spear 'igh up 'is leg – in the groin." The air rattled in his laboring lungs. "It never 'ealed. Got ulcerated and 'e could never sit an 'orse again."

That would have been a crippling blow to any man in the Dark Ages, but surely even worse for the High King himself. My gaze flicked toward Arthur and Cadwy. They both stood motionless, glaring at one another.

"It's troubled 'im bad ever since, it 'as, but this year it got worse." The bony hand in mine felt cold and already dead. Dark patches spotted his scrawny neck, like vicious bruises. "The ulcer spread. His 'ole leg began to go black. Then it moved onto 'is body. That's what the smell is, me dear, that's what the smell is."

If only they'd had antibiotics. Though it was probably too late now for them. Was it gangrene? Most likely.

I looked again at Arthur and Cadwy. Arthur was the taller of the two, but Cadwy the more powerfully built. The padded tunic and mail shirt bulked Arthur out, but Cadwy still looked twice as wide.

Cadwy broke the silence between them with an angry snarl. "I didn't think you'd have the barefaced cheek to show yourself here, after all these years."

Arthur bristled in response. "It wasn't my father that kept me away. It was you, poisoning him against me. I'd have been here all the sooner if you'd been gone."

"Well, I am here, and you'd better get used to it. I've been Father's War Leader since he took that wound – when you were just a boy. I'm the one the soldiers follow – the one who makes the decisions here."

Arthur sneered. "That'll be why the Saxons are making such inroads to the East then, won't it? Because you're the War Leader and they're scared of you."

I thought Cadwy was going to hit him. His hands balled into great fists by his sides and the tendons in his neck tightened. His face suffused with blood. His eyes bulged.

"And what about the West?" he snapped back, "Have you been so successful in keeping out the Irish?"

"At least I'm not employing Saxons as Foederati to help my warriors do their jobs. I've met with your Saxons, and I wasn't impressed. Did you think I wouldn't know you sent them? Did you think I'd take it lying down?" He turned and gestured at Morgana. "Did you think I wouldn't know it was she who warned you of our arrival?"

Cadwy seized on that last sentence. "You've got Merlin. I need someone with the Sight. She's more gifted than Merlin, and she's mine."

"She only knows what Merlin taught her," countered Arthur. "And that won't have been everything he knows, by any means."

"She saw the coming of the Lady of the Ring," Cadwy spat. "She warned me you were bringing her."

"So you could prepare a reception committee."

"You've no proof of that."

"Do I need it?"

"I'm the favored son. I'm the firstborn. I told you – it's me the men follow."

Arthur gave a scornful snort of laughter. "Not out of choice. D'you think they'd be so keen to do so if there was a choice? D'you think they wouldn't turn to me if I called them?"

"They're my men. They know where their allegiance lies."

"To the High King, not you."

"Your time in the West has addled your brains, brother. You forget who you're talking to."

"And you forget that our father still lives. You're not King yet. And you'll never be High King."

"I soon will be. And then I'll deal with you."

"You think the Council will elect you High King?"

Doubt slid across Cadwy's face. It was plain this thought had already occurred to him. "They will enact my father's instructions."

"You think our father will have told them to make you High

King?" Arthur's voice rang with mockery.

Cadwy opened his mouth to form a retort, but the words didn't come. Dubricius came hurrying into the chamber followed by Euddolen. The archbishop took in at a single glance the suppressed fury emanating from the two brothers and stepped between them, forcing them apart.

"You sent for me?" he addressed Cadwy. "Is he worse? Am I to administer the Last Rites?" He had a hand pressed hard against the chests of each of them.

The bony hand beneath mine stirred and Uthyr opened his eyes. "I'm not dead yet," he snapped. "You're here to witness a marriage." He followed this with another coughing fit.

"What?" I almost snatched my hand back from Uthyr's. I hadn't forgotten about the fate hanging over me, but it had been gone from the forefront of my thoughts for several days, as I didn't think Arthur believed in the prophecy or was that interested in me or marriage. Especially not after the bath house incident.

To say that Arthur was taken aback as well, seemed to be an understatement. "Now?" he asked, his face off with Cadwy all but forgotten. "You want us to marry *now*?"

Uthyr's thin dry lips drew back in a travesty of a smile, showing his yellowed teeth. They were in a surprisingly good state compared with the rest of him. "Now," he repeated. "Fulfill the prophecy and marry the Lady of the Ring."

Cadwy's face contorted with rage for a moment before he could get it under control. With an enormous effort he schooled it into something resembling compassion. If I'd been Uthyr, I wouldn't have been fooled.

"We can't do a wedding here," he protested. "And you're too weak to officiate."

The fiercely alert eyes flashed at him. "I won't be doing it," Uthyr said. "You will."

An expression of furious shock flashed across Cadwy's face, and he looked at Morgana as though appealing for help.

She shrugged her slender shoulders. "You'll be head of the family after he dies. He's right. You can carry out the ceremony."

The old man gave a snort of laughter. "To fulfill the prophecy one of you has to do this. You can hardly marry her yourself, can you?"

*Thank God.*

"Being already married, that is." Uthyr closed his eyes again. That outburst had taken it out of him. His chest rose and fell as his breathing labored.

Cadwy blustered. "I could put aside Angharad."

"Well, you haven't. It's too late for that. Arthur will wed her."

No one had thought to ask me what I thought about it. I let go of Uthyr's hand and got to my feet. "I don't want to get married," I said, but I might as well not have bothered, for all the good it did me.

Arthur glanced at me, then back to his father. "I don't need anything to forge my future. And I don't believe in prophecies. Especially not this one."

He was paid as much attention as I was.

"The chest," Uthyr grunted. "In the chest."

It was old Breanna who went to the iron-bound chest up against the far wall. She lifted the lid, and after a few moments, stood up. In her hand was a length of soft rope. What the hell was that for?

"What you believe does not matter," Euddolen said to Arthur. "What is true is what matters. And this prophecy is true."

Arthur gave a snort of derision.

Cadwy looked back at his father. "You're not thinking straight," he tried. "We can't have a wedding at such short notice. It needs to be done in front of our people."

Uthyr's brows came together in a deep frown worthy of either one of his sons. "You know I can't do that." He gasped for breath. Anger was exhausting him. He began to cough again, and Breanna put a cloth to his mouth. This time the fit went on for longer, his breath becoming more and more wheezy. At last he collapsed back onto his pillows, eyes shut, chest heaving. Bright blood stained the cloth. Was he even going to last long enough to see this wedding?

I was trapped. I was in a strange land with no way of getting back home to Nathan, whose very existence felt more and more like a distant dream. This was my reality now. I couldn't escape it any more than I could fly to the moon. It was no use protesting. No one was listening. That bloody prophecy was the thing directing my life, and I had no control.

Morgana cast her eyes over me again. I felt like a piece of meat being assessed for quality. How dare she look at me like that?

Breanna held out the length of rope to Cadwy. For a moment he just stared down at it, then, very reluctantly, he took it.

Euddolen came over to me. "Take my hand."

I hesitated. What I really wanted to do was run away, but where to? I put my hand in his. I was surprised. For a Seneschal, who I assumed was the equivalent of a Prime Minister, it was very rough and calloused.

He led me to the foot of the bed. "Morgana, bring your brother."

Morgana took Arthur by the arm none too gently, and steered him to stand facing me, at arm's length. Uthyr's eyelids fluttered open. He gave a small nod of satisfaction. "Get on with it. My strength ebbs."

I looked up at Arthur, and his dark eyes held mine. Was that exultation there, hidden in the depths? I blinked in shock. Had he engineered this? Was all his protestation feigned?

Cadwy stepped up to us, the rope lying over his outstretched hands like a dead snake. It was creamy white, too slender to be of any practical use. Dubricius was at his elbow, a frown of disapproval on his face. Neither of them wanted to do this.

Of course. It was giving Arthur a step on the road toward the coveted High Kingship. And Arthur's apparent reluctance had only made his father the more determined to carry this marriage out right now. Clever. I was impressed. How could I not be?

"Clasp hands."

Arthur reached out and caught both my hands in his. Was that a tremble of excitement running through them?

Cadwy laid the rope over our clasped hands. Behind him, Morgana was as angry as he was, her face white with suppressed fury. But neither of them dared to cross their father, even on his deathbed. How easy would it have been after his death to have refused to carry out this wedding? Very, I suspected. Had she intended me for Cadwy? To replace this unknown Angharad? Should I look upon this hasty marriage as a rescue? After all, Uthyr himself had put aside Cadwy's mother to take Eigr as his wife, so it must be easy to do.

Cadwy cleared his throat and began. "Arturius Pendragon, son of Uthyr Pendragon, High King of all Britain, grandson of Aurelius Ambrosius last Emperor of the Western World, great-grandson of Constantine, third of that name, you have come here today to plight your troth to this woman—" He looked at me questioningly. Close up like this I could see the hairs in his nostrils and smell the rank sweat of his body. Marrying Arthur looked more and more like a lucky escape.

"Guinevere," I managed.

"To this woman, Guinevere." Cadwy's gruff voice was loud in the quiet bed chamber, only the rasping breath of the dying High King competing with it. He looked at me again. "Guinevere, you are come here today to plight your troth to this man, Arturius Pendragon. To vow to be his wife, to serve him all your days, to bear him strong sons, to honor his household, to obey his law."

He took one of the ends of the rope and wrapped it around and over our hands.

"Arturius Pendragon, do you take this woman into your house to be your wife, with this promise of the knot of marriage?" He took the other end and similarly wrapped it under and over our hands, tying it in a loose knot on top. "Do you vow to return in twelve months to make this contract binding?"

I looked into Arthur's face. He had four days' stubble on his chin, his hair was unkempt and tangled, there were dark shadows beneath his eyes and the sharp smell of horses and winter clung to his clothes. I thought of Nathan – of his flopping fringe and his boyish smile, and my heart ached for him. But the image of his face shimmered and dispersed. Instead I saw Arthur, still frowning, as totally different to Nathan as any man could possibly be.

"I take this woman," he said.

From the bed came a grunt of satisfaction.

Cadwy wrapped the ends of the rope around our wrists and tied another knot, binding us ever more closely together.

"Guinevere, do you vow to obey all the laws of the house of your new husband, until this knot be broken?" Cadwy was having difficulty getting the words out. They must have been choking him.

I pressed my lips together. What could I say? I had no viable alternative, and perhaps being bound by marriage to Arthur would make me safe in the dangerous place this palace looked to be. Perhaps it was my only hope. Without it, what was to stop Cadwy taking me for his own? That was what Morgana wanted. I knew without a doubt that it was what Cadwy wanted, too.

"I take this man," I said, into the silence.

# Chapter Fifteen

A FTER THE MARRIAGE ceremony was done, Uthyr lay back sleeping on his pillows, his haggard face even more drawn than before. Arthur nodded to Dubricius. "Fetch Merlin."

After a moment, Merlin appeared in the doorway, but stopped short, as though up against a solid but invisible wall. He stared – not at Arthur and me, still hand-fasted together by the rope – but at Morgana, who had gone to sit beside her father on Breanna's stool. She gazed back at him out of hostile, dark eyes. No explanation was needed. His feelings were written across his face for everyone to see.

He loved her.

All the stories I'd read about Merlin and Morgana came flooding back to me. She'd been his pupil. She learned his magic. She used it to help destroy her brother, King Arthur, and against her old teacher, Merlin. Or was that Nimuë? I needed to warn him.

However, most of that could be a load of bollocks. Yet some of it might be grounded in fact. If you traced old legends back to their roots, you almost always found some grain of truth in their origin. And here were Merlin and Morgana in the same room, two people connected inexorably by their timelines. Two people of legend made flesh before me.

The question was, did *she* love him?

After an awkward pause, he seemed to remember himself and tore his eyes away from Morgana. He made a small, stilted bow to Cadwy and Arthur, and a bigger one to the sleeping figure on the bed.

"He lives," Arthur said. "For now."

Merlin's eyes slid down to the rope that joined our hands and his eyebrows rose. Did I detect a look of triumph?

Arthur nodded. "It was my father's wish."

Merlin glanced at Cadwy, who was still scowling. Hadn't his mother ever warned him that if the wind changed, he'd stick like that? On second thought, maybe the wind had already changed, and he *was* stuck like that.

"Take Gwen away and find her some food and somewhere to sleep," Arthur said, sliding the knotted rope off our hands. "I'm staying with my father. The end is near."

⤜⪤⪥⪤⪤

MY BEDROOM OPENED off the wide garden courtyard on the side opposite the King's bedchamber, so any comings and goings in the night passed me by. I certainly didn't get a visitation from Arthur to demand his conjugal rights, which had been worrying me a bit, so as a wedding night, I suppose it was a bit of a flop. Not that I minded. I was more than happy to be left to myself.

I woke to the timid touch of a young servant girl.

"My Lady." The girl had a sweet, soft voice.

I opened my eyes and looked up at her. She was only in her early teens, fourteen at the most.

She stepped back from me and bobbed a little bow. "I was asked to waken you. The King commands your presence in the audience chamber."

In the audience chamber? Surely not. Didn't she mean in his bedchamber? I was confused, which stopped me putting two and two together and realizing the obvious – that the old king must be dead, and she meant the new king.

I sat up and pushed back the covers. The room was pleasantly warm, the tiled floor beneath my feet even warmer. Of course, there must be a hypocaust, that under-floor heating system the Romans invented. I was very glad they were so clever. Who'd have thought there'd be central heating in the Dark Ages? Good old Romans.

"I've brought you food and wine." She indicated the table in the center of my bed chamber, where a chair with a basket work seat and back had been drawn up. A tray stood on it with a carafe of wine, a loaf of dark bread, a small bowl of yellow butter and a basket of dried figs. I went over to the table and sat down in just my long undershirt.

Breaking off a steaming hunk of the still warm bread, I spread it liberally with butter and ate it.

"What's your name?" I asked as I ate, washing the bread down with a draught of the wine. It still seemed odd to drink wine for breakfast, but I was getting used to it. Everybody here must be operating in a permanent state of inebriation, bolstered by the intake of alcohol every few hours.

She blushed and looked at her feet. "Kinna, my Lady."

I smiled at her and took a sip of wine. What I would have really liked was a cup of strong coffee. Unfortunately, the advent of the coffee bean in Britain was still some thousand years off.

When I'd finished eating, Kinna helped me into my blue gown, lacing it down the back so it clung to me as alluringly as Morgana's had. I wished I had a full-length mirror; I really wanted to see what I looked like in it.

Having undone my plait, she brushed out my hair until it hung in a shining chestnut mane down to my waist, thick and wavy and luxuriant. More than a match for Morgana's dark locks. Was I trying to show her that I could look as feminine as she did, to prove I didn't always look like the bedraggled waif she'd seen the night before? Had she made me feel so inadequate? Well, quite frankly, yes.

As an afterthought, I took the dagger Merlin had given me and slipped it, in its sheath, down the side of one of my boots. Doing so was actually more uncomfortable than I'd expected. They made it look so easy in films. You never knew when a weapon might come in handy in a place like this.

A knock on the door signaled the arrival of an escort. To my surprise, it was Gwalchmei, the flute player, which made me wonder what Cei and Arthur and Merlin were doing that they had to send someone else to fetch me. Kinna draped a long, fur-lined cloak around my shoulders and pulled the hood up over my head against the cold.

Gwalchmei led me along the colonnaded walkway surrounding the square garden, my booted feet clacking on the paving slabs, his soft leather boots almost silent. On the side opposite the atrium we came to a halt. Behind us, a wide, paved pathway lined with box hedges and statues led from the steps where we were standing, back through the center of the gardens to the atrium. In front of us, a pair of ornately carved doors stood open, two armed soldiers standing guard outside. Was this the audience chamber?

Gwalchmei propelled me through the open doors and into a crowded chamber twice as wide as it was long. Opposite the doors, on a raised dais, stood a stark, wooden throne. And on that throne sat Cadwy, a golden crown resting on his grizzled head.

I hesitated on the threshold, staring at him. His bulk filled the throne to capacity. The dais being several feet above the level of the floor, the height accentuated the impression of menacing power. Instinct warned me to caution. I was learning fast.

Down the sides were ranged all the men I'd seen the night before, and more besides, as well as Arthur's own men, with a few women scattered amongst them. To one side of the throne stood Arthur and Morgana. He'd changed his clothes and shaved, and his dark hair was brushed back from his face, but nothing could disguise the shadows of exhaustion beneath his eyes. Had he slept at all? The smell of smoke from the lamps and the stink of men's sweat pressed in on me.

I looked quickly at Gwalchmei by my side. "Is Uthyr dead?" I whispered. He gave a brief nod. I knew what that meant – Cadwy was now king in his place. That didn't feel like a good thing.

"You must go and pay your respects to the new King," he whispered back. "Walk to the foot of the dais. Bow to him. He is Lord of Viroconium now."

Bowing to anyone comes as difficult to a twenty-first-century girl, and I was no exception. I might have felt more willing to do so if I'd thought Cadwy in any way merited it, but I didn't. From what I'd seen of him, he was little more than a spiteful thug and a bully. He'd tried to intercept our party and kidnap me, he'd wanted to prevent Arthur from marrying me last night, and he was brim full of aggression and jealousy that was directed at my new husband.

My husband. I looked down the hall at Arthur. I didn't really feel as though we were married. Our eyes met. His solemn face softened a little. He winked.

What?

I blinked. Had I imagined it?

Gwalchmei took my cloak, revealing my hair spilling down my back.

"Go on." He gave me a slight push.

I began to walk toward the throne, my footsteps loud on the mosaic floor. A murmur of surprise echoed through the throng, and heads on all sides turned to look at me. Most of them had already seen me the night before, but then I'd been in dirty braccae and tunic, looking like a grubby boy. Now I was all woman, and I knew it. The knowledge gave me confidence and I stepped out proudly, head held high, my long hair rippling down my back.

On the dais Cadwy rose to his feet, and Morgana's look of bewilderment was quickly replaced by one of consternation. But the one I was paying most attention to was Arthur. He didn't take his eyes off me as I reached the dais and then dropped to one knee before Cadwy, as gracefully as I could, my head bowed, my hair hanging about me in a curtain.

I remained there, unmoving, waiting. It worked. Cadwy came down the three steps from the dais, and, taking my hand, raised me to my feet. The gold dragon ring shone on my finger. He couldn't fail to have noticed it.

"So, the Lady of the Ring is here amongst us," he said, as though he'd never seen me before. "The one foretold by the wisemen of the Usurper." He turned me to face the assembly. My heart beat so hard in my chest, surely he would hear it.

To my left, Archbishop Dubricius stood with Euddolen the Seneschal. To my right, in the crowd, I'd already spotted Cei and Theodoric, the latter standing beside a small, heavily pregnant young woman. I was glad to see the now familiar faces of Arthur's other men scattered amongst the rest of the crowd.

Cadwy ushered me to the left-hand side of his throne, away from Arthur and Morgana.

"You are welcome here, my Lady of the Ring, and by the ancient laws of hospitality, my home shall be as yours."

Releasing my hand, he returned to his throne, leaving me standing there alone. I felt very exposed and vulnerable.

Euddolen stepped forward and made a bow to the throne. With a flourish, he drew a scroll out of the front of his long robe. "If I may speak?" He looked at Cadwy for permission. The King inclined his head, clearly puzzled at this interruption.

"I have here the last testament of High King Uthyr," the Seneschal announced, holding the scroll above his head for all to see.

A muffled murmur went round the chamber. Cadwy's scowl darkened. Dubricius looked furtive. Morgana's dark eyes narrowed. Cei's huge face broke into a toothy smile. Theodoric held the little pregnant woman closer to his side. Only Arthur's face remained unmoved. He was clearly not surprised and neither were his men.

Euddolen looked expectantly at Cadwy. He was waiting for his permission to read out the testament. Was it the same as a will? Was it as binding as a modern will would be?

Cadwy looked very much as though he would like to refuse. However, he gave a short nod to Euddolen, his face a picture of suppressed anger. Had he thought his father had died without leaving any kind of instructions? It looked as though that might be so.

Euddolen turned to face the crowded chamber. The aisle that had been left for me to walk up, closed, and the people surged forwards in their eagerness to hear what he had to say. The Seneschal raised his right hand, and they subsided, silence falling.

He unrolled the scroll. It wasn't long, and from where I stood I could see it held less than a dozen lines of close writing. Whatever Uthyr had decided, it looked as though it might be concise and to the point.

Euddolen began to read. His strong, clear voice carried across the heads of the assembly.

"I, Uthyr Pendragon, King of Powys at Viroconium, King of Dumnonia at Din Cadan, High King of all Britain by the grace of the Council of Britain, son of Ambrosius Aurelianus, last Emperor of the Western World, grandson of the Emperor Constantine, being sick unto death, yet of sound mind, do decree the following." He paused for effect. Everyone hung on his words.

"Having to my certain knowledge got two sons on my two wives, I own paternity of them both. I therefore invoke the customs of old." A communal indrawn gasp shivered through his audience. Presumably they had some intimation of what that meant. Unlike me.

"I divide my kingdoms as my forefathers did, before the Legions came. I give to my sons, in equal part, the kingdoms of Powys and Dumnonia. To Cadwy, the elder, I give Powys and Viroconium. To Arthur, the younger, I give Dumnonia and Din Cadan. May they rule them wisely and well." He looked over the top of the scroll. "He signs it with his own hand, Uthyr Pendragon."

The crowd erupted. I looked at Cadwy. He gripped the arms of his throne with whitened knuckles, and his face suffused with dark color. He hadn't been expecting this. His territory was effectively halved. Dubricius pushed his way to Euddolen's side to seize the scroll and scrutinize it closely, as though he suspected it might be a forgery. From his place beside his sister, Arthur met my eyes, a wicked sparkle in his own. He'd known. He'd been expecting this.

From within the crowd, voices rose above the din. "Long live our kings!"

"Long live King Cadwy!"

"Long live King Arthur!"

A cheer went up, and then a din of stamping feet on the mosaic floor. It was noticeable that there were more calls for Arthur than his brother. His men must have been placed with careful consideration to influence the crowd. Could Cadwy not be popular here, despite his ten years as War Leader? Or maybe because of it?

The penny finally dropped. Of course. I saw it all. Merlin had said that Arthur could never be elected High King because he wasn't a king, because Cadwy would inherit the throne as he was the older brother. But this had turned the tables. Uthyr had neatly overcome that hurdle for Arthur. Whatever the customs of old were, they'd allowed him to name his younger son as a king as well. And now Arthur would have a place on the Council as a king in his own right, and he could be elected High King, as Merlin's prophecy said he would.

And I would be his queen.

# Chapter Sixteen

THE COUNCIL OF Britain was to be called in two days' time. That much I learned as I stood alone and forgotten in the midst of the chaos that followed Euddolen's shock announcement.

The room swiftly divided into two factions – those supporting Cadwy and those supporting Arthur. There were a surprising number of the latter. I'd have thought there would have been few more than the men he'd brought with him since he'd been absent from his father's court for so long. But this wasn't so. Which was just as well, because if he'd not had such support, I think Cadwy would have turned on him there and then, and that would have been it for us. It dawned upon me now why he'd brought so many men.

There was a stir as Cadwy got to his feet, towering over the assembly. For a moment he stood looking at us all, his lips curled in an angry snarl, and then he swept down the steps, Morgana following in his wake. The crowd parted for him like the Red Sea before Moses, his own faction falling in behind as he stormed out of the chamber. Silence fell as the last of his men hurried out after him. Then everyone who was left started talking at once.

Merlin shouldered his way through the crowd to stand by my side. His eyes were alight with excitement, and a flush had risen to his cheeks.

"That was well played," he said, leaning close to me so that I could hear him over the racket. "Neatly carried out by the Seneschal."

"Was this all planned?" I asked. "Did you know there was a testament?"

Merlin tapped the side of his nose.

Euddolen, who had carried out the coup, was beside Arthur, talking volubly.

There was a lot I wanted to know. I put my hand on Merlin's arm. "How come Cadwy didn't know his father had left a testament?"

Merlin grinned. "Because he hadn't. At least not until last night. Our timely arrival – with you – brought about that change of heart. Uthyr always loved Arthur's mother more than he loved Cadwy's, and Arthur's very like his mother. It's natural he wouldn't want to leave her son with nothing."

There was something he wasn't telling me. "But Arthur had fallen out with his father. It doesn't look as though it took much to make his father welcome him back."

Merlin frowned at me. "Well, he did."

Theodoric emerged from the throng. He had his arm around the shoulders of the little pregnant woman, who clung to him for support. In her pale face her brown eyes were wide with anxiety. Theodoric thrust her into my arms. "This is my wife, Morgawse," he almost shouted at me. "Take care of her. Get her to somewhere safe. I have to return to Arthur." And he was gone.

Morgawse pressed herself against me, shivering with fear. Her body felt small and delicate, fragile as a little bird – at odds with her massive swollen belly. She looked as though the birth might be imminent, although I was no expert on pregnancy. My only experience was vicariously through my best friend, Sian, from university, whose baby was now four months old. Or rather, she would be in about fifteen hundred years. I'd had the description of her delivery in rather too graphic detail, and it didn't sound at all like a pleasant experience.

I put my arms around the girl and held her tight. "Don't worry," I said into her ear. "It'll be all right. Merlin and I will keep you safe." Only that wasn't true, because when I looked round, Merlin had gone, following Theodoric back into the press. I was alone with a frightened, heavily pregnant girl whom I didn't know.

A decision had to be made. Where we were standing wasn't the safest place. My arms still around her, I moved back toward the wall where we were less likely to be jostled, and we watched from there.

Arthur mounted the dais, head and shoulders above the crowd, who were still all shouting at him and at one another. He raised his hands above his head and stood there, waiting for them to fall silent.

When the room was quiet, he waited a few seconds longer until he had their total attention.

"My father has made me a king," he began, his gaze sweeping the room. "And a king I intend to remain. My brother has gone to call his warriors. I must do the same. Your support is invaluable." His eyes fell on a tall man near the back of the crowd. "Eudaf, call out the City Guard. We have need of their numbers."

In my arms, Morgawse turned her head. "He's the Captain of the City Guard," she whispered. "My husband said he would declare for us."

So this was a planned coup. The headlong rush to get here before his father died was all because Arthur had wanted Uthyr to name him king. Had this been planned for a long time? Was Theodoric, who had all this time been in Uthyr's court, the architect of it? No wonder Cadwy was angry. His brother had been in virtual exile for years, and Cadwy had thought his father's entire kingdom was his birthright. Only now it wasn't. If I were Cadwy, I'd be planning to fight back and finish this once and for all.

Eudaf made Arthur a quick bow, and with half a dozen other men hurried out of the audience chamber.

"The rest of you, to arms!" Arthur finished.

The chamber emptied like water down a plughole. What was I

supposed to do? No one was paying any attention to Morgawse and me. I followed the last of the men outside, taking her with me. The guards by the doors had gone. Arthur's followers were running down the colonnaded walkway. Armed soldiers came charging up the pathway through the gardens from the vestibulum. They had swords in their hands and dragon shields on their arms. They didn't look at all friendly.

I gave up being gentle, and dragged Morgawse after me. With a sob of terror she followed, waddling as fast as her enormous belly would allow. Behind us, the soldiers charged into the now empty audience chamber. I ran. We were nearly at the corner when the soldiers came out again. On the far side, some of Arthur's men charged back into the courtyard with drawn swords, heading toward the soldiers. In front of us, a half-open door beckoned. Without stopping to think, I dragged Morgawse through and closed it behind us.

My breath came fast and my heart pounded. Morgawse was sobbing. I put my finger to my lips, and she made a brave effort to be quiet.

Then I looked around. We were in a kitchen. Four servants stared at us in surprise. It wasn't a large room. In the center stood a worktable. At one end a young girl had paused in the act of chopping vegetables into large heaps. Beyond her, a sweaty, red-faced man stopped rolling out pastry on the floury tabletop to wipe large hands on his grubby tunic. A middle-aged woman stood beside a pot bubbling on a stove, and a spotty teenage boy gawped at us over a large bowl he'd been scouring with sand. A strong smell of onions and freshly baked bread pervaded the air.

I put my arms around Morgawse again in the hopes it would soothe her. If she were terrified into an early labor, I didn't know what we would do. All the men who were supposed to protect us had buggered off doing their own thing.

Footsteps sounded on the paving slabs outside the door. Hobnailed boots struck stone.

Then came a voice. "Check all the rooms. Root out the traitors to the king. Get to it." I looked at the four dumbfounded servants.

There was nowhere to hide. Pans of all shapes and sizes hung on the plain plastered walls, amphorae and sacks stood in the corners, and shelves bearing glass vessels and ceramic bottles lined the walls. Nothing that would give cover to even the smallest person.

I pulled Morgawse flat against the wall, where the opening door would cover us, holding her close, and putting my finger to my lips, glared at the servants. The door swung open. Morgawse gave a little whimper. I clamped my free hand over her mouth.

Someone was standing on the other side of the door. I couldn't see him, but I could hear his heavy breathing. If only he couldn't hear mine. I fixed my gaze on the servants. They remained still and silent, eyes wide, staring back at the open doorway.

"Nothin' in 'ere sir," said a loud voice close to my ear. "It's just the kitchens. No room to 'ide a cat." He was inches away, only the oak separating us. Morgawse trembled in my arms. The four servants sat impassive, frozen in their food preparations.

"Hurry up then, get a move on." That was the commander's voice again, rough and impatient. "Get out of there before more of 'em arrive." The door slammed shut behind the retreating soldier. I heaved a sigh of relief and released Morgawse's mouth. She took a great indrawn gasp of breath, and a shudder ran through her.

I looked at the servants. "Thank you."

The woman by the stove pushed her pots onto the side where they wouldn't burn, and came round the table to us. Her straggly grey hair was scraped back from a doughy wrinkled face, and her tunic, tied at the waist with a length of cord, gave her the look of a sack of corn someone had given a head to. She'd have made a good Guy for Fireworks Night. But she had a kind face.

Morgawse broke away from me and collapsed into the woman's

arms with a sob. The woman looked at me over Morgawse's head, patting the girl on the back. The red-faced man wiped his hands again and approached.

He put a floury hand on Morgawse's back. "Don't fret yerself, milady Morgawse. Ye're safe wi' us." She gave another convulsive sob, and huddled in close to the woman's ample bosom.

The woman looked at me. "What's goin' on out there? And who are ye, if I can be bold enough to ask ye?"

"My name's Gwen. The Seneschal read out the old king's testament. He said Cadwy should get Powys and Prince Arthur should get Dumnonia. They're fighting. Theodoric gave Morgawse to me to look after and left."

The man noticed the dragon ring on my finger. His eyes went round as saucers.

"Tis true what the boy said last night," he hissed, jerking his head at the spotty youth. "She 'as the dragon ring. This be the Lady of the Ring 'erself, Karstyn."

Karstyn looked across at the boy. "Be this the maid ye saw last night?" she barked. Anyone would think he'd done something really bad.

He nodded. "Tis 'er awlright. I seed 'er comin' out the king's chambers, I did. She were there wi' Prince Arthur. I 'eard Old Breanna sayin' 'oo they woz."

"King Arthur," Morgawse said with a sniff, raising her tear-drenched face and speaking for the first time. "My brother is named King of Dumnonia by my father." Her quavery voice was full of pride.

So she was also Arthur's sister. What did I know about Morgawse? I racked my brains.

"We'd best bar the door if there's to be fightin'," the man suggested, going to a big beam that lay against the wall. The boy ran to help him, and together they slotted the beam into place in metal wall brackets on either side of the door. I began to feel a bit more confident.

Which was when Morgawse doubled up with a cry of pain, clutching her swollen belly.

*Oh fuck*. Now what were we going to do?

Karstyn's arms tightened around the girl. "Fetch that stool, ye idlers!" she snapped at the two men. "Don't ye just sit there gawping! 'Aven't ye ever seen a woman birthing?"

I certainly hadn't, but she wasn't talking to me.

"We'll need hot water and clean cloths," I said hopefully.

Karstyn gave me a funny look.

The boy passed her a small, three-legged stool, and she lowered the girl onto it gently.

"It's all right," Morgawse managed. "The pain's gone again now. I feel better. I think it was just indigestion. I've been having a lot of that lately. It can't be the baby – it's not due for two weeks."

Karstyn pushed back a wayward lock of her steely grey hair. "Two weeks is nothin' to a babby," she declared. "'Tis comin' now whether ye like it or not."

Morgawse opened her mouth to refute this, but another pain swept over her and instead she groaned in anguish. "Oooh, make it stop."

Karstyn dragged up another stool and set it beside Morgawse. "Here," she said to me. "Sit ye down aside of 'er and tell 'er it'll be all right. That's the best ye can do. I'll find the necessaries for a birthing and these two lollies'll find us all somethin' to eat. Can ye do that?"

I nodded and sat down on the stool. Morgawse shot out a small hand and seized mine in a vice-like grip. Who'd have thought such a fragile looking girl could turn out to be so strong?

After a bit, her grip relaxed as the pain subsided. I might have had a friend with a baby, but I'd never seen anyone in labor before, so this was all new territory – territory I was fast deciding I never wanted to navigate for myself. Perhaps a distraction would help.

"How long have you and Theodoric been married?" I asked,

searching for the sort of small talk you could share with an in-labor mother.

She looked at me out of still puffy eyes, and managed a besotted smile. "Four years now. He's wonderful, don't you think?"

Well, what I thought was that with a wife like this waiting for him, Theodoric was a fool to be with other women when he was away from her. Of course, I didn't say so. She was very obviously in love with him.

"He doesn't look British. He's so blonde. He looks like a Saxon." I knew he was a Goth, but I wanted to give her something to talk about, and couldn't think of anything else to say.

She nodded, glowing with pride. "People often think that. But he's not. He's from Gaul. He was a general in the army of King Syragius of Gaul. But when the Franks came, under King Clovis, the Goths were driven out. Syragius was killed. Clovis executed the old king's generals, but he didn't get Theo." She massaged her swollen belly with one hand and managed a smile, before screwing her face up in pain as another contraction took her.

I waited for it to pass. "So he's a Goth?"

She nodded.

"Have you any other children?"

She shook her head. "This is my first. Morgana says I didn't quick-en because Theo is away so often. I think she's right. He's always away with the fleet. For months at a time."

Yes, and I had a good idea what he was up to when he was away. How many of the women he'd been with had fallen pregnant by him while his wife waited hopefully to do the same? A fair few, I imagined. Men. I wasn't sure I liked Theodoric much.

She tightened her grip on my hand again.

"Oooooh. Morgana gave me a potion to put in his wine –" She doubled up in pain, both hands cradling her bump. "It hurts!"

Karstyn came back with two wooden beakers of wine. She passed one to me and took a long swig out of the other. We waited while the contraction passed.

"That's better," Morgawse managed with a weak smile. "I'm sure it's just indigestion. I had it all day yesterday and all night. But I managed to sleep a bit. It'll go soon. I get it a lot. Morgana would know what to do."

"I'd not let that one give me anything," Karstyn said with a disgusted snort. "I'd not trust 'er as far as I could throw 'er. Which int far."

I was with Karstyn on this. Morgana didn't look to me like the sort of person whose potions I'd trust.

Morgawse went on. "She's my sister. She helped me conceive. She says this child will be a boy. A son for Theo. He'll be so proud. We have a name for him already."

I patted Morgawse's small hand and gave her a sip of the wine. I'd heard that first babies took a long time. Certainly my friend Sian's labor had taken a good twenty-four hours. We'd be out of this kitchen long before any drastic action was needed.

The spotty boy had gone to stand by the doors with his ear to the crack. "I can 'ear fightin'," he said suddenly. "And shoutin'."

"Stay there and keep listening," Karstyn said. "But it sounds like we may 'ave to stay in 'ere a while. We're fairly safe. They'll know this is the kitchens. I doubt anyone else'll come looking in 'ere." She looked at Morgawse worriedly. "But ye'll 'ave to keep as quiet as ye can, and that won't be easy."

I hoped she was right.

"Oh no, here it comes again." Morgawse's face crumpled into pain and her grip on my hand tightened like a vice.

Karstyn came back to her side. "Did ye say ye'd 'ad this indigestion since yesterday?"

Morgawse nodded, her lips compressed together.

"Like this?"

She shook her head. "Not so bad," she managed through gritted teeth. "A bit like the pains you get at your time of the month. Morgana said it was indigestion. She said she'd give me a potion."

Was this girl an idiot? Surely she knew Morgana was in Cadwy's camp. Morgawse had seemed to know about the planned coup her husband had engineered. Did she think Morgana could mean her any good? But of course, they were sisters. She must have allowed her familial feelings to get the better of her. And she must be gullible.

Karstyn put a hand on Morgawse's belly. "I think she's bin in labor longer than she thinks," she said to me. "They say ye're a healer. D'ye know anything about childbirth?"

Well, I'd watched every episode of *Call the Midwife*. And Sian had given me *all* the unnecessary details of her delivery. But that was it. My first aid course hadn't taken into account the fact that I'd be shut in a primitive kitchen with a woman in her first labor. Feeling inadequate, I shook my head.

"Morgana would know what to do," Morgawse said, rather unhelpfully. "That's better, it's wearing off now."

"Aren't her contractions coming really close together?" I asked. Sian's had been every twenty minutes when she'd started and had escalated to every two by the time she was ready to give birth, some hours later, and even without a watch, I was sure these were less than two minutes apart.

"I think I need to go to the latrine," Morgawse said. "I'm sorry. I told you it was indigestion."

Crap. Literally. Well, not crap, *baby*.

"D'ye need to push?" Karstyn asked.

"Jupiter, I've wet myself!" Morgawse's cheeks flushed pink with embarrassment as water gushed over the stool and the flagstone floor around her feet. Even I knew it wasn't wee.

"Yer baby's nearly 'ere," Karstyn said, going down on her knees beside the girl, "when ye feel the next contraction ye need to push as 'ard as ye can."

On television, when mothers in dramas start pushing, they get the baby out in seconds. It felt like Morgawse had reached this stage with only a few contractions, whereas in reality she'd been at it since the day before, so it wasn't a quick labor at all. Had nobody told her what to expect? But now she was trying to push the baby the rest of the way out, everything seemed to stall.

Karstyn got another stool and shoved the two of them together so Morgawse was sitting half on each one, legs apart, with a clear run for the baby between them. She crouched there, face ruby red, in the position you'd take if you were monstrously constipated, which was exactly how Sian had described it to me.

The boy stayed by the door, listening, his eyes averted from the scene being enacted in the middle of the kitchen floor. The red-faced man had cleared away the pastry he'd been rolling and given the table a scrubbing. The girl had piled her vegetables into a couple of pots. I sat beside poor Morgawse as she alternately pushed herself purple in the face for a minute or two, then sagged onto me in an exhausted heap. She valiantly stayed as silent as she could, her poor lips bitten and bleeding. Karstyn had cut a strip of leather from a butcher's apron hanging on a peg on the wall and given it to Morgawse to put between her teeth and bite down onto.

After what seemed like ages, Karstyn went down on her knees, and lifting Morgawse's skirts, took a look at what was going on down there. Thank goodness she didn't want me to do that.

Eventually, she looked up with a big beam on her face. "Well done, girl, I saw the 'ead that time!"

Morgawse collapsed back into my arms. "You only just saw the head?" she squawked in exhausted shock. "I thought he was nearly born! I can't do this. It hurts too much. I can't do it."

Well, there wasn't much of an alternative.

"Yes, ye can," Karstyn said positively. "Not long now. Just a few more pushes. And then ye'll be saying 'ello to yer son."

Morgawse emitted a long groan, and then doubled up again as the pains rose once more. She gritted her teeth and strained hard.

Watching her was strengthening my resolve not to get put in the same situation. The trouble was, I was now a married woman, and it was unlikely that my new husband was going to want our relationship to remain platonic. My contraceptive injection could be counted on to last at least a few months, and its aftereffects maybe as much as a year, but beyond that I'd be at high risk of pregnancy. Sex was a problem I was going to have to face sooner rather than later.

"That's right, give it all ye've got."

When her next contraction started, Morgawse did as she was told, her small white teeth grinding into the thick leather.

But the good thing was that Karstyn had been right. Only a few more contractions brought the baby's head out in a rush of bloody liquid, and another contraction brought its body.

"Tis a boy," Karstyn said delightedly. "Ye've a son."

"Jupiter," Morgawse cried, tears streaming down her face. "He's here. Medraut is here."

Karstyn put the baby in her arms. It was a little purple and red creature like a frog, crying lustily.

But I was staring at the baby. At little Medraut. To give him the name by which he was known in my time – Mordred. I knew that name well. What reader of Arthurian literature doesn't? Arthur's nephew – in some stories his bastard son by incest – the man who would bring Arthur to his final battle at Camlann where both of them would fall. Except in the stories, Arthur wasn't really dead – he was carried away by three queens to the Isle of Avalon where he supposedly lived on, ready to come to the aid of Britain in her hour of need. A load of claptrap most of it, yet here was little Medraut, Arthur's nephew.

I sat back and looked at Morgawse, her hair sticking to her sweaty forehead, her eyes bright with love for the little bundle in her arms, her ordeal all but forgotten. Maybe none of the stories were true. Maybe Medraut had just got a bad press. Maybe he would grow up into one of Arthur's staunchest supporters.

Maybe.

# Chapter Seventeen

S EVERAL BODIES LAY in the colonnaded walkway, and one was sprawled on the steps up to the audience chamber. An eerie silence filled the courtyard.

Lann, the red-faced man, set the bar he'd just removed down beside the door and came and stood beside me, looking at the empty courtyard. He had a big kitchen knife in his hand. That there'd been quite a fight was obvious, although we'd been unaffected by it, walled up as we'd been in our little delivery room, and concentrating on something that had seemed far more important. Where had everyone gone? The spotty boy sidled up to stand beside us.

Blood had pooled on the floor tiles, smeared as though someone or something had been dragged through it. I put my hand down to my boot and felt the comforting presence of the dagger stuffed into its top.

Inside the kitchen, the baby set up an angry wailing. Glancing over my shoulder, I saw Morgawse put him to her breast, where he began to suck hungrily. He was a strong little thing. Too strong. It might have been better if he'd died. But that was presuming all I knew about Medraut's future was true, and no one could tell me that. Guilt washed over me for wishing dead a defenseless baby, who might be quite innocent of all I was attributing to him. Hindsight is a terrible thing, and I was full of it. I alone knew all the stories that had adhered to Arthur down the ages, from the ridiculous medieval inventions to the ones that might have had some basis in truth. And that knowledge made me afraid. Afraid for myself, and afraid for Arthur and this baby.

"Someone will have to go and find out what's been happening," I said, to no one in particular.

Lann nodded, and the boy looked frightened. They were probably both worried I was expecting them to go. But I wasn't.

"I'll go," I said firmly. "I need to see what's going on for myself."

They didn't argue. Perhaps they were too used to taking orders to cavil.

I glanced back at Karstyn and Morgawse. The girl's dark head was bent over her suckling baby. Karstyn had her hand on her shoulder in reassurance. They made a pretty picture. But if Cadwy had won, and Arthur and his men had been killed or put to flight, she and I were in terrible danger here in the Imperial Palace. I had to get us out, and that wouldn't be easy with a baby and a woman who'd just given birth.

"Go back inside and lock the door again," I said to Lann, who looked relieved at my words. He was a cook, not a warrior. "And keep the Lady Morgawse and her son safe at all costs. I'm going to find out what's happened. It looks safe enough for the moment. Go on." I gave him a little push, which was all it took. He and the boy retreated inside the door and closed it behind them, shutting me out. There was a thump as they slotted the beam back into place.

I was all alone.

For a moment, I stood listening. Now that it was just me, I could hear more. From somewhere distant came the sound of wailing, and the howl of a dog. I bent down and drew the dagger out of my boot. It was warm in my hand, a living blade, shimmering in the late afternoon light. I tightened my fingers around the handle, glad to have it and convinced that if I had to, I would use it. You can change a lot in just a few days. Our primitive selves are lurking still, just below the surface, and mine had fought its way through to the top.

Caution sent me creeping round the edge of the garden under cover of the colonnade, dodging from pillar to pillar, afraid of each closed doorway I passed. But nobody emerged. If there were people behind the doors, they weren't coming out.

I made it all the way round to the atrium. A soldier with a red-dragon emblem lay sprawled on his back across the entrance. As I moved closer he opened his eyes.

I stopped.

He was young, with short brown hair curling about his forehead and a shadow of stubble on his chin. No older than the Saxon foederati we'd captured two nights ago. Why were they all boys? Did no old men fight? His eyes, somewhere between grey and blue, were dim with pain and fear, and fixed on the dagger in my hands. I stayed well back, as frightened of him as he was of me.

But he wasn't going anywhere. The broken shaft of a spear protruded from just below his ribcage, rising and falling with every labored breath, and bright blood bubbled in the corners of his mouth. I lowered the dagger.

His lips moved. "Help me." It was scarcely more than a whisper. His lungs must be punctured. More bloody froth bubbled up. There was nothing I could do for him; he was going to die.

I went down on one knee beside him, heedless of the spreading red pool.

"I'm here. Don't try to talk." I took his hand, slick with his own blood, and held it tight. "Everything will be all right," I lied. "Someone will come in a moment and you'll be looked after." I laid the dagger down on the tiled floor and smoothed his forehead. "I'll stay with you."

Raised voices came from beyond the doors into the vestibulum, and fear prickled across my skin. Common sense told me I needed to get up and run.

His lips moved, and I had to bend close to hear his words. "Are you an angel?" His voice was weak and thready. The end must be near. I couldn't leave him.

Someone was shouting right outside the vestibulum's doors.

"Yes, I am," I lied. "Come to take you home. You can sleep now. Your work is done." I don't know why I said this; it just came into my head. Was I wicked to lie to a dying boy? I didn't think so. His expression softened, and a look of peace came over his bloodless face.

"Thank you," he whispered. And then he died.

I'd never been *with* anyone who'd died before. I'd seen my father's body, but I hadn't been there when he died. The Saxon had been taken away before he'd been killed. Uthyr had died after I'd left.

For a long moment I knelt there in his blood, lost in the tragedy of so young a death. Then propriety stirred me, before fear could take its place. You had to close the eyes of the dead. I'd seen it done in films and on the television. His gazed sightlessly up at me, the unblinking stare unnerving. I put a trembling hand over his eyelids and tried to close them. They wouldn't stay shut, and I was seized with rising panic. Was he staring at me? Was he accusing me of having lied? I tried again, holding the lids down for longer, and this time they stayed shut. I heaved a sigh of fleeting relief.

Raised voices once again came from the vestibulum, as though someone had opened the doors into the street. The voices drew nearer. Heart hammering, I struggled to my feet. My dress was stained dark with the boy's blood. A wave of nausea at the metallic stench of it rose in me. I mustn't be sick. I had to pull myself together. My eyes fell on the dagger lying on the tiles by my feet. I bent and picked it up, and nearly retched. I was in no fit state to cope with anything, but I had to. There was nowhere to hide. Hot tears burned in the corners of my eyes, tears for the dead boy, tears for myself, tears of fear.

Arthur came striding out of the vestibulum in full armor. For a moment, I stared, unable to believe he was alive and unhurt. And then anger took over. Oblivious of the press of his men behind him, I marched up to him and thumped him hard in the chest.

"You left me!"

His dark eyes opened wide in surprise, and as I went to thump him again he caught my wrists. Probably he was worried I might even try stabbing him as I was still clutching the dagger in my right hand.

"You bastard!" I shouted, letting all the tension of the last hours pour out of me. "You left me with a pregnant girl and just buggered off!" I struggled in his grasp as Merlin, who'd come up beside him, carefully prised the dagger out of my hands. I shot him a furious look – he'd left me too.

Arthur took me by the shoulders and held me at arm's length, looking at me carefully. Behind him, I was dimly aware of a sea of blurred faces.

"Where are you hurt?" His voice was strained with concern. It might well be, considering the amount of blood that had soaked into my once beautiful blue dress.

"I'm not," I blurted. "It's his blood." I pointed to the dead boy. "And Morgawse's."

Theodoric was by my side in an instant. "Morgawse's blood? Where is she? What's happened?"

I twisted in Arthur's grip, angry with all of them, particularly Theodoric. Shoving his poor, pregnant and in labor wife into my arms, and then clearing off, was not the done thing, surely, even in this world. "She's fine," I snapped. "She's had her baby, that's all. I helped deliver it."

His eyes widened in surprise. "She told me it wasn't due for two weeks." It was a protest, an excuse, a shifting of the blame onto her. *Bastard.*

Arthur was looking unmistakably impressed. With me? Perhaps.

"Well, she was wrong," I returned, feeling even more angry with him. "And it's born, and before you ask, it's a boy."

Arthur released his hold on me and clapped Theodoric on the back. "A fortuitous day for your son to be born. It will bring him great luck."

*Really? Not if I was right.*

I considered hitting Arthur again, but decided against it. I rubbed my forearms so that he'd see he'd hurt me, but he was too busy congratulating Theodoric.

The big blond Goth looked smug as several more of Arthur's warriors also clapped him on the back. As if he'd done any of the work. *Bastard.*

"What's happened?" I asked. "Where's Cadwy? Is it safe now?"

Arthur nodded. "It's safe. There was fighting. We have the City Guard under Eudaf on our side. Along with my warriors from Din Cadan, and Theodoric's men. Cadwy has the Palace Guard."

"Are there many dead?" I asked, glancing back at the dead boy.

Arthur shook his head. "We don't know yet. Too many. Luckily Cadwy saw it was only going to get worse, fighting in the confines of his city streets. We've come to an agreement with the help of Dubricius on Cadwy's side and Euddolen on ours. Cadwy's not happy. But if he hadn't agreed, he would have lost everything. I've settled for Dumnonia as my father decreed. I don't want Powys. I never did. He doesn't seem to understand that even now."

"Because he's always wanted all of it," Merlin put in. "He thought you did too."

I shivered. My anger was waning and shock taking its place. "So it's all over?"

Arthur shook his head. "Not really. We've still the Council of Kings to come. When a new High King should be elected." He grinned, but his eyes remained serious. "That should be fun."

"What about the kings who were already here?" I asked. "What did they do when the fighting was going on?"

Arthur flashed a wry smile. "Stood back and watched, that's what. It's none of their business what happens between Cadwy and me. They just waited to see who would come out on top."

"So none of them supported him?"

"Not a one. But you could say the same thing about them not supporting me."

Theodoric interrupted. "Where is my wife? I want her with us. We're going to the Domus Albus, Euddolen's house. Where is she?"

We went together to collect Morgawse, followed by a score of heavily armed warriors.

Outside the door, I called out. "Lann, it's me, Gwen. I've come for Morgawse."

After a moment Lann answered me, but he didn't unbar the door "Did ee get 'elp, milady?" His voice was muffled, and afraid.

"It's all right," I said, as reassuringly as I could. "I've got King Arthur with me." As soon as I said his name – his proper name – I realized with a jolt how strange it sounded coming out of my mouth. When he'd been a prince it hadn't felt quite real, as though the stories I knew of his future couldn't apply to him. Now he was a king, all those stories suddenly hung on his name like lead weights dragging him down. And me with him.

The thumps of Lann unbarring the door sounded, and then it swung open. His ruddy face paled when he saw how many heavily armed warriors were standing outside.

Theodoric barged in before anyone, pushing Lann rudely to one side, and hurried to Morgawse, who was sitting on a bed Karstyn had made for her on flour sacks. The girl burst into floods of tears and flung her arms around his neck like an octopus enveloping its prey.

To do him justice, Theodoric was all consideration and concern, but I couldn't get the thought of him with the doxies out of my head. However, Morgawse's small, pale face was wreathed in smiles as she showed him the baby, wrapped in some cloths Karstyn had found for her.

Arthur followed Theodoric inside, and so did I.

He looked at Karstyn. "Can she be moved?"

She bobbed a respectful bow to him. He was a king, after all. "She be an 'ealthy young leddy, milord King. An' the babby be the same. I'd say twas safe to move 'er." She glanced toward the doorway where the other warriors were peering inside. "Safer than for 'er to stay 'ere, that's for certain."

Arthur nodded to Theodoric. "Fetch her." Then he looked down at me. "And you, come with me." Before I could stop him he grabbed me by the wrist again and pulled me after him out of the kitchen. I was angry – again – but I'd only look foolish if I struggled, so I went with him.

"Where are we going?" I asked, but was ignored.

Behind us, Theodoric lifted Morgawse as though she were light as a feather and carried her and the baby with us, back through the still deserted courtyard of the Imperial Palace, through the atrium and the vestibulum, and out into the street. I hurried in Arthur's wake, having to almost run to keep up with his longer strides, the wet folds of my bloody gown flapping round my legs uncomfortably.

In the street, we came upon the rest of Arthur's force, which by now was considerable in number and filled the roadway. All of them were on foot: the warriors from Din Cadan whom I vaguely knew, Eudaf's City Guard, recognizable by their red cloaks, and a number of other supporters from Viroconium, mainly men of Arthur's age or younger. Some of them just boys.

When the men saw Theodoric cradling Morgawse and the baby in his arms, a great cheer went up, as though this event was the icing on the cake to their success. The baby began to cry lustily, and Theodoric's face was a grin of pride from ear to ear.

Arthur raised the hand that was holding mine into the air. "The Lady of the Ring!" he shouted. "The Queen of Dumnonia, as the prophecy foretold!" Another great cheer went up, and before I could stop him, Arthur swung me deftly into his arms, pressing my body against his chainmail shirt, and his mouth came down on mine.

For a second, I froze with surprise. Then anger took over, and I struggled in his arms, but there was nothing I could do to escape. His mouth was hard on mine, the smell of his masculinity all about me. A treacherous hot feeling slithered through my body and my knees felt weak. Just as I'd decided it was actually very nice to be kissed like this by an undeniably attractive king, after a bloody battle, he released me. The cheer was deafening.

He didn't seem to notice that he'd left me flustered and breathless.

"To Domus Albus!" Arthur shouted above the din.

I was swept up in the victorious march, bowled along like a piece of driftwood on the tide of men, the only woman there but for Morgawse.

After the triumph of the baby's safe delivery – and that kiss – I was seized by an impulse to shout and wave my arms in the air in jubilation, which wasn't at all like me. The excitement got into my very soul, exposing a long-hidden side I'd never known existed. An inner, more primitive side that the Dark Ages were bringing to life. I wasn't the same woman who'd climbed Glastonbury Tor to scatter her father's ashes just a week ago.

# Chapter Eighteen

THE DOMUS ALBUS, Euddolen's house, stood on the western side of the city, close by the walls which overlooked the riverfront wharves.

All along the narrow streets, people peered out cautiously as we passed. Here and there the bravest inhabitants came out to stand in the road raising sporadic cheering and cries of "Long live King Arthur!" Even though he'd been gone from Viroconium for years, he'd not been forgotten. Or it may have been that Cadwy's unpopularity had endeared their prodigal son to them the more.

I scanned the wary faces of the citizenry. "Whose side are they on?"

Merlin, walking by my side, gave a shrug. "The winning one. They're merchants, artisans, and craftsmen, not warriors. They'll hide behind their doors until they think it's safe to come out, and then congratulate themselves on backing the victor."

"And this army marching with us now?"

"Needs accommodation and food. Arthur can't afford to let them disperse. Cadwy will be keeping his troops close about him, waiting for any sign of weakness. Euddolen will have to find the space for all these men."

When we arrived, Arthur had only three words for me. "Go with Theodoric."

Although it went against the grain, and my newfound confidence, I did as I was told, leaving him to organize his forces. There was nothing for me to do in the bustling courtyard, apart from get in the way, and Morgawse could probably do with another woman to help her. So I hurried after Theodoric's long striding legs, through a gateway and into a garden courtyard that was a smaller version of the one at the Imperial Palace.

We were halfway across the central garden when a door off the colonnaded walkway swung open, and three women came out. One was grey-haired, the other two, by the looks of them, her teenage daughters, all finely dressed in flowing gowns. Theodoric strode up to them, Morgawse's head resting on his shoulder, and I ran up beside him.

"What's this?" the older woman asked.

"My wife," Theodoric said curtly. "She's just had the babe. She needs your help, Ummidia."

The two young women's eyes widened with shock. As well they might. There was blood all over Morgawse's clothing, just as there was over me.

"Bring her in," Ummidia said, swiftly taking charge of the situation. "Albina, fetch Cutha. Cloelia, fetch hot water from the kitchens and bring it to the dolphin bedroom." The two girls ran to do her bidding without a second asking. "This way, Theo."

He followed her along the walkway, with me trailing in his wake. In the corner, she flung open a door, and we entered a large bedchamber with a mosaic of a leaping dolphin underfoot. She began to light the little clay oil lamps set in recesses in the walls.

"Set her on the bed."

He did as he was told, laying his wife down gently. In her arms the baby awoke and began to whimper.

"Where are we?" Morgawse asked. Perhaps she, too, had been asleep.

Ummidia bent over her. "You're with me, my dear, and you're

safe now. Nothing can hurt you here." She soothed Morgawse's brow with her hand. "We'll soon have you feeling better. Give me the baby and get out of those filthy clothes." She turned to Theodoric. "Well, you can go now. This is women's work. Off with you." And, baby in arms, she shooed him out of the room.

After only a few minutes, Albina, Ummidia's elder daughter, returned with the promised Cutha, who turned out to be a proper midwife, thank goodness. Shortly after that, Cloelia arrived back with two maids carrying buckets of hot water, which Cutha used to clean Morgawse up. A fresh undershirt was supplied, her tangled hair brushed out and rebraided, and the baby wrapped in a clean shawl and returned to her to feed. Morgawse sat up in bed looking glowing and happy, as every new mother should.

To my surprise, instead of a nappy, they wrapped the baby's bottom in a rabbit skin stuffed with dried moss, from a pile of them that Cutha had brought with her. Cozy, at least, though probably a bit of a nightmare to get the poop out of the fur.

This done, they turned their attentions to me. More hot water. A clean undershirt and dress, and exclamations over my walking boots and dagger, which Merlin had returned to me once he was sure I wasn't going to use it on Arthur. My own hair, which was considerably more tangled than Morgawse's, was also brushed out. Without protesting, I let them get on with it. I think I was in delayed shock, despite the euphoria of the triumphal march. So much had happened I was having difficulty processing it. Their conversation went over my head until I heard Arthur's name mentioned, and then I pricked up my ears.

"Did you see Prince Arthur – I mean King Arthur, in the stable courtyard when you went for the water?" Albina, a tall girl with large, hazel eyes and a wide, friendly mouth, asked her younger sister, who was teasing through my hair with a bone comb.

Cloelia nodded and a flush crept up her round cheeks. She was smaller and chubbier than her sister, but otherwise very like her. A dusting of freckles covered her nose.

"What's he like?" Albina asked, also coloring. She was tidying up my dirty blood-stained clothing into a pile.

"So handsome," Cloelia breathed, "Oh, he's so handsome. A dream."

Goodness. They sounded like a pair of modern teenage girls talking about some pop star. How times don't change. Maybe the idols do, but not the language in which they're discussed. They made me feel old.

Cutha, a middle-aged woman with a long grey plait of hair, passed the dirty buckets of water to the maid. The bedchamber was getting pretty crowded. She tutted loudly, reminding me of Cottia. "They do say as 'e's wed the Lady o' the Ring."

"No, really?" Albina's voice rose in consternation. "The prophecy's come true after all this time? Did you ever think it would?"

Cloelia shook her head and managed to give my hair a sharp pull.

"Ouch," I complained, curling my fingers around the dragon ring so they wouldn't see it.

"I'm sorry." Cloelia said, with true feeling. "It's just that all the girls I know wanted to get a look at him. We didn't live in Viroconium when he was here before. Our father's from Rheged. We are, too, I suppose, although we live here now. Father is the Seneschal."

"I don't suppose he'll be that now," Ummidia put in. "Not now he's come down on the side of Arthur." She sounded a little bitter. I supposed she had reason. It must have been good to be the wife of the Seneschal, the most important man after the king. "We'll probably have to go back to Rheged."

Cloelia began to braid my hair.

"I wonder if there're nice boys in Rheged?" she mused.

I glanced across at Morgawse, but she'd nodded off, the baby sleeping at her breast.

It was time to leave the new mother to herself, with Cutha to take care of her.

Such a lot had happened, yet it all felt compressed into a rush of activity. Above the courtyard garden a myriad of stars sparkled in the blue-black sky, and the cold nipped at my nose and fingers. I was wearing one of Albina's cloaks around my shoulders, as mine had been left behind in the audience chamber. With a shiver, I pulled it closer. The bedroom had been warm with the heat from the hypocaust and the number of people in it.

"I need to change for dinner," Ummidia said. "Do you mind waiting a moment while I do so, Milady?"

Why would she think I'd mind? I was a guest in her house. But of course, she knew I was a queen even if her daughters didn't. That thought was sobering. Embarrassed, I murmured my assent. The girls went skipping off down the walkway chattering excitedly about seeing Arthur at dinner, and we went into her bedroom.

Her preparations took Ummidia a full twenty minutes, so a bit longer than a moment. At last, wearing a diaphanous gown beneath a fur-lined cloak, she was ready to go.

My stomach certainly was.

I was relieved to discover that we were not expected to lounge on indigestion-inducing couches to eat, but sat at a long trestle table in Euddolen's dining room.

There was no need for a fire, thanks to the hypocaust, which, to judge from the pleasant warmth, must have been in full swing. Euddolen had given up his place at the head of the table to Arthur, who was sitting there in a somber tunic and braccae, a plain gold circlet in his dark hair. As we came in, he met my eyes just a tad defiantly and got to his feet. My heart gave a little skip and my cheeks warmed. I could still feel the heat of his lips on mine.

"My Lady Guinevere." He held out his hand. I crossed to the table and took it, a little frisson coursing through my body at his touch. A servant pulled out a sturdy wooden chair for me. I was pleased to see there was a well-padded cushion on it. As graciously as possible, I took my place between my husband and Theodoric, who, if I was not mistaken, was already the worse for wear. Presumably he'd been wetting the baby's head. Opposite me sat Euddolen, with his daughter Albina on his left between him and Cei. Ummidia took her place at the foot of the table, between Merlin and Cloelia.

It was a festive meal. The men were euphoric after their victory, and the women caught the mood. Conversation flowed. I learned that the troops had been fed and deployed to guard the house, the horses had been retrieved from the Imperial stables and were grazing in the pens that lay up against the city wall, and Cadwy was back in the palace licking his metaphorical wounds, accompanied by Morgana.

I was intrigued by the relationships between the three brothers and their two sisters. It would have given any modern reconstructed family a run for their money. So I asked Arthur about it.

He'd been drinking more than usual as the meal progressed. Not that I had a vast experience of his drinking habits. Perhaps his previous abstinences had been the exception, and this was the norm. He might be my husband, but I didn't know him at all.

"Why don't you get on?" I asked as I put down my knife with which I'd been cutting up roasted pork in a rich savory sauce. "You and Cadwy and Morgana? You and Cei seem good friends."

He looked at me over his goblet, then carefully set it down on the table. Euddolen was listening to Theodoric's version of the attack on us at the ruined way station the other night. It was turning out to be a very loud story. We couldn't be overheard.

"It's complicated." Arthur's eyes gave away nothing. Albina, ignored by her father and Theodoric, was staring up the table at us, but I ignored her. She must have realized who I was by now.

"Try me."

He pulled a wry face. "Cadwy is the firstborn. My father was already married to Cadwy's mother. He'd had other mistresses before, but my mother was different. Merlin told him so. He told my father he had to marry my mother and make me legitimate."

So Merlin was in the habit of arranging marriages.

A servant leaned over us and filled our goblets to the brim again. I was feeling a bit squiffy myself, and more than a little attracted to Arthur. Triumph is a great aphrodisiac. He took another long draught of the wine, eyes glittering in the lamplight.

"So he put Cadwy's mother aside. I think she went into a house of God. I don't know."

I had to admit, that was a pretty awful thing to do to a small boy just to ensure you got your way with another woman. A bit Henry the Eighth. Could I blame Cadwy for how he felt about the other woman's son? I was still enough of an outsider to be able to see both sides in this argument.

"But didn't your father kill Cei's father so he could marry your mother?" I knew the story well. It was enough to make the most lurid soap opera seem tame.

He nodded.

"Then how come you get on so well with Cei?"

His dark eyes met mine, sending a pleasing shiver down my spine.

"I was brought up with him." He wiped his mouth with the back of his sleeve. "He's always been my brother. My proper brother, that is, with scarcely three years between us. There was never any rivalry. Cei always knew he would get Tintagel when he came of age. But he chooses to stay here with me. He leaves it to our mother to govern his people as she sees fit."

Another course, this time of stuffed birds, was brought to the table, and he took one. I waved the servant with the tray away.

"Why is Cadwy jealous of you?"

He smiled, pulling the legs off the bird's carcass with greasy fingers. "Because he is the son of a loveless marriage, and he's always worried that I was our father's favorite, because I'm my mother's son. He's always known his mother was put away so mine could become queen."

He paused to take another mouthful of wine. "Cadwy was responsible for my exile in Din Cadan. My mother was long gone to Tintagel, but my father had already received the wound that would eventually bring about his death. Cadwy was a man grown and War Leader. He had power. I had no one to fight for me except Merlin. Cadwy accused me of treachery, of seeking to kill our father and trying to seize power. It was a lie." He took a bite from one of the legs and was silent a moment, chewing.

"Did your father believe him?"

He gave a shrug. "If he had, would I be sitting here today with you? But he had to act. I was a constant trouble to him. I didn't do what he wanted. He couldn't rely on me. He needed a son he could rely on. Like Cadwy. All these things he said to me when I came to his quarters as an angry boy."

He was silent again for a moment, reflecting on the past, his gaze fixed on somewhere distant.

"So he sent you away?"

He nodded. "To Din Cadan. I was sixteen. I thought I'd been banished and that Cadwy was behind it. I was right. He wanted me gone. He wanted me dead. As Merlin pointed out so sagely, I was safer away from Cadwy than walled up with him in the Imperial Palace of Viroconium. He said I was lucky to have reached sixteen without falling victim to some mysterious sickness."

That was probably true.

I smiled at him. "But you've got the better of him now. You've got Dumnonia, and you're a king."

Triumph kindled in his eyes. He took my hand where the dragon ring sparkled. "Thanks in part to you." My heart did a somersault of excitement at his touch.

Yet I was puzzled. "Why me?"

He turned the ring on my finger. "Because even though I'm not superstitious, my father was. He had the prophecy of the Lady of the Ring carved onto his heart. I knew that if I brought you to him, it would make things so much easier."

"So you wanted him to make you marry me? That was why you brought me along? Not because you thought I was a healer – and by the way I'm just a first aider, which is something quite different – but because you knew if he saw me, he'd want to see the prophecy fulfilled?"

He nodded, and this time he gave me a wide grin. I could sense the collective sigh emanating from Albina and Cloelia.

"Neatly done, wasn't it?" His voice held a hint of smugness.

Hadn't Merlin said something similar when he'd come upon us hand-fasted together?

I was curious. "So how did you get him to write the testament in your favor?"

"Simple." He looked proud. "He didn't write it. Merlin did."

Of course. They'd gone prepared.

He must have sensed my next question because he forestalled it. "He wrote it for me back in Din Cadan, and all we had to do the night of my father's death was to get him to sign it. Cadwy was stupid enough to leave me alone with him. He thought he wouldn't waken again. I got the testament out, and my father signed it. It wasn't underhand. Well, not much underhand at any rate. He meant me to have Dumnonia. He told me so as I sat with him, but I knew Cadwy would disregard his spoken wishes. So I had to get it in writing. He was glad to do it. He knew what Cadwy is."

Hence the confident wink when I was walking toward the throne on the dais to pay my respects to Cadwy. Something presumably I'd never have to do again. Because if Arthur was a king, then I, as his wife, must be a queen.

The meal was nearly over. Euddolen, Theodoric's story finished, turned back to Arthur, and I pushed my plate away, unable to eat anything more.

Arthur leaned back in his seat, stretching his arms above his head and yawning widely. "It's been a long day and I'm ready to turn in. I started it out as nothing and finished it as a king, and it's high time I took my queen to bed."

He turned his head, looking at me appraisingly, and my stomach lurched. His eyes were like dark peaty pools, reflecting the glow of the torches set in the wall sconces, and I was falling into them. Had I been looking forward to this?

Albina and Cloelia looked at me in open envy. Their mother must have revealed my identity to them before the meal, because they'd been shooting me envious glances whenever they could.

Arthur got to his feet and made a bow to Euddolen.

"Let me thank you, Euddolen, for all your help and planning. Without you, none of this would have come about. Nor you, Theodoric. Without you riding to fetch me from Din Cadan, this would never have succeeded." He raised his goblet. "To Euddolen and to Theodoric. The best of allies." We all got to our feet and raised our goblets, repeating the toast. Euddolen beamed round the table at his family and guests like the Cheshire Cat.

Arthur took my hand as I set down my goblet. "And now to bed."

# Chapter Nineteen

L ITTLE CLAY OIL lamps sat on every surface in the bedchamber. The room was suffused with their warm glow, and our shadows leapt up the wall in every direction. Arthur closed the door behind us, shutting out the cold night air.

I took a few steps inside and halted, looking at the bed. Our bed.

On soft footsteps he came up behind me. I could sense him standing there, not touching me, just quietly breathing. I didn't know what I was feeling. Was I afraid? Excited? Both? To one side stood a long, carved wooden bench spread with colorful cushions. I went and sat on it, hands folded in my lap.

He sat next to me. He smelled clean and freshly scrubbed from the villa bath house, with a hint of the herbs his clothes had been kept in. But overlying it all he smelled very masculine. It was a heady mixture. He took my hand, threading his fingers between mine in a curiously intimate gesture – the same way I'd held hands with Nathan.

A lump rose in my throat. Would I ever see Nathan again? Or was I stuck here forever, lost in time, part of a yesterday that was now my today? Tears formed in the corners of my eyes and trickled down my cheeks. Arthur put a gentle hand up and wiped them away.

I turned my head and looked at him. His face was close to mine.

"Why are you crying?" His voice held unaccustomed tenderness. "Are you afraid?"

I shook my head. "I'm – I was thinking about my boyfriend."

"Boyfriend?" He might well look puzzled. I don't think "boyfriend" was a concept he could understand.

"I was going to be married," I explained, lying judiciously. "Back where I come from. We were going to be married. And I miss him."

He was silent. What was he thinking? Another tear rolled down my cheek. He leaned toward me, and before I could move, kissed my cheek where the tear was. It was a strangely gentle gesture after the hard kiss he'd given me outside the Imperial Palace. I was too surprised to recoil.

"Don't be afraid."

I gave him a damp smile and wiped my eyes and nose on my sleeve. "I'm not." No such thing as hankies in the Dark Ages.

His solemn face softened into a smile. "That's better."

He was very close to me. I could almost hear his heart beating. Wait, maybe that was mine, hammering in overtime in my chest, the blood pounding in my ears.

He had enviably long dark eyelashes and flecks of gold in his brown eyes, the shadow of stubble on his chin, and unruly dark hair just like his son's.

His smile vanished. "Will you undo your hair for me?" His voice was husky and low.

Should I? Would that herald the betrayal of Nathan? Half of me felt it would, but the other half was protesting that he wasn't even born yet, nor would he be for another fifteen hundred years, so I couldn't betray someone who didn't exist. And Arthur was undeniably attractive, made more so by his recent triumph, which had cloaked him with the confident air of the victor.

And I was lonely. Surrounded by people, but so lonely. I longed for the closeness of human intimacy, for the feel of comforting arms around me, of a warm body next to mine. I missed Nathan. Not just for himself and his companionship, but for his protective arms embrace, for his warm body in my bed, his slight snore when he was drunk, his clothes spread about the bedroom floor, his smell, his touch. I craved the feel of someone touching me, and me touching them.

I pulled my long plait over my shoulder and undid the cord that bound it in place. He lifted a hand, and, taking the plait, pulled it through his fingers until every lock fell loose in a luxuriant veil.

I heard him catch his breath and felt my cheeks color.

He cupped my chin. "You're very beautiful." And he bent forward and kissed me gently on the lips.

I'd been kissed lots of times, of course. But this was different. His lips touched mine, barely brushing them, warm and dry, and light as thistledown. A quiver of desire ran through my treacherous body.

His mouth was close to my ear, his breath warm and intimate. "Don't think of him, think of me."

He kissed me again. I closed my eyes and opened my mouth under his, my body responding. His tongue flicked over my lips, exploring, finding my tongue. It was a long time before he released me.

I was breathless. Not because of the length of the kiss, but because of the way it had made me feel, stirring all the inner longings that I'd never thought I could have for anyone but Nathan. It no longer mattered to me that he wasn't Nathan. My lonely soul cried out for Arthur.

I was pleased to see that he was breathless as well.

"Get up," he said.

We got to our feet together, and he gently turned me around. His fingers were on the lacings of my dress. My heart thundered in my chest so loud he must have heard. Before he had them all undone, he leaned forwards, and moving my hair to one side, kissed the back of my neck. His lips felt hot and firm as his tongue traced a path across my skin. I shivered with excitement at his touch, and his suddenly clumsy fingers fumbled on my laces. Was he nervous too?

He tore them undone. The dress loosened and his hands slid over my skin and round to my breasts. I felt an ache of reciprocal longing.

There was no getting away from it. I wanted him as much as he wanted me. Maybe for similar reasons. Maybe he, too, was lonely. I didn't care. He was the connection I was looking for.

The dress fell to the tiled floor; my undershirt slipped off my shoulders and followed, leaving me naked in my walking boots. For a moment he looked down at them in surprise, then he dropped to his knees to unlace them. His head was below my waist. I put my fingers in his thick hair as he pressed his lips against my naked thigh. Covering my skin with kisses, he got slowly to his feet, working his way up to my breasts, exploring my body with his mouth.

It was my turn now, and I was impatient. I undid his belt and let it fall to the floor, then pulled his tunic over his head and discarded it. He took me in his arms and kissed me again as though this was something he'd wanted to do for a very long time. I kissed him back, sliding my hands under his loose undershirt to touch his skin, taut over his ribs, the muscles firm beneath it. His whole body quivered. I pulled him to me, pressing my body against his, feeling his arousal hard against my naked belly.

We had somehow found ourselves by the bed and now he pushed me down onto my back. Still standing, he pulled off his undershirt and dropped down on top of me. For a moment our eyes met, and then he bent and kissed me again, his tongue on mine. I opened my legs and felt him slide between them. He was still wearing his braccae. I could feel him pushing at me through the soft material. I wanted him. Badly.

I pushed his mouth away. "Take your trousers off." I could only manage a gasp.

He stood up and there was the sound of him hurriedly pulling off his boots and braccae. Then he was back between my legs and his mouth was hard on mine and he was hard against me and then inside, pushing and questing and filling me up. I let out a groan of pleasure and dug my fingers into his back as he thrust into me again and again. My whole body had been crying out for this, for the closeness of becoming one flesh, for the intimacy of sex, for the relief that sex can give. Our bodies were slick with sweat, our breath coming in pants, as in unison we galloped toward the conclusion.

At last it was over. He rolled off me, spent and tired, and I lay on my back with his seed running down my inner thighs. I'd just been fucked by King Arthur. Not a nugget of information I would want to have shared with my father.

After a few minutes he turned onto his side and looked at me. "You're no virgin bride, are you?"

I shook my head. "I never pretended to be." I paused. "Do you mind?"

He gave a shrug. "You're mine now. And you're the Lady of the Ring. What do I care what you did before?"

That was a relief, although I wasn't so sure about the possessive "mine". I'd put him right about that later.

An unmistakable twinkle sparkled in his eyes. I rolled over to face him and slid my hand down his stomach toward his groin. "Would you like me to show you what I've done before?"

He blinked at me. Doubt showed on his face, doubt mixed with curiosity. I gave him a squeeze and felt his arousal. "Yes." His voice was hoarse.

So I showed him. And when we made love the second time, it lasted much longer, and he learned quite a bit about what women want in bed, and what women can do if given a free rein. It was altogether a resounding success.

Afterwards we lay side by side, exhausted and naked, the sweat beginning to dry on our bodies.

"Are you sure you weren't ever a whore?" he asked after a while, when he'd got his breath back. It wasn't meant as an insult. I think it was praise for my bedroom skills.

"Of course not. It's just that where I come from, there's lots of advice about sex. You can read about it in books, and we talk about it a lot. So people just know a lot more." Difficult to explain where I'd learned what I'd just shown him without compromising myself. Better not mention television porn channels, the internet and Cosmopolitan.

"I'm very impressed, although I don't think my mother would approve of me even knowing a girl with your skills. It's lucky you're the Lady of the Ring, otherwise, I don't think I could have married you."

"That's a bit judgmental. Anyhow, you wouldn't have known until it was too late and we were married, would you?"

He laughed, and I saw the boy he'd once been. "You're right. I'm rather glad you're the Lady of the Ring and you're married to me. It's..." he paused, "fun."

Something I felt the Dark Ages lacked.

He lifted his arm and I moved in close, snuggling up to him. He smelled of sex. He pulled the covers up over my nakedness and I put my leg across his, getting as close as possible. For the first time since I'd arrived in the Dark Ages, I felt happy.

We made love again in the early morning, sleepily, languorously, fulfillingly. And then we lay in one another's arms, listening to the sounds of the villa coming to life.

At last, we got up and dressed. A servant brought us bread and wine and cheese for breakfast, which we ate sitting on the cushioned bench side by side. Curiously, clothes had made us shy of one another, as though without them nothing had stood between us, but with them we were different people, and the barriers were immense. We ate in silence, the gap widening. When Arthur had finished, he got up and picked up his cloak.

"I need to see to my men." And he was gone.

Left alone, I finished up all the remaining food. Sex three times in one night certainly gives you an appetite.

I was just picking up all the crumbs with a licked fingertip when there was a knock on the door, and without waiting for an invitation, it opened. Albina and Cloelia came in on a gust of cold air. They were wearing padded jackets over their dresses and beneath their cloaks.

They stopped on the threshold, and both performed a rather clumsy bow.

"My Lady," Albina began. "Mother sent us to apologize for how we talked about King Arthur yesterday in front of you. We should have had better manners. It was behavior unbecoming of young ladies of noble birth."

She must be quoting her mother.

"Me too," Cloelia said and managed another bow.

I couldn't help but smile. "That's quite all right. It doesn't matter. Yesterday was…a bit of a whirl for me. I just didn't know how to break it to you about who I was."

They looked at one another for a moment, and then both broke into smiles.

"Thank goodness. Mother said you'd be furious with us. I'm so glad you're not," Albina said.

"No, I'm not."

They ventured further into the room, emboldened by my lack of anger.

"I've never met anyone who was the outcome of a prophecy," Albina ventured.

"Me neither," added Cloelia.

"That goes for me too." I grinned. "And I don't even believe in prophecies."

They looked surprised. "But everyone does. They're true. Look at you. You've transformed Arthur into a king." Albina seemed to be the spokesperson.

I sighed. "I did nothing of the sort. He did that all by himself. And if his father hadn't wanted him to be a king in the first place, it wouldn't have happened whether I was there or not."

They didn't believe me. I could see from the shocked expressions on their faces. It was no use arguing with the blindly faithful. I changed tack. "Come and sit down."

They hurried forwards and sat, one on either side of me on the cushioned bench seat, rapt.

I smiled at them again. "I don't know much about what goes on. I'm – I'm from far away and it's quite different there." I took a deep breath. "You could start by telling me how your father came to be seneschal to King Uthyr." I might glean some useful information.

Albina started. "He's from Rheged. There was a Council of Kings and he came here with his own king. I mean *our* own king. Meirchion the Lean. Years ago. In the time of the old High King."

"She means High King Ambrosius, King Uthyr's brother."

"Yes, I do. Don't interrupt. I'll lose my track."

"Well, you weren't going to say." Cloelia's jaw had a stubborn set to it.

"I was. Shut up and let me talk. It was when Meirchion was a young man and had just become king in Rheged. He's an old man now, like Father. He brought Father to the Council of Kings in his retinue, and Father met Mother. And they fell in love."

"She was Grandfather's only child. He didn't want her to marry a man from Rheged. Grandfather was High King Ambrosius's seneschal," Cloelia elaborated.

"You keep on interrupting!"

"Well, you keep on leaving out important bits."

"Just be quiet. Yes, she's right, Grandfather forbade the marriage. Father had to go back to Rheged without her. He was really sad because he loved Mother so much."

"You wouldn't think it now, but she was really beautiful when she was young."

I didn't think she was too bad now.

"Just let me. I'm the oldest. I get to tell the story." Albina cleared her throat. "He pined for her. Then there was another Council of

Kings and he had to come back here, and he found she was pining for him, and finally Grandfather let them marry because he thought she might die! Isn't that romantic?"

I nodded dutifully. I wanted to ask them more about the Council of Kings but held my tongue, waiting for their story to finish.

Albina continued. "They went back to Rheged together, and Father worked for King Meirchion for years. He didn't want to be a warrior – he says he's too clever for that."

"He says only stupid men want to fight. But I don't think that's true. All the heroes in the stories are warriors, not seneschals." Cloelia did like to put in her pennyworth.

"Shut *up*. He worked for King Meirchion's seneschal – sorting out taxes and things like that. It's what he does now. He makes money for the King."

"Mother says kings are nothing without a good seneschal. But I think seneschals are nothing without good warriors."

"Cloelia! Anyway, we were born. We lived in Caer Ligualid, the capital of Rheged, up beside the Wall. It's an old Roman city like this, only nowhere near so big or so splendid. And then there was *another* Council of Kings and Grandfather retired, so King Uthyr persuaded Father to come and work for him as seneschal to the High King, not just to the king of Powys."

"Mother says it was promotion."

"So we all came south. Grandfather was really pleased. We came to live here, with him. In Domus Albus. It's our family name – Albus – well, Grandfather's family name. He was a Roman. It's why I was named Albina. To keep the family name alive. He isn't here now. He died three years ago. Mother says we made his old age happy."

I was sure they had. They seemed like exceptionally nice girls.

They appeared to have finished their narrative, so I asked, "What can you tell me about the Council of Kings?"

Albina started. "It's held once every two years unless something special happens. Always here. I don't know why, but it is."

"Because the kings of Powys have always been the High Kings. That's why, stupid."

Albina glared at her sister. "I'm not stupid. You are. Well, the High Kings have come from Powys for a really long time. Before Uthyr, it was his brother Ambrosius, and then, before him it was the Usurper." She gave a shrug. "Heraclion, our tutor, showed me a map of Britain and said this was like somewhere called Delphi, near where he was born. He said Viroconium is the navel of Britain."

Heraclion must be a Greek. So, in a fledgling way Britain was as cosmopolitan in the Dark Ages as it was in my time. I'd like to get a look at Heraclion's map. I could probably tell him a thing or two about the shape of the British Isles that he wouldn't know, even as an educated Greek.

But should I? At the moment, I'd really done very little in the past except for fulfilling part of an old prophecy, which might mean I was supposed to be here, which in itself might mean that anything I did shouldn't matter in the grand scheme of things. Could it? Could I do that classic kill-your-grandfather thing?

"What happens at a Council of Kings? Who comes?" I needed some information on this, as it was due to happen the very next day.

Albina gave her sister a triumphant glare. "All the kings come, of course, with their retinues. And lots of really important men – their advisors. Lots of young warriors, too. Sons of important men. They bring all sorts of people with them."

"And some are here already?"

She nodded. "Mother says King Cadwy told Father to send out messengers to all the kings when he realized King Uthyr was dying. She says he wants to strike while the iron is hot and get himself elected High King after his father."

But he'd sent no one to tell his brother in far off Dumnonia. The-odoric had been forced to sneak away with his small force of men and ride hell for leather to Din Cadan.

Albina went on. "Father says they're being housed all over the city. The ones that arrive today will have to make camp outside the walls. There isn't room for them all."

Cloelia interrupted – again. "Normally not every king comes. Sometimes they just can't be bothered – Father says – and sometimes they have other things they have to be doing. But this time, because it's going to be an election, they're all coming."

Albina frowned at her. "We weren't born when they had the last election, so we don't really know how it happens. You could ask Father if you want to find out more."

I could have, but I didn't, mainly because he wasn't around until that evening when we all ate together again in the warm dining room. He and Arthur had been absent all day and the only person I'd seen who I knew had been Merlin, and even he'd been distracted and disinclined to answer my questions.

Arthur was not at the meal, though, and Euddolen took the seat at the head of the table. I was still beside Theodoric, so after a while, I took my courage in both hands and asked where Arthur was.

Theodoric looked surprised I'd spoken. He'd been deep in a dull sounding discussion with Cei on the contrasting merits of hunting boar or deer.

"Matters of state," was his terse reply, and he turned away from me and started talking to Cei again.

Well, that could have been anything. Theodoric certainly seemed to have no intention of enlightening me. Maybe the well-informed Albina knew what "matters of state" might entail. She was sitting almost opposite me, busily tucking into a plate of salted cod in garlic sauce.

However, just then a troop of agile jugglers arrived. They took everyone's attention for the remainder of the meal, tossing balls into the air, juggling with fiery torches, doing somersaults and balancing on each other's shoulders. And when they'd finished, it was time to retire to our bedchambers.

The oil lamps had been lit again and the room glowed golden in their light. But without Arthur's vibrant presence, it felt empty and lonely, doubly so after last night. A maid came and unlaced my gown, and, wearing just my long undershirt, I climbed into the big bed alone. She extinguished most of the little lamps before she left, just leaving me the ones beside my bed and near the door, plunging the room into great wedges of shadow where no light penetrated between the islands of golden glow.

I lay back on my pillows on the comfortable bed. Probably after time it would develop lumpiness, but right now it was really very good.

But I was alone in it.

I hadn't realized how much last night had meant to me. I wanted Arthur back here, warm and alive beside me. I was confused by the aching void in my heart, sure I didn't love him. Nathan was the man I loved. The trouble was, he was far away, so far away I might never get back to him. I'd always thought it was human nature not to give up, even in the face of insurmountable odds. So I clung resolutely to the belief that there'd be a way back for me, just as there'd been a way here.

But Nathan's face was fading. If I thought back to our last night together in the hotel in Glastonbury, I could only see the hump of his body in the bed, his tousled sandy hair on the pillow. I had to fight to conjure his image, and when it came it was just of a photograph hanging on the wall in our sitting room at home. He was on the beach in Tenerife last year, his hair wet from the sea, sand stuck to his skin, nose peeling slightly, sunglasses resting on the top of his head. I held that image to my heart as though it would bring me closer to him.

It didn't.

I rolled onto my side and curled up, drawing my knees to my

chest. Instead of Nathan's face, Arthur's rose before me. As he'd been this morning while we were still in bed. His dark eyes full of humor, crinkling at the corners, his grin infectious. I could still feel the warmth of his body under my hands. A little shiver of excitement coursed through me at the memory.

I shook myself crossly. Why was he so much more real than Nathan? I didn't understand my feelings, and it upset me. I wanted to stay the woman I'd been when I'd climbed Glastonbury Tor, but it was a losing battle. I was changing, and there was nothing I could do about it.

I blew out the lamp on the stool beside the bed and closed my eyes. Sleep crept over me.

I was standing on a windswept hillside with mounted men all about me, carrying shields and wearing helmets, swords glinting in the sunlight. My own beast pranced beneath me, chaffing at the bit and impatient for the off, and I realized that I, too, had a shield and helmet, with a ferocious-looking sword gripped in my right hand.

A sea of faces swam all around me, close up, far away, milling. Arthur's face came close. I wanted to shout to him, to tell him it was me, but he rode past without a backward glance, unrecognizing.

A battle horn sounded, deep and rich, echoing through my head. In the valley at the foot of the hill a mass of mounted soldiers galloped toward us. My vision zoomed to show me their faces, dark and angry. Their banner rippled in the wind; a red dragon leaping across a green field.

Suddenly, we were galloping down the hill. Hooves thundered, and the wind pulled at my hair, which streamed out behind me. I was filled with the lust for blood, uncontrollable and basic. Men shouted. I couldn't hear the words. I wanted to shout too, but nothing came out. I was mute.

With a terrible crash, we came together. Horses shrieked, men screamed, swords clashed, the air stank of blood and sweat and shit. It was in my ears, up my nose, in my eyes. Confusion and noise and yet more noise.

Then silence. All around me lay the dead and dying. Low moaning ululated in the breeze that blew across the battlefield. I heard quiet sobbing and the harsh call of carrion crows that hung in the air like bundles of windblown black rags.

I was on my knees, my armor gone, and in its place a muddy, blood-stained gown. A man lay beside me, sprawled under a dead horse that had once been white but now was dark with blood. Its weight had trapped his left leg beneath it. His head lay in my lap. I looked down into his face. He'd lost his helmet, and dark hair flecked with grey spilled out. His eyes were closed, and blood veiled the left side of his face. But I'd have known him anywhere. It was Arthur.

"Arthur!" I found my voice, and with it, came starting awake. Someone had their arms around me, holding me. For a moment I struck out, but the arms held me tight.

"It's all right," a voice said soothingly. "It's all right. You were just dreaming. You're all right now. I've got you."

Arthur.

In the dark bedchamber I couldn't see him, but I recognized the scent of lavender and reassuring masculinity and sweat. I clung to him. With one hand he lifted my chin, and his mouth came down on mine, gentle and warm. I melted into his body, my arms going up around his neck and holding him close, driving away the image of him lying dead on a distant battlefield. He was here and Nathan wasn't. And he was mine.

# Chapter Twenty

THE COUNCIL OF Kings was held where the Roman forum used to stand. The stone foundations of the Roman buildings were visible here and there, but an enormous thatched wooden hall had transformed the whole center of the city. To the east lay the marble-faced remains of the public baths, towering in decaying splendor over the city's houses. How odd to think I'd walked in those ruins fifteen hundred years in the future.

Arthur's party consisted of his right-hand men – Cei, Theodoric, Merlin, plus Euddolen, and a number of heavily armed warriors from the band of fifty who'd accompanied him from Din Cadan. And me. To my surprise, I hadn't had to ask to be taken with him, although he'd told me in no uncertain terms that being a woman, he wanted me to look and listen and not say a thing.

Not wanting to give him a reason to leave me behind, I had to bite back the stinging retort that leapt to my lips. Consumed with curiosity about the Council, I wanted to see the other kings, hear what they had to say, witness the process that would elect the next High King. That morning I was all historian again, and Arthur all king.

We rode in horseback procession to the Hall, with me perched up behind Merlin on a leather pad attached to the back of his saddle, sitting sideways, in a gown. I managed to achieve a rather elegant appearance with my skirts and cloak gracefully flowing down the sides of Merlin's horse.

In the Domus Albus's crowded courtyard, Arthur had lifted me up effortlessly into the saddle, and as we rode through the narrow streets, I could still feel the hot imprint of his hands on my waist. The feeling gave me a pleasant glow that was more than a little disturbing to my inner equilibrium.

The marketplace around the hall bustled with activity. Servants hung onto clusters of horses, men held forth with self-importance to those around them, and the townsfolk watched with interest. Barking dogs and shouting children ran everywhere. Market stalls thronged with customers drawn by the mouthwatering smells of freshly baked pastries. A babble of noise rose toward the wintry sky.

Arthur jumped down from his horse, and, coming back to Merlin, held out his arms for me. I slid down into them, and just for a moment he held me close, before turning and leading me toward the hall. Servants from the Domus Albus had taken our horses' bridles, and now all of Arthur's men followed him up to the hall's open double doors. Two of our Dumnonian warriors took charge of collecting all our party's swords and remained outside as we passed into the hall.

A horse could have been ridden round inside this hall. From an open-plan ground floor, stairs climbed to a galleried level already filling with people. However, it was the center that riveted my attention.

For standing in it was a round table.

A genuine round table. Probably *the* Round Table. It was very large and made of wide, knotted planks of silvered wood. Around it stood about two dozen high-backed seats, all the same, except for one, which was larger and more ornately carved than the rest – a throne more than a seat.

Already, some of the kings had taken their places, heads bent together in conversation, or simply sitting aloof. Cadwy sat in his seat on the opposite side to the throne, his glowering gaze fixed on us as we made our entry.

Arthur turned to me. "You'll have to go with Merlin. I need to take my place at the table. He'll look after you." And he was gone, striding across the paved floor of the hall to take his seat, three down from Cadwy, ignoring his brother's angry glare.

Cei and Theodoric were already pushing their way through the crowd to get positions behind Arthur's seat, our warriors following them. I turned to Merlin.

"This way," he said, pulling me after him.

It was standing room only. The only seats were for the kings themselves, who came in through the double doors to take their places whilst their retinues jostled for position behind their lords. Merlin elbowed his way to the front with me.

Once there, he bent his head to my ear, pointing a discreet finger. "That's Euddolen's old king – Meirchion the Lean."

A gaunt middle-aged man, whose only hair was a sparse ring of iron grey, took his seat beside Cadwy. The skinny youth standing behind his seat must have been his son, by his appearance.

Merlin nodded toward the doors. "Natanleod, of Caer Gwinntguic on the River Itchen."

Did Merlin mean Winchester? In my time that was the name of the town which stood on the River Itchen. A swarthy young man, built like an ox, with tattooed, bare arms bulging with muscles, swaggered into the hall.

Behind him came a group of noisy young men, one of whom wore a plain gold circlet on his head. "Cynfelin," Merlin said, bending closer. "King of Cynwidion. He's not long succeeded his father. He's great-grandson to Coel the Old. He served his father at the last Council. Now he's on it himself." He might have been young, but he looked every inch a warrior, his dark auburn hair bound in a tail that reached his waist, and rings of heavy gold skulls dangling from his ears.

Another man followed close behind Cynfelin. "Masgwid the Lame and his son and heir, Prince Llaenog. Masgwid's a nephew of Meirchion of Rheged, and king of Elmet in his own right." This king walked with a stick, his left hip and leg twisted and stiff. Close behind followed four youths. "Those young men there are Llaenog's four younger brothers." Each one of them, even the youngest who was only a boy, had the same hungry look as Llaenog.

I thought perhaps that was all the kings, but then a tall man with very straight black hair lightly flecked with grey at the temples came striding in. He paused on the threshold, staring around the hall with lazy, heavy-lidded eyes. A hooked nose in a long, narrow face and a thin-lipped, cruel mouth gave him the look of a ferocious bird of prey. Of all the kings I'd seen so far, his was the only face I took an instant dislike to.

Merlin seemed to be of the same mind as me. His lip curled in disdain. "Melwas, King of the Summer Country, Lord of the Mount of Frogs. Overlord of Caer Baddan and sub-king of Dumnonia."

I looked at him with more interest. Sub-king or not, he walked across the hall as though he owned it, his expression haughty, his contempt for the watching rabble obvious. One of his entourage pulled out his seat for him, and he sank into it with conscious elegance, leaving only one place still empty apart from the throne.

The press of the audience grew greater. Merlin put an arm about my shoulders to steady me as those behind pushed against us, eager to get a better look at the kings seated about the round table.

The man who came in last wore Roman dress of a deep red tunic beneath a cream toga. His ascetic face was clean-shaven and his grizzled, dark hair cut severely short.

Merlin leaned toward me again. "Aurelius Caninus, King of Gwent. Cousin to Arthur – and to you now – and son to the great Ambrosius himself."

Aurelius Caninus took the last empty seat, beside Arthur, and their heads came together. They had their backs to me, but even if they'd been facing me, with so much noise in the hall, I could never have heard them. I hoped when the Council started it would be different.

It was.

As the son of Ambrosius, Caninus began the proceedings by getting to his feet to stand motionless, waiting for silence to fall. This had the desired effect. The noise died away as the mass of people realized the Council was about to start. Caninus didn't speak for a full minute. You could have heard the proverbial pin drop. All eyes rested on him.

"Fellow kings," he began. He had a deep, sonorous voice. He'd have been good on the stage. "People of Britain." He paused again, encompassing everyone with his gaze. "We are gathered here with much sadness to honor the passing of a great man. The wise King Uthyr, brother to my father, Ambrosius." A ripple of agreement ran through the crowd. Caninus waited again for silence to fall.

"His funeral rites will be held tomorrow. Today, we meet to acknowledge his heirs and to elect a new High King."

Cadwy's profile was visible from where I stood. His bushy, black hair had been bound back from his face in a long sausage of a plait, and it was evident from his expression that he'd softened nothing toward his younger brother. His jaw jutted forwards belligerently, and he appeared to be grinding his teeth. Not a good idea when there's no chance of any dental care.

Caninus looked down at Arthur in the seat beside his, and then at Cadwy, still glaring angrily round the table. He was Cadwy's cousin as well as Arthur's. Whose side did he favor? His thin face gave away nothing.

His voice boomed out. "I have seen the testament of King Uthyr Pendragon and declare it just and true. Today we ratify his wishes."

Beside me, I heard Merlin give a sigh of relief. Had he doubted it would be so?

Caninus went on. "He leaves as his heirs his two sons. We welcome to our Council King Cadwy Pendragon, elder son of King Uthyr, now ruler of the kingdom of Powys."

CADWY GOT TO his feet and tried to school the scowl off his face, not very successfully.

Caninus inclined his head. "We welcome you to our Council."

The kings echoed Caninus' words in some disunity. Cadwy made a rather curt bow to the table and sat down again, his cheeks now flushed an unbecoming blotchy red.

Caninus looked down at Arthur. "And we welcome, also, King Arturius Pendragon, younger son of King Uthyr, now ruler of the kingdom of Dumnonia."

Arthur got to his feet far more gracefully than Cadwy had done. Only the back of his head was visible, but his spine was ramrod straight.

Caninus allowed his solemn expression to slip into a half smile. "We welcome you to our Council."

And again, this was repeated by the other kings, except for Cadwy, whose mouth stayed firmly shut.

Arthur made a bow and sat down again. Applause rumbled from the watching people. Standing at the front of the crowd of Cadwy's supporters, Morgana briefly allowed her beautiful face to contort in anger before she had it back under control. What did she have against Arthur? He did, after all, share both parents with her, whilst she and Cadwy just had the same father. I couldn't imagine not loving your brother.

That seemed to be Uthyr's last wishes accounted for. But would acceptance by the Council of Kings be enough to quiet Cadwy's yearning for both kingdoms? I doubted it.

Merlin's body stiffened beside me, and I glanced sideways at him. His eyes were shining brightly, but he wasn't looking at the round table. Instead, he stared at Morgana, her face now a picture of innocence, and she looked back at him, her long hair hanging in a veil of darkness to her waist. I was struck again by her beauty, and by something else that lurked beneath that show of perfect womanhood –

her wickedness – as though a shadow of darkness rippled beneath her alabaster skin.

Caninus had begun to speak again. I had no time to speculate. My gaze returned to the round table.

"Now it is my task to call for nominations for High King. It is long since we had the last election – twenty years ago Uthyr took the title by fair vote. Many of you will not remember what it is to elect a new High King. I myself was just a boy." He looked round at the crowd on the lower level of the hall. "Any man who has today come with their king may make a nomination. Any king may do the same. A king may even nominate himself. A king and only a king may be nominated. After nominations we will hear from each man why he is suitable to rule. And then we will vote by show of hands. Our decision this day will be final."

Caninus sat down.

A buzz of excited conversation filled the air.

The kings began to talk amongst themselves.

I gave Merlin's sleeve a tug. "Are there likely to be many nominations?"

He dragged his gaze away from Morgana. Should I warn him to stay away from her? Would he believe me? Since he knew where I'd come from, he ought to take anything I said very seriously.

"I said, are there likely to be many nominations?"

He shrugged. "Difficult to say. It depends on whether there are many who have delusions of grandeur."

There were a few.

Cadwy was not the first one to be proposed, though. Archbishop Dubricius judiciously waited until Meirchion the Lean's lanky son had nominated his father to much shouting and cheering from the Rheged faction. After Cadwy's name had been cast into the ring, someone proposed Natanleod of Caer Gwinntguic, and before long there were four nominations in the air because the five sons of Masgwid the

Lame, probably with an eye to his kingdom for themselves, jointly proposed their father. Not a single person proposed Arthur.

Perhaps he'd been away in Dumnonia too long. Cadwy had been ever present in Viroconium. The kings knew him. They'd seen him every couple of years at the Council by his father's side. What would they know of his younger brother? Perhaps being a king wouldn't be enough. Perhaps having me by his side wouldn't work as Merlin had thought. But why hadn't one of Arthur's own followers nominated him?

Caninus got to his feet again. "We have four candidates for High King. Meirchion of Rheged, Cadwy of Powys, Natanleod of Caer Gwinntguic and Masgwid of Elmet. Each of them in turn will tell us why they would make the best High King. Firstly, I will call upon the oldest of the four – Meirchion."

But he didn't get the chance to say any more, because Arthur sprang to his feet, pushing back his seat with a clatter across the stone slabs.

Everyone looked at him, and Caninus put his hand on his arm as though to restrain him. Arthur shook it off.

"Fellow kings," Arthur began. "Will you allow me to address this Council?"

Caninus sat down. The attention of every person in the hall fixed on Arthur. The silence was deafening.

And not without reason. He had prepared well for this moment. His long hair was tied back from his face, and he'd dressed in plain dark clothes devoid of any ornament that might have emphasized his kingship. In this hallowed gathering of all the kings of Britain, every man wore his finest tunic; arms and throats and ears were hung with gold, and yet in his plain attire Arthur stood out amongst them, a crow amid a gathering of birds of paradise.

Arthur turned slowly on his heel, scanning the crowd, for the moment ignoring the kings seated round the table, gathering in his audience. His eyes were bright with an inner fire, his body taut with scarcely suppressed excitement and determination.

His gaze came to rest on me, and for a moment his expression softened. He raised a hand and held it out to me. "Step forward, Guinevere."

Merlin gave me a little push from behind. Conscious of the gaze of hundreds of people, I stepped forward and put my hand in Arthur's, my head held high. He gave me the full wattage of his smile and I couldn't help but smile back.

Holding my hand, he turned back to the round table where the kings were all looking at him in open curiosity.

"I will tell you an old tale," he said, with the air of a father about to read his child a bedtime story. "You all know it well. Long ago, when Guorthegirn the Usurper ruled Britain, he invited the Saxons to our shores." He shot an accusatory glance at Cadwy. "But he could not control them. There were too many of them. Keel upon keel arrived, lured from their homes across the seas by tales of the riches of our lands. Frightened, Guorthegirn called for his wisest men because he wished to build, in the mountains at Dinas Emrys, the fortress that stands there now. But it would not stay built. Every night, what they'd achieved during the day was rendered rubble by morning, and they had to start again."

Every eye was on him. His deep voice filled the hall.

"Guorthegirn consulted with his wise men, and they told him that he must send far and wide to find a boy with no father, and sacrifice him and scatter his blood over the foundations to bless them. Only then would the fortress rise on the rocky hilltop." He looked at Merlin, who was listening intently in the crowd.

"The boy he found is here today. Merlin Emrys, for whom the fortress is named. A boy without a father. The wise men brought him before the Usurper, but when the king questioned him, he showed that he knew far more than the wise men. He asked the wise men what lay beneath the fortress, but they knew not. Smiling, he told them that beneath the hill they would find a lake, and when they dug down, they discovered a black lake. He then asked them what was in the lake, but they could no more answer that than his first question. He told them to drain it down, and they would find two dragons, one red, one white, fighting to the death."

Not a whisper disturbed the hall.

"They drained the lake. And sure enough, uncovered were two great dragons, fighting to the death. The wise men had no idea what the fighting dragons signified, first the white gaining the advantage, then the red. But Merlin knew."

Arthur's hand was warm, his fingers tight around mine. I could feel the excitement pulsing through him. My own body quivered in recognition of what I instinctively knew to be a pivotal moment.

His eyes held Merlin's. "The white dragon symbolized the Saxons, whose superior strength and numbers were defeating the Usurper's armies. The red dragon symbolized the people of Britain who would not be defeated, and who would rise again as surely as the red dragon rose above the white."

Cottia had told me a version of this story.

"Guorthegirn asked the boy Merlin what this signified. He told the king that for a time the Saxons would seem to be winning but that eventually a line of kings, who could trace their lineage back to Rome, would drive them back. He foretold the advent of my uncle, Aurelius Ambrosius, who would become High King after the Usurper, and his brother Uthyr. It was these kings who would turn the tide of raiders, these kings who would lead we Britons in the defense of this island."

Merlin stepped out of the crowd. "And after them would come another," he said, raising his voice to the rafters. "Another greater king, the son of Uthyr Pendragon. And this king would be the one who would finally drive the Saxons out of our lands, who would defend our northern borders against the savage Painted People from beyond the Wall, and our western shorelines from the Irish raiders, heralding a new golden age."

Dubricius the Archbishop pushed his way forward. "And I say," he shouted, throwing a furious glare at Merlin, "that king is Cadwy, Uthyr's firstborn son. He is the king who will drive out the Saxons."

There was a muted rumble of agreement, mostly from Cadwy's own men.

Merlin waited until they fell silent again. "No, Cadwy is not that king," he said. "Because the prophecy says that the king will come with a queen by his side, a woman with no family, a woman from nowhere bearing the ring of the Pendragons. You all know the story. She is the Lady of the Ring."

Goosebumps prickled my skin.

Merlin stepped up beside Arthur and me, and taking my free hand in his, raised my arm into the air. "Behold the Lady of the Ring."

Uproar filled the hall. Advisers from the ranks of the kings' followers rushed to discuss this new portent with their lords, and everyone in the public viewing areas talked or shouted to everyone else.

I stood still, letting the sound wash over me. No wonder Arthur and Merlin had thought it a good idea to bring me. The importance of this moment, which hinged on my presence, both weighed me down and buoyed me up. I couldn't help but be infected by Arthur's confidence, but at the same time a little knot of fear curled itself in my stomach.

Caninus got to his feet and, standing with raised arms, managed to quieten the noise. At last, the hall fell silent again.

"You have seen the Lady of the Ring," he said. "You have seen the prophecy come true. She is the Queen of Arthur Pendragon. She is the Lady of the Ring."

He was about to lose the crowd, which was buzzing with excitement. Arthur might not believe in prophecies coming true, but his audience definitely did, and were very keen to talk about it. Arthur released my hand and, in one bound, was up on the round table, standing in its center where all could see him. Out of the corner of my eye I saw Morgana fix him with a baleful stare.

"I am Arthur Pendragon, king of Dumnonia, son of King Uthyr." His voice penetrated to every corner of the hall and snatched back the attention Caninus had almost lost. "This is my wife, the Lady Guinevere, my Queen. I am the one the dragons foretold. I am the red dragon who will drive back the Saxons and free our kingdoms from their yoke. And she will be by my side."

My heart galloped at breakneck speed, stirred by his rousing words. Surely none of his audience could be immune to his message.

"But I do not ask you for the High Kingship here today."

*What?* I'd thought that was exactly what he wanted.

"I ask instead that you give me the ancient title – Dux Britanniarum. It is an ancient Roman title, and I am a Roman born. My great-grandfather, Constantine, wore the purple and ruled the Western Empire, and yet the bloodline of Cunedda runs in my veins." His gaze dared anyone to challenge him. No one did. Not even Cadwy.

"I'll tell you what I ask of you today, every one of you. An army of young men who will follow me across Britain from one kingdom to the next, fighting not just for me or for my brother or for my neighbor, not for one kingdom, but for all. The Dux Britanniarum should guard every kingdom from far off Alt Clut in the north, to Caer Dore in the furthest tip of Cornubia. And so that I may do this, I ask you to provide me with warriors. I've proven myself in Din Cadan these past seven years. My father rewarded me with the kingship of Dumnonia. Din Cadan will be the base for my army – an army comprised of young men sent by each of you, ready to defend not just their own, but every kingdom."

The five sons of Masgwid the Lame gave a shout of agreement as one. Proving that then, as now, young men's lust for action is easily roused by a good speech. "We'll join your army!" the eldest, Llaenog, called. Immediately amongst the younger followers of the kings there were echoed similar shouts. But the kings themselves were not so easily convinced.

One of them got slowly to his feet and looked up at Arthur. "You speak well, young man," he began gruffly. "Your words are enough to rouse an army for you, I can see. But can you hold them? Can you bring home your promises? If we invest in you, will we get a return?" His age was difficult to gauge because his rugged face was devoid of wrinkles, although he had snowy white hair, thick and long like a lion's mane.

Beside me, Merlin leaned close enough to whisper in my ear. "King March of Caer Dore." Of course. King Marcus Cunomorus of Cornwall. I knew that name. My father had once taken me to the circle of grassy banks that was Caer Dore in my time.

From behind March, a young man with a mass of wild auburn curls to his shoulders stepped forward. Little more than a boy, he sported a fine fuzz of down on his strong chin. He gripped the back of March's chair with whitened knuckles and burst out. "I'll join you. Let me become one of your warriors."

King March turned to glare at the young man. "Drustans! You will not volunteer for anything unless you have my permission."

Tristan. Near to Caer Dore stands a stone known as "the Tristan Stone" engraved with the name Drustans, son of Cunomorus, and thought to be the origin of the Tristan and Iseult stories. I'd stood beside it with my father. This boy's grave. It was a sobering thought.

The boy reddened. "I'm sorry, father, but if King Arthur becomes our Dux Britanniarum, then I will join him whether I have your permission or not." His jaw jutted in defiance, and for a moment there was a prickly silence while it occurred to the rest of the kings that maybe they might not be able to stop their younger warriors rushing to Arthur's standard.

"A vote!" someone cried. "Put it to the vote."

There was a chorus of agreement amongst the kings, followed by a roar of approval from the watching crowd and a thunder of stamping feet. They couldn't have made their approval more obvious.

Caninus got to his feet again. "Come down off the table now, Arthur." The noise almost drowned out his voice, but Arthur, his peacocking at an end, jumped down to the flagstone floor and resumed his seat, head held high, challenging anyone to go against him. He looked very confident, and confidence wins hearts. Merlin took a few steps back with me until we were amongst our own men again.

Caninus held up his hands, and gradually order was restored. He waited until he had total silence.

"We will vote on what my cousin has proposed." He paused for effect. "And I say that if we have a Dux Britanniarum once again, a War Leader for all the kingdoms, not just one, then we have no need of a High King."

I was struck by the cleverness of all this. Had he planned it with Arthur?

I could no longer see Arthur's face, but Merlin was standing right beside me. His face glowed with triumph. He'd known this was coming, which surely must mean Caninus was part of it. Maybe that was where Arthur had been all day yesterday and part of the night.

Uproar broke out again. I couldn't tell whether it was in agreement or disagreement. Several of the kings jumped to their feet. Morgana's face contorted in fury. She certainly hadn't seen this coming. So much for her having the power to see the future. She'd been check-mated, good and proper.

Caninus at last managed to restore silence. He turned to his fellow kings.

"What say you on this?"

The young, tattooed warrior, King Natanleod, got to his feet.

There was nothing of the Roman about him. More Conan the Barbarian. Would he want a Roman office reinstated? He nodded to Arthur. "If I were not a king, I would join you myself. My vote is for the creation of the Dux Britanniarum." Behind him, his assembled supporters cheered their approval. "I will send six of my best young warriors to Din Cadan with arms and shields, and six of my best horses." He sat down again.

Masgwid the Lame lumbered awkwardly to his feet. "I have five sons who have already said they wish to join you. But my question is this: who will pay to feed and house your warriors? If we send our young men to you, will it cost us?"

A murmur of approval buzzed round the hall. It looked like the economics of this was foremost in the minds of many of the kings. Perhaps money lay at the root of all things, even back in the Dark Ages.

Arthur rose to his feet. "The lands of the southwest, in Dumnonia, are rich. We have wheat and grass, we have herds of cattle and sheep and horses, and we have good hunting. As Dux Britanniarum I will ask tribute from each kingdom we defend. If you have no need of us, you will not pay."

Apparently he'd done some working out beforehand of how he was going to run this army he was intent on recruiting, which showed common sense.

"And if we do not send warriors to you, what then? Will you still come to our aid?" The black-haired king, Melwas, to whom I'd taken an instant dislike, got lazily to his feet and stood surveying his fellows out of his hooded eyes. "Will you pass us by and leave us to our fate?"

Arthur shook his head. "My *combrogi,* this brotherhood, will defend all who ask for help. We will turn no one away who is in need. You have my oath on that."

Surely that was a dangerous promise to make. If he planned to defend whoever asked, whether they'd contributed men or not, what was there to ensure anyone would send him their warriors?

Arthur sat down and Caninus stood up once more. "If we agree to reinstate the title and role of Dux, then we must all vow to send warriors to carry out Arthur's pledge. There can be no abstentions. I too, like Natanleod, have six warriors ready to send with Arthur to Din Cadan. We must vote, and if we agree to Arthur becoming Dux, then we must also agree to send him men, just as Natanleod has said, with horses, arms and shields." There were murmurs of agreement. I had the distinct feeling some of these kings had known this was coming.

Natanleod jumped to his feet again. "And I vow that when one of my warriors falls in the service of the Dux, I will send another to replace him."

Feet stamped in agreement from the crowd.

"Let us vote." Caninus looked around the kings. "All those in favor of creating Arthur, king of Dumnonia, our Dux Britanniarum, raise your right hands."

Cadwy was one of only three who kept their hands down, the others being Melwas of the Summer Country, and another, who Merlin told me was Owain White Tooth, king of Gwynedd, great grandson of Cunedda and so Arthur's distant cousin. There was no need for a count. Caninus took Arthur's arm and raised him to his feet.

A great cheer went up – enough to raise the thatched roof. I looked around at the applauding crowd, carried away by a rousing speech, and a man who, by his plain clothing, looked more like one of them than a king, convinced that this, like Arthur's inheritance of the throne of Dumnonia, had all been cleverly engineered.

# Chapter Twenty-One

U THYR'S FUNERAL WAS to take place the following day. He'd been three days dead, and the stink he'd had when alive hadn't improved any when Arthur and I went to pay our last respects as custom decreed. In fact, the smell met us out in the courtyard garden like a solid wall, bringing us up short in shock.

Merlin, Theodoric and Cei exchanged worried glances. I didn't think any of them wanted to brave the bedchamber where the corpse now lay in state. Arthur must have seen their discomfiture because he waved them away to wait in the courtyard with the rest of the warriors who'd accompanied us.

"The Queen and I will go in alone."

I'd much rather have stayed outside with the men. But as his queen, I couldn't argue, even though I'd have quite liked to.

Breanna was sitting in the antechamber on a little stool beside a burning brazier. Strongly scented smoke drifted upwards, eddying about the room, insufficient to mask the putrid stench of death. Hearing us enter, she got to her feet, her face creased with sorrow and confusion. Arthur went to her.

"Mother Breanna, it's me, Arthur."

She clasped his hands in her own gnarled grip. "Arthur? How can it be? My Arthur is just a little boy. You can't be him."

Had Uthyr's death addled her brains?

She licked her thin, dry lips. "You're too late, whoever you are. My sweet king is dead these three days since. You're too late."

"I know, Old Mother. I was with him when he died." His voice was gentle.

She raised cloudy eyes to his face and peered at him myopically. "Were you?" Her voice wavered. "Were you really?" She tottered on scrawny legs. Had she sat here in this antechamber whilst the world passed her by, forgotten, cast aside like an old pair of shoes?

My heart ached for her.

Arthur guided her to the cushioned seats. "Sit down and rest, Old Mother. You're shaking. When did you last eat? Gwen, fetch her some of that wine from the table."

A tall, earthenware pitcher stood on the table next to four intricately embossed pewter goblets. I poured a generous amount of the rich red wine and carried it over to the bench.

Arthur took the goblet and held it out to the old woman. "Here, drink this. You'll feel better for a draught of good wine." He spoke as though to a child. She wrapped her bony hands around the stem of the goblet. Wine ran down her chin as she took one gulp and then another, to quench her thirst.

"'Tis indeed good wine," she muttered, taking a third long pull, and smacking her lips together in appreciation. "From the king's own cellars. Prince Cadwy brought it 'ere 'imself not an hour since. Fit for a king, 'e said. For 'is brother the king." She looked up at Arthur. "Are ye the king 'e meant? If ye are, should be me pourin' for you, not t'other way round."

A moment of awful silence stretched between us as Arthur's stricken eyes met mine over her head. Then Arthur snatched the goblet from her hands.

"Cadwy sent it? For me?"

She peered up at him. "Are ye his brother? Are ye a king?" Her rheumy old eyes held no recognition.

He sniffed the wine in the goblet. I stared at him. He went back to the table and, taking the pitcher, took another long sniff.

I followed him and did the same. It smelled like ordinary wine. I dipped my finger.

"Don't." He held my hand down, and the wine dripped from my fingertip. Our eyes met again; his brimmed with anguish.

On the bench, Breanna gave a cough. Together, we swung round to look at her. She coughed again, then hawked and spat onto the mosaic floor.

I ran to her. Her breath heaved in desperate wheezes, one hand up at her throat, terrified eyes appealing for help. I looked back at Arthur, but he still stood immobile beside the table, his face dark with anger.

"I can't breathe," she spluttered, her yellowed nails scratching at her convulsing throat, her eyes wide and staring.

"Arthur!" I cried out, terrified. "We have to help her. What shall I do?"

He came. Dropping to one knee in front of the old woman, he looked up into my eyes. "There's nothing we can do. It's too late."

She slumped forward, and he caught her in his arms like a bundle of twigs. Around her mouth, wine-stained froth bubbled as she fought for breath.

Shock numbed me. She was dying in front of my eyes, and I could do nothing. But worse than that came the certainty that the poison she'd imbibed had been meant for Arthur...and me.

Even as I wrestled with my fear, her body stiffened and arched, her breath came in a bubbling rasp, and then faded to nothing. Silence fell. Slowly, her body relaxed, and Arthur was left holding just a bag of fragile bones.

He knelt motionless, his head bent over the tiny form. The silence stretched between us.

At last, he lifted her and laid her on the cushions as you would a sleeping baby in its cot. With life extinct, she seemed to have shrunk, as though her very soul had given substance to her frame. With a shaking hand, he closed her staring eyes and stood up, his head bowed. Tears streaked his cheeks. Was he praying?

I touched his arm. "Was that poison?" The evidence was clear. But I wanted to say the word out loud.

He nodded. For a moment longer, he stood in silence gazing down at her, and then he looked up at me sharply, brows knit in a heavy frown that gave him a sudden look of his brother. "This goes no further. Tip away the wine. She's an old lady who died from the shock of her lord's death, that's all."

"But Cadwy meant for us to die!" Gasping for breath that wouldn't come, clawing at our throats the way Breanna had, last breaths bubbling out. Guilt washed over me – guilt for the relief I felt that the old woman had died and not us.

He nodded again, dark brows still knitted together, brooding. "He did indeed. But it'll do no good to accuse him publicly. He'll deny everything, and there'll be no proof." He sounded very certain. Did he speak from experience?

"There must be proof. There always is. She said he brought the wine himself. Someone will have seen him."

"Who? This is his palace. The people here are his. Why d'you think he brought it himself? To involve no one else – no one who could give evidence against him. There's no point in pursuing this. We're not dead. Be thankful."

My strong twenty-first-century sense of right and wrong came to the fore. No one, especially not Cadwy, whom I really didn't like, should get away with murder. Anger rose in me.

"So you'll just let him get away with this?"

He shook his head. "There are ways and means of taking revenge that don't involve accusations of poisoning. I'll bide my time. I should have realized this would force his hand, that he'd feel he had to act because of what happened yesterday at the Council. This is the way he works – nothing out in the open. I should have been more vigilant. It's my fault Breanna's dead. I should never have given her that wine."

"You didn't know."

He frowned. "That's no excuse. A king should know. I failed her."

My voice trembled. "You failed her only because you don't think the same way Cadwy does. Because you didn't suspect him of doing something you would never do."

He raised his eyebrows at me. "Wouldn't I?"

I stared at him, shocked. Would he do the same? Had he already tried it? What did he mean?

He gave himself a little shake. "We came to say goodbye to my father. Nothing can help Breanna now. Come." He held his hand out.

I hesitated. The lines had somehow smoothed themselves out of Breanna's old, tired face like the wrinkles from an ironed shirt. She looked different. Hollow, just an empty shell. She was the second person I'd seen die. How many more would there be?

I put my hand in Arthur's and let him lead me through the doors into his father's noisome bedchamber.

⟫⟨⟨

THE FUNERAL SERVICE seemed to take forever. I couldn't stop thinking about Breanna's body lying on the bench in the antechamber. The image of her empty face wouldn't go away. We were burying one person, but another lay dead, and one of the mourners was her murderer.

The press of people was immense. A chill wind blew through the city, but it looked as though the entire population had turned out for the interment of their king. A sea of faces pressed in on us as we passed by, following the cortege that bore Uthyr's bier. The stink of putrefaction hung over everything. No one could do anything to dispel it, even though the young boys walking beside the bier carried burning incense. Maybe everyone was used to the stench of death.

The burial ground lay outside the city gates. That was where the Romans had buried their dead, and the custom had continued. Stone tombs and grave markers lined the paved road, some ornately splendid, many just small, inscribed stones. Uthyr's tomb was the biggest and the newest – the size of a small house. In the front, four white marble pillars supported a portico carved with battle scenes. The solid oak door stood wide open, gaping on the darkness within.

Archbishop Dubricius led the procession, walking ahead of the stinking bier. Following behind, Cadwy, as the oldest son, took precedence over Arthur. The cloaked and hooded figure of Cadwy's wife walked behind him, the wife he would have put aside so willingly for me. And I followed my husband. Behind us came a line of chanting monks. A long column of dignitaries, including the visiting kings, trailed in their wake.

At the tomb, we halted, and Dubricius, carrying his incense, climbed the three steps to the portico. In front of the door, he swung his censer three times, then turned toward the bier, on which rested the wrapped and rapidly decomposing remains of the king. Silence fell. Dubricius cleared his throat.

"Lord Jesus Christ, by your death you hallow the graves of all those who believe in you. You have made the grave a sign that promises resurrection as it claims our mortal bodies. Grant our brother, Uthyr Pendragon, peaceful sleep until You awaken him to glory, for You are the resurrection and the life. He will sit at the right hand of God in Your holy kingdom and know the splendor of God, for You live and reign for ever and ever."

I was struck by how very much like the modern funeral service it was, having not long ago been to my father's. But presumably this was in Latin. I couldn't tell the difference, as the ring had bestowed understanding of both Celtic and Latin.

A mumbled refrain of "Amen" rose from the assembled mourners.

Dubricius nodded to the six grizzled warriors who carried the bier.

Arthur and I stepped to one side. I took the opportunity to put myself between the brothers as the bier moved to the doors of the tomb.

Dubricius swung his censer three times more.

"In sure and certain hope of the resurrection to eternal life promised through our Lord Jesus Christ, we commend to Almighty God our brother, Uthyr Pendragon, and we commit his body to its resting place here: earth to earth, ashes to ashes, dust to dust. May the Lord bless him and keep him, the Lord make his face to shine upon him and give him the peace of everlasting rest."

"Amen." Arthur's voice rose loud and clear above the hushed murmur. I glanced up. He was watching Cadwy, and Cadwy was watching him. Cadwy's wife, her hood pulled well forward, was praying.

One by one the assembled kings stepped forward to pay their respects, going on one knee to honor him as High King, and then retreating into the mass that filled the narrow roadway. Finally, Cadwy and Arthur stepped forward together and, side by side, went down on their knees on the steps of the tomb.

As the brothers knelt, the bearers carried the bier with its shrouded body into the tomb and Dubricius followed them in. The bitter wind soughed in the branches of the nearby trees, and the murmur of five thousand people's breathing and shuffling filled the air.

Only I was close enough to hear what Arthur said to Cadwy as they knelt there waiting for their Archbishop to emerge.

"Thank you for the kind gift of the wine, brother." Arthur kept his voice low.

Cadwy bristled like a porcupine. "I need not ask if you enjoyed it," he hissed back.

"You'll need to try harder than that."

"I was not even trying. It was too good a chance to miss."

"And miss you did. Your aim, as ever, was poor. There's a body in my father's chambers – no, your chambers now – that you'll need to take care of."

Cadwy's look of surprise was genuine. "A body?"

Arthur gave a nearly imperceptible nod. "A certain old woman. She was tired and melancholy. She drank the wine you meant for me."

"Not Breanna!" Cadwy's voice rose, and several people turned their heads to look at him.

"Yes. Breanna." Arthur kept his voice low. "Harmless Mother Breanna. But she was old and of little use, wasn't she? Her master's death had addled her brains. What does her loss matter to King Cadwy? What was she worth to her king?" There was contempt in every word. Cadwy quivered with suppressed fury.

Two and two came together for me. Arthur had called Breanna mother and yet she hadn't been. Could she, like Cottia, have been his nurse? And if so, could she have been Cadwy's as well? A woman as close to the children in her care as their mother would have been.

"You made her drink the wine on purpose." Cadwy hissed.

Arthur shook his head. "You put the wine in her hands when you brought it to our father's rooms. The best wine. Fit for a king. Did you not expect her to try some for herself? An old woman who had been a slave all her life."

His twisting of the truth impressed me. In his place I'd have done the same. No one needed to know he'd given Breanna the wine, least of all his murderous older brother.

By his sides, Cadwy's fists clenched until the knuckles whitened. Clearly he was fighting to control his emotions. Could he have loved her too? It's all too easy to demonize someone and deprive them of all the emotions that by rights are theirs. I was guilty of doing that to Cadwy. I didn't like him; he'd tried to murder both me and Arthur by stealth, so in my head he'd been incapable of human feelings. Now, I saw that he wasn't quite the ogre I'd made him out to be. Tears glistened in the corners of his eyes.

Dubricius emerged from the dark doorway of the tomb, the bearers filing out behind him. The oak doors closed. Uthyr Pendragon had been committed to his final resting place.

⇶⇷

WE WERE TO leave the following day to get back to Dumnonia before the worst of winter fell upon us. We'd been lucky so far, but the weather wasn't going to stay like this. Arthur saw old Breanna interred with due respect in a little cemetery outside the city walls reserved for slaves, close to where her lord and master lay at rest. Cei went with him because it turned out she'd also cared for him as a small boy. Neither of them told Cadwy.

The next morning at first light, a hammering shook the door of our bedchamber in the Domus Albus. Arthur was already dressing, but it seemed someone had been up before him that morning.

Picking up his sword, Arthur threw open the door, and Cei came striding in, already in his travelling clothes of mail shirt and leather braccae, his helmet tucked underneath his arm.

Arthur put down his sword.

Cei briefly glanced at it. "You need to come and see this."

I was still in bed, the furs drawn up to cover my nakedness, but Arthur had been lacing up his braccae. He'd gone barefoot to answer the urgent pounding.

"Give me a moment. What's so important? What's happened?"

Cei handed Arthur his undershirt from the floor where he'd discarded it the night before. "There's something strange in the old forum. You need to come and see."

Arthur pulled his shirt over his head. "All right. I'm coming. Go and ask Theodoric to come too. I won't be long."

Cei disappeared, and I got up. Arthur turned back, and his eyes took in my naked body. I sensed his eagerness to discover what was in the forum fighting with his desire for me. Good. I wanted him to want me. It fed my desire for connection with another human being. I, too, wanted the closeness sex brought. With him in particular. The belonging. I'd wanted it last night and now I wanted it again. I could see he did too. Against all my instincts, I was beginning to like him a lot.

Temptation lured him, and he crossed the room and put his hands about my waist.

"I need to go."

I buried my hands in his hair.

"I know." The smell of him was intoxicating. My body's instincts prevailed. I leaned forward, pressing myself against him. His arousal pushed hard against my belly. My hand slid down and held him. He gave a little groan of desperation.

"I can't." He released me and stepped back. "Help me with my armor, will you?"

I wasn't going to win this one. "Can I come with you?"

He nodded.

I helped him with his armor and then dressed in my travelling clothes of braccae, tunic and heavy cloak, tying my long hair back in a thick braid.

Outside in the misty, late autumnal morning, we found Cei and Theodoric waiting for us with most of Arthur's original men. Added to their number were faces I recognized from the Council chamber and others I'd never seen before. It looked as though our ranks had swollen considerably.

We marched on foot through the narrow streets until we came to the forum. Long before we arrived, we heard the roar of a crowd up ahead of us.

Though still early morning, the forum was packed. The city had risen at dawn, it seemed, and made the discovery straight away. The crowd of onlookers parted to let us pass, and Arthur and Cei led the way into the center of the marketplace. Already the smell of cooking filled the air, and, having gone without breakfast, my empty stomach grumbled.

The onlookers had left a clear space, holding themselves back a good ten paces from what stood there. And as we came out of the throng of people, I saw straight away what had fired up Cei.

A sizeable rock had appeared in the center of the forum. It must have weighed several tons. Out of the top of the boulder protruded part of the blade and hilt of a sword. And it was there because of what I'd told Merlin about the sword in the stone legend.

A group of men already clustered round the stone, and as we watched, one of them seized the hilt and tried to pull it out. Of course, the sword didn't budge. One of his fellows elbowed him out of the way and tried his luck with the same result. That sword was going nowhere.

Arthur had no idea what was going on. The only expression on his face was one of puzzled surprise.

"See what I mean?" Cei said with an air of triumph. "I told you something strange had happened."

"Where did it come from?" Theodoric asked as a third man wrestled with the sword to no avail. "How can something like that have appeared overnight?"

"Exactly." Cei looked pleased to be vindicated. "No one knows."

I looked round at the crowd. They weren't just the local inhabitants; all the kings and their followers seemed to have gathered there, too. In fact, bold young King Cynfelin of Cynwidion, his dark auburn tail of hair swinging with the effort, was now trying to draw the sword out of the stone. I could have told him not to bother.

His muscles bulged, the tendons in his neck stood out and his face went from red to purple, but nothing happened. Of course. Only one man would ever be able to pull that sword out.

Cynfelin released his hold on the sword and stood back, panting. "It's no use. The cursed thing won't budge. If magic put it here, then magic will be needed to pull it out, whatever it says on the stone."

There was writing?

Masgwid the Lame's five sons pushed forward for a chance to try their strength. Someone in the crowd shouted. "What does the inscription say? Read it out, can you?"

Llaenog, the oldest son, his hand already on the hilt, bent down to read, then straightened up, his hand still on the sword, keeping his brothers at bay. "'*When the time is right, he who draws this sword from this stone shall be the true born High King of all Britain'.*" He gave a shrug, "I might as well try my hand. It could be mine as much as anyone's." He bent and set his back to it, heaving as hard as he could, but again, nothing happened apart from him looking as though he might have a heart attack.

Arthur looked at Cei. One thing about my husband – he was quick on the uptake. "'*When the time is right*'," he quoted. "So not now. Futile to try to draw this sword from its stone before the time is right. The Council has just voted to institute the title of Dux – so why would we want or need a High King now?"

He was right. I saw it clearly. And I knew who'd put that stone there. Merlin, of course. He'd stolen my telling of the modern legend and created history. Was this how it came to be a legend in my time? Because I'd made it happen? Had I just changed something, my butterfly wings of knowledge molding the course of history?

The crowd filling the road to the Imperial Palace parted, and Cadwy, flanked by the Palace Guard, arrived, Morgana accompanying him. She wore a flowing, creamy white gown, adorned only with a chain of heavy gold links about her slender waist, and a white cloak lined with pale fur. Cadwy didn't hesitate but strode up to the stone, Morgana following close behind. The men around it stepped back respectfully – this was his city, after all. He walked around the stone, examining it. Morgana stood still and scrutinized the inscription for several minutes.

Cadwy stopped, his bulk making her look delicate as a flower.

"Well?" he said to her, his voice deep and gruff and full of irritation. He was a man who didn't like things he couldn't understand, that was clear.

The crowd had fallen silent, watching their king, watching his sister.

She ignored everyone but him. "Strong magic brought this stone here," she said, her clear voice carrying across the crowded forum. "I feel it in my bones." She reached a slender, white hand to touch the hilt with her outstretched fingertips. With a start she snatched her hand back as though the sword had bitten her, a momentary look of fear on her lovely face.

"What is it? What's wrong?" Cadwy's face mirrored hers.

"Some force protects it," she managed, her face paling even further. "Whoever set this here has spun spells all about it in a defensive web. I cannot touch it. It knows me."

Cadwy looked from her to the sword in the stone, then back again. "Can I touch it? Does it know me?"

She shook her head. "It knows you not. The protection is against other practitioners of magic. I cannot see beyond the outer trappings of this strange stone, nor see who set it here."

Cadwy put out a big square hand and laid it on the hilt of the sword. He hesitated a moment, as though unsure whether she was right, but no jarring shock came, so he closed his fingers tightly round it.

"This sword is meant for me," he said, over loudly. "My father was High King before me, and I shall be the next High King. This sword will prove it." He gave an enormous heave.

Big mistake. The sword didn't budge. He pulled harder.

He was a big and very strong man, possibly the strongest there. The sword remained planted firmly in the stone. And now everyone had seen that he couldn't draw it out – all his fellow kings and all his own people. Everyone knew he was not meant to be High King.

Archbishop Dubricius stepped forward. "This is a heathen object," he cried. "Tear it down."

Morgana rounded on him. "Silence, priest," she snapped. "These are forces you know nothing about. And you could not destroy sword or stone even if you tried. Didn't you hear what I said? It is protected."

I looked over my shoulder searching for Merlin. Surely this was his work. And if so, why wasn't he here to see the effect it was having? But there was no sign of him.

A well dressed, middle-aged man stepped out of the crowd. "I'm Morfael the weaver, citizen of Viroconium, my lords. I say leave the sword be. The Lady Morgana speaks wisely. Here in the old forum any man may try his hand at pulling it out. When the time is right, when we need a High King, someone will pull it from the stone."

A chorus of agreement buzzed around the watching crowd.

Dubricius blustered. "Only God can decree the next High King, God and the Council. This object is a pagan idol. It must go."

Theodoric bent his head to Arthur's ear. "Why don't you try? You have as much right as any man. More than most."

Arthur shook his head. "Not now. I'm no Cadwy to make a fool of myself. Look at him. He's belittled himself in the eyes of his people, whatever Dubricius may say. They've seen him fail. His quest to become High King is over. When the time is right, I'll know, and come back here and draw that sword from the stone. The sword is marked for me."

And he turned on his heel and led us all out of the old forum and back to our horses at the Domus Albus. While the rest of Viroconium was still busy trying their hand at the impossible, we were riding out of the eastern gate, onto the road toward Din Cadan.

# Chapter Twenty-Two

A S THERE WAS less urgency about our return journey to Din Cadan, we took our time. Each day we rode only thirty miles, which, after the headlong rush north to reach Uthyr's deathbed, seemed easy stages. Euddolen and his family, whose safety had been promised by Cadwy, along with Morgawse and her baby, rode with us for the first ten miles in a heavy ox-drawn wagon until we reached their country estate.

Morgawse seemed to have taken to me.

"I wish you didn't have to go back to Dumnonia," she said, as we stood together in the outer courtyard of Euddolen's villa, under a leaden sky. I felt awkward, because I didn't feel the same way about her. The baby being held by Cutha, the midwife, might have been the reason for that.

"You saved my baby's life," Morgawse said, throwing herself into my arms and clinging on with the strength of a limpet.

I prised myself free of her, and she flung herself at Arthur. "Send Theo back as soon as you can," she gushed. "I need him more than you do."

Theodoric received her next enveloping hug. Tears streamed down her cheeks. "Come back soon."

It was an emotional farewell, on her part, at least. We remounted our horses, and with much waving from Morgawse, and Albina and Cloelia as well, rode out of the villa courtyard and onto the road south.

The end of the first day brought us back to the hostelry at Caer Luit Coyt, and on the second, we progressed to another small town, Alauna. The hostelry there was smaller, and, as the inhabitants found it hard to house all our warriors and horses, they were glad to see us on our way the next morning.

At the end of the third day, we stopped at a villa near the ruins of Corinium, then headed south toward Caer Baddan and the dubious hospitality of Bassus for the next night.

The weather deteriorated to depressing rain that soaked through to our very bones and made riding uncomfortable. But the five days on the road to Din Cadan allowed me to get to know Arthur better, in person instead of just in bed.

Due to my new status, Merlin no longer flanked me, and I took pride of place at the head of the column, riding side by side with my husband. He'd shrugged off his serious demeanor like an unwanted cloak. Instead, he seemed light-hearted and buoyant, even on the most miserable of days, and realization dawned on me that he was probably no older than I was.

He was an informative and interesting companion. Once he discovered I knew next to nothing about the surrounding countryside, he took great pleasure in telling me about it. An abridged version, I guessed, composed specially to entertain me, making even the longest day seem short. And the more time I spent with him, the more I liked him.

Loved him?

Did I? Could it really be love, or was he my safety net? A very personable and charming one, but a safety net, nevertheless. I couldn't tell. If I still loved Nathan, how could I be in love with someone else? But Arthur made me laugh. He made me happy. He made me feel safe – this last being the most important to me, a stranger in a strange land. Craving the security he could give me, maybe I was guilty of mistaking that for love. But whatever it was, it felt good.

On the last day of our journey, with the sun breaking through the heavy cloud cover, the bitter wind finally died. As we left the Fosse Way to ride toward Din Cadan, I realized with a start that I would be sad when this journey ended. I no longer looked on Din Cadan as the only haven of safety. Arthur had taken its place, and when I was with him, I felt safe. But at Din Cadan, his kingly duties would separate us, leaving me alone and vulnerable again.

What bothered me the most was the fear that he might not feel the same. I couldn't forget that goodbye kiss he'd given Tangwyn, or the loving way he'd held little Llacheu in his arms. I liked the little boy, but he and his mother were now my rivals. Which made me wonder if Arthur could ever love me in the way I wanted. He obviously desired me. In fact, he desired me every night, and I desired him. But desire wasn't the same as love. As unsure as my own feelings were, I was doubly unsure about his.

The drizzle had cleared a couple of miles back, and the plain before us, scattered with its myriad of little farmsteads, lay grey in the late afternoon light. Smoke rose from every chimney to hang pungent in the cold air, and here and there herdsmen were driving their animals home from pasture, to pen them safely up for the night. The threat of wolves wasn't just an idle one. The evening we'd ridden into Alauna, I'd heard them howling in the distance. As a big party of mounted horsemen, we were safe, but flocks of sheep or goats, and herds of cattle were not.

Din Cadan's bulk rose from the plain before us, and behind it the hills rolled away into the mist. Our road wound between the fields and began its climb to the summit.

"Are you glad to be back?" I asked Arthur as we rode abreast on the narrow road, his warriors strung out behind us, the last of them still at the foot of the hill.

He smiled. "What do you think? I left them as a prince, here by my father's grace, and I return as their king. This is all mine now. I've the freedom to do as I choose."

But what would he choose?

I twisted in my saddle, but the hump of Glastonbury Tor was invisible. Instead, I looked up at the gates coming into view as we neared the summit. This was where I'd longed to get back to when we'd been on our way to Viroconium, but now, who knew?

The gates swung open to shouts of welcome from the guardsmen on the walls, and we rode underneath the gatehouse and into the fortress.

Despite the cold and the lateness of the day, every inhabitant had come out to welcome us home. We rode up the cobbled road to the Great Hall amidst a crowd of men and women, their children nearly getting under the feet of our horses. At the stables, we dismounted, and there followed a confused period where the warriors found accommodation for all the new animals. I think I'd expected Arthur, as a king now, to have a groom to look after his horse, but he knuckled down and cared for it himself. Which meant his queen had to, as well.

Not that it bothered me; my horse had carried me a good three hundred miles, and I'd grown fond of him. I took my time rubbing the sweat from his body, covering him with his makeshift rug and making sure he had a good portion of grain and hay, and a leather bucket of water. I was in no hurry to face the Great Hall as its new queen. The knot of nerves that resided in my stomach was only growing tighter.

Arthur eventually came to find me.

"What're you doing? He's fine now. Leave him to eat in peace."

I looked up from where I'd been squatting, brushing the mud from my horse's shaggy fetlocks. "He needs to be clean, or he might get mud fever."

He reached a hand down and took me by the wrist, pulling me upright, laughing. "Enough's enough. You can come out here and brush him again in the morning when the mud's dry, but right now we have to go and celebrate with my people."

He gave me a tug, but I resisted, stubbornly.

"What's wrong?" His voice softened. Did he guess the turmoil in my heart?

I shrugged. "Nothing. I'm – I'm just a bit nervous." My feet became suddenly very interesting.

Putting a hand under my chin, he raised my face to his. "What about? This is my home. And now it's yours. I am its king, and you, its queen. There's nothing to be afraid of."

How could I expect him to understand? My lower lip trembled, much to my annoyance. "Suppose they don't like me?"

It was already gloomy in the stables. He was only a silhouette against the open doors. "How could they not? I..." He paused for a long second. "I like you."

My breath caught.

He went on, a little hastily. "But it isn't for my people to decide if they like you or not. You are their queen, and they have no say in the matter. Of course they will."

"You think so?"

He drew me into his embrace, holding me close against his rough mail shirt. One hand caressed my face. I wanted to melt into him. "They will," he said. "Have no fear. You're beautiful, and you're the long-awaited Lady of the Ring."

I looked up at him. "But you don't believe in prophecies."

I felt him smile even though his face was hidden by the gloom.

"I may not," he said, "but they certainly do. The story of how I've become both king of Dumnonia and Dux Britanniarum will be round the whole fortress by now. You're their lucky charm."

He bent his head and kissed my lips. My mouth opened under his, and I clung to him, wanting that embrace to go on forever. But after a moment, he gently released me. "Come, let's get you out of these travel clothes. You're not fit to be seen as a queen when you're dressed as a boy. Inside."

I let him lead me into the Great Hall. Torches burned in brackets on the pillars, and in the hearth, a fire glowed beneath the carcass of a roasting deer. The feeling of never having been away was strong.

We went through the door into Arthur's bedchamber. Our saddle bags lay on the end of the bed. Someone had spread out a beautiful dress of deep red.

I hesitated. "I can't put that on. I'm dirty." The bath house at the villa was two long days of riding behind me. I wanted to wash my hair, as my scalp had begun to itch.

"Let's bathe," he said firmly, gathering up our clean clothes. "Come on."

Steam filled the bath house. But instead of going to the women's side, Arthur led me to his side, and we went in together, hand in hand. A male slave waited there with an array of small, exquisitely made bottles. After the man had helped him take off his mail shirt, Arthur dismissed him with a wave of his hand.

The big wooden bath in the center of the room brimmed with temptingly hot water scented with lavender. With no need for an invitation I slithered out of my travel-stained clothes and stepped into the water. A moment later, Arthur got in with me and sat down at the opposite end, sinking in up to his neck. I reached round and undid my plait, letting my hair float across the surface. Then, holding my breath, I ducked under for a moment and came up gasping.

Arthur laughed at my wet face, and did the same, emerging with his dark hair plastered to his head. His face sobered for a moment. "Come here."

I went to him, the water sloshing over the edge of the enormous bathtub. I slipped into his arms, and he bent his head and kissed me hard. I kissed him back, my body responding as fast as his. A long moment passed where neither of us came up for air. I was jubilant. He was home in Din Cadan, the offer of Tangwyn there between us, but he'd chosen me. I wriggled round until I straddled him, head, shoulders and naked breasts above the water. His mouth found a nipple as I slid down onto him, and he groaned with pleasure.

We splashed a great deal of water out of that bath between us. It was a good thing it was so big because it gave us ample room to maneuver, which we took full advantage of. And then we washed each other. He massaged the contents of one of the glass bottles into my hair – soapwort, he told me – and I did the same to his, then we rinsed it off, ducking beneath the water together and coming up laughing.

Finally, with the water cooling, we emerged slick and wet and feeling cleaner than either of us had been for days. And then we slowly dressed one another.

Hand in hand, we walked back to the Great Hall through the gathering darkness and a fine rain. Inside, servants were preparing the tables, with bread already laid out on wooden boards and the smell of roasting meat heavy in the air. My stomach rumbled with hunger. Who'd have thought taking a bath could work up such an appetite?

This was the first meal at Din Cadan that I actually enjoyed. Yes, I'd liked the food before, but underlying everything had been the nagging feeling of not belonging, of being a cuckoo in their nest. As Arthur and I took our places at the table on the dais, I realized with a start that the constant knot in my stomach had vanished at last. Even Tangwyn, sitting on one of the benches near the door and spending much of the evening staring at me, couldn't make it return. Fresh from our lovemaking, the feel of Arthur's hands and mouth on me still, I felt she was no threat at all.

Dish after dish was served, first to us, then to the crowded tables – tables seating men I now knew. Not all of them, but dotted amongst the faces of strangers were the familiar ones of the men who'd accompanied us to Viroconium. I didn't know all their names, but their presence made me feel at home, as though I finally belonged here.

Then came the entertainment. The fat little man I remembered from before came tumbling in, head over heels, to land on his feet in front of the dais. His capering brought gales of laughter from his audience. Even I, with my twenty-first-century sense of humor and political correctness, found him quite funny.

A singer with a lyre followed. He sang a jolly song about three brothers in a brothel. Everyone joined in the chorus. It went on for a long time, each verse bawdier than the last. Several young men jumped up and accompanied it with increasingly explicit actions. The audience greeted its end with shouts of "Another verse!" but he retired from the floor to pick up a thirst-quenching flagon of ale.

Three jugglers came next, but we were nearing the end of the meal by then. I'd eaten well and drunk rather too many goblets of wine, and felt too sleepy and content to pay them much attention.

One of the warriors who'd ridden with us to Viroconium raised his voice above the general hubbub of eating and talking. "Gwalchmei!"

Immediately more voices joined in. "Gwalchmei!"

"A tune!"

"Gwalchmei!"

With a show of reluctance, Gwalchmei got to his feet halfway down one of the long tables, and climbed over the bench to stand in the aisle.

"I don't have my flute," he protested, as several of his neighbors gave him a shove toward the dais.

"Give us a song, then," Theodoric boomed. "Sing us the song about the last giant."

Gwalchmei squared his narrow shoulders.

He had a pure, sweet voice, unusually high for a man. Everyone in the hall fell silent under its spell.

*Over rivers deep and mountains old,*
*With feet that roam and eyes that seek.*
*Through snowy pass and shadowed vale*

*Comes the last giant of them all, Gwawl. Mighty Gwawl.*

At the end of each verse everyone in the Hall joined in with the final mournful refrain, their hushed voices echoing to the rafters.

*He leaves behind the silent halls*
*Where ne'er a voice will sound again*
*With footsteps echoing in the gloom*
*He follows the road of ages past, Gwawl. Mighty Gwawl.*

*Long, have his people ruled the north*
*Long, have their wide halls rung with song*
*Long, have they watched the ice giants' gate*
*But now they're gone, leaving only one, Gwawl. Mighty Gwawl.*

*The valleys echo to his mournful cries,*
*And his voice ascends the towering peaks*
*To the arch of the sky where the eagles call*
*But there's none to hear, the voice of Gwawl. Mighty Gwawl.*

As he sang, I thought of my own predicament. My own people were yet to be born. Stuck here, I would live and die and be long buried before Nathan became even a twinkle in his parents' eyes. A great chasm gaped between me and my world, just as it had for the poor giant, driven away by the people who'd invaded his country.

*Through ancient forest tracks he roams,*
*Past lake, and hill, and white flanked fort*
*Rivers and roads lead him ever on*
*Toward the place where his people are gone, Gwawl. Mighty Gwawl.*

*But the people he finds are not his own,*
*He's strayed too far from the lands of his birth,*
*It's stones and spears and shouts that are his*

*As all alone he wanders on, Gwawl. The Mighty Gwawl.*

*At last his gaze rests on new mountains tall*
*Whose ice-capped peaks reach to the sky.*
*On tired feet he hastens toward his goal*
*Surely the giants will welcome him here, Gwawl. Mighty Gwawl.*

*But the mountains offer no giant's call*
*Only cold silence echoes from peak to peak*
*And deep in the valleys he wanders alone*
*While high on the crags he cries for his home, Gwawl. Mighty Gwawl.*

Gwalchmei's song sobered me. Fueled by alcohol, I'd been in danger of allowing this world to swallow me, but who was I fooling? Only myself. No matter how I might try, I didn't belong here any more than the giant who'd faded away in the savage mountains.

*Many a day and many a day*
*The last giant calls to an empty sky*
*Many a day and many a day*
*For no giants answer the lonely cry, of Gwawl. Might Gwawl.*

*Down in the lowlands they hear his voice,*
*The farmers and wives who drove him away.*
*The voice of the storm, the voice of the wind*
*And they bar their doors to keep him at bay, Gwawl. Mighty Gwawl.*

*Alone in the mountains, alone and sad*
*The last giant falters and falls to his knees*
*Then stretches himself on the top of the crag*
*And lays down his head in his final sleep, Gwawl. Mighty Gwawl.*

I looked sideways at Arthur, who was listening intently still, on his face a look of rapt concentration. I'd been wrong. For a few short hours it had felt like I belonged, but I didn't. How could I? How could a woman from the twenty-first century ever belong in the fifth? How could my feelings for Arthur be real? It was all an illusion. Nathan was where I belonged. Nathan, waiting for me, grieving, his entire world turned upside down by my disappearance. For the first time since we'd left Viroconium, Nathan's face became clear in my head, sharp and real. Dodging it was impossible now – I had to get back to Glastonbury and find the way back to my world. So why was my heart aching?

*Down in the lowlands they hear his voice die*
*And slowly they walk up the valley to see*
*Why the storm's passed, the wreckage, the cause –*
*The hump of the body on top of the crag, Gwawl. Mighty Gwawl.*

*Great rocks they bring to the top of the crag*
*Small rocks to cover the dead giant's face*
*Dark rocks to build a great cairn over him*
*The last of the giants from the frozen north, Gwawl. Mighty Gwawl.*

*The last giant's grave still stands wide and long,*
*Lying alone on the steep rocky crag*
*The wind that still whistles down through the pass*
*Is the song that now lulls the sleep, of Gwawl. Mighty Gwawl.*

A cheer went up as Gwalchmei's song came to a close. He did a solemn bow, first to Arthur and me, and then to the room. I joined in the applause, but my sore heart was no longer in it.

I left the Hall before Arthur, and with Maia's help, undressed and climbed into bed. I'd hoped to be genuinely asleep when Arthur arrived, but sleep wouldn't come, only tears, and when I heard the door open and his quiet footsteps approach, I closed my eyes tightly and tried to slow my breathing.

I felt him sit on the end of the bed and heard him grunt as he pulled off his boots. They thudded onto the floor, followed by his belt and then his tunic and shirt. In bare feet, he padded to the table where Maia had left a bowl of water, tepid when I'd had it but surely cold now, and I heard him throw water on his face. I knew what came next – cleaning his teeth with a frayed twig and powdered charcoal mixed with dried mint leaves, spitting the black residue and then rinsing and spitting again.

He came back to the bed, and removed his braccae, unlacing the ties that held them up and stepping out of them. Then came the sound of him blowing out the oil lamp. Naked, he slid into bed. Strong arms encircled me, and his body curled around mine. It was impossible not to like the sensation as his hands explored my breasts and his mouth nuzzled my neck. Only a heart of stone could have withstood that, and I was just a weak woman with an aching heart I didn't understand. I rolled over and succumbed to temptation.

# Chapter Twenty-Three

I T WAS SEVERAL weeks before I had the opportunity to carry out my plan of escape, weeks in which I struggled with the growing bond between Arthur and myself. Back in his own kingdom, he continued to surprise me. Most mornings he held a meeting in the Great Hall to discuss the affairs of his kingdom with his captains, to which any of his subjects could come. Once a week, he held a court where people presented grievances for his judgement, and he tried anyone who'd committed a crime. Justice was administered. I was impressed.

The extra warriors who'd accompanied us from Viroconium, and those who kept arriving in twos and threes from the other kingdoms, slept mostly in the Great Hall. Once the tables had been cleared away in the evenings, they laid out their bed rolls on top of the reeds. The ever-blazing hearth fire made it a warm and cozy, if pretty smelly, place to sleep as Christmas approached. I was getting used to the smells.

I now understood more about the workings of the fortress. The whole place buzzed with an industry that I hadn't taken in at first. Potters churned out day-to-day utensils, although Cei had the finer ware for the Great Hall imported from the Mediterranean. Metalworking shops clustered together near the stables – some forging weapons, others tools for farming. Woodworkers pedaled lathes to turn bowls and table legs, or produced spear shafts, shields and ploughs. Women busied themselves with weaving, and making or repairing clothes, or cooking. At this time of year, men, women and children alike winnowed wheat every day, in preparation for taking it to the mill at the foot of the hill. Leatherworkers constantly labored over new saddlery and the mending of broken tack. Armorers hammered ring mail shirts, helmets and gloves. And each day the livestock had to be cared for.

The fortress ran like a well-oiled wheel, and in those weeks, I became a part of it. Cottia took me under her wing, although criticism lurked never far from the surface because I had her precious Arthur's attention so much of the time.

As far as I could tell, Arthur went nowhere near Tangwyn in those weeks. He slept with me every night, and during the day, when he wasn't busy running his kingdom, he took time to be with me. I liked to think it was out of choice. On fine days, we rode out together, winding our way down the paved road to the farmsteads and then branching out into the forest or across the open plain. Sometimes Cei or Theodoric or Bedwyr came with us, or a larger party made up of Arthur's warriors. Merlin accompanied us every time. It was as if he didn't trust me when we were outside the walls of the fortress.

Then one day, the opportunity at last arose for Arthur and me to ride out alone.

Mid-morning came, and the business of ruling the kingdom had been quickly accomplished. The only plaintiff had been a gaunt middle-aged woman named Mabina.

"Me 'usband upped and left me fer a slip of a girl, an' now 'e's gone an' set up an 'ousehold with 'er, leavin' me on me tod wi' three girls to get married off, and no man ter 'elp me," she began, and then continued to ramble on at length about every perceived fault he possessed.

The husband, Einion, a stocky, grizzle-bearded farmer, on the other hand had been terse. "She be a right scold. Couldn't live with 'er a day longer. An 'er girls takes after their mother."

Arthur's judgement had been swift.

"A wife should never be a scold," he said, after careful consideration of the facts and the surly countenances of the two opponents.
"But a husband is responsible for her upkeep for the whole of her life."
He fixed the husband with a hard stare. "You will work four days on
the property you share with your new woman, and two for your
lawful wife, who needs you less as she has her three unmarried
daughters to work the fields with her."

Mabina opened her scantily toothed mouth to protest, but Arthur
held up his hand to silence her. "And it is the duty of a husband to
provide dowries for his daughters and see them well married. From
the flocks Einion has taken to his new farmstead, I allocate four
breeding ewes to each daughter, to be handed over on their wedding
days."

It was Einion's turn to look aggrieved – twelve sheep would seriously diminish his flock. He opened his mouth, but Arthur silenced
him with a look.

Reluctantly the two plaintiffs bowed before their king and one of
Arthur's warriors escorted them from the Great Hall. No one else
seemed to be awaiting audience with the king.

We got to our feet. Outside the Hall the weather was fine, and I
was itching to be astride my horse and away from the fortress's
confines.

In our chamber, Arthur tossed his crown onto our bed while I
changed swiftly into braccae and a tunic that had been Arthur's as a
boy, pulling on the new calf-length boots he'd had Elfydd, the cobbler,
make for me. My walking boots stood forgotten underneath the bed,
cast off remnants of the twenty-first century. Feeling like a pair of
truant schoolboys, we walked down the slope to the stables where a
servant had our horses ready.

Seeing there were only two horses, I turned to Arthur with a question on my lips.

He forestalled me. "Just us today. Merlin's engaged with teaching the boys. Theo and Cei are organizing the warrior training. And it's too nice a day to miss out on a ride."

My heart gave a nervous bound. "Shouldn't you be helping with the warrior training?" There'd been days when we'd not ridden out at all because he'd been too busy training his new recruits himself.

He flashed a wicked grin. "I'm king. Delegation is one of the perks. And I feel like a ride with you today, not setting myself up for all those would-be warriors to knock lumps out of me with a wooden practice sword."

He gave me a leg up into the saddle, and I settled into my place, hardly able to believe that at last I was free of Merlin and might be able to persuade Arthur to take me to the Tor.

We jogged side by side down the cobbled road to the smaller north-eastern gates. Two guards swung them open for us.

With a wave to the two men, we passed through the north-eastern gatehouse and started down the hill. Small clouds scudded across a pale blue sky, and a red kite rode the wind above our heads. Below us, the plain stretched away into the distance, patchworked with small fields and farmsteads nestled between tracts of forest and rough grazing. It was clear enough to see the distant hump that was the Tor.

I pointed. "Could we ride that way? I'd like to see Ynys Witrin." With an effort, I kept my voice relaxed and natural.

I held my breath. Would Merlin have warned Arthur not to take me anywhere near it?

He smiled, seemingly unaware of the implications of what he was agreeing to. "If you want. The track goes through the forest, and it'll be a long and muddy ride at this time of year, but we can go that way."

There. It was done. I was on my way back to Glastonbury at last. My heart, which I'd expected to soar, sank down into my new boots. The familiar knot tied my stomach up like a piece of crochet.

As the crow flies, it was a good ten miles from South Cadbury to

Glastonbury, farther by the winding back roads of modern Britain, but still not much longer than half an hour in a car, tops. Arthur and I, on horseback, took nearer two hours than one.

We didn't take the route I'd ridden with Corwyn and the lay brothers from the abbey all those weeks ago. Instead, we branched westwards, skirting the edge of the marshes until we came out of the trees into a wide clearing beside open water. We were on the edge of a lake, the far bank just a hazy line of trees. At the water's edge a plank causeway led out to an artificial island – a village built on stilts above the lake. A frill of small, flat boats decorated the island, tethered by their noses and shifting on the current. Scattered between the forest edge and the shore lay a jumble of animal pens and barns. The men working there paused to look up at us in curiosity.

Arthur swung himself down out of the saddle. "Our horses can go no farther. We'll have to leave them here and cross by boat from the village."

Some of the workmen hurried forward. "Milord Arthur, welcome to our village."

I slid to the ground, and a big, bald man took my horse's reins. "Milady Guinevere." He bowed almost to his knees.

"Thank you." The words came naturally to my lips despite six weeks of servants running round after me. I still couldn't quite get used to the deference they accorded me.

A few women came out of the sheds and stood whispering amongst themselves. I smiled at them in as friendly a way as possible, but they were shy, and backed away. I was a queen, after all.

A small, wiry man hurried up, pulling off his leather cap and bobbing up and down in his effort to be respectful. "Milord, milady, welcome to our 'umble village. What can we do for ye? We've food and cider if ye're 'ungry. We 'ave fodder for yer 'orses." He waved at the other men, who obediently led our horses toward an open-fronted barn.

Arthur nodded. "Thank you, Nial. Fodder for our horses would be much appreciated. But not for us. The Queen and I would like to go to the Holy Island. She has a fancy to see it for herself."

"Of course, of course. Come this way, milord, milady. 'Tis an honor to see ye here. I'll be 'appy to take ye meself." He ushered us to the start of the timber causeway. It was about twenty yards long and less than two wide, with no handrail. Weather had warped the timbers, so it didn't look like the most fun thing to walk on. I hesitated.

Arthur took my arm. "Come along."

Well, if I wanted to get to Glastonbury, it looked like I would have to brave that wobbly walkway. Presumably, the inhabitants did so every day, maybe even the old and infirm and the small children.

Hanging onto Arthur, I negotiated my way across the dark waters.

The village was constructed on a wide platform that in the center rested on a huge pile of rocks and earth and at the edges on a lot of rickety-looking stilts. The buildings clustered cheek by jowl, narrow walkways running between them, the clutter of the villagers' lives piled everywhere – crayfish pots, nets, tall jars, coils of rope, piles of firewood. A wider path ran straight through to the center, where a small public area was set around a single upright pillar carved like a totem pole. Women sat here in a circle mending fishing nets, while small children played about their feet.

They looked up as we entered with Nial, and there was a general chorus of "milord, milady", though the bone shuttles in their callused fingers never stopped flying through the nets.

Nial led us across the tiny square and down some steps on the far side to where a platform dipped toward the water's edge. Drawn up against a ramshackle landing stage was a long, flat-bottomed boat.

Arthur handed me down into it. There was a plank for a seat, so I sat down. I'd never much liked boats, and this one looked as dilapidated as the island village. Arthur climbed in and sat down beside me, drawing his cloak about him. Then Nial untied the ropes and hopped in at the stern, a long pole in his hand.

"Be like old times, won't it?" our escort said with a lopsided grin.

Arthur nodded. "It's long since I was a boy here, fishing with you."

"A sight too long." Nial pushed us off from the jetty, out into the deeper waters. I hung on tight to my rickety plank seat.

Arthur shifted a little, and the boat rocked. "I'm no longer the boy you knew."

"Kingship be an 'eavy burden to bear. But one I know ye can."

Arthur's hand covered mine reassuringly, as though he sensed my trepidation.

Nial stood at the stern, propelling the boat forwards with his long pole as we skimmed out across the wide waters of what must have been part of a river. He made it look easy, which I'm sure it wasn't. The only comfort I got from his steering was the knowledge that the water couldn't be all that deep or he'd not have been able to reach the bottom with his pole.

Our course took us upstream, against the current, but we made steady progress and gradually the two shores drew together. Little channels broke off to left and right and the bankside trees grew stunted and misshapen. As we passed into the marshes, shreds of mist rose to hang over the water, and a curlew's lonely call broke the silence. The air was damp, and the smell of rotting vegetation strong. The cold seeped into my bones. Like Arthur, I drew my cloak close about me.

Up ahead, the river twisted to the right, and as we rounded the bend, a low wooden landing stage came into view, deserted now but surely our destination. Nial guided the flat-bottomed boat in until it lay up against it. Seizing the bow rope, Arthur leapt out onto the jetty and wrapped it round a wooden stanchion. Nial took the stern rope, and we moored as easily as that.

Arthur held out his hand. "Welcome to Ynys Witrin, the Holy Island."

I took the proffered hand and warily disembarked. It was good to stand on dry land again. Good to be at Glastonbury. And if all went to plan, I wouldn't need to brave that threadbare boat again. The knot which had been slowly untangling itself in my stomach while I concentrated on not being frightened, retied itself with alacrity. Why was I so worried? Surely, if all went well, I could be back where I belonged within a few hours? Wasn't that what I wanted?

But where did I belong?

Arthur's hand in mine was warm and solid and real. I squeezed it tightly, feeling the bones beneath the skin, the calluses on his palms, my fingers sliding between his. I didn't want to let him go.

He didn't seem to have noticed. "This is the monks' wharf," he said, gesturing around expansively at next to nothing. "Where their goods come in and out. A lot of their cider comes our way in late autumn, but that trade's over now, just like the year."

The landing stage stretched to twice the length of our boat. The bank it abutted was muddy and pocked with prints made by the cloven feet of cows and sheep. Beside the landing stage, the traffic of animals had hollowed out a muddy watering place. Beyond, tall bare trees marched away from us, scattered over a long tongue of rising land.

"Wait here for us, Nial." Arthur took my hand. "I'm off to show the Queen what there is to see. We'll be stopping by the abbey to offer our prayers to the Virgin, so we might be quite a while."

Nial nodded and, pulling a fishing rod out from where it had been lying along the bottom of the boat, prepared himself for some leisure time.

We walked away from him along the rise through the trees. Before we'd gone very far, we could no longer see him or the river. The island that was Glastonbury lay spread out before us.

"Why's it called the Holy Island?" I asked. The big trees had thinned, and now we were walking through apple orchards, the trees bare of both apples and leaves, but standing in regimented rows plainly planted by human hands. Ynys Afallon – the island of apples. Avalon. How appropriate to find it thick with apple trees. And magic, of course. That was the reason for my visit here. The magic of the place.

"It's always been a place of worship." He paused. "A place where you can be close to God. Before it was His, it was the sanctuary of the old gods, and they don't easily give up their hold." Glancing around myself, I got the distinct impression they'd never left. He went on. "It's said the entrance to the otherworld, Annwfn, is here, and that if you find it, you'll meet Gwynn ap Nudd, its ruler. My people worshipped the old gods a lot longer than they've been worshipping the Christian God at the Abbey."

I'd been to Glastonbury on many occasions, but in my time it was full of tourist attractions, gaudy shops, the museum, and nutcases who thought they were being spiritual. The magic was muffled. But it was still there, flowing beneath the ground, camouflaged by modern life.

Now, standing alone with Arthur on the slopes of the island, the magic of the place hit me in waves like a spring tide rolling up the beach. Surely, here I'd find what I wanted?

Arthur gave my hand a tug. "Come on, I'll show you the abbey. Abbot Jerome is a good man. You'll like him."

I hung back. Now, at last, was the time for some honesty. Abbot Jerome wasn't likely to have forgotten me. I'd rather it was me who told Arthur than anyone else.

"I know he is." I tried to sound matter of fact. Not to make a big deal out of it. "I met him when I was here before. It was he who sent me to Din Cadan."

Arthur turned around and looked at me, eyes full of surprise. "Why didn't you tell me?"

Maybe he was wondering why Merlin hadn't told him either.

The wind soughed in the branches of the apple trees, making them chatter together in a curious clicking language.

I swallowed. "I didn't think you'd bring me here if I told you."

"Why would I not have?"

I wrestled with my conscience. I didn't want to tell him too much, yet I wanted to be honest. I owed it to him, didn't I? But how much could he cope with? Not the whole truth, that was for sure, because it had taken me all this time even to come to the stage of acceptance I'd now reached.

"Because I came from here." I watched his face. "And Merlin's afraid I might go back."

He didn't understand. I could see it in his eyes.

"Well, you're back, so what does it matter?"

"Everything." I kicked at the dead apple leaves littering the grass.

"Tell me."

I swallowed again. "I – I come from somewhere else – somewhere a long way away. Merlin brought me here to fulfill the prophecy. He'd been watching me since I was a child, waiting for the right time to bring me here, to Ynys Witrin."

He shook his head as though to clear it. "He brought you here? How? With what?"

I held up my right hand, on which the dragon ring shone deep and warm even in the wintry light. "With this."

He reached out and took my hand, staring at the ring as though for the first time. "With the dragon ring?"

I nodded. A great lump welled up in my throat. I didn't want to lose control and dissolve into tears, so I dug the nails of my other hand into my palm.

Understanding dawned on his face. "And you want to use it to take you back." There was bitterness in his voice.

"I don't know," I said, the tears spilling unhindered down my cheeks. "For a long time I thought I did, but now I'm here, I just don't know. It's so different where I come from. When I first arrived here, everything was strange and frightening. I wanted to go home, to the place where I grew up, to my – my betrothed."

"You're speaking of how you felt then, not how you feel now." His face was guarded, his voice uncertain. Above our heads a bevy of crows rose screeching out of the nearby naked chestnut trees.

"Well, then I met you."

"Am I not enough to make you stay?" His voice was deep with emotion.

We looked at each other for a long time in silence, his words writ large between us in the cold air.

Was he giving me the chance to grab what I wanted? But what was that? I looked hard at him from top to toe, willing myself *not* to want him. At his expressive eyes that could hold mirth or anger or justice – or love. At his mouth that knew the intimacies of my body as no other did except for Nathan. At his long slim horseman's frame and all the muscles that knotted it together in whipcord strength. At his thick dark hair, and his solemn brows, his determined mouth, the little pulse beating at his throat. Was I committing him to my memory? Was today the last day I'd ever see him?

I struggled to think of Nathan. His face wouldn't come. I tried to think of our life together, but everything about my old life seemed suddenly trivial. What was it I'd loved? I didn't know.

Maybe that was it. Maybe its very triviality was important. Maybe I wasn't cut out to play the bigger role. Maybe I was just plain Gwen Fry, destined to be a librarian, housewife and mother, to one day retire and have grandchildren who would never know what I'd once been – Guinevere, Queen of Dumnonia. A woman who would be spoken of down the ages, a legend, a name known throughout the English-speaking world, forever linked with King Arthur.

Was he enough to keep me here?

"I just don't know," I said.

For another long minute, he stood motionless, and then he put up a hand and wiped my tears away. "Don't cry. If it means that much to you, I'll take you where you want to go."

# Chapter Twenty-Four

I N UNSPOKEN AGREEMENT, we skirted the abbey and Geraint's village, and made our way up the steep slope of the Tor, following a narrow path that wound its way around the hill like a twisting mountain road. The bitter wind whipped at us, and we held our cloaks close.

I wanted that climb to last forever, but all too soon we reached the summit, and I saw once again the small circle of gaunt grey stones where, in my time, the ruined tower of St Michael stood. I halted beside Arthur.

"Well, here we are," he said, with a lightness that rang false.

I looked at the stones, and the knot in my stomach twisted and tightened. My hands trembled. There, between the stones, lay my way home. Perhaps. But did I want it? My heart was ripping down the center.

Arthur held out his hand, lean and brown, the nails short and none too clean, the hand of a man who knows physical work. Instantly, I had an image of Nathan's hands – the palms soft, nails neatly trimmed and clean, the hands of an intellectual, a man for whom the daily grind is books and lectures, not spears and swords and horses. I put my hand in Arthur's.

I couldn't move. Gently, Arthur put his hand in the small of my back and pushed me forwards. I took one step and then another. The stone circle drew closer, every jagged stone pointing to the grey sky, accusing fingers from another age, daring me to enter.

Arthur stopped just outside the circle, dropping his hand from my back to take my hand again. Tension quivered through him. I wanted to ask him to tell me what *he* wanted. I wanted him to tell me he loved me, and he couldn't let me go.

He said nothing.

I stood still, as uncertain now as I had been at the foot of the hill. The wind whistled forlornly between the stones. Below us, smoke drifted westwards from the hearth fires of the village and abbey, rising above the trees that embraced the foot of the Tor. My heart thundered in my chest, and my stomach roiled.

"It's all right," he said, a tremor in his voice. "Do what you have to. I'll stay here."

I looked up at him. "I don't even know if it'll work. Merlin said it might not."

He stared at me out of solemn dark eyes. I couldn't read his expression. He licked his lips. "I...I need to ask you something. Before you...before you go." His long hair whipped across his face, and he brushed it aside with an impatient hand.

I nodded. What was he going to say? *Please make him ask me to stay.* But if he did, would I?

A succession of emotions flitted across his face: confusion, fear, hope, unhappiness. He cleared his throat awkwardly. "Are you...? Have you come from...from Annwfn? Are you one of the fairy folk?"

That wasn't the question I'd been expecting.

I shook my head vehemently, almost relieved. "No. No, I'm not." Nerves put me on the edge of manic laughter. "I'm a person...like you. I just come from somewhere different. A place Merlin brought me from. These stones are a doorway into my world. At least, I hope they are."

If I'd tried explaining this to anyone in my time, they would have laughed in my face, but Arthur had grown up here, in a land steeped with tales of magic. And we were standing at the gates to Annwfn. All of this he'd taken in his stride. So much so, he'd suspected he might have married a fairy.

His eyes held mine. "Will I be able to see this doorway?"

"I don't know. I didn't see it when I came here. I fell through and rolled down the hill, and here I was. It was…terrifying." How to convey to him the utter confusion and fear I'd felt on finding myself in his world? I couldn't put it into words.

"And the man you're going back to; do you love him still?"

I wished I'd never told him about Nathan. Did he think I was going because I preferred Nathan to him? How could I even begin to compare them? They were so different.

Just weeks ago my answer would have been a resounding "yes", but a lot can change in even so short a time. It was another question I didn't have the answer to, but this time it was the most important question of all. Because if I loved Arthur more than Nathan, why was I going back? Once through the door, I had no guarantee that if I found I no longer wanted my comfortable modern world, I could just come back and take up my life in Dark Age Britain where I'd left off. I had an awful feeling that this choice might be a final one.

"I did," I said in a low voice. "I-I loved him…when I was with him."

"But you're not with him now."

"I know."

He turned my hand over in his, lifting it to his lips. "Does he honor you, as is your right? Will he make you his queen? Would he fight for you to the death – his death, if necessary?"

He kissed my palm. His breath was warm on my skin, his lips soft. For a long moment, he pressed them hard to my hand.

I snatched my hand back. It was unfair. His very touch electrified, sending a current through my body that threatened to overpower me. Every moment longer in Arthur's company made it harder for me to make this decision. I had to make it for myself. I couldn't let him make it for me.

He fixed me with his gaze, his eyes refusing to drop. I drank him in. If what I'd long hoped for happened, then I'd never see him again. In the blink of an eye, he'd be dead and buried – long gone, lost, just a myth. Only I would know he'd been real. Only I would know he'd been flesh and blood, a man prepared to fight to save my life from Saxon raiders. A man who'd made me his queen.

"I don't know." I could barely get the words out. How could I compare what I'd had with Nathan to what I had with Arthur? Which was more real? Which was the life I wanted?

I'd liked my life until that fateful day on the Tor. I'd been happy working in the library amongst my books, going home to my little modern box of a house, along busy roads in my second-hand car, and cooking dinner with Nathan in our tiny kitchen. Our yearly foreign holiday, my iPhone, Wi-Fi, the NHS, Income Tax, useless political parties, our soldiers fighting in far-off war zones, the BBC, going to the cinema to watch the latest new release... how trivial everything seemed. What, of all that, was truly important?

He took a step back. "If you want to return, then go. I won't make you stay with me." He swallowed. "But you need to know one thing, Gwen." He hesitated as though marshalling some sort of resolution. "I...I care for you." He paused, and when I remained silent, he hurried on. "I didn't know it until today. I thought I'd married you to please my father and gain my kingdom. I wasn't looking for love." He hesitated. "But now that I have to let you go, I don't want to. I want you to stay. Because..." He seemed to be struggling to get the words out. "Because I love you."

My heart was thudding so hard, he must have been able to hear it. "You love me?" He'd never spoken those words before, not once in all our lovemaking. Saving it unfairly for now was something I'd never expected.

He nodded. "With every bone in my body."

"You never said." I couldn't keep the accusation out of my voice. Above our heads a buzzard's mewing cry rose above the wind, as accusatory as I was.

"I didn't know it myself. Did you not suspect?"

I shook my head. "I didn't know."

He swallowed again; he was still clearly struggling with expressing his emotions. "But because I love you, I know I have to let you go. You love another. Go to him. I won't stand in the way of your happiness."

My heart was breaking. I wanted to tell him I loved him, but how cruel would that be, to give with one hand and snatch away with the other? Because I didn't love only him, did I? I loved Nathan, too. Faraway Nathan, just a distant memory.

He lifted his hand. I thought for a moment he was going to reach out and touch me, snatch me back. But then he let it drop again, his lips closing in a grim line.

I looked at the stones. If the door opened for me, could I step through it and leave him behind?

The world as I'd left it lay on the other side. What difference had my disappearance made to Nathan and my brother Artie, the only two people who would have mourned my loss? Would they cope if I never returned? Perhaps. My loss would fade in their memories and their lives would go on. I'd be just another story, like Arthur. A mystery, forever unsolved.

I choked on a sob. "I need to know. I-I need to know if I can get back. That's the only way I can choose. D'you understand?"

He shook his head. "You've been happy here, haven't you? I thought you were happy."

"But I still need to know."

Tears sparkled in the corners of his eyes. "And if the door opens for you, will you step through it?"

"I won't know until I try. If I walk away now, never having tried, it'll be as if I never had the choice. I don't know how I feel. I – I want to stay with you. I think. Most of me does. But out there..." I gave a great wave of my arms. "Out there is somewhere you could never comprehend. I miss it. The world I come from is so very different, I don't know if I could be truly happy here without it. And I'm frightened. Frightened I'll make the wrong choice, and there'll be no going back."

For a moment, he stood in silence, absorbing what I'd said, and then he stepped up to me and roughly took me in his arms, pinning my body against his. He bent his head and kissed me on the mouth, hard and long and hungrily. I melted into his arms, my hands coming up to hold his head to mine, fingers deep in his hair, eyes closed.

*Never let it end. Let me stay like this forever.*

But it ended. He released me, stepping back, panting. Every cell in my body tingled and my heart was hammering. My breath came in gasps.

*Unfair.*

"I want you to remember what we had." His voice was rough and choking. "Remember every moment you've spent with me. Back in your own world, think of me every day – think of me in your bed at night, when you're alone, when quiet is upon you. Think of my touch and my voice and my loving. Because that's what I'll be doing, here, alone, in Din Cadan."

I could bear it no longer. I turned away from him and stepped into the circle of stones, the fingers of my left hand tight around the golden dragon ring.

Damp mist rose out of the ground, curling around my feet and swirling about the stones in a silken veil. In moments, the top of the hill was cloaked in dense, grey fog – a fog so thick that when I turned around to look for Arthur, he'd vanished. My heart gave a lurch of searing pain. All around me, the stones rose out of the mist like jagged islands out of a foaming sea, but beyond them, all was a blank curtain.

For a moment, I stood indecisive. Merlin had never said how he'd found me in my world. Maybe there was more to it than standing inside the stones, hoping. Maybe I had to do something with the ring? I turned around slowly on my heel. Only the stones existed. Arthur was wiped away as though he'd never been.

My heart broke in two.

Although it was the middle of the day, darkness was falling fast, the fog shrouding what faint winter sunlight there'd been.

Whispers sibilated in the mist. The hairs on the back of my neck stood on end.

I spun round. Nothing there.

Whispers again, shifting and formless. Was there someone here, in the fog, with me?

"Show me the way back," I called out. "Please." But my voice died on my lips, muted by the fog.

Fear grasped my entrails, an instinctive fear of the unknown, and for a moment blind panic threatened to take me. Then, just as when I'd been here before, a pure musical note seared through the mist. My fear fell away as a light glimmered, faintly illuminating the two biggest stones. It drew me like a magnet, and as I stepped toward it, the note rose and the light grew, burning their way through the mist. I wavered, unsure of what I was being shown, and took another faltering step.

Within the ragged circle of light, a shape took form as the musical note continued to rise, impossibly pure and sweet. I was dazzled for a moment, before beyond the brightness I saw the walls of the ruined church tower that stood on Glastonbury Tor in my time, closing in about me. Through the archway, a grim grey winter sky loomed.

My world.

My feet rooted me to the spot. I tried and failed to conjure Nathan's face. But he no longer existed in my head. I couldn't recall his touch, his kisses, his lovemaking, his voice. Something, *someone*, had gradually erased him. Did I want this man I could barely remember? Did I want the security of twenty-first-century life? A life of safety, a life without peril.

Or did I want the life of a Dark Age queen? The uncertainty, the danger, the risks? Did I want Arthur with his half-suspected tragic future, which already had its foundation stones laid by the birth of Medraut? With his rough-and-ready home at Din Cadan, a brother who wished him dead, a sword waiting for him to draw it from its stone in dangerous Viroconium, and not just his own kingdom to defend, but every kingdom in Britain?

If I went home, I would be a nobody – a single ant in a gigantic anthill. With Arthur I could be the Queen Ant – Arthur's Queen. I alone knew the fate that lay ahead of him, knew his destiny; and if I stayed, I could perhaps bend events away from tragedy toward a different outcome.

But if I stepped through this ragged hole, I would return not just to Nathan but to Artie, my carefree, careless twin brother, my womb companion, my childhood friend, the only family I had left. Could I separate myself from him forever?

I stared at the hole, its edges silvered and crackling as though lightning had been harnessed in its creation, and took an uncertain step toward it. The edges expanded to swallow me. Under my feet were solid paving slabs, and if I reached out my hand, I would be able to touch the rough stone walls of the tower. *But was that what I wanted?*

I halted and all about me the edges of the hole shimmered and broke and reformed into new shapes. Could I do this? Could I leave Arthur behind and never see him again?

And then I knew. With a clarity I'd never felt before, I knew where I belonged, and it wasn't with Nathan. I belonged with Arthur. The realization swept over me that I was and always had been Guinevere, his queen, even as a child walking up here with my dying mother. My destiny lay with my lover, my husband, my king – in the world that was my home.

Was it already too late? Desperately, I turned back, back toward the mist, back toward the man I loved – and he wasn't there. Fog, thick and dense and dark, stretched before me, and behind me the world of the twenty-first century dragged me inexorably toward it.

"Arthur!"

The End

# Acknowledgements

*With thanks to everyone at Critique Circle who helped me perfect my craft and without whom I would not be here today.*

## About the Author

After a varied life that's included working with horses where Downton Abbey is filmed, riding racehorses, running her own riding school, owning a sheep farm and running a holiday business in France, Fil now lives on a widebeam canal boat on the Kennet and Avon Canal in Southern England.

She has a long-suffering husband, a rescue dog from Romania called Bella, a cat she found as a kitten abandoned in a gorse bush, five children and six grandchildren.

She once saw a ghost in a churchyard, and when she lived in Wales there was a panther living near her farm that ate some of her sheep. In England there are no indigenous big cats.

She has Asperger's Syndrome and her obsessions include horses and King Arthur. Her historical romantic fiction and children's fantasy adventures centre around Arthurian legends, and her pony stories about her other love. She speaks fluent French after living there for ten years, and in her spare time looks after her allotment, makes clothes and dolls for her granddaughters, embroiders and knits. In between visiting the settings for her books.

Social Media links:
Website – filreid.com
Facebook – facebook.com/Fil-Reid-Author-101905545548054
Twitter – @FJReidauthor

Printed in Great Britain
by Amazon